TRISTEN WILLIS

Eden's Rise

Chains Of Conformity Book One

ISBN (paperback): 9781764072601
ISBN (hardcover): 9781764072618

Editing by Cecelia Connaughton
Cover art by Katelyn Groombridge at Design by Kage

This book was professionally typeset on Reedsy.
Find out more at reedsy.com

This book is dedicated to my children.
A world where my heart is no longer capable of loving you both is
one I can scarcely imagine, and it is the very essence of terror.
Your love makes everything worth living for.

Contents

Foreword

Please be advised that although this story is intended for a mature audience (18+) it does contain content which may be triggering to some readers.

Please see below list of potential triggers:

- *Violence*
- *Emotional and psychological abuse*
- *Explicit sexual content inclusive of on page sex scenes (open door spice)*
- *Profanity (my characters swear **a lot**)*
- *Oppression*
- *Suppression*
- *Blood/gore*
- *Psychological torture (happens off page)*

Acknowledgments

Firstly, thank you to my husband, my biggest supporter, who has helped me navigate every moment of imposter syndrome.

Thank you to my Alpha and Beta readers, as well as my editor, for your invaluable feedback and support in making this book the best it can be.

To my street team—thank you for your unwavering encouragement and belief in me.

Thank you to my hype team for shouting into the void of social media on my behalf. Your support and encouragement mean the world to me.

To my author bestie, Stephanie Fernandez—thank you for agonizing over every small detail with me when I was overcome with crippling indecision.

Lastly, to my readers—thank you for joining me on this

journey. I hope Ziva and Myall's love story captured your heart as much as it did mine. Your support means the world.

Prologue

Excerpt from The Emotional Regulation Act

Ratified Year 47 After Establishment (A.E.) by decree of The Harmonization Authority

Preamble

To preserve order, unity, and the enduring peace of humanity, it is hereby declared that unregulated emotion poses a direct threat to the welfare of all citizens. History has proven that unchecked grief, rage, longing, and desire give rise to violence, instability, and the collapse of collective progress. The Emotional Regulation Act (ERA) exists to prevent such failures.

Article I: Universal Compliance

- All citizens, upon reaching their tenth year of life, shall be fitted with a NeuroMod device approved by The Authority.

- The device shall monitor, regulate, and when necessary, chemically suppress destabilizing emotional states.
- Noncompliance constitutes a breach of civic duty and is subject to corrective intervention.

Article II: Prohibited States

The following emotions, when expressed beyond the thresholds approved by The Authority, are deemed hazardous and shall be subject to recalibration:

- Anger in excess of tolerance.
- Grief in excess of mourning period.
- Desire that interferes with assigned duties.
- Attachment that supersedes loyalty to The Authority.

Article III: Correction

- Citizens found in violation shall undergo recalibration at designated facilities.
- Persistent offenders may be subject to detainment in the interest of collective stability.
- Recalibration is not punishment; it is restoration.

Article IV: Continuity of Peace

Freedom from the burden of harmful emotion ensures a unified society. The individual is safeguarded through compliance; the whole is strengthened through obedience.

Historical Note

Though the majority of civilization embraced the Emotional Regulation Act as the sole path to peace, dissent arose among certain governing regions. Declaring independence, these territories formed what is now recognized as *The Sanctum*. While rejecting The Authority's reliance on chemical dosing and forced suppression, The Sanctum embraced its own doctrine of emotional restraint. Through conditioning, indoctrination, and structured environments, they claim to achieve harmony without reliance on pharmacological intervention.

Despite this divergence, both The Authority and The Sanctum affirm a single truth: left ungoverned, human emotion endangers stability. Where methods differ, purpose remains the same. *Control in service of order.*

Chapter One

Ziva

The hum of the NeuroMods fills the facility, a constant, droning presence as the cold air wraps around me. At my workstation, I run a routine diagnostic on the NeuroMod, watching its small screen flicker with data. The beeps, the readouts, the movements of my hands—it's all second nature now. There's comfort in the routine, but also a suffocating predictability. I imagine smashing the wrist device against the wall, watching it explode into sparks and shards.

But that's just a fantasy. For now.

A burst of awkward laughter slices through the monotony of the workroom. I glance over and see Anders, one of the senior Technicians, holding a printout. It's likely one of the so-called "humor bulletins" our supervisors distribute at the behest of the Harmonization Authority.

"Did you hear the one about the NeuroMod and the mood chip?" he calls, voice flat beneath forced enthusiasm. "It's a real shocker."

His laughter is mechanical, a hollow mimicry of joy. I catch a flicker of despair in his eyes, just before it vanishes behind a familiar, medicated glaze—his NeuroMod no doubt pumping him full of emotional suppressants. The woman nearest Anders looks calm, but her hands tremble slightly, her jaw clenched tight as if suppressing a reaction.

My stomach knots, an instinctive response to the absurdity, as if my body knows how wrong this all is. No one laughs. Here, silence weighs more than words. The air itself seems to crush any attempt at genuine interaction.

The NeuroMods represent control, conformity, a life without the messy complications of *real* emotions. A life without the violence that unbridled emotions can cause. At least, that's what they tell us. I can almost see the thought bubbles forming over my colleagues' heads: *Do I need to laugh? Will someone report me if I don't?*

I return my focus to the NeuroMod, my hands moving with dull efficiency. The joke wasn't funny. But that's not the point. The point is, we're expected to laugh. We're expected to respond on cue, display the right reactions at the right times. It's all so painfully obvious. The Authority scripts our lives, our feelings. And I absolutely fucking hate it.

Images of my parents flicker in my mind—my mother's laughter echoing in our small apartment, my father's protective embrace. Fleeting, raw moments of emotion that felt like warmth on the coldest days. So different from the icy numbness of now.

A deep ache blooms in my chest, grief heavy and solid,

like I'm carrying their absence with every breath. I dare not voice it. Grief is just another feeling to be corrected.

My NeuroMod vibrates, registering the spike in emotion. I draw a deep, steadying breath.

Anders shrugs and returns to his work, the printout already crumpled and discarded. I try to follow suit, stealing a glance at the wall clock. Two more hours of this shift, then I can retreat to my apartment and tinker with the salvaged NeuroMod. Maybe tonight I'll make a breakthrough. Maybe I'll find a way to bring back what they took.

Or maybe it's just another empty hope.

I sigh and close my eyes, letting the harsh overhead lights bleed through my lids. When I open them, the world looks even more washed out and drained of color, of life. I wonder what this place looks like to someone who believes in the Authority's vision. Do they see order where I see desolation?

I don't know how much longer I can keep going through the motions without dying inside.

I turn back to my work and adjust the NeuroMod's settings. The cool metal feels foreign against my skin—a constant reminder of its invasive presence.

The soft whir of machinery surrounds us, blending with the rhythmic beeps that mark another life dulled into submission. My jaw tightens with each adjustment, a quiet tug-of-war between duty and the longing for something more.

Neurotransmitter levels. Emotional outputs. Brainwave patterns. All must fall within acceptable parameters, per the Authority's strict regulations.

A woman enters the workroom, her movements stiff and mechanical. She sits across from me, eyes dull and lifeless. I attach cords to the NeuroMod at her wrist and to her temple, the electrodes clicking softly as they adhere to her skin.

"State your designation," I say, my voice flat and monotonous, just like I was trained.

"Citizen 47299," she responds, her tone equally devoid of inflection as she brushes a strand of golden hair away from the electrodes at her temple.

I nod and enter her ID into the Sentinel database. The screen flashes red, indicating heightened emotional activity. I adjust the settings, dampening her feelings and replacing them with a carefully curated mix of synthetic emotion.

The woman's sun-warmed face remains blank as I finish the calibration. She stands, thanks me in a flat voice, and walks out with measured, mechanical steps. I watch her go, something unnamed tugging at my chest.

I lean back from the console, my long brown hair falling over one shoulder, posture straight. Perfect. Just like they taught us—efficiency and conformity, the twin pillars of our society. I resist the urge to roll my eyes.

"Emerson, status report." The voice of my supervisor crackles through the comm at my workstation, stern and demanding.

"Citizen 47299's NeuroMod recalibration is complete, ma'am. Neurotransmitters normalized, irrational impulses suppressed. Ready for re-entry." The words flow out automatically, coldly, as if spoken by the machine itself rather than a living, thinking human.

"Good. The Authority expects nothing less than perfect efficiency from its citizen's."

"Understood, ma'am." I keep my eyes on the Sentinel programming console, another successful realignment, another glowing data point on my record of flawless service to the cause of artificial harmony and peace. My supervisor's presence retreats, and I allow myself a small sigh of relief.

Around me, the other Technicians work with the same practiced efficiency, faces blank with obedient masks. The room hums with machinery and the soft beeping of NeuroMods in recalibration. No one speaks unless absolutely necessary—not even the citizens. And when they do, it's clipped, precise, drained of anything real.

I turn back to my workstation, my mind churning with forbidden thoughts.

NeuroMods are supposed to keep us safe—protect us from chaos, from emotional volatility.

But at what cost?

Are we alive...or just drones, drifting through a life stripped of meaning?

I inhale for four. Exhale for five.

"Next," I call out, voice crisp and professional.

A middle-aged woman with slightly graying hair shuffles forward, eyes downcast. She settles into the chair, and I attach the sensors to her device and temples with efficiency.

"Please state your designation," I recite, the familiar words rolling off my tongue.

"Citizen 38290," she murmurs.

I nod, entering the identification number into the system. "And how would you rate your mood today, on a scale of one to ten?"

Citizen 38290 hesitates. "Um...a six, I suppose."

My eyebrows raise a fraction. Anything above a five is cause for an immediate reprogramming session. "I see. And what's troubling you today?"

"Nothing in particular," she says quickly. Too quickly. "Just…life, I guess."

Forcing a reassuring smile, I initiate the emotional dampening sequence, praying that the Sentinel system doesn't flag her heightened readings. The last thing I want is a Compliance Monitor involved. "That's okay. We'll have you feeling nice and balanced in no time."

As the recalibration begins its work, the women's eyes glaze over, tension visibly draining from her body. Another successful adjustment. Another citizen rendered blissfully numb.

Recalibration days are the worst. I'd rather spend the time fixing NeuroMods than suppressing someone's humanity.

But this is my job.

I try to ignore the twist in my gut—the voice inside me screaming that this is wrong.

"How do you feel now?" I ask as the sequence ends.

"Fine," she replies, her voice flat. "Everything is fine."

Of course it is. It always is.

As she leaves, I fight the urge to sigh.

Is this it? Just an endless stream of empty shells, stripped of everything that makes us human?

Did the Authority really *fix* us?

Or just hollow us out?

Twenty years ago though, the world was a different place. Or so the older generation claims. The Harmonization Authority came into power with a promise to eliminate the chaos and pain that unchecked emotions brought. To restore order to a society that was out of control.

People resisted, at first. They fought to keep their emotional freedom, refused to trade their pain for manufactured calm.

But the Authority was relentless. Uprisings were crushed. Dissenters reeducated. Step by step, they brought the population into line.

That's the official history, anyway.

The version they drill into us in mandatory Harmonization Classes. The version I pretend to believe to keep my job. My apartment. My life.

In reality, the NeuroMods have taken more than they've given. They've stripped us of our passion, our joy, even our sorrow. We've become a society of emotional zombies, going through the motions of a life that's been pre-scripted for us.

I risk a glance at my co-worker, Lena, her auburn hair pulled back in a tight bun, her eyes focused on the NeuroMod in her hands. We've worked side by side for years, but I've never seen her smile or heard her laugh. It's as if all the color and vibrancy has been drained from her, leaving behind a hollow shell.

"Ziva, have you completed the recalibration on the latest batch of citizen's?" she asks when she notices me staring, her voice flat and emotionless like always.

Nodding, I force myself to hold her gaze. "Yes, they've been recalibrated accordingly."

Lena doesn't acknowledge my response, simply turning back to her work. Her hands move with precision, yet I notice a slight tremor, as if her body remembers what it once felt. Does she feel the same longing I do, the same desire for something more than this monotonous existence?

I keep watching her, wondering what kind of life we might have had. What friendships we could have formed—if only we were allowed to feel it.

But these days, authentic connection is a fantasy. Don't even get me started on true love.

Because how can you truly know someone when you're numb? When every word, every look, is monitored?

My fingers itch for the calibration dial. Just one nudge. A tiny shift in the settings—enough to let a flicker of something real slip through.

Just enough to prove the human spirit can't be silenced.

But I hold back.

Even the smallest act of defiance could cost me everything.

My hands move on autopilot while my mind drifts to forbidden places. A world where we could love, laugh, cry—where our feelings were truly ours. Not muted, not controlled by these cold, unfeeling devices strapped to our wrists.

A sudden commotion by the entrance pulls me back.

Two black-uniformed Harmonization Enforcers drag a middle-aged man into the room.

His face is twisted—half fear, half defiance. "Please, I didn't mean to feel! It was an accident!" he pleads, his voice raw with emotion.

Watching in morbid fascination, they force him into a chair beside a workstation, restraining his limbs with cold efficiency. One of the Enforcers adjusts the man's NeuroMod, and his cries fade into a dull, lifeless monotone.

"Citizen, you have violated Emotional Regulation Code 371. Your NeuroMod will be recalibrated, and you will be monitored closely for further infractions."

The man's eyes glaze over, his face slackening into the familiar mask of apathy. A shiver runs down my spine as I witness the brutal suppression of his emotions.

Marcus, a fellow Technician, is tasked with the recalibration.

From across the room, I see the tension in his neck, the reluctance in his movements.

The restrained man is led away, his spirit crushed.

A flicker of anger ignites inside me.

How can they do this to us?

How can they erase the very essence of humanity?

My NeuroMod vibrates sharply, warning of my rising emotions.

My fingers itch with restless energy, my heart hammering against my ribs.

The urge to defy the system surges. I have only seconds before the NeuroMod doses me into numbness.

Each second ticks down like a countdown.

Sweat beads at my temples, trickling down my cheek, reminding me of the risk I'm about to take.

Instead of a full rebellion, I settle for a small, subtle one.

I reach up and tug at the collar of my dark gray uniform, loosening it just enough to reveal a sliver of skin at my neck.

It's tiny—barely noticeable—but it makes me feel alive, holding on to a shred of individuality in this sea of conformity.

I glance around carefully. No one has caught the slight transgression.

Fuck it.

I make a snap decision.

A few quick taps, and I lower my NeuroMod's sensitivity— just enough to let a trickle of real emotion slip through.

For a brief, thrilling moment, fear, excitement, hope rush through me. It's intoxicating.

A glimpse of the life I've been denied.

But I know I can't hold this without the Sentinel system flagging me.

Reluctantly, I reset my NeuroMod to its standard numbness.

My face returns to its mask of dutiful compliance.

Turning back to my workstation, my gaze meets a pair of deep green eyes across the room. Compliance Monitor Myall Hansen.

He watches me, a flicker of curiosity in his expression.

He pushes his unruly dark brown hair from his eyes, biceps flexing beneath his uniform.

My heart skips.

For a moment, I'm thankful for the muted emotions the NeuroMod forces on me—without it, my flushed face would betray me. Myall steps around his workstation and approaches, his movements fluid and graceful despite his rugged exterior.

"Everything alright, Ziva?" His voice is low, meant only for my ears as he leans his tall, muscular frame against my workstation's bench.

I nod, my tongue suddenly feeling too large for my mouth. "Everything's fine. Nothing I can't handle." The words come out more breathless than I intend.

A ghost of a smile plays at the corners of his lips. "I have no doubt."

His gaze lingers on mine for a moment longer than necessary, and I feel a flutter of something in my chest, a whisper of an emotion that shouldn't be possible.

But the moment shatters with the sharp click of heels against the tile floor. My supervisor, Penn, her face pinched with disapproval, strides towards me—no doubt making her final rounds for the day.

"Emerson, what's the meaning of this?" She gestures to my slightly disheveled uniform.

Shit.

Straightening, my fingers fumble to adjust my collar and cover up the sliver of tawny skin peeking out. "Apologies, ma'am. It won't happen again."

Her eyes narrow, but she doesn't press further. "See that it doesn't." With a final, pointed look, she continues on her rounds.

I exhale, heart pounding in my ears.

Catching Myall's eye, he gives a small, almost imperceptible nod before returning to his work.

Chapter Two

Ziva

As the day winds down, I'm alone in my section of the workroom, waiting for the next group of employees to arrive. Glancing around to ensure no one is watching and no cameras are swiveled in my direction, I carefully pry open the casing of the device on my wrist.

The closer I lean over the circuitry, the heavier the weight of what I'm doing feels, a cold sweat trickling down my spine. I wish I could do this in the comfort of my own home, but the necessary tools are restricted to this facility and closely monitored by security.

I trace my calloused fingers along the wires, trying to discern their purpose. Each component seems to hold the key to our emotional suppression. It's why I became a NeuroMod Technician in the first place—to understand how it all works. I've been surviving here for the past four years since completing my education. If I can just figure out the right combination, the right sequence to disable the NeuroMods hold…

Lost in thought, I barely register the click of heels approaching. I hastily snap the casing back into place, my hands trembling slightly as I look up to see my supervisor standing before my workstation.

Her eyes narrow, lips pressing into a thin line as she stops before my workstation. The silence stretches between us, thick with unasked questions. She doesn't speak right away. Instead, her gaze flits to my NeuroMod, then back to my face. The silence between us stretches, and I wonder if she can hear my pulse pounding in my throat.

"Emerson, what are you still doing here?" Her voice slices through the silence—sharp and accusatory, laced with authority that makes my skin crawl. Her scrutiny pins me like a spotlight, each second stretching into eternity as my mind scrambles for an excuse.

Forcing myself to meet her gaze, I swallow hard, my mind scrambling. My heart is a wild animal in my chest, desperate to escape. "Just running some final diagnostics, ma'am. Wanted to ensure everything was in order before I left for the day."

My NeuroMod vibrates in warning as she looms closer, the air turning thick and suffocating.

"Is that so? And what exactly were you doing with the casing open?"

I force myself to meet her stare. The pulse in my temple throbs like a drum, drowning out the sounds around me. My device vibrates a second time. "I noticed a slight irregularity in the output. I wanted to check for loose connections before reporting it."

I take a deep steadying breath, forcing my heart rate to slow. For a moment, she says nothing, and I fear she sees right through my lie. But then, miraculously, she gives a curt nod. "Very well. But in the future, any irregularities should be reported immediately to a Compliance Monitor. We can't have our Technicians taking matters into their own hands."

"Of course, ma'am. It won't happen again." I keep my voice steady, even as relief floods through me.

She gives me one last, lingering look before turning to leave. "See that it doesn't. I'll see you tomorrow, Emerson."

As her footsteps fade, I release a shaky breath, my knees still wobbling. That was too close. I know I'm treading on dangerous ground, but I can't stop now. Not when I'm so close to understanding the truth behind these devices that control our every emotion.

As I readjust the NeuroMod casing, a flicker of movement at the edge of my vision catches my attention. It's Myall, his piercing green eyes locking onto mine with an intensity that makes my spine stiffen. Something unnamable flickers in his expression as his gaze stays fixed on me across the row of workstations.

I thought he'd left. Did he see what I did? The way he watches me, it's like he's weighing a truth I'm not ready to share. I've worked in close proximity to Myall for years, and I still turn into a fumbling mess whenever he's near.

A flush creeps up my neck as I realize I'm still staring at him. I drop my gaze, pretending to focus on the device in my hands. But even as I pack up my belongings, I can feel his eyes on me, studying me.

Please, don't report me.

I risk a glance and find myself drawn to the strong line of his jaw, to the way his dark, unruly hair falls across his forehead. He's not like the others—with their blank stares and robotic movements. There's something alive in him. Something different. Maybe that's why I've always been so drawn to his presence.

Lost in thought, I almost miss the hushed conversation nearby as employees trickle in for the next shift. As I strain to listen, snippets of their words reach my ears. Two Technicians, their voices hushed and urgent.

"Did you hear about the graffiti in Sector 7?" The Technician with a stock of dark curls says. His voice dropping to a whisper, urgency lacing every syllable as if the very walls might betray his words. I lean closer, straining to catch every word.

"No, what happened?" his companion replies, glancing furtively around to ensure they're not overheard.

"Someone spray-painted a message on The Authority's Detention Center. 'Emotions are not a crime,' it said. Can you believe it?"

I don't register the approach of heavy footsteps until it's almost too late. Jerking my head up, I see a patrol of Authority Enforcers marching down the aisle, their black uniforms and gleaming badges a harsh reminder of the power they wield.

Panic surges through me, setting my nerves alight. My heartbeat roars in my ears, drowning out everything else. They're headed straight for the workstation where the hushed conversation happened.

Acting on instinct, I lurch to my feet, sending a tray of tools clattering to the ground. The noise echoes through the cavernous room, drawing every eye in my direction—including those of the Enforcers.

For a heartbeat, I freeze, certain that my guilt is written all over my face. As the squad leader's gaze bores into me, I force myself to meet it with a look of wide-eyed innocence.

"I'm so sorry," I stammer, my voice trembling with a carefully measured mix of fear and contrition. "I didn't mean to disturb the peace. It won't happen again."

His helmeted gaze lingers, and my throat tightens as I fight to stay calm. Behind that visor, he could be calculating my every move, deciding if I'm a threat. With a curt nod, he motions for his squad to continue their patrol through the room, leaving me weak-kneed with relief.

As I bend to gather the scattered tools, I catch a glimpse of the two Technicians who had been discussing the graffiti. They're studiously focused on setting up their workstations, their faces carefully blank, but I can see the glimmer of gratitude in their eyes as they meet my gaze for the briefest of instants. I glance back at Myall's station, hoping he's gone—but he's still watching, his expression unreadable.

Shit.

I quickly gather the rest of my tools and head out, passing through the security checkpoint with my head down and expression carefully blank.

The streets are empty when I exit the facility at last, as they usually are after work hours. In a truly harmonious society, there's no need for socializing or recreation. Everyone goes home, eats their prescribed meals, and sleeps the recommended eight hours. It's efficient. It's predictable. It's absolutely fucking soul-crushing.

On my way home, I pass The Authority's propaganda

lining the city walls. Bright posters plastered on the walls depict idyllic scenes of citizens smiling vacantly, their eyes glazed with compliance. The slogans—'Harmony is Happiness' and 'Balance is Bliss'—seem to mock those who dare to feel anything deeper than surface-level satisfaction.

I've seen the broadcasts too many times to count—smiling, vacant faces proclaiming the joy of submission, the bliss of emotional regulation. It's absurd, almost laughable, but beneath it all, I know that's what they want us to believe. The real tragedy is how many of us do. They tell us harmony is happiness, but I wonder—what's the point of a world that only wants you to feel what it's told you to?

I still remember the day The Authority took my parents. I was six years old, and we were eating dinner. Real food, not the nutrient packs we have now. I remember the warmth of my mother's laughter, rich and full, mingling with the aroma of her favorite strawberry pie baking in the oven. That night felt like a dream, one that shattered into a thousand pieces when the door swung open. A squad of Authority Enforcers marched in and declared my parents emotionally unstable. They gave them a choice—submit to recalibration or face indefinite detention.

My parents chose detention. I never saw them again. I've asked the detention center for updates more times than I can count—always told my parents aren't on any list.

They were fools. Brave, beautiful fools.

Reaching my building, I take the stairs two at a time. There's an elevator, but I prefer the exertion. Unlocking the door to my apartment, I slip inside, shutting out the world and its oppressive calm.

Inside, my apartment is small and sparsely furnished, just

enough to meet The Authority's standards for a single occupant. The walls seem to close in around me, a monochrome palette of grays and whites. I tell myself it's a blank canvas, though I've never had the courage to add color.

I head to the tiny kitchen and pour myself a glass of water, then make my way to the bedroom. There, in the bottom drawer of my worn dresser, beneath a pile of old clothes, is my most dangerous possession. A notebook.

Taking it out, I run my fingers over the leather cover. It's worn and soft, like an old friend. Opening it to the last page, I read the words I wrote last week.

Why do we fear our own feelings? Are we even alive if we can't feel?

I grab a pen and start writing, the words spilling out like a burst pipe.

I miss them so much. It's been eighteen years now. Every day I wonder if they're still alive, if they're still the people they were. Would things have been better if they'd just submitted instead of resisting? Would I be better off if I gave in too?

The pen feels foreign in my hand, heavy with the weight of unspoken truths. Each stroke on the page is a rebellion, a tiny act of defiance against the numbness that threatens to envelop me. These are questions I already know the answers to, but admitting them, even in the privacy of my own home, is dangerous. Closing the notebook, I press it against my chest, as if somehow the paper and ink can protect me. It's all I have left of the real me, the part they can't touch.

A knock startles me. I shove the notebook into the drawer and check the peephole. It's Wren, my neighbor two doors down. She's holding something, but I can't tell what.

I open the door a crack. "Yeah?"

"Ziva, hi." Wren's voice is too bright and annoyingly cheerful, the kind that makes me wonder if her NeuroMod's malfunctioning. Her voice rings loud in the quiet I cling to. Maybe that forced cheerfulness is just a mask, one hiding the same fears that gnaw at me at night.

"Do you have any sugar? I'm all out."

Sugar.

The black market for contraband items like sugar and spices has grown in recent years, a sign that people are starting to crave more than just emotional variety. I have a small stash, but I hesitate.

"Since when do you bake?" I ask, eyeing the empty cup in her hand.

She shrugs. "Thought I'd give it a try. Something to do, you know?"

I sigh and open the door wider. "Wait here."

I grab a small container of sugar from the back of the cupboard. I don't know why I hoard it—I never use it. Maybe it's the idea of having something illicit. Something with flavor.

Walking back to the door, I hand Wren the container. Her eyes light up. "You're a lifesaver. I'll bring back whatever I don't use."

"Keep it," I say. "I don't need it."

She starts to turn away, then pauses. "Hey, Ziva…a bunch of us are getting together to watch the new Balance is Bliss episode. You should come."

I suppress a groan. Balance is Bliss is a fabricated reality show created by artificial intelligence. The last thing I want is to sit through an hour of propaganda, especially with a group of true believers. But saying no outright would raise suspicions.

"I'll see if I have time," I say, noncommittally.

Wren smiles, and for a moment I think it looks genuine. "We'd love to have you. It's always more fun with friends."

Friends.

I force a smile, close the door, and lean against it, exhaling slowly. I've made it this far by keeping to myself, never letting anyone get too close. The more you care, the more vulnerable you become.

I think of my parents again, of the life they wanted for me. A life with real connections, real community. A life with friends.

The thought of friends, of connections, leaves a hollow ache in my chest. I know I can't risk exposing my true thoughts and feelings about The Authority. But this loneliness—it's a weight I can't carry anymore.

Chapter Three

Myall

The shrill beep of my alarm pierces the darkness, dragging me from sleep. I suppress the groan that rises in my throat. Even alone, emotional restraint is mandated.

"Citizen 24601, it is time to begin your day," the AI assistant drones from the ceiling speaker, each word a mechanical reminder of my obligations. "The current time is 06:00. You have precisely 27 minutes to complete your morning routine before reporting for work."

"Acknowledged," I mumble, my voice still rough with sleep. I swing my legs over the side of my warm bed, feeling the soft sheets against my skin as the lingering scent of lavender from my sleep aid fills the air. My bare feet hit the cold floor, the chill sending a shiver up my spine, but I quickly stifle the reaction.

I move through my apartment with practiced efficiency, each step carefully timed and measured. Teeth brushed for exactly two minutes. Shower set to 38.5 degrees Celsius, lasting no more than five minutes. As I lather regulation-issued soap over my skin, my mind wanders to Ziva Emerson.

She was acting strangely yesterday, giving off an unsettling vibe. Against my better judgment, I checked her emotional compliance stats on Sentinel. They were within normal parameters. So what was causing her odd behavior?

I know I should report her behavior, but something holds me back. Maybe it's the curve of her smile or the spark in her eyes when she thinks no one is watching. Her smile lingers in my mind, a warmth I both crave and fear. Shaking my head, I banish the thought.

"Stop thinking about her, Myall," I mutter to myself as I step out of the shower. "You can't afford to slip up."

Dressing quickly in the standard-issue uniform, I smooth out any wrinkles with meticulous care. The uniform is designed for efficiency rather than aesthetic appeal and the dark gray fabric seems to blend in perfectly with the equally drab walls of my living space.

The AI's voice interrupts my dressing. "Citizen 24601, you have 17 minutes remaining in your morning routine. Please proceed to the nutrition station for your daily sustenance."

I sigh, squaring my shoulders. "Understood."

As I choke down the flavorless nutrient bar, I can't help but wonder how much longer I can keep up this charade.

"Another day in paradise," I groan to myself, adjusting my collar before stepping out into the world beyond my door.

The chill morning air bites my face as I merge into the stream of citizens, all moving like shadows toward the maglev station. The streets stretch like lifeless veins beneath dull gray concrete, echoing with the distant drone of machinery. The only splashes of color come from the digital advertisements that flash on screens above the streets.

"Good morning," a woman beside me intones flatly.

"Good morning," I respond, my voice equally devoid of emotion. Our eyes meet briefly, and I catch a flicker of… something. Longing? Fear? But it's gone in an instant, replaced by the vacant stare we've all perfected.

Joining the flow as I approach the maglev station, I catch glimpses of AI monitors flashing messages of obedience and efficiency. The maglev train glides into view as it slices through the morning fog, its sleek, silver body a serpent winding through the heart of the city. We all move in perfect synchronization as we board, like a well-oiled machine. No one speaks above a whisper, no one makes unnecessary physical contact. The silence is deafening, the air hanging thick with unspoken thoughts. Eyes cast down, faces are blank, yet I can almost feel the simmering emotions beneath the surface, like a pressure cooker ready to explode.

"Remember, citizens," a soothing voice announces over the speakers, "emotional stability leads to societal harmony. Report any signs of deviance to your local Authority Enforcer."

Clenching my jaw, I fight the urge to scream. Instead, I stare out the window, watching the landscape blur into a wash of gray and green, my thoughts far from the glass and steel structures rushing past.

The Harmonization Authority wasn't always in control. Grandma used to tell me stories about a time when people could feel whatever they wanted, when emotions ran wild and free like untamed rivers. It sounds chaotic, but also beautiful. That's the world she grew up in, the world she believed in, even as The Authority tightened its grip and turned feelings into something dangerous.

They started as a small committee, a group of so-called experts who convinced the public that emotional instability was the root of all societal problems. Their arguments were seductive in their simplicity: Remove the highs and lows, and you remove conflict. Create a balanced, harmonious populace, and you create a utopia. People bought into it, slowly at first, then with the fervor of true believers.

Once The Authority had enough support, they moved quickly. Laws were passed, first encouraging and then mandating emotional regulation. Those who resisted were labeled dissidents, enemies of harmony. Rebellions flared up like brushfires, including the one my parents foolishly threw themselves into. Each was crushed with a precision that grew more ruthless over time. The last of the resistance was snuffed out when I was a boy, or so The Authority claims.

I shift in my seat, uncomfortable with the direction of my thoughts but unable to stop the flow. The maglev cart is sparsely populated, citizens in their gray uniforms sitting in silence, eyes vacant. Most are likely on Tranquil, the state-issued drug that flattens emotional peaks and valleys into a manageable plain. I'm one of the few who can maintain the facade without it, who can pretend to be less human than I am.

The maglev slows as it approaches my stop, the Compliance Monitoring Division looming large and oppressive against the skyline. Sighing, I attempt to center myself. Each day is a balancing act, the weight of my emotions threatening to tip me over.

The doors hiss open, and I stand, straightening my gray jacket. One more day of pretending. One more day of planning. One more day of surviving in a world where survival is the only thing left to experience. Stepping onto the platform, the crowd moves with the mechanical precision of a wind-up toy, and I let myself be carried along, just another cog in the machine.

My stomach churns as I pass through the biometric scanners, praying my rebellious thoughts aren't somehow detected.

"Welcome, Compliance Monitor Hansen," the AI greets me as I enter the sparce lobby. "Please proceed to your workstation."

Nodding, I carefully keep my expression neutral as I push through the revolving door and into the facility, where a giant screen displays the latest emotional balance statistics.

I head toward my workstation, noticing a small crowd gathered near the break room. Curious, I wander over and peer through the glass wall. On the vid-screen, the newscaster discusses the latest Harmonization campaign before cutting to Regent Colvin, the public face of The Harmonization Authority. A hush falls over the room.

Colvin speaks with his usual clipped tone, outlining new measures to ensure emotional stability. His words are a dagger wrapped in velvet, each one designed to pierce our hearts and drain them of feeling.

"...in these turbulent times, we must remember that true harmony requires sacrifice," Colvin says. "The NeuroMod is not just a tool; it is a symbol of our collective commitment to a balanced and orderly society. Those who resist harmonization endanger not only themselves but all of us."

A hand lands on my shoulder, and I turn to see Kellan, a fellow Compliance Monitor. Kellan's a big guy, always wearing a frown. Today, though, his expression is cold and unreadable.

"Can you believe this shit?" he says, his voice low. "Colvin's turning the country into a police state." Kellan's face is stone, brow deeply furrowed, as if he carries the weight of the world. His disillusionment radiates like heat from a furnace.

Shrugging, I keep my expression blank. "He's just trying to maintain order."

Kellan shakes his head and walks away, muttering something I can't make out. I take one last look at the vid-screen. Colvin's speech has ended, and the newscaster is reading a list of recent detentions.

Around me, my colleagues are already reabsorbed in their tasks, their faces as blank as the white walls surrounding us as I move toward my workstation.

"Morning, Mr. Hansen," Tara mumbles from the workstation next to mine, her tone flat and lifeless.

"Morning," I reply, matching her disposition.

Staring at the reports in front of me, the numbers blur together. Another day. Another stack of data to push through. The world outside this workroom feels so distant, as if it's happening in another lifetime, or another place entirely.

I let my mind wander—just for a second—away from the endless rows of data. And in that instant, I'm not in this sterile workroom anymore. I'm back in my grandmother's living room.

The first time Grandma Elara told me about love, I was

ten, sitting cross-legged on the worn rug in her living room. She held a faded photograph in her hands, a relic from the time before Harmonization. In it, a young couple stood arm in arm, their faces unguarded and joyful.

"This was your grandfather and me," she said, her voice a soft rasp. "We were so happy then."

I looked at the picture, then at her. "Why don't you look like that now?"

She smiled, but it was the kind of smile that hurt to see. "The NeuroMods make sure we don't feel too much of anything. It's safer this way, though it means we can't experience true happiness—or true sadness."

As a child, I couldn't fully grasp what she was telling me. The idea that people once lived with unregulated emotions seemed as fantastical as a bedtime story. But even then, a seed of doubt was planted in my mind. If they had been so happy, why had things changed?

Over the years, Grandma Elara fed that seed with countless stories that wrap around me like a warm blanket—each word a whisper of forgotten freedom, leaving a hollowness in my chest: an aching reminder of what was and what can never be again.

She spoke of a time when people laughed freely, cried openly, and loved with their whole hearts. A time when every day was an adventure, full of unpredictable highs and lows. She never outright condemned The Harmonization Authority, but her nostalgia for the past made it clear where her sympathies lay.

It was Grandma Elara who explained the concept of freedom to me. Not the kind enshrined in laws and regulations, but the deeper, more personal freedom to be oneself—to feel and express every emotion without fear of reprisal. Her wisdom came from a place of lived experience, and I drank it in like a man in a desert finding a hidden spring.

I blink, the memories fading as quickly as they came. My throat tightens. She was right. Looking around at my colleagues, I see nothing but empty shells, going through the motions of living without truly feeling alive.

"Hansen," a sharp, feminine voice cuts through my reverie. "Your productivity has decreased by 3.7% in the last five minutes. Is there a problem?"

Swallowing hard, I force my face into a bland expression, glancing up at my morning supervisor. "No, ma'am. Just recalibrating my focus." I say as she continues on her rounds.

Glancing up from my workstation, I catch sight of Ziva across the aisle. Her long, light brown hair cascades down her shoulder as she bends over her NeuroMod console, nimble fingers adjusting its controls. A familiar ache blooms in my chest.

"Ridiculous," I mutter, forcing my gaze back to my screen. "Quit staring, Myall."

But my mind wanders, wrestling with the constant internal conflict. The regime's mantra echoes—emotions lead to chaos. Control brings peace. Yet every fiber of my being strains against it.

Ziva looks up, catching my eye. She quirks an eyebrow, the tiniest hint of a smirk playing at her lips.

"Excuse me, Myall," she calls out, her voice carefully measured. "I need your input on this compliance report, please."

Standing, I approach her station, wiping my sweaty palms on my pants as I walk. "Of course, Ms. Emerson. What seems to be the issue?"

As I lean in to examine her screen, I catch a whiff of her scent—clean and slightly floral. It takes every ounce of control not to close my eyes and breathe deeply.

"See this anomaly?" Ziva points to a graph, her finger barely brushing mine. The contact jolts through me. "It doesn't fit the standard pattern."

Focus on the data, not how close you are to her.

"You're right. It could indicate a malfunction in the citizens NeuroMod, or—"

"Or non-compliance," Ziva finishes, her hazel eyes meeting mine with an intensity that makes me wonder if we're still talking about the report. For a moment, I see a flash of something in her eyes before it's quickly masked.

"Thanks for flagging it," I say, careful to hide the resentment from my tone, "I'll review the data."

Ziva's lips curve upwards in a small, almost melancholic smile. My gaze drifts to her lips, noting the fullness of her bottom lip and the faint scar on her warm tawny skin, right where a dimple would be.

Returning to my workstation, my mind wanders again. Is it possible Ziva feels the same frustration, the same longing for freedom? Or am I projecting my own desires onto her, seeing what I want to see?

One thing's certain—this growing attraction, this connection—is dangerous. But as I steal another glance at Ziva from across the aisle, I can't bring myself to care. In a world of emptiness, she makes me feel alive.

Leaning back in my chair, I scan the rows of data scrolling across my screen from the citizen that Ziva reported. My fingers fly over the keyboard, inputting complex algorithms to detect even the slightest deviation in emotional patterns. It's ironic, really. I'm using my intelligence to maintain the very system I despise.

"Hansen," my supervisor's voice crackles through the intercom at my workstation. "Report on Sector 7's compliance levels. Now."

Taking a deep breath, I suppress my irritation and steady myself. "Right away, ma'am." My voice is calm, betraying none of the turmoil beneath.

I compile the report, acutely aware of the weight of my actions. Each number represents a person, a life constrained by the regime's iron grip.

"Compliance levels in Sector 7 are at 98.7%," I announce, my tone neutral. "There's a slight anomaly in sub-section C, but it's now within acceptable parameters."

"Good work, Hansen. The latest dissent appears to have been squashed," comes the reply. "Keep monitoring."

I exhale slowly, relief mingling with guilt. I've just condemned countless people to continued emotional abuse.

When I landed my job at eighteen in the Compliance Monitoring Division, my goal was to make a positive impact. It's been six years now, and I have yet to make a difference for anyone. Each report I process feels like a chain tightening around my chest, squeezing the breath from my lungs. It makes me question whether I am the instrument of my own oppression.

As the lunch hour approaches, I feel a desperate need for solitude. Grabbing my regulation nutritional packet, I slip away to a secluded corner of the building's rooftop garden.

Sitting on a cold metal bench, I stare out at the stark

cityscape. The towering gray buildings seem to close in around me, a physical manifestation of the oppression we all live under.

What am I doing here? Am I really making a difference?

Grandma's stories spoke of a time when people felt freely—laughing, crying, loving with abandon—before The Authority. I think of Ziva, and the spark I see in her eyes. And I feel the weight of all those who can't feel at all.

There has to be another way. I can't keep living like this. None of us can.

As lunch ends and I head back to my workstation, I know I have no choice. For now, at least, I must continue to be the perfect Compliance Monitor. It's the only way to stay close to the heart of the system, and the only way I might one day find a way to bring it down.

The rest of my shift passes in a blur of data and compliance reports. When the end-of-day signal finally sounds, a weight lifts from my shoulders.

Gathering my things, I nod goodbye to my colleagues. I step out into the crisp evening air, my steps quickening as I head towards the security checkpoint, leaving this hellhole behind for the day.

Chapter Four

Myall

The streets are empty and eerily silent, the cool air biting my cheeks as I trudge home from another mind-numbing shift. Gray buildings loom on either side, their blank facades like a mirror to the emotional void we're forced to endure. I clench my fist, pushing against the heavy weight in my chest. There has to be more than this hollow excuse for a life.

My grandmother's stories of a time before The Harmonization Authority echo in my mind, taunting me with glimpses of a life I'll never know. I try to steady my thoughts, reminding myself of the potential consequences for even thinking such rebellious ideas.

I'm so lost in my bitter musings that I almost miss it—a flash of movement in a shadowy alley. My instincts kick in and I slow my pace, peering into the darkness.

A lithe woman crouches in the shadows, vibrant red hair spilling from beneath her dark hood. Her slender fingers work frantically, the dim light flashing off a small metal tool as she tampers with her NeuroMod. My breath catches as I realize what I'm seeing.

She's defying The Authority by sabotaging her device. Or at least, she's trying to.

I should report this immediately—it's my job, my duty as a Compliance Monitor. Yet I stand frozen, drawn in by the fierce boldness of her actions. My mind races with conflicting emotions and thoughts as I struggle with what to do next.

Before I can decide, she glances up, her eyes locking onto mine. It's like time has frozen, the air thickens between us, charged with the thrill of rebellion and discovery. The shadows of the alley dance around her as her lips curve in a mischievous smile.

"See something interesting?" Her voice carries a hint of challenge.

My words catch in my throat. "I…what are you doing?"

She holds up her wrist, the NeuroMod's screen flickering erratically. "Living. You should try it sometime."

The distant wail of a siren echoes through the night. I watch as her eyes widen in fear, slowly backing away from me.

"Fuck," she mutters, pocketing the small blade she was using to tamper with her NeuroMod as she continues her retreat down the alley.

"Wait," I call out, surprising myself. "I'm Myall. What's your name?"

She hesitates, then grins. "Arden. Catch you around,

Myall—if you're brave enough."

With a wink, she disappears into the shadows, leaving me standing there with my world turned upside down. I stare at the spot where she vanished and take a deep breathe before resuming my walk.

As I round the corner to my apartment, a patrol drone buzzes overhead. I freeze, heart pounding in my throat.

Did it see me? Does it know what I just saw?

The small gray drone pauses, its scanning beam sweeping the street. I hold my breath, willing my face to remain as impassive as always.

"Citizen, state your purpose in this area," the metallic voice of the drone demands, slicing through the evening air like a knife. Swallowing hard, I force my voice to remain steady. "Returning home from work shift. Compliance Monitor Myall Hansen, ID 24601."

There's a moment of agonizing silence as the drone processes my response before it responds. "Verified. Proceed."

As it zips away into the night with a soft whir, I exhale shakily. Close call. Way too fucking close. My mind races as I hurry home, Arden's defiance echoing in my thoughts. A tangled mix of hope and fear tightens in my chest. I've never seen anyone challenge the system so openly before.

I know I should report her. It's not just my job—failure means severe consequences. If anyone finds out that I knew about her bold act of rebellion, I could end up in one of The Authority's detention centers, facing possible recalibration.

"Living. You should try it sometime." Her words echo in my ears, stirring something long dormant inside me.

Unlocking my apartment door, my hand trembles slightly as I hold it up to the biometric scanner on the wall. I step inside, catching my reflection in the mirror—my green eyes, wide with a mix of awe and trepidation—stare back at me. My normally tan skin looks pale and lifeless under the harsh light.

My fingers twitch, itching to do something, anything. But what? Report her? The thought makes my stomach churn.

"There have to be others," I mutter, running a hand through my mousy brown hair. "Other people who want more than just…to exist."

The implications of Arden's actions hit me like a shock wave. If she's willing to tamper with her NeuroMod, what else might be possible? My mind kicks into overdrive, considering possibilities I've never dared entertain before.

But the risks.

I slump onto the dark gray sofa, my fingers clenching and unclenching in my lap. Every muscle in my body trembles with indecision.

The room around me suddenly feels suffocating, as if its walls are closing in on me. A faint sheen of sweat appears on my forehead as I try to calm my racing thoughts. My NeuroMod vibrates against my wrist, sensing my rising emotions. Every part of me pulls in a different direction, uncertain which way to turn.

Yet the memory of Arden's fierce smile, the glimmer in her eyes, stirs something in me. A yearning for genuine connection with real emotions, for the depth of emotions I've only glimpsed in my grandmother's tales.

There must be a way to challenge the system, to feel again.

Standing, I pace again, my mind awhirl with questions and possibilities.

The shrill wail of sirens jolts me from my thoughts. They're getting closer. I rush to the window, peering out cautiously.

"No, no, no," I groan, spotting the telltale blue and red flashing lights of Authority Enforcer vehicles converging on the area where I last saw Arden.

I should turn away, pretend I saw nothing. But my feet are rooted to the spot, my eyes fixed on the scene unfolding right outside my apartment complex. A flash of red hair catches my eye, darting between shadows.

"Come on, come on," I urge under my breath, willing her to escape. If she's caught, she could easily rat me out.

Suddenly, an Enforcers gaze locks onto me. I duck instinctively, heart pounding.

Shit, did he see me?

I force my breathing to slow, knowing I need to appear calm, compliant. I'm just another law-abiding citizen, nothing to see here.

A sharp knock at my door a minute later makes me jump, my stomach bottoming out. "Compliance check!" a stern voice calls out. "Open up!"

Fuck.

Taking a deep breath, I school my features into a mask of placid neutrality.

The NeuroMod on my wrist emits a warning beep, taunting me with the knowledge that it can sense my true frame of mind, despite my efforts to appear composed.

"Coming!" I call back, my voice steadier than I feel. My hands shake as I smooth my hair and approach the door.

"Good evening, Enforcer," I say, opening the door with a practiced smile.

The Authority Enforcers cold eyes scan my face, then peer past me into my apartment as if searching for something—or someone.

"We're investigating a disturbance in this sector that has been reported by multiple citizens. Have you witnessed any suspicious activity in this area tonight?"

Swallowing hard, Arden's face flashes in my mind. "No, sir. Just a quiet evening at home."

"Really?" he asks, his tone skeptical. "You didn't see a woman with red hair in the area?"

My heart pounds so loudly I'm sure he can hear it. If other citizens reported Arden, they might have reported me too.

"I…I'm not sure," I stammer. "I thought I saw someone earlier, but I didn't get a good look."

The Enforcers eyes narrow. "Where exactly did you see this person?"

"Near the maglev station on Fifth," I lie, pointing in the opposite direction of where I actually saw Arden. "But it was just a glimpse, so I can't be certain."

He studies me for a long moment. I force myself to meet his gaze, praying my face and my NeuroMod don't betray me.

"Very well," he says finally. "If you remember anything else, report it immediately. Failure to do so is a violation of the Emotional Harmony Act."

I nod, relief washing over me, but I keep it hidden. "Of course, Enforcer. I understand."

As the door closes, I lean against it, my legs weak.

What the fuck am I doing? I just lied to an Authority Enforcer. For her. For a stranger.

Panic swells within me, accompanied by a flicker of exhilaration. I slump back onto my sofa, heart still racing from the close call. The echoes of sirens fade into the distance, but the image of Arden's defiant act burns bright in my mind.

I've spent years playing it safe, burying my doubts deep beneath a veneer of compliance.

Standing abruptly, I pace the small confines of my apartment.

If I say something, do something...I could lose everything.

But a voice in my head, one I can almost hear like my grandmother's, asks, 'What are you really living for if you do nothing?'

I pause by the small window in my living room, staring out at the cityscape. The NeuroMod on my wrist feels heavier than ever, like a cold metal shackle binding me to a life without choice. Its constant thrum pulses against my skin, reminding me that freedom is just a fantasy.

"There has to be more than this," I murmur, touching the cool glass. "A life where emotions aren't controlled, where fear isn't the only constant."

My reflection stares back at me, eyes conflicted.

I can't take this any longer.

I want out.

I want freedom.

I want her.

I square my shoulders, determined. I can't stand by any longer. But I have to be careful. I return to the sofa. If there's one person willing to fight back, there have to be others. Perhaps we can band together and form a network. Leaning forward, elbows on my knees, I begin to plan—searching for a way forward.

Chapter Five

Myall

The next morning, I arrive at the Compliance Monitoring Division, my heart racing beneath a carefully composed exterior. My NeuroMod vibrates in warning of the elevation in my mood, but I tune it out. The antiseptic smell of the place hits me as I pass through security, and I inwardly cringe.

Making my way to my workstation, I scan the room for any sign of unusual activity. That's when I spot her—Ziva Emerson, her long, light brown hair cascading down her back. She leans over her workstation, and the light catches her hair, making it appear more golden than brown. There's an indescribable quality about her that I'm drawn to.

A sudden beep from the communication system overhead grabs everyone's attention.

Our supervisor's voice cuts through the air, tense and

urgent. "Attention all personnel. We've received reports of a potential NeuroMod sabotage last night in one of the outer sectors. Be on high alert for any irregularities. All Compliance Monitors are to begin scanning for irregularities immediately."

My breath catches in my throat, a lump of dread forming as I digest the announcement. The realization that they know about Arden sends a chill through me. There's a growing sense of dread as I struggle to maintain a mask of composure. I can't help risking a glance at Ziva from across the aisle. What I see makes my heart skip a beat.

Her hazel eyes widen, revealing a mixture of fear and something else. She quickly schools her features, but not before I catch a glimpse of something that mirrors my own inner turmoil.

Interesting.

"Emerson," our supervisor barks through her desk comm. "I want you to run a full diagnostic on the affected sector."

Ziva nods, her voice steady. "Right away, ma'am."

Now's my chance.

She turns to her screen, fingers flying over the datapad as I approach.

Leaning in, I keep my voice low. "Quite a stir this morning, huh?"

Ziva looks up, her eyes meeting mine before her usual mask of indifference slides back into place.

"Just another day in paradise," she replies, her tone dripping with sarcasm and her full lips pursing.

Leaning in, I pretend to examine her screen so that Lena at the workstation beside us thinks we are discussing compliance data. "Ever wonder what it would be like? To live without these things?" I gesture subtly to the NeuroMods on our wrists, holding my breath as I wait for her reaction.

Please let me be right about her.

Her fingers pause mid-keystroke. She looks at me, really looks at me, and I feel exposed under her piercing gaze.

"Those are dangerous thoughts, Hansen," she murmurs, but there's no reproach in her voice. Instead, I hear a note of curiosity.

Nodding, I return to my station, my mind lingering on Ziva's reaction. Her words echo in my head, but it's the look in her eyes—curiosity, maybe even hope—that lingers.

During the lunch hour, I find myself gravitating towards her in the cafeteria. My shoes squeak softly against the linoleum as I cross the room toward Ziva's table.

"Mind if I join you?" I ask, lunch tray in hand.

Ziva shrugs, a small smile playing at the corners of her mouth. "Free country, isn't it?" The irony in her tone is unmistakable.

Sitting beside her, I lean in close. "About earlier..." I begin, my voice barely above a whisper so that none of our coworkers or the cameras on the walls can overhear. "I've been thinking. There has to be more to life than this, right?"

Ziva's eyes dart around, checking for eavesdroppers. "Careful," she warns, but there's an undercurrent of excitement in her voice. "Walls have ears here."

"I know," I murmur, my heart racing. "But don't you ever wonder about the resistance? About a world without NeuroMods?"

Her eyes narrow slightly, studying me. I can almost see the gears turning in her head, trying to decide if I'm a threat or something else entirely. She leans back, continuing to study me as the internal struggle plays out across her face.

Finally, she speaks, her voice low and measured. "Meet me after work. Northeast corner of Sector 7. We'll talk then, not here."

Nodding, I try to contain my excitement. This is it—the first real step toward rebellion. Would my parents be proud? Or would they be concerned that I'm following in their footsteps?

The rest of the day passes in a blur of anticipation and nerves. I find myself watching the clock, counting down the minutes until I can learn more about whether Ziva feels the same way about this world as I do.

I spend the remainder of my shift weighing my every word, the consequences of a single mistake heavy on my mind. But the chance for freedom, for real connection—it feels worth the gamble.

As our shift ends, I casually make my way to Sector 7 with an outwardly composed appearance. But inside, my heart is beating rapidly. The NeuroMod tracks my elevated heart rate. I know I'll need to erase the data tomorrow. I take a series of deep breaths in an attempt to steady myself before my NeuroMod takes over to dose me.

That's when I spot Ziva leaning against a wall, one leg braced upon the wall and her eyes scanning the area with practiced nonchalance.

"Beautiful weather we're having," I say as I approach, using the coded phrase we'd agreed on earlier.

Her lips quirk. "Could use more sunshine," she replies, completing the exchange.

She steps out from the wall and we fall into step together, walking as if we're simply two coworkers heading home.

"I saw your face when they announced the NeuroMod sabotage this morning," I murmur, keeping my voice low in case of any cameras or drones flying overhead. "You looked...hopeful."

Ziva stiffens slightly, her pace faltering for just a moment. "And what if I did?" she challenges, her voice a mix of defiance and caution, but I can see the color draining from her light brown skin.

I take a deep breath, bracing myself for what I'm about to confess. "Then I'd say you're not alone. I've been questioning things for a while now. And after seeing what happened with Arden..."

Her head snaps toward me, "You actually know the person sabotaging their NeuroMod?"

I should not have said that.

I shake my head, "No, I have absolutely no idea who she is."

Ziva's sharp intake of breath tells me I've struck a chord. "Then...you saw it happen?" she whispers, piecing it together.

I realize then just how intelligent Ziva actually is. Nodding, my eyes meet hers. "It made me realize there are others out there who want change. Who believe we deserve more than this...existence."

For a long moment, she's silent as we walk. It's like the gears are turning in her mind, weighing the risks against the potential of finding an ally versus the consequences of if we're caught.

Finally, she speaks. "This is dangerous territory, Myall. You know that, right? Are you sure you want to go down this path?"

"I've never been more sure." As soon as I say it, I know it's the truth.

Ziva's hazel eyes widen, a mix of surprise and intrigue flickering across her face. Her lips purse slightly, the tension in her posture mirroring the precarious balance of our conversation. Her fingers wrap tightly around my arm, pulling me towards a dimly lit alcove. As we enter the alleyway, I can feel her excitement radiating through her grip, but also a hint of caution as she leads us into the shadows.

"You're serious about this?" she whispers, her voice trembling slightly. "You really want to challenge the system?"

I nod. The silence between us stretches, heavy with the gravity of what we've just said. "I can't keep living like this, Ziva. Pretending I don't feel, that I don't want more. Can you?" Each word feels like a vow, a commitment to the unknown. The NeuroMod on my wrist feels heavier now, reminding me of what we stand to lose, but also of what we might gain together.

She bites her lip, her face tense with conflict. When she speaks, her voice is a whisper, each word laced with fear and resolve. "I've been trying to modify my NeuroMod in secret for a while now," she confesses, her eyes darting around to check we're alone. "Trying to find a way to break their hold on us so that I can experience the full extent of my emotions."

My breath catches as I realize the risk she took in confessing this. "That's brilliant. And incredibly risky."

"Says the man proposing rebellion," she retorts, a hint of a smile tugging at her lips.

I can't help but grin back. "Maybe we're both a little crazy."

"Maybe we're the only ones who haven't given up on feeling anything at all," Ziva muses. She looks at me intently.

"If we do this, there's no going back. Are you prepared for that?"

I offer my hand. She takes it, and I feel the warmth of her skin against mine. "I am if you are. Together, we might actually have a chance."

Ziva squeezes my hand, her eyes shining. "Alright, Hansen," she says softly as she squeezes my hand once more, her grip warm and steady. "Let's start a rebellion."

Chapter Six

Ziva

Watching Myall's steady, fluid movements as his slender fingers glide over the tools, he places each one with meticulous care, and I can't help but smirk, even as my own NeuroMod dulls the amusement I should be feeling.

We're gathered around my workstation, conducting our repairs on malfunctioning devices. Thankfully, it means we won't have to subject any citizens to the mind-numbing recalibration process today.

"You know," I say, keeping my voice low, "I think you missed a spot. That micro capacitor is at least half a millimeter out of alignment."

Myall's green eyes flick up to meet mine, a ghost of a smile playing at the corners of his mouth before he quickly schools his features. "Very funny, Ziva. I'll have you know this system is perfected to maximize our repair efficiency."

"Oh, I'm sure," I drawl, picking up a precision screwdriver and twirling it between my fingers. "Because heaven forbid we have to reach an extra inch for a tool."

Myall shakes his head, his messy brown locks falling into his eyes—but I catch the slight upturn of his lips. "Mock all you want, but when we're neck-deep in repairs later today, you'll be thanking me for this organization."

I open my mouth to retort, but the words die in my throat as the screwdriver slips from my grasp. Time slows as the tool clatters to the floor, the sound echoing through the cavernous workroom like a gunshot. My heart rate spikes, a flash of panic breaking through the emotional dampening of my NeuroMod.

Before I can react, Myall is there, his rough hand brushing mine as we both reach for the fallen screwdriver. I freeze, my pulse quickening as our fingers brush, the brief touch sending a ripple of feeling through me that my NeuroMod can't quite suppress. It's a warmth that spreads from our fingertips, awakening something long dormant within me.

"I've got it," Myall says, his voice low and gentle. He retrieves the screwdriver, our hands still close enough that I can feel the warmth radiating from his skin.

Swallowing hard, I try to regain my composure as a flush creeps up my neck. "Thanks," I manage. As Myall straightens, our eyes meet, and for a moment, I see a flicker of something in his gaze—a depth of emotion that shouldn't be possible with our dampened states. I blink and the emotion vanishes from his face.

"No problem," he replies, clearing his throat and taking a step back as he holds out the screwdriver. "Wouldn't want to disrupt the perfect organization, right?"

Taking the instrument, my fingers brush his once more. "Right," I say, attempting to inject some levity into my tone. "Can't have chaos in the sacred order of things."

As we return to our work of repairing the NeuroMods, I can't help but steal glances at Myall. My mind races, trying to make sense of the connection I just felt. Is it my imagination, or was there something different in the way he looked at me today?

Since our meeting at the abandoned factory last night, where we proposed the idea of starting a rebellion, he's been looking at me almost…wistfully? No, that can't be right.

I refocus on the NeuroMod, but my mind keeps drifting. My hands move automatically through the familiar motions of repair, but my mind can't seem to let go of that brief touch with Myall and the way he keeps looking at me today.

There's something about him, something I can't ignore, no matter how much my conditioning demands I suppress it. Our interactions have always been strictly professional— even with our workstations across from each other—but this morning there's something different, a connection that I never expected to feel.

And here I am, unable to stop thinking about it.

Myall continues working beside me, seemingly oblivious to the turmoil in my mind. He hums softly under his breath, and I find myself drawn to the sound. It's a simple tune, one that we've all heard countless times during our daily routines here.

But now it sounds different, almost like a melody that wraps around me, pulling me into its rhythm. The familiar tune, once a mere backdrop to our daily routines, now stirs something deep inside, a longing for freedom that thrums in sync with the beat.

I shake my head, my long hair swaying back and forth as I try to clear my thoughts. This is ridiculous. I'm supposed to be immune to these kinds of feelings. That's what the NeuroMods do, they suppress these burning emotions. We've all grown up being warned about the dangers of uncontrollable feelings.

"Something on your mind?" Myall's soft, husky voice breaks through my thoughts, and I jump slightly in surprise.

"Uh…no," I reply quickly, hoping he didn't notice my distraction. I grab the NeuroMod before me, turning it over and begin prying open it's casing. "Just…lost in thought."

He gives me a curious look before shrugging and returning his focus to his work. But even as we continue our tasks in silence, I can't shake off the questions swirling in my mind.

How many others feel this way? How many of us are silently yearning for something more, something real? And more importantly, what would happen if we dared to reach for it?

The sharp click of heels on the polished floor shatters my reverie. I cringe as I recognize the sound—Supervisor Penn approaching. Glancing at Myall, I see my own tension mirrored in his eyes.

"Status report, Technicians," Supervisor Penn demands, her voice as cold and sterile as the room around us.

I swallow hard, heart stuttering. We've been talking more than working, and our progress is behind. "I'm just finishing up the repairs on this batch, ma'am," I lie without hesitation, gesturing to the half-repaired NeuroMods before us.

Supervisor Penn's eyes narrow suspiciously. She glances

at Myall who paused his retreat to his workstation when Penn glanced his way. "Is that so? Your efficiency metrics seem…lacking today, Emerson."

Thinking quickly, I grab the nearest NeuroMod. "Actually, ma'am, Mr. Hansen and I encountered an unusual malfunction. See this fluctuation here?" I point to a random readout laying sprawled on my workstation bench, praying she doesn't look too closely. "We've been working to isolate the cause. It could indicate a larger systemic issue."

Myall picks up on it, adding, "Ms. Emerson decided it was best to investigate thoroughly before proceeding with repairs, and asked me to examine the fluctuations from a compliance standpoint."

Supervisor Penn's expression shifts from suspicion to interest. "I see. Carry on then, but I expect a full report by end of shift."

As she walks away, I exhale slowly, relief washing over me. *Thank god she bought that.*

Turning to Myall, a small smile plays at my lips as I bump his shoulder with mine. "Quick thinking," I mumble.

"You started it," he replies, his voice equally low.

Seizing the moment, I discreetly reach for a small, folded paper from my pant pocket and slide it across my workstation bench. "Something you should see," I whisper, my heart pounding. "Later."

Myall's fingers close around the note, and I see a flicker of curiosity in his eyes as he expertly tucks the note away, concealing it from sight. What I've just done is dangerously reckless, a foolish gamble that could unravel everything. But as I watch him stride back towards his workstation, excitement bubbles within me.

The rest of the morning passes in a blur of routine repairs and diagnostics, and I find my gaze constantly drawn to Myall. Our eyes meet across the workroom, brief stolen glances that send a flutter through my chest despite the dampening effects of my NeuroMod. Each time, I quickly look away, focusing intently on the tools in my hands, but the connection lingers—and so does his searing gaze.

I'm reaching for a micro-spanner when Supervisor Penn's voice cuts through the noise of machinery over the comm system at my workstation. "Emerson, Hansen. My office, now."

My stomach drops. Did she suspect something about our earlier exchange? Did one of the camera's catch the note that I passed to Myall? I shoot a worried glance at Myall, but his face remains impassive as he places his tools on the workbench and begins walking towards our supervisor's office.

Inside her office, Penn gestures sharply toward a complex array of circuitry on her desk, the polished surface reflecting the harsh overhead lighting. The intricate network of wires and components hums softly, like a mechanical heartbeat.

"We've got a priority repair at the request of Regent Colvin. Highly sensitive equipment from Elysium. I need your combined expertise on this."

Myall and I exchange curious glances. Priority repairs are rare, reserved for high-ranking projects or emergencies. And we are being assigned one together. If Regent Colvin, figurehead of The Harmonization Authority is requesting this personally, it must be important.

"Of course, ma'am," Myall responds smoothly for the both of us, his tone neutral.

The thrill of being assigned to work with Myall on a project that could have far-reaching implications sends a rush of adrenaline through me as Supervisor Penn begins briefing us on the details of the repair.

As she talks, I lean in, examining the intricate web of connections. My fingers trace the delicate pathways, feeling the coolness of the components beneath my touch, each one a potential key to unlocking the mysteries of the NeuroMod system.

"This is…different," I mutter, my curiosity piqued.

Myall nods as he points to a section, his presence close enough that I feel the warmth of his body. "Look at how these relays are configured. I've never seen anything like it."

Supervisor Penn dismisses us back to our workstations to start the repairs, and we make our way back, Myall's pace easily matching mine in our usual synchronized rhythm.

"What do you think this is all about?" he murmurs out of the corner of his mouth as we stand huddled back at my workstation, examining the small machine before us.

Neither of us has any clue about the function of this machine, and Supervisor Penn purposely kept us in the dark. This must mean that its use is something truly terrifying.

I shrug, keeping my voice equally low. "No idea."

We fall into a seamless rhythm, our hands moving in tandem as we discuss possible approaches.

"If we reroute through here," I suggest, tracing a path with my finger, "we might be able to bypass the damaged section entirely."

Myall's eyes light up. "Yeah. And if we couple that with a recursive feedback loop—"

"We could potentially boost the overall efficiency by at

least 15%," I finish, a hint of excitement filling my voice before it's quickly suppressed.

We move with an unspoken rhythm, our thoughts and hands aligning effortlessly.

I catch Myall's eye, a flicker of mischief sparking between us. "You know, I bet I could repair a NeuroMod faster than you," I say, my tone flat but my eyes glinting with challenge. Myall began as a NeuroMod Technician—before he became a Compliance Monitor—so I know he will be a decent component.

Myall raises an eyebrow, the corners of his lips twitching. "Is that so? Care to test that theory?"

"Why not?" I reply, clearing some space and reaching for two identical NeuroMods at my workstation. "First one to recalibrate and restore full functionality wins."

We position ourselves at the workstation, tools at the ready. I am hyperaware of our coworkers' eyes frequently darting towards us, but I tune them out.

"On three," Myall says, his voice low. "One…two…three."

Our hands move swiftly, deftly manipulating the delicate components. I steal glances at Myall, admiring the intensity of his focus, the precise movements of his fingers. My heart rate quickens, but the NeuroMod quickly dulls the edge of the feeling.

As I work, my mind wanders. What would this feel like without the dampening effects of the NeuroMod? Would my hands shake with excitement? Would I feel a rush of adrenaline?

I finish a fraction of a second before Myall, setting down my tools with a soft click. "Done," I announce, my voice betraying only a hint of satisfaction. I catch Marcus's eye from a few workstations away. His lips curl into the hint of a smirk as he watches Myall and me. My cheeks flush as I realize that he's been observing us this whole time. I pray that he won't say anything to Supervisor Penn.

Turning my attention back to Myall, he glances up, his eyes meeting mine. "Well played," he says, his tone warm despite its subdued nature. "You're remarkable, Ziva."

The compliment catches me off guard, a rush of warmth spreading through my chest. I lower my voice, leaning in slightly. "Do you ever wonder what it was like before? Before The Harmonization Authority I mean."

I'm putting myself in danger by asking him a question like this, especially since anyone can overhear and report me to The Authority.

Myall's expression shifts, his lips pursing in thought. "Sometimes," he admits softly.

I give a silent nod, understanding the implications of his vague response and realizing I shouldn't have asked him while we're at work. But it's a question I've been dying to ask someone for years now.

Before The Harmonization Authority, the world was chaotic, communities on edge, always afraid of losing control and causing fear and disorder. But even with that knowledge, I can't help but feel a pang of curiosity about what life was like before. Now that I have Myall to talk to, it's like I can't help all these burning questions from slipping out.

"Do you think we were happier then?" I ask quietly, biting my lower lip.

This isn't the time or place, stop pushing Ziva.

Myall's gaze softens as he looks at me, an unspoken understanding passing between us. "It's hard to say," he replies thoughtfully. "There were certainly more…ups and downs. But happiness is a relative concept."

We fall into comfortable silence once again, neither of us wanting to voice our true thoughts so openly with fear of being overheard. My mind still lingers on Myall's words though, wondering what it would be like to experience those 'ups and downs' moments without the dampening effects of the NeuroMods.

Redirecting my attention to my workstation, I zero in on the damaged machine scattered across the bench. The cold metal feels familiar in my hands as I turn it over, studying its lifeless display. Myall stands beside me, his presence both comforting and unnerving, the weight of Penn's expectations pressing down on us both.

"We need to figure out what's wrong with this thing," I mutter, more to myself than to Myall. My fingers trace the edges of the machine, searching for any obvious defects.

He leans in closer, his warm breath tickling my ear and making the hairs on my neck prickle. "What if we approach it from a different angle?" he suggests softly.

I turn to look at him, raising an eyebrow. "What do you mean?"

He glances around furtively before continuing. "Instead of trying to fix it, what if we try to understand how it works at its core?"

Is he suggesting what I think he is?

I force my voice to stay steady."That's…not exactly what Penn assigned us to do."

And its way too fucking dangerous if Regent Colvin finds out.

Myall's green eyes lock onto mine, filled with an intensity that slows my heartrate. "No, but it might be more valuable in the long run."

Biting my lip, I consider. The rebellious part of me thrills at the idea, while the rational side warns of the dangers. But as I look down at the machine again, a new perspective occurs

If we want to start a rebellion, we need to actually start rebelling.

"You're right," I whisper. "If we can understand its inner workings, we could…"

I trail off, not daring to voice the rest of that thought aloud.

Myall nods, his mouth quirked with a small smile. "Exactly."

Carefully, I pry open the casing of the machine's circuitry, the sharp snap of the casing breaking the silence. I peel back the layers and am met with a confusing tangle of wires and components.

As I examine the machine's innards, my fingers brush against a tiny component that went unnoticed before. It's nestled behind the main circuitry, almost invisible to the naked eye.

"Myall," I breathe. "Look at this."

He leans in close, his warmth radiating against my skin. "What is it?"

"I'm not sure, but…" I squint, examining the minuscule component. "It looks like some kind of failsafe. Or maybe…"

My mind races with possibilities. Could this be the key to understanding how the NeuroMods truly function? Or better yet, how to disrupt them?

Myall's voice drops to a whisper, a soft, urgent tone. "Is it a way to switch off our NeuroMods?" he asks, his shoulder brushing against mine as he peers closer.

I nod, heart pounding. "Possibly. If we could figure out how to manipulate this…"

Glancing around, I'm suddenly aware of how exposed we are in the workroom—but the thrill of this new discovery outweighs my caution. My NeuroMod vibrates in warning, quickly dampening my emotions.

"We need to be careful," Myall murmurs, his eyes meeting mine with concern. "If anyone found out we were even looking into this…"

"I know," I reply, my voice equally low. "But think of what this could mean, Myall. If we could find a way to exploit this…"

I can't finish the sentence, but I don't need to. The possibility of freedom, of genuine emotion, hangs unspoken between us.

As I carefully reassemble the machine, my mind is already formulating plans. This tiny component we found could be the first step towards dismantling the entire NeuroMod system. For the first time, I feel a surge of something I'd almost forgotten—hope.

Chapter Seven

Myall

The crumpled note burns in my pocket, Ziva's hurried scrawl seared into my memory. She used a basic code that could easily be decoded, using numbers to represent letters. She said we need a hidden place to talk freely, because our conversations at work are restricted, and it would be too conspicuous if we continue to meet in secluded areas like the outskirts of sector 7.

My gaze drifts to her station across the aisle. Her long, golden-brown hair falls over her shoulders, her gray shirt slightly untucked which is against regulation.

We can't exactly meet at each others apartments, one of our neighbors could easily rat us out for suspicious activity. I considered taking her to Grandma Elara's house, the safest and most obvious option for us to meet and talk. But, I couldn't quite bring myself to do it. It wasn't that I didn't want her to meet my grandmother. I just wanted some time alone with her, like the other night.

I clear my throat softly. "Ziva."

She looks up, hazel eyes sharp and questioning. Gesturing for her to come closer, she approaches my workstation.

"I have an idea," I whisper. "About what was in your note."

Her eyes widen almost imperceptibly, a flicker of vulnerability crossing her face as she leans in closer, her breath warming the space between us. She leans forward, ostensibly examining my monitor as she pretends we're discussing compliance data. "Go on."

I keep my eyes on the screen, words measured. "There are places in the city, hidden places. Remnants of…before. We could explore them. See if we could find a suitable location to continue to meet and talk."

Her breath catches, and for a moment, the world fades. It's just her eyes, locked on mine, the unspoken understanding between us deepening. My gaze drops to the rest of her face, seeing a mix of excitement and apprehension.

"That sounds…interesting," she says carefully.

I nod, swallowing. "It could be dangerous. But worth it. To find a safe place we can meet. To also understand where we came from. What we've lost."

Ziva straightens, her face a mask of professional indifference. But I catch the gleam in her eye, the slight tremor in her voice as she replies, "I look forward to discussing your findings at shift's end, Compliance Monitor Hansen."

As she walks away—her hips swaying softly—I stare at my hands, willing them to stop shaking. What we're planning is beyond risk—it feels like teetering on the edge of a cliff, the thrill of the fall mingling with the terror of what lies below.

If Authority Enforcers catch us we will be brought straight to the detention center. But the thought of showing Ziva those forgotten places, of sharing that connection—it makes me feel more alive than I have in years.

Taking a deep breath, I force myself back into the emotionless facade expected of us before my NeuroMod can dampen my mood. I can barely focus for the rest of my shift, my constantly thinking about the risks. As the final minutes tick by, I gather my things, taking great care to appear nonchalant.

"Goodnight, Mr. Hansen." Tara mumbles from the workstation beside mine as she heads for the exit.

"Goodnight," I reply, watching her leave as Ziva appears beside my workstation, her face a carefully constructed mask of neutrality.

"Shall we walk home together today, Compliance Monitor Hansen?" she asks, her voice steady but her eyes alight with barely contained excitement. She blinks once and the excitement vanishes from her features which makes my jaw clench.

"Of course, Technician Emerson," I reply, matching her professional tone as we make our way casually towards the exit.

We exit the building, our footsteps echoing in unison as we pass the security checkpoints and step out into the cool, evening air, the hum of the city surrounding us.

"So," Ziva murmurs, her words barely audible, "where are we really going?"

Resisting the urge to look around, I keep my gaze forward. "First, towards the maglev station. After that, nowhere specific. Just...exploring. Looking for possibilities."

She nods, a ghost of a smile playing at her lips as she walks in sync beside me. "Sounds intriguing. I've always been curious about the city's…less regulated areas."

"It's a risk," I warn, keeping my voice low. "But if we're careful, we might find what we need."

Ziva's hand brushes mine, a touch that's gone too soon. "I trust you, Myall."

I swallow hard, fighting to keep my expression blank. "Keep an eye out. We need to look like we're just taking a casual walk home."

We reach the maglev station and wait for a short while before the sleek, silver train arrives to take us towards my sector of the city. Ziva sits next to me, looking out the window at the rapidly passing cityscape.

I ensure we get off at my station, keeping up the illusion we're heading home together. We go through the security checkpoints and emerge onto the streets, which are now shrouded in twilight.

Guiding Ziva towards the outskirts of the sector, my eyes scan for potential meeting spots—abandoned buildings, secluded alleyways, anywhere that might offer a moment of privacy. Ziva's presence beside me is both comforting and terrifying. I'm leading her into danger, but the connection between us feels more real than anything I've ever felt before.

"What do you think that was?" Ziva whispers, nodding towards a crumbling structure.

At the outskirts, remnants of old buildings stand like ghostly sentinels, relics from the time before The Harmonization Authority took control. It's forbidden for citizens to come here, but I've managed to sneak out enough times during my childhood to explore. From my experiences, I know it's not as heavily guarded as The Authority wants us to believe.

Squinting, I try to imagine its original purpose. "Maybe…a theater? A place where people used to gather and listen to music or watch things."

Her eyes widen, drinking in the forbidden sight. "It's beautiful, even in ruins."

I nod, a hollow feeling in my chest. "Yeah. It is."

Or at least, it was.

Glancing around, ensuring we're alone and that there are no drones flying overhead, I guide Ziva towards a narrow alley tucked between two dilapidated buildings.

"This way," I say, as we step over the cracked pavement. "I've explored some of these passages before."

Ziva follows close behind, her curiosity palpable, and I can see her excitement bubbling just beneath the surface, mirroring my own.

"How did you find these?" she whispers, her slender fingers trailing along the rough brick walls as we step into a hidden alleyway.

"Desperation," I admit, ducking under a low-hanging pipe. "And a lot of sleepless nights spent wandering as a teenager."

We navigate a maze of forgotten alleyways. The air is thick with dust that clings to my skin, and the remnants of a world that once thrived seem to hang in the air. I can't help but marvel at Ziva's agility as she maneuvers through the obstacles with ease. She almost seems…graceful.

"It's like a whole other world down here," Ziva breathes, her eyes glistening in the dim light.

I nod, feeling a surge of warmth at the wonder on her face. "It's a glimpse of what once was, before—"

"Before Harmonization," she finishes, her tone bitter.

We round a corner, and my breath catches. There, hidden behind years of neglect, is a rusted metal door. "This is it," I whisper, my hand hovering over the handle. "Beyond this… it's territory The Authority has abandoned. It's forbidden to all citizens."

Ziva's expression is guarded. "Are you sure about this, Myall?"

Meeting her gaze, I see my own conflicted emotions reflected back at me. "No," I admit. "But I'm sure I want to find out what's on the other side. With you."

Her hand finds mine, squeezing gently before intertwining our fingers. The simple touch sends a jolt of warmth through me, grounding me in a way I hadn't expected. "Then let's do it."

With a deep breath, I push open the door and step into the forgotten space, my eyes widening as they adjust to the dimness. My NeuroMod registers the darkness of the room, and a soft blue light emits. The room is filled with relics of another time, each item a silent witness to a world lost to the ages, reflecting a time when art and passion thrived, unshackled by the cold hand of regulation.

"Look at this," I murmur, gesturing with the light of my NeuroMod to a large canvas propped against the wall. It's a riot of colors, vibrant and chaotic, each stroke pulling me deeper into the artist's turmoil. "Can you imagine creating something like this now?"

Ziva turns, her fingers hovering just above the surface of the painting. "It's…chaotic," she says, her voice hushed. "But beautiful. I can almost feel the artist's emotions pouring out of it."

I nod, unable to look away from the intensity in her eyes, trying to read the unspoken thoughts behind her gaze. "That's what art used to be about. Expressing the inexpressible."

Ziva's eyes soften, her face a mirror of longing and something else—something raw. "How do you think it made people feel? To look at something like this every day?"

"Alive," I respond automatically, the word catching in my throat. "I think it made them feel alive. Like they were truly here, in the moment."

We move deeper into the abandoned room, discovering sculptures twisted into impossible shapes, their forms defying the rigid structure of our current world. Ziva runs her hand along the curve of one, her touch reverent.

"It's so different from anything in the city," she muses. "Everything there is so…sterile. So calculated."

Emotionless.

I feel a pang in my chest, recognizing the longing in her voice. "That's the point though, isn't it? To keep us from feeling too much, from questioning The Authority and what they've taken from us."

Ziva's eyes meet mine in the dim light, a glimmer of defiance in them. "But…we're already questioning, aren't we? Just by being here, standing in the middle of all this," she says, gesturing around the room.

Swallowing hard, I'm suddenly aware of how close we're standing and how good it feels, holding her hand in mine. "Yeah, we are."

She nods, her gaze dropping to a small figurine cradled in her other hand. "Do you ever wonder what it would be like? To feel everything, without the restraint of the NeuroMods?"

"All the time," I admit. "But I think…I think I'm starting to understand it a little better now." I take a deep breath, the musty air of the abandoned building filling my lungs. "You know, my grandmother used to tell me stories about The Transition," I say, my voice low, cautious even though we're alone. "How it wasn't sudden, but a slow erosion of what people thought was acceptable to feel."

Ziva nods, her eyes shadowed with a mix of curiosity and shared understanding. "The salami-slice approach," she murmurs. "Take away one small freedom at a time, until there's nothing left."

"Yeah," I say, swallowing. "Over time though, people forgot what it was like to feel. They came to see the NeuroMods as a natural part of life, as essential as breathing. Anyone that rebelled was erased from history, their names and deeds consigned to oblivion."

"Just like my parents," she whispers, her voice filled with emotion that is quickly suppressed by her NeuroMod.

"Yeah. Mine as well," I whisper back in understanding.

We move through the room, our footsteps echoing in the emptiness when I spot a doorway. "Shall we?"

We step into the cavernous remains of an old theater, its rows of decaying seats staring back at us like forgotten witnesses to a lost era. The air is heavy with the scent of mildew and nostalgia as dust motes dance in the dim light.

"Can you imagine?" Ziva breathes, her voice filled with wonder. "Hundreds of people, all experiencing the same emotions together. Laughing, crying, feeling it all."

Closing my eyes, I try to picture it—the hundreds of people filling these seats and the music that would have filled the air.

"It must have been noisy," I say, opening my eyes to find Ziva watching me intently.

"But beautiful," she adds, a wistful smile tugging at the corners of her mouth.

We make our way to the stage, our footsteps stirring up dust motes that dance in the dim light of our NeuroMods. I help Ziva up, and for a moment, our hands linger together.

"You know," I say, my heart beating rapidly, "they say this is where the first protests against emotional regulation happened. Right here on stages like this one."

Ziva's eyes widen. "Really? I always thought it started in the factories."

I shake my head. Grandma Elara always told me stories of the resistance, I think it was her way of keeping my parents memories alive. "That came later. But it was artists who first understood what was happening, who tried to warn everyone."

We stand there in silence for a moment, the weight of history pressing down on us. Each dusty seat and frayed curtain tells a story of resistance and loss, and I can almost hear the whispers of those who dared to dream before us.

"Do you think we could ever get back to that?" Ziva asks, her voice almost a whisper, even though we're the only two people in the room.

Meeting her gaze, something stirs inside me—an unnameable sensation that grows harder to ignore. "I don't know," I admit, rubbing my thumb along the outside of her hand. "But being here, with you…it makes me want to try."

Ziva's eyes lock with mine, a flicker of something raw and unguarded passing between us. For a moment, we're suspended in time, the crumbling theater fading away until it's just us, standing on the precipice of something dangerous.

"Look," she whispers suddenly, breaking the spell. Her slender fingers point to a faded mural on the wall behind us.

We approach it carefully, mindful of the dusty chase and rotting floorboards that creak ominously beneath our weight. As we draw closer, I can make out vibrant splashes of color emerging from beneath years of grime and neglect. It's a scene of people—dancing, embracing, laughing. Their faces are alive with emotion, so different from the carefully controlled expressions we're used to seeing.

"It's…fascinating," I murmur, drinking in the sight. "I've never seen anything like it."

Ziva reaches out, her fingertips hovering just above the surface of the painted wall. "They look so free," she says, her voice thick with longing. "Can you imagine feeling that much, Myall? Without fear?" Ziva's voice trembles with a longing that resonates in my chest, her eyes wide and bright, as if she's peering into a future she can barely fathom.

I swallow hard, acutely aware of the NeuroMod on my wrist. "It would be terrifying," I admit. "But also…incredible."

She turns to me, a fierceness in her voice. "This is what we're going to fight for, isn't it? The right to feel like this?"

My heart pounds in my chest, each thump echoing in my ears as if it might betray me to the watchful eyes of The Authority. I want to tell her yes, to match her passion with my own. But caution holds me back.

"It's dangerous to think that way, Ziva," I warn, even as every fiber of my being rebels against my own words.

Isn't this why I brought her here? To share these very thoughts with someone else who feels the same way as I do?

"And living like this—half a life—feels safer to you?" she

challenges, her sleeve of her uniform shifting as she gestures emphatically. "Look around us, Myall. This is what we've lost. Don't you want it back?"

I close my eyes, overwhelmed by the conflicting emotions surging through me moments before my NeuroMod dampens them. When I open them again, Ziva is watching me intently, waiting for an answer I'm not sure I'm ready to give.

I inhale slowly. "You're right," I say heavily. "This is what we should be fighting for. But we need to be smart about it."

Ziva's eyes light up, a smile tugging at the corners of her mouth. "I knew you felt it too," she says, her tone a mix of triumph and relief.

Glancing around the abandoned space, reality settles back in. "We can't keep coming here, though. It's too far, too risky."

She nods, her expression turning thoughtful. "We need somewhere closer, somewhere where we don't need to rely on the Maglev. Somewhere that's within walking distance, where we can meet regularly without raising suspicion."

"I know," I agree, my mind already running through possibilities of old factories and buildings that are within walking distance from the Compliance Monitoring Division. "Maybe there's a place near work that's less monitored. We'll have to be careful, but—"

"But it will be worth it," Ziva finishes, her gaze intense.

A surge of warmth flares in my chest, quickly tamped down once more by my NeuroMod.

"We should head back," I say reluctantly, my voice barely a whisper. "It'll be curfew soon and we don't want to risk any drones or Authority Enforcers on our way back." The reality of our situation crashes over me like a cold wave, and the thought of leaving this sanctuary fills me with a profound sense of loss.

Reluctantly, we make our way through the winding passages. I'm hyper-aware of every sound, every shadow. We can't leave a trace, or let any cameras catch us. Ziva glides through the darkness, blending effortlessly into the shadows.

"Remember," I whisper as we approach the border of the controlled zone, "act natural. We were never here."

Ziva nods, her face a mask of calm compliance. But I catch the glint in her eye, a spark of defiance that no amount of Harmonization can extinguish. Together we hurry through the streets, making our way back to the maglev station.

We pause at the threshold of the entrance to the station, the stark white corridors stretching endlessly in both directions. The night is eerily silent, interrupted only by the faint whir of drones and the distant approach of the maglev.

When I meet Ziva's gaze, my breath catches. Her hazel eyes, brimming with hope, stir something deep inside.

"Today was..." I start, struggling to find words that won't trigger the NeuroMods dampening sequence.

"I know," she says softly, her eyes meeting mine. There's a world of understanding in that gaze, a shared secret that makes my heart race dangerously.

I clear my throat. "We should do this again. Find somewhere...to discuss work matters."

Ziva's lips quirk in a barely-there smile. "Wasn't that the plan for today? We need to stay productive."

The double meaning in her words sends a thrill through me. I want to say more, but not here. Not now.

She whispers, "I'll figure out how to create a secure channel for us to communicate through. It will be easier than constantly searching for isolated meeting spots."

I nod, excited about the prospect of being able to communicate more openly and frequently with Ziva. The sound of the approaching maglev pulls me out of my dangerous thoughts.

"Goodnight, Ziva," I manage, my voice rougher than I'd like.

"Goodnight, Myall," she replies, her fingers brushing mine as she turns to enter the station.

Walking away, I try to keep my steps steady, though the storm inside me threatens to break. As I round the corner, out of sight of the cameras, I lean against the wall, eyes squeezed shut against the crushing reality. Ziva's laughter, the vibrant mural—both haunt me, vivid reminders of what we're fighting for. Her smile, the warmth of her touch, the fire in her eyes when we spoke of freedom—they crash over me in a wave of longing.

What is this feeling? This ache in my chest, this lightness in my step? I've never experienced anything like it before. It's dangerous, I know. Feeling this strongly about anything—let alone another person—is strictly forbidden.

But as I make my way to my living unit, I can't bring myself to regret it, the thrill of feeling something—anything—pulls me forward into the night.

For the first time in my life, I feel truly alive. And it's all because of Ziva Emerson.

My NeuroMod begins vibrating, a low, ominous hum that sends a chill down my spine, signaling a warning moments before another hit of the dampener is injected, and my emotions disappear.

Chapter Eight

Ziva

I lean over my workstation, eyes narrowed as I scrutinize the delicate inner workings of the NeuroMod before me. My fingers, calloused from years of tinkering, deftly manipulate the tiny components.

"Careful with that one, Ziva," Myall's voice drifts over from his workstation. "Heard it's been giving false readings all week."

Glancing up, I catch his eye across the row. A warmth radiates from his gaze, a silent understanding that sends a flutter through my chest. Clamping my lips together, I force down the flush creeping up my neck. I push the feeling down, focusing back on my work.

"Thanks for the heads up," I mutter, trying to keep my tone neutral.

As I adjust a minuscule wire, my mind wanders to last

night—the hidden corridors, the thrill of discovery, the way Myall's hand held mine in the darkness. I shake my head, forcing myself to concentrate.

Suddenly, a spark jumps between two connectors, leaping between the device I'm working on and my own on my wrist—a brilliant flash that lights up the space around me. The shock courses through my wrist and down my body, leaving a tingling sensation that makes the hairs on my arms stand on end.

I jerk back, breath catching in my throat. The NeuroMod's display flickers, then goes dark. A quick look at my own NeuroMod confirms that it, too, has stopped working—a silence falling over my workspace as the world sharpens into focus around me.

"Everything okay over there?" Myall calls, concern evident in his voice.

"Fine," I reply quickly, perhaps too quickly. My pulse quickens as I realize what's happened. The dampeners are offline. Every emotion bursts forth—the sharp pang of fear, the thrill of excitement, and the deep ache of longing that pools in my chest. Each one crashes over me like a relentless wave, threatening to drown me.

I force myself to take a deep breath, to appear calm as I examine the device. My mind races. This is it—the vulnerability I've been searching for. But I can't let anyone know, not yet. Not even Myall.

"Think this ones just glitching," I say, keeping my voice steady. "Nothing I can't handle."

Lena's piercing gaze from her workstation is fixed on me, curious about the commotion.

Get it together, Ziva. Compose yourself before she reports you.

I grip the edges of the workstation, my palms damp with sweat. A slight tremor of adrenaline courses through me, likely a response to the sudden influx of emotions. Each heartbeat resonates in my ears, a steady reminder that I am alive, that I feel everything I've long suppressed. It's as if a dam has burst, flooding my senses with sensations I've never experienced so vividly before.

"Ziva?" Myall's voice cuts through the chaos in my mind. "Are you sure you're alright?"

Lifting my gaze to meet his, the concern in his eyes hits me like a physical force. My heart races, desire and fear intertwining in a dizzying dance.

"I'm…I'm not sure," I breathe.

Myall strides towards me, the warmth of his presence enveloping me, and I instinctively back away, my back pressing against the cool metal of the workstation. The air thickens between us, charged with unspoken words and feelings, leaving me breathless. His gaze softens, but I look away, unable to meet it.

"What's wrong?" he asks, his brow furrowed.

Cautiously, I glance over at Lena and see that she is still watching me. I know I'd be stupid to discuss what just happened in front of her, as she may be listening.

I turn back to the NeuroMod, my heart racing with a mix of determination and nervous energy. "Just a glitch that requires a closer look," I mutter, reaching for my tools and deliberately ignoring how close Myall is.

As I carefully prod the circuitry, I sense his eyes still on me. His presence is both comforting and unnerving. I want to share everything with him, but years of caution hold me back.

Myall steps closer once more, his eyes darting between me and the NeuroMod. "Let me take a look," he offers, reaching for the device.

"I've got it," I say firmly, pulling the NeuroMod closer to my chest. Myall raises an eyebrow, but doesn't push further. Risking another quick glance at Lena, she quickly averts her gaze, pretending not to be watching.

"What exactly are you looking for?" he asks, keeping his voice low.

Hesitating, I choose my words carefully. I know I should tell him—about what just happened, but something holds me back.

"I'm not sure yet," I say softly, not looking up from the NeuroMod, "I think I've found something. But I can't discuss it here. We need somewhere safe."

I hear him shift from one foot to the other, sensing his eagerness to know more. "I might know a place," he murmurs. "It can't be today though cause I'll need to confirm it. Tomorrow, after shifts end?"

Nodding, I will my heart rate to slow. "Tomorrow."

As Myall turns to leave my workstation, Lena approaches me with a concerned look on her pinched face.

"What happened here?" she asks suspiciously, glancing at the NeuroMod in my hands.

"Just a minor glitch," Myall replies smoothly before I have a chance to say anything.

Lena's eyes narrow, but she doesn't press further. She knows better than to challenge a Compliance Monitor. Still, I can feel her watching me as she moves to walk away.

"It was just a minor malfunction that surprised me," I assure her with a forced smile. "I'm working on fixing it now."

Lena eyes the device suspiciously but doesn't press further. "Well, make sure you fix it quickly. We have a lot of work to do today, and you can't afford to get in trouble again for your lack of productivity, Ziva."

Myall and I nod in agreement as Lena stalks back to her own workstation.

As soon as she's out of earshot, Myall turns to me with a worried expression. "Are you sure you're alright? You look like you're about to faint."

Taking a deep breath, I force myself to calm down. I can't let my emotions control me like this—especially not around Myall. But every time I see him, every time he speaks, a dangerous desire grows within me, pushing against the walls of my carefully constructed defenses.

"I'm fine," I assure him with a forced smile. "Just a bit overwhelmed with work lately and Lena's constant hovering isn't exactly helping."

Myall nods understandingly before turning back to his workstation. But I can sense that he's still studying me carefully—his gaze lingering just a second longer than necessary and I can feel a warmth spreading through my chest.

I shake my head, trying to clear my thoughts. This is not the time or place for these confusing feelings.

With renewed determination, I turn back to the Neuro-Mod and start running diagnostics tests. But no matter how much I try to focus on my work, I can't seem to shake off the strange sensations that are still coursing through my body—leaving me both exhilarated and terrified at the same time.

I pull up the schematics of my NeuroMod on the Sentinel terminal to review the data of my emotional input from the last few minutes since the malfunction. My eyes scan over the rows and rows of data, searching for any anomalies in my emotional state, but nothing stands out. I scroll through to read the live data on my current emotional reading.

'Emotional output is stable,' it declares.

Even though my NeuroMod is not functioning properly, it's still sending signals to the Sentinel system that it is working and my emotions are within normal ranges.

A smile tugs at my lips as I read the data again. My emotions may be unchecked, but this—this is freedom. The kind I've been searching for.

Chapter Nine

Ziva

My fingers tremble as I pack up my tools, a storm of emotions raging inside me. I discreetly slip the broken NeuroMod and a few tools up the sleeve of my uniform, praying that I'll make it through the security checkpoint without issue.

I know I need to share what happened with Myall. But the ever-watchful cameras and Lena's scrutinizing gaze hold me back. I force myself to maintain a neutral expression as I gather my things, acutely aware of Myall's gaze on me.

"Goodnight, Ziva," he calls out, his voice carefully casual.

I turn, meeting his eyes. "Goodnight, Myall." The words carry a hidden promise.

I'll tell him tomorrow.

I leave the facility, the possibility of dismantling the system that has controlled us for so long sending a rush through me.

But with it comes the terrifying realization of what we're risking. I quicken my pace, desperate to return home and continue my research in the safety of my unit.

Once inside my unit, I barely pause to remove my boots before diving back into my research. I spread the NeuroMod components across my small kitchen table, the rough wood surface worn from years of use.

I work quickly, the cool night air wafting through the window, carrying distant sounds of the city. Hours slip by unnoticed as I lose myself in circuits and code trying to figure out how the glitch happened, and how I can replicate it.

"If I can just isolate this frequency," I mutter to myself, adjusting a tiny component. "There has to be a way to—"

A sudden beep from my datapad startles me. It's a generic reminder about tomorrow's work schedule, but it snaps me back to reality. Glancing at the time, I'm shocked to see how late it's gotten.

Leaning back, I rub my eyes.

Focus, Ziva. This is bigger than you. Bigger than Myall. This could change everything for a lot of people.

But even as I dive back into my work, Myall's face floats in my mind. His gentle encouragement, the intensity in his eyes when we spoke earlier. The warm sensation that floods through my body every time he touches me.

Even now, just thinking about him, I feel a warmth spreading through my body, a flutter in my stomach. I shake my head, trying to clear the distracting thoughts.

"Emotions are a liability," I remind myself, echoing the mantra we've been taught since childhood. But for the first time, doubt stirs within me.

I make another adjustment to the NeuroMods circuitry. A

small light flickers, then stabilizes. "Yes!" I whisper, a rush of triumph surging through me. It's a tiny victory, but it feels monumental.

Leaning in closer, I scrutinize the inner workings of the device. "If I can replicate this malfunction…trigger it at will…" My voice trails off as the implications hit me.

Freedom from constant emotional regulation. The ability to feel, *truly feel*, without fear of detection. My hands shake slightly as I reach for my notebook, scribbling down my findings. "Myall needs to see this," I murmur, then catch myself. The mention of his name sends a warm flutter through my chest once more.

I pause, pen hovering above the page, a deep ache growing in my chest.

What are we doing, Myall?

I imagine his deep green eyes, the way they seem to see right through me.

This isn't just about dismantling the system anymore, is it?

Closing my eyes, I allow myself a moment to indulge in the fantasy. Myall and I, free to explore our emotions, our connection…our bodies. No hiding, no fear. The image is so vivid, so achingly desirable, that it almost hurts.

We need to meet. But where? How?

The logistics of finding a safe meeting place seem insurmountable. Every public space is monitored, every private conversation potentially overheard and recorded.

I return to my work. As I tinker with the NeuroMod, I find myself imagining Myall's hands instead of my own, his fingers brushing against mine as we work together to unravel the secrets of the device.

Stop thinking about him.

The longing lingers, sharp and unyielding, beneath every thought. Now that my emotions aren't muted, it's easier to see how these thoughts and feelings toward him have been hidden beneath the surface. It's like they have always been there, but now they're magnified tenfold. I'm not sure how to handle it.

I know I need to share my discoveries with him, but it's not just that. I need to see him. I need to switch his NeuroMod off and confirm if this connection between us is real, that I'm not alone with these burning feelings and desires.

As the night wears on, my determination grows alongside my breakthroughs. I set down my tools. The NeuroMod lies before me, its inner workings exposed, vulnerable. Just like me.

I glance at the clock on the wall, its soft blue glow a reminder of the passing hours. It's late, but sleep is the furthest thing from my mind. My thoughts drift to Myall again, wondering if he's lying awake too, grappling with the same restless energy that courses through me.

I imagine his face, those deep green eyes that seem to see through the mask I wear. Pacing the small confines of my unit, my mind whirls with possibilities.

The old industrial sector or even the old recycling plant. Maybe there's a blind spot in the surveillance there?

My fingers itch to grab my datapad, to send Myall a coded message right now. But I resist. Caution has kept me alive this long and I can't abandon it now, no matter how much I want to.

With a heavy sigh, I reluctantly cease my pacing and head towards my bedroom. As much as I hate to admit it, I need some rest if I'm going to be able to continue my research tomorrow.

Stepping into the shower, the hot water washes away the fatigue that clings to me. After toweling off, I slip into my cozy pajamas. The warmth seeps through me, comforting and calming after a long day.

I collapse onto my bed and stare up at the ceiling, my mind still racing with thoughts and ideas. But eventually, exhaustion takes over and I drift off into a fitful sleep.

** * **

The shrill sound of my alarm slices through the haze of sleep, dragging me awake. "Citizen 26304, it is time to begin your day," the unit's AI assistant drones from the ceiling speaker. I groan, wishing for just a few more minutes of sleep. But then I remember the important task at hand— sharing my discovery with Myall.

Dressing in haste, I head to work, eager to see Myall and discuss a safe meeting spot. But as soon as I step inside, I can tell something is wrong.

The usually quiet corridors are bustling. People are rushing around with purposeful expressions on their faces, their voices hushed in urgent conversations. And there's an uneasiness in the air that makes me feel like something is about to go terribly wrong.

Fuck, what if someone has reported me?

Myall is already at his workstation, but he looks tense and preoccupied. As soon as he sees me, he rushes over.

"Ziva, we need to talk," he says urgently, gesturing for us to move away from prying ears and I quickly follow him down the corridor to the nearest supply closet.

He makes a motion with his hand, signaling for me to enter.

Shit, it must be bad if he wants to talk in here.

I don't waste any time and step inside, with Myall following close behind. He shuts the door behind us, trapping us in the room. Each second stretches, the silence amplifying the sound of our quickened breaths as we huddle close.

A sour taste rises in my throat, thick and bitter. "What's going on Myall?"

Myall takes a deep breath before speaking again. "There's been a breach in our security system."

A breach?

The enormity of the threat sends chills down my spine. I can almost hear the ticking clock of our impending doom, the weight of the knowledge pressing heavily on my chest, constricting my breath.

"Do they know what was accessed?" I ask quietly, already dreading the answer but needing confirmation.

The air in the closet feels thick, suffocating. I hear Myall's breath, quick and shallow, matching my own. Every second feels like it could unravel everything. My heart pounds louder than my thoughts as I wait for him to respond.

Myall nods grimly. "Yeah. Someone stole all the schematics for the NeuroMod and Sentinel systems."

Standing so close to Myall, I'm sure he can hear my heart pounding. Panic starts to bubble inside me as we both realize the severity of the situation.

Someone else is looking to dismantle the NeuroMod system besides us. Someone else is planning a rebellion. My heart races, torn between the intoxicating thrill of fighting back and the heavy weight of the risks involved.

"Do they know who did it?" I ask, my voice shaking slightly.

Myall shakes his head. "Not yet. But they have reason to believe that it was an inside job."

My heart sinks when I come to the realization that I won't be able to work on my NeuroMod plans during work any longer. Not with so many watching eyes and security likely tightening. "What are they going to do?"

"They're conducting an investigation to determine who did it, but in the meantime, security has been tightened even more," Myall explains and confirms my suspicions. "They're also warning everyone to be on high alert and report any suspicious behavior."

I glance at Myall, his face taut with the weight of what we've just learned. He looks at me, eyes wide, as if searching for answers. But there's nothing more to say. Not here, not now. We both know the risks of staying too long. Without another word, we step back into the corridor, the harsh buzz of the lights almost mocking the stillness that followed our conversation.

The sound of hurried footsteps, the murmur of voices, all the usual noise feels louder now. I'm acutely aware of the space around me, of the eyes that might be watching. My skin prickles, as if the walls themselves are listening. I force myself to breathe, to appear normal.

I walk towards my work station, mentally bracing myself for another monotonous day of recalibrating and continuing the cycle of emotional abuse.

Chapter Ten

Myall

Dust motes dance lazily in the stale air as I scan the rows of data on the Sentinel system.

I can't stop glancing at Ziva across the aisle. Her tense posture and jerky movements make it clear something is off today.

Yesterday she was distracted, today she's downright jittery. My mind churns with possibilities. Did she have a breakthrough? Crack the NeuroMods code somehow? Was Ziva the one who stole the NeuroMod blueprints?

I want to rush over and ask her, but not here. Not with cameras, Technicians, and Compliance Monitors everywhere. We need a safe place to talk, but I haven't been able to find one yet.

Yesterday we made a plan to meet in private after our shift was over, and I spent most of the night awake, trying to think of possible places where we could talk without being overheard. Mentally, I mapped out the city, but each location that came to mind was quickly dismissed as unsuitable.

My fingers move over the keypad on autopilot, inputting citizen emotion data, but my thoughts are elsewhere. Only three hours until our shift ends, and I can take Ziva to meet Grandma Elara, the only place I've deemed safe enough.

"Hansen!" A sharp male voice cuts through my reverie and I glance up at the imposing figure of Supervisor Sant standing before my workstation. "Your productivity is down 4% this week. Explain."

I swallow hard against the dryness in my throat, forcing my face into a mask of calm even as my heart thuds painfully against my ribs. "Apologies, sir. I've been experiencing some eye strain. I'll increase my output immediately."

The afternoon Compliance Supervisor nods curtly and moves on. I breathe a sigh of relief, but my heart is pounding.

Sneaking another glance at Ziva, her tense posture betrays her calm facade. Her fingers tap against the desk in a rhythmic, nervous pattern, a sign she's trying to hold herself back from asking what Sant wanted.

The minutes crawl by like hours. I try to focus on my work, but my mind keeps drifting to what's to come. Will Grandma's stories affect Ziva the way they affected me? Will she understand the beauty, the power of unbridled emotion? And most importantly, will Grandma Elara approve of Ziva?

Finally, mercifully, the end-of-shift bell rings. I stand, stretching cramped muscles, and make my way to Ziva's workstation.

"Ready?" I ask softly, nodding farewell to Lena as she glares in our direction.

Ziva nods, her face carefully blank, but I catch a tremor in her hand as she gathers her things. Something is definitely off with her today.

As we walk towards the exit of the building, I murmur, "We're going to visit my grandmother. She hasn't been feeling well."

Ziva's dark eyebrows raise slightly, but she plays along. "That's kind of you. I hope she gets better soon."

We pass through the security checkpoint unscathed and step out of the stark, sterile building of the Compliance Monitoring Division and into the open streets. Ziva's eyes dart around, scanning for potential eavesdroppers as we slowly walk. I can sense her unease, the tension radiating from her body.

"So, where exactly are we going?" she asks, her voice low and guarded.

Leaning in close, my lips barely move as I respond, "Like I said, we're visiting my grandmother. She hasn't been feeling well lately."

Ziva's eyebrow arches skeptically. "A sick grandmother? How convenient," she says, voice laced with thinly veiled skepticism.

She thinks it's a cover story, but little does she know, we're actually heading to see Grandma Elara. We walk down the street, away from the building and from prying eyes and ears.

Leaning in close, I feel the warmth from her body as our shoulders touch. "Are you okay? You seemed…off today."

Ziva's eyes dart around nervously. "Not here," she whispers. "But yes, we need to talk."

Whatever Ziva's figured out must be big if it's got her this jittery. We continue walking, our footsteps echoing off the concrete buildings that line the streets. Holographic ads flicker as we walk, reminding citizens to maintain harmony.

I steal glances at Ziva as we navigate the crowded sidewalks from the work-time rush. Her eyes are constantly moving, taking in every detail of our surroundings.

"It's not what you think," I murmur, careful to keep my voice down. "My grandmother...she's different. Special. You'll see when you meet her."

Ziva's hand brushes mine briefly, sending a tremor through me. I try to ignore the flutter in my chest. "I hope you know what you're doing, Myall," she whispers back. "If we're caught..."

Swallowing hard, I push down the fear that threatens to rise. "We won't be. Trust me."

As we turn down a quieter street, the imposing facades give way to older, more weathered buildings. It's like stepping into a different world, one where the relentless march of progress hasn't quite erased all traces of the past.

"It's strange," Ziva muses, her eyes lingering on a crumbling brick wall. "I've never been to this part of the city before, even though my unit isn't that far from it. It feels...different."

I nod, a mix of pride and nostalgia washing over me. "This is where my grandmother lives. It's one of the few areas of the city they haven't 'modernized' yet."

As we approach Grandma Elara's house, I suddenly begin second guessing myself. I'm about to introduce Ziva to the person who shaped my worldview, who planted the seeds of rebellion in my mind. I only hope that Ziva is ready for what she's about to experience.

We approach the modest dwelling, it's faded blue paint

and slightly overgrown garden standing out in against the sterile uniformity of the surrounding buildings. I can't help but smile, remembering countless afternoons spent here growing up, basking in the warmth of Grandma's love and wisdom.

"This is it," I say to Ziva, gesturing towards the house. Her eyes widen slightly, taking in the uniqueness of the place.

Pushing open the weathered wooden gate, its hinges creak softly. Ziva follows close behind as we approach the small cottage. I knock, three quick raps followed by two slow ones. It's the secret code Grandma and I came up with when I was little. The door creaks open, revealing Grandma Elara's kind face, her eyes crinkling with a smile that makes my chest ache with a forbidden surge of affection.

"Myall, my sweet boy," she says, her voice as soothing as always. Her gaze shifts to Ziva. "And who's this lovely young lady?"

"Grandma, this is Ziva," I say, ushering us inside as Grandma Elara closes the door softly behind us. "Ziva, meet my grandmother, Elara Hansen."

Ziva extends her hand as we stand in the entryway of Grandma's house, ever cautious. "It's a pleasure to meet you, Mrs. Hansen."

Grandma bypasses the handshake, pulling Ziva into a tight hug. Ziva's tense posture instantly relaxes, her shoulders dropping as if a weight has been lifted. Grandma Elara has that effect on people—it's like her very presence radiates comfort and understanding.

She chuckles as she releases Ziva, ushering us further inside the house. "Please, call me Elara. Or Grandma, if you'd like. Any friend of Myall's is family to me."

The interior of the cottage is a stark contrast to the city outside. Warm light spills from mismatched lamps, illuminating the array of furniture and the walls are adorned with faded photographs and hand-painted landscapes. The room is filled with the scent of cinnamon, mingling with the musty, comforting smell of old books.

We settle onto the worn sofa as Grandma Elara instructs us to wait while she brings over a tray of steaming tea.

"Now," she says, taking a seat in her favorite armchair, her eyes twinkling with mischief, "I suspect you two didn't come just for tea and pleasantries. You want to hear about the old days, don't you?"

Ziva leans forward, her curiosity palpable. "The old days? You mean…before the NeuroMods?"

Grandma Elara nods, her expression turning wistful. "Oh, those were different times, my sweet girl. Imagine a world where your heart could soar like a bird on the wind, or plummet like a stone in a still pond. Where a smile wasn't just a facial expression, but a burst of sunlight breaking through storm clouds."

A lump forms in my throat, tightening with each of Grandma's words. Even with my dampened emotions, Grandma's words paint vivid pictures in my mind. I glance at Ziva, seeing the wonder in her eyes.

"But wasn't it chaotic?" Ziva asks softly. "That's what they always told us."

Grandma Elara's laugh is like windchimes in a gentle breeze. "Oh, it could be, certainly. But that was the beauty of it—life was a tapestry, each thread a distinct hue, each emotion a vital part. Joy, sorrow, anger, love—they all had their place, their purpose."

Grandma continues to weave her tales of a world unbound by emotional regulation, and I feel my breath catching as wonder lights up Ziva's eyes, her fingers clenching the fabric of the sofa as if anchoring herself to this moment. The usual guardedness in her eyes is melting away, replaced by something I've never seen before—hope.

I lean forward, captivated by Grandma Elara's every word. Her stories are a lifeline to a world I long to understand.

"Tell us more about love," I say, my voice thick with longing. "What was it like when people could feel it freely?"

Grandma's eyes sparkle. "Love, Myall? It was like standing at the edge of a cliff, heart pounding, knowing you could fall at any moment. But instead of fear, you felt...alive."

Looking at Ziva, I catch the wonder in her eyes. She's sitting on the edge of her seat, brow furrowed in concentration. I can almost see her mind working, trying to reconcile these vivid descriptions with our reality.

"But how did people function?" Ziva interjects, her tone a mix of curiosity and disbelief. "With all those...feelings rushing around?"

Grandma chuckles softly. "We managed, dear. In fact, those emotions drove us to create, to connect, to live more fully than you can imagine."

A strange tightness grips my chest, a ghost of an emotion pushing against the NeuroMods control. "It sounds beautiful," I murmur.

For a moment, I catch a flicker of something raw and unguarded in Ziva's gaze. My heart rate spikes, warmth spreading through me as a longing I didn't know I had rises.

"It does, doesn't it?" Elara whispers, more to herself than to us.

Ziva's expression softens, her shoulders relaxing as a tentative smile begins to form. It's like watching a flower bloom in fast motion, each petal of curiosity and wonder unfurling before my eyes.

"But if emotions were so powerful," Ziva asks, leaning forward, "why did people let them be silenced?"

Grandma's smile falters as she rests her hands on the armrests of her chair. "It wasn't all at once, dear. Little by little, they convinced us it was for our own good. Safety. Stability. Progress."

The words land like a punch. I've heard them a thousand times in Harmonization Authority propaganda, but coming from Grandma, they sound hollow, sinister.

"We can't let this continue," I blurt out, surprising even myself with the intensity in my voice. "There has to be a way to fight back."

Ziva's eyes lock onto mine, blazing with a newfound determination. "You're right," she says, her energy rising. "We can't just accept this. We need to do something."

I feel a surge of…something. Not quite an emotion, thanks to my damned NeuroMod, but a sense of connection, of shared purpose. It's intoxicating. *Ziva* is intoxicating.

Grandma reaches out across the armchair, taking my hand in hers. "You two," she says, her voice thick with emotion that I know will be gone in a moment, "you give me hope. But be careful. The path you're considering is a dangerous one."

Squeezing her hand, I notice how Ziva watches us intently. "We will be," I promise. "But we can't back down now."

Ziva's eyes dart between Grandma Elara and me, her fingers twitching nervously at her sides. She takes a deep breath, her chest rising and falling rapidly.

"I have to tell you something," she blurts out, her words tumbling over each other in a rush. "Yesterday, when I was working on the NeuroMods, there was a glitch. Mine malfunctioned, and so did the one I was repairing."

My heart races, even as my NeuroMod struggles to dampen the surge of adrenaline. "What do you mean, malfunctioned?" I ask, leaning towards her on the sofa.

Is this why she's been acting so strange?

Ziva's eyes are wide, her cheeks flushed. "I've been experiencing full emotions since then. Everything. It's overwhelming and terrifying and...beautiful."

She has her emotions back.

Grandma's hand flies to her mouth, eyes brimming with tears. "Oh, my god," she whispers.

"That's not all," Ziva continues, her voice dropping to a hushed whisper. "I've been working to replicate the glitch. I'm *so* close to figuring it out. If I can, we could free others and show them what it's like to truly feel again."

"Ziva, that's incredibly dangerous," I say, even as part of me thrills at the possibility at being able to feel freely.

Grandma Elara rises from her armchair and shuffles over to sit beside Ziva on the sofa, taking Ziva's hands in hers. Her eyes are filled with a fire I've rarely seen.

"Ziva, listen to me," she says, her voice low and urgent. "What you're experiencing now, it's precious. It's who you truly are, beneath all the control and regulation."

Ziva nods, tears forming in the corners of her eyes. Grandma continues, "Embrace these emotions, every single one. They're your birthright, your humanity. And if you can find a way to share that with others, to fight for a world where we can all feel freely again…"

She trails off, her face slowly becoming blank as her NeuroMod doses her with suppressants. For a moment, Elara's expression turns to one of confusion, as if she's suddenly lost her train of thought.

Ziva's face hardens, fear giving way to burning determination as her jaw tightens. "I will," she says fiercely. "We will. Whatever it takes."

Looking at Ziva, I see the raw emotion on her face. A wave of longing washes over me, something I didn't know I was capable of. In that moment, I know that I'll do whatever it takes to make that happen.

My NeuroMod vibrates in warning.

I swallow, my chest tight as a lump forms in my throat. "Ziva," I say, my voice hoarse, "I'm with you. All the way."

My hands tremble slightly as I reach out to her, hesitating before gently grasping her shoulder. "We'll figure this out. Whatever it takes to escape this…this numbness."

Ziva's eyes lock onto mine, an ocean of raw emotion reflected in her gaze. "Myall," she whispers, her voice thick with gratitude. "I…I don't know what to say. I've never felt so…so…"

"Alive?" I offer, thinking back to our conversation the other night.

She nods, a single tear escaping down her cheek. I hold back from wiping the tear away, feeling the weight of her vulnerability.

Grandma Elara watches us, her weathered face creased with a knowing smile. "My dears," she says softly, "you give an old woman hope. Hope for a future I thought lost forever when your parents died."

A pang of sadness fills my chest as Elara mentions my parents. She has always been so open about their deaths in the resistance, but I can't help wondering, if she truly felt the full extent of her emotions, would she still be able to speak so openly about it if she could feel the true pain of their loss?

Ziva turns to her on the sofa, clasping Elara's wrinkled hands in her own. "Elara, I can't thank you enough," she says fervently. "Your stories, your wisdom…they've shown me what's possible. What we've lost, and what we could regain."

Something passes between them, a connection deeper than words.

I clear my throat, reluctant to interrupt the moment but mindful of the time. "We should go," I say softly. "But Grandma, we'd like to come back. Maybe…once a week on our day off? To check on you, of course."

Ziva's eyes light up, catching onto my plan. "Yes, we'd love to visit regularly. If that's alright with you, Elara?"

Grandma's knowing smile widens. "Nothing would bring me more joy, dears. My door is always open to you both."

As we step out into the fading light, the city's oppressive atmosphere seems less stifling. Ziva walks close beside me, her fingers occasionally brushing mine. The contact sends a fluttering feeling in the pit of my stomach.

"Once a week," Ziva muses. "A safe place where we can speak freely, plan our next moves."

Nodding, I scan the emptying street for prying eyes or ears. "It's perfect. No one would question us visiting my sick grandmother on our day off."

It's an ideal arrangement. Ziva and I have shared shifts for years, meaning we always have the same day off. It will provide us with a whole day each week to spend together, and I find myself looking forward to our next day off.

We walk in comfortable silence, my eyes occasionally drifting toward Ziva. I marvel at the subtle changes in her demeanor. Her steps are lighter, her eyes brighter. Even with my muted emotions, I feel a warmth spreading through my chest.

As we near Ziva's living complex, she turns to me. "Myall," she says, her voice low so that it doesn't carry into the night. "Today…it changed everything for me. I feel like I'm truly awake for the first time."

I swallow hard, fighting against the artificial calm of my NeuroMod. "I know," I reply. "Grandma's stories, they've always affected me, but seeing you experience them…it's different. More real somehow."

Ziva reaches out, her fingers ghosting over my wrist where my NeuroMod pulses steadily. "Soon," she promises. "Soon you'll experience it all too. We'll bring down this whole system, Myall. Together."

I nod, unable to find words to match the fire in her eyes. As she disappears into her building, I'm left standing in the growing shadows, my mind filled with possibilities of what it would be like to experience love for the very first time.

Chapter Eleven

Ziva

The warm morning light filters through my small bedroom window, casting a soft glow on the NeuroMod lying dormant on my bedside table. I stare at it, my heart mingling with a mixture of excitement and fear. It's been a week since it malfunctioned, a week since I've truly felt everything.

Running my fingers through my long, thin hair, I detangle the knots as I try to calm the storm of emotions inside me. The intensity remains overwhelming. I clutch at the edge of my bed, willing the sensation to lessen, yet part of me craves the chaos. Myall flashes in my mind—his deep green eyes, his strong jawline.

Stop thinking about him, Ziva.

Dressing in long dark pants and a soft cashmere sweater, the anticipation builds within me. Today's our first planned visit to Grandma Elara's, and the thought of spending more time with Myall and his grandmother sends a warm flutter through me.

I pause, catching my reflection in the mirror. My eyes seem brighter, more alive.

Is this what it means to truly feel?

Every second spent walking to the maglev station in my sector feels like an eternity. All week I've been counting down the days until our next trip to Grandma Elara's, where we can finally talk openly without fear of being overheard.

Growing up in an orphanage meant I had no family members who could recall a time before The Harmonization Authority took control. And I've always been too afraid to befriend my classmates or coworkers for fear of them discovering my true thoughts about The Authority.

I understand Myall's reasoning for choosing his grandmother's house as our meeting place. It's the perfect cover. Meeting at either of our own apartments will surely raise suspicions among our neighbors, who are not used to seeing unmarried couples spending so much alone time together. Since all our emotions are regulated by the NeuroMod system, true relationships are a rare occurrence. Love, lust, and desire are all muted, leaving only biological instincts and societal expectations driving most intimate connections.

Most teenagers are allowed some leeway to experiment, a nod to the reality that young people will seek out intimacy regardless of The Authority's regulations. But I never did. I couldn't stomach the thought of being physically close to someone without fully experiencing what those feelings truly felt like. It's like trying to read a book with the pages glued shut—no matter how much you want to read, you can't access the story.

The country has seen a massive decrease in babies being born since the NeuroMod system was mandated. It makes me wonder what will happen if our population continues to decrease.

The direction of my thoughts are interrupted as I reach the towering maglev station, my eyes immediately landing on Myall's figure, silhouetted against the sterile, white wall.

It's strange seeing him out of his uniform, dressed in dark pants and a matching tunic. His posture is casual but alert, as though he's constantly surveying his surroundings. We meet at the entrance of the station, its doors looming above us like a monolithic gate that leads to another world. He gives me a subtle nod, his dark, unruly hair falling into his eyes like always.

"Ready?" he asks, his voice low and measured.

I nod, trying to keep my voice steady. "Can't wait to hear more of your grandmother's stories."

We set off and as we walk, I sneak glances at Myall.

Does he feel this too, or is his NeuroMod dampening the connection I'm starting to sense?

"You seem...different today," Myall observes, his eyes studying me intently.

I tense, worried I've given my thoughts away. "Do I? Must be the anticipation of more illegal storytelling or the fact that you're seeing me in my non work attire for the first time," I quip, deflecting with humor. A quick scan of my surroundings confirms that no one caught my rebellious words.

Myall chuckles, the sound sending a warmth through me. "There's something about Grandma's stories that makes you forget about the world outside, isn't there?"

Nodding, my voice softens. "It's like stepping into another time. A time when people could just...feel."

We fall into a comfortable silence as we walk, but my thoughts churn. I want to tell him about the overwhelming emotions I've been experiencing in his presence. The ones that send my stomach fluttering and a warmth to spread through my chest. But fear holds me back. What if he doesn't understand?

As we approach Elara's house, I inhale deeply, the rich scent of blooming jasmine wafting around me, mingling with the earthy aroma of the cottage. I knock on Elara's door, following the rhythm Myall showed me, my heart bursting with excitement. Myall stands close, his presence comforting. The door creaks open, revealing Elara's warm, wrinkled face.

"My dears," she says, her voice soft but filled with genuine warmth despite her dampened emotions. "Come in, come in."

The moment we step into Elara's cottage, I am enveloped by its warmth. The walls are lined with shelves of dusty books, each whispering stories of the past. The earthy scent of dried herbs wafts from the kitchen. Elara's warm smile reaches her eyes, a softness that reminds me of long-forgotten joy.

"How are you feeling, Grandma?" Myall asks, his tone carefully neutral as he steps further into the house.

"Oh, just fine," Elara responds, waving a hand dismissively as she bustles into the living room. "Now, sit down. I've been thinking about what stories to share today."

Chuckling, we settle onto the sofa as Elara lowers herself into her favorite armchair, her eyes distant as if looking into the past.

"Today," she begins, her voice taking on a dreamy quality, "I want to tell you about joy. Real, unbridled joy."

Leaning forward, I hang on her every word. "What was it like?" I ask, unable to contain my curiosity.

Elara's eyes sparkle. "Oh, my sweet girl. It was like sunlight bursting through your chest. Like every cell in your body was singing." She pauses, lost in the memory. "I remember the day my son—Myall's father that is—was born. The moment they placed him in my arms, it was as if the whole world disappeared and time stood still. There was only him, that perfect little face."

Glancing at Myall, I wonder if he can even begin to imagine the depth of emotion his grandmother is describing. His face is impassive, but there's a tension in his jaw that makes me wonder what's going on beneath the surface.

Elara continues, her voice growing more animated. "And laughter! Oh, how we used to laugh. Not the polite muted chuckles you hear now, but deep, belly laughs that would leave you gasping for air. Your whole body would shake with it, tears streaming down your face."

As she recounts the laughter of long-lost friends, I can almost hear the echoes of their joy ringing in the air, feel the sun-warmed grass beneath our feet, and see the vivid colors of a world bursting with life.

I try to imagine it—uninhibited joy. My laughter's always been muted, controlled by both my NeuroMod and societal conditioning. But with my malfunctioning NeuroMod, I've glimpsed what Elara describes.

"What about love?" The question slips out before I can stop it, and I feel Myall stiffen beside me.

Elara's smile falters slightly, an unspoken memory reflected in her gaze. "Love was… everything and more. It could lift you to the highest heights and plunge you into the deepest despair. It was messy and complicated and… absolutely beautiful."

A surge of emotion nearly takes my breath away. Is this what I feel for Myall? This wild, uncontrollable force? No, that can't be it. My emotions have been dulled for so long, I just don't know how to correctly interpret them anymore.

A tumult of thoughts swirls in my mind. What if my feelings for Myall are just a fleeting rebellion against a lifetime of suppression? What if, in seeking freedom, I jeopardize the very connection I crave? The fear tightens like a vise around my chest.

I steal another glance at him, only to find him already looking at me. Our eyes lock, and I swear I see a flicker of something in his gaze. Something that makes my heart race even faster.

I can't take it anymore. The tension, the unspoken words, the weight of Elara's memories—it all comes crashing down on me at once.

"How can they justify this?" I burst out, my voice trembling with barely contained fury. "Stripping away everything that makes us human, choking us with their sterile, lifeless policies?" My voice trembles and I feel the heat rising to my cheeks.

Myall's eyebrows shoot up, surprise flickering in his eyes. "Ziva," he warns, glancing at Elara.

But I'm beyond caution now. "No, Myall. We need to talk about this. The Harmonization Authority claims they're *protecting* us, but they're just…neutering us. Making us docile. Compliant. They wrap around us like a suffocating blanket, promising safety while stripping away the very essence of what it means to be human."

Myall leans forward. His voice drops to a low murmur. "I understand. But we need to be careful. The consequences—"

"Consequences?" I scoff, feeling a rush of bitterness. "We're already living the consequences. A world without joy, without passion, without—" I catch myself, almost saying 'love.' My eyes flick to Myall, and I see something flicker in his gaze.

"You know it's not that simple," he argues, running a hand through his messy hair. "The system keeps order, prevents conflict. You've heard the stories of what it was like before when the world was filled with so much violence and death. Wars caused by hatred and fear."

I shake my head vehemently. "But at what cost? We're not really living, Myall. We're just… existing."

His shoulders slump, and for a moment, I see the weight of his own doubts. "I know," he whispers. "But what can we do? Two people against the entire Authority? They squashed the resistance, thousands of people, as if it were nothing more than an irritating fly."

Reaching out, I almost touch his hand before pulling back. "We start small. We find others. We…we…we show them what it's like to feel again."

Myall's eyes meet mine. "Do you really think we can do this, Ziva," he murmurs, but I can hear the wavering in his voice.

"I can't keep living half a life," I counter softly.

For a long moment, we just stare at each other. I can feel my heart pounding, my palms sweating. With my malfunctioning NeuroMod, every emotion is so raw, so intense.

Does Myall feel even a fraction of this?

"I want to experience it all," I admit, my voice barely audible. "The highs, the lows. Everything."

Myall swallows hard. "Even if it hurts?"

I nod, feeling suddenly vulnerable. "Especially then. Because at least then I know I'm alive."

Grandma Elara clears her throat, startling me. I hadn't realized how close Myall and I had gotten, lost in our conversation. She's moved to stand in the doorway, her eyes twinkling with an understanding that makes my cheeks flush. Myall and I both stand abruptly.

"Myall, dear," she says, her voice gentle but firm. "Would you mind fetching some herbs from the garden? I'd like to make us all some tea and I have none left in the kitchen."

Myall nods, seemingly oblivious to Elara's motives. As he leaves, Elara turns to me, her warm eyes searching my face. "Ziva, come sit with me for a moment."

My stomach knots as I take a seat on the worn sofa once more. What if she disapproves of my outburst? I twist my hands in my lap, trying to calm my racing thoughts.

"You know," Elara begins, her voice soft and melodic, "there was a time when people didn't hide their feelings. When love wasn't something to be feared or regulated."

I look up sharply. "Love?" The word feels foreign on my tongue.

Elara smiles, reaching out to pat my hand. "Connection, dear. The spark between two people that lights up the world around them."

"But it's dangerous," I whisper, echoing Myall's earlier

words.

"Oh, it's always been dangerous," Elara chuckles. "But it's also the most powerful force in the universe. It's what makes life worth living."

Tears prick at my eyes. "How can you be so sure?"

"I've lived it, Ziva. Felt love, loss—everything in between. And I wouldn't trade any of it for all the 'harmony' in the world."

Her words sink into me, resonating with something deep inside. "But what if…what if I'm misinterpreting my feelings. Or what if he doesn't feel the same?" I ask, finally voicing my deepest fear. Elara looks at me patiently, waiting for me to continue.

A deep breath steadies me, and I steel myself to confide in Elara. "I'm so confused," I admit. "These feelings, they're overwhelming. One moment I'm elated, the next I'm terrified or angry. Is this…normal?"

Elara's eyes crinkle with understanding. "Oh, my sweet girl. That's the beautiful chaos of emotions. It's perfectly normal, especially when you're experiencing them so intensely for the first time and don't know how to process them. Right now, you're like a toddler, learning to deal with your emotions."

I nod, grateful for her reassurance. But there's more gnawing at me. "It's not just that. I'm scared of what these feelings mean for starting a rebellion. What if they cloud my judgment? What if they put us all at risk?"

My chest tightens with the realization of how deep my feelings for Myall have become in such a short amount of time.

"I want to fight for our freedom," I continue, my voice

trembling slightly. "But now, when I think about the dangers we face, I'm not just worried about myself. The thought of anything happening to Myall…" I trail off, unable to finish the sentence.

A war rages inside me—desire clashes with fear, each side pulling at my heartstrings, as I ponder the weight of what it means to care for someone this intently versus the reality of starting a rebellion.

Elara takes my hand, her touch both comforting and grounding. "Ziva, love doesn't weaken our resolve. It strengthens it. It gives us something to fight for."

Elara's voice carries a soothing rhythm, each word wrapping around me like a blanket, coaxing my fears into submission. I meet her gaze, searching for answers. "But how do I balance this? How do I keep my head clear when my heart is so…full?"

Elara's eyes twinkle with a knowing glint as the sound of the back door closing reaches us. She pats my hand gently and rises from the sofa. "You know, I think I'll go ready that tea now. Why don't you two chat for a moment while I prepare it?"

As she shuffles out of the room, I catch a hint of a smile playing on her lips. My suspicions are confirmed—she's giving us space on purpose. Myall, oblivious to his grandmother's scheming, turns to me, his eyebrows drawn together.

"Are you alright?" he asks. He reaches out, fingers hovering over my arm, as if waiting for permission to touch me, his voice is low and filled with concern as he takes a seat beside me.

I nod. "Yeah, I'm fine. Just…processing a lot."

Myall shifts closer, his knee brushing mine, sending a jolt through me that threatens my composure. "I know what you mean," he says sheepishly. "Sometimes it feels like we're carrying the weight of the world on our shoulders."

Looking into his eyes, I see the same mixture of determination and vulnerability I feel. Without thinking, I reach out, my fingers brushing against his, and his hand envelops mine, warm and reassuring.

"At least we're in this together," I whisper, the words barely escaping my trembling lips.

Myall nods, his thumb tracing small circles on the back of my hand. I lean in, drawn by an invisible force, and rest my forehead against his. We stay like that, the rhythm of our breaths a quiet bond between us. I close my eyes, savoring the closeness.

When I open my eyes, Myall is looking at me with an intensity that takes my breath away. Our gazes lock, and in that shared moment, a thousand unspoken words hang between us, weaving a tapestry of hope and fear that threatens to unravel with the slightest touch. Slowly, hesitantly, he raises his free hand to cup my cheek. I lean into his touch, my skin tingling where his fingers make contact.

This is madness. Beautiful, terrifying madness. And still, I can't bring myself to pull away.

The full weight of my feelings for Myall crashes over me like a tidal wave. It's exhilarating and terrifying all at once. I've never felt anything this intense before. I glance at Myall, my resolve hardening. This isn't just about us anymore—it's about everyone silenced by The Authority.

"Myall," I say softly, my voice trembling as I pull away from him. "I...I think I'm falling for you."

His eyes widen, a flicker of surprise crossing his face before it's replaced by a warmth that makes my heart soar. "Ziva, I—"

I press a finger to his lips, silencing him. "Wait. Before you say anything, I need you to know something. Obviously, all my emotions are heightening right now. And it's okay if your feelings don't match mine, or at least not to the same degree. This… us… it changes everything. It makes our fight even more dangerous, but also more important than ever."

Myall nods, his gaze never leaving mine. I take a deep breath and continue, "We can't fight for ourselves alone anymore, can we? We have to fight for everyone robbed of the chance to feel this way."

He meets my gaze, and in his eyes, I see the same mix of resolve and uncertainty that's been swirling inside me. We've made our choice. It's not just about us anymore. But the weight of it presses on me. I wish we could hold onto this connection, just a little longer.

But if we want to start a rebellion, if we want to free everyone from this emotional oppression, we have to be willing to put our wants and needs last. The rebellion must come first.

"That's why we need to put these confusing feelings aside." The words taste bitter on my tongue, but they're necessary. We can't afford distractions now.

Myall nods, a tense muscle twitching in his jaw.

"Our focus needs to be the rebellion, finding a way to break the cycle so we can create a better future for everyone. Only then can we think about…whatever this is growing between us."

"You're right," he says after an awkward pause. "Emotional

freedom for everyone comes first."

"Okay," I breathe, as relief floods through me. "But where do we even start with this rebellion?"

Myall rubs the back of his neck. "I guess…we need to expand our rebellion. Find others who share our beliefs."

I nod eagerly, my mind already planning possibilities. "Yeah. And I think I know where to start with that. We need to find someone who can help me replicate the glitch in my NeuroMod. If we can do that—"

"We could free everyone," Myall finishes, a hint of excitement in his eyes before it's washed away.

And I will finally know if you feel the same towards me, without your NeuroMod.

Squeezing his hand, I feel more determined than ever. "Are you with me? No matter how dangerous this is going to get?"

Myall leans in, pressing his forehead against mine once more. "I am," he promises. "We're in this together, now. Until the very end."

His warmth radiates against me, a silent promise that we are not alone in this fight.

Grandma Elara returns, clearing her throat, a tray of tea in hand. My cheeks flush as Myall and I quickly create distance between us on the sofa.

"Tea anyone?" she asks, placing the tray on the small coffee table in front of us.

* * *

As we step outside, the cool evening air hits my face, a harsh reality to the warmth of Elara's home and carrying with it the artificial scent of regulated purity that permeates our city.

I turn to Myall, my heart beating with a newfound excitement I'm still getting used to.

"Same time next week?" I ask, trying to keep my voice casual despite the flutter in my chest.

A small smile plays at the corners of his mouth. "Wouldn't miss it for the world. Grandma's stories are always… enlightening."

"They're more than that," I say, my voice dropping to a whisper. "They're a window into a world we've been denied. A world I want to fight for."

We start walking toward the maglev station, our footsteps echoing in the eerily quiet streets. The silence between us is comfortable, filled with an unspoken understanding and shared purpose.

As we walk—Myall's hand brushing mine again—I'm overwhelmed by a rush of emotion that almost stops me in my tracks. The connection with Myall, with Grandma Elara, it's changing me. I'm not just a cog in The Harmonization Authority's machine anymore. I'm becoming something more.

"You know," I say, "a week or two ago, I couldn't have imagined feeling this way. About anything. Or anyone."

Myall's hand brushes against mine once more, a gesture so subtle it could be mistaken for accidental. But I know better.

"Neither could I," he admits. "It's…strange."

Turbulent emotions swirl within me as I glance at the gray buildings looming around us. "We're going to change this world, Myall. One person at a time if we have to."

As we near the point where we'll part ways, a pang of reluctance twists in my chest. I turn to him, meeting his gaze in the dim light.

"I guess I'll see you at work tomorrow," I say, my voice filled with reluctance.

He nods, his expression mirroring my own. "Yeah. Goodnight, Ziva."

"Goodnight, Myall."

Standing there, I watch him disappear into the maglev station, the air cool against my skin as my mind formulates plans—each one more daring than the last.

We need to be smart about this.

My fingers brush the outline of my malfunctioning NeuroMod through my pocket. I know I should be wearing it, especially with my wrist exposed, but the relief of not having it on is almost too great. My thoughts drift back to everything we discussed in Elara's home.

We need to find the right people. People who question, who wonder...

Entering my building's complex, I mentally begin to catalog potential allies.

There's Marcus from the tech division at work. He always asks too many questions.

I stop at my door, hand poised over the biometric scanner.

But how do we approach them without raising suspicion? One wrong move and we could end up in a detention center.

The thought sends a shiver down my spine, but it's quickly replaced by a rush of determination. For the first time, I'm not afraid of what the future holds.

Chapter Twelve

Ziva

A few days later, I slip into the Compliance Monitoring Division repair lab, my heart pounds against my ribs as my eyes scan the room, searching for him. *There.*

Marcus Holt hunches over a workbench, his wiry frame taut with concentration as he tinkers with a NeuroMod's innards. I've been watching him for days, observing how he bends the rules—an impulsive twitch here, a glance that lingers too long there.

Approaching, I clear my throat. "Excuse me, Marcus?"

He startles, dark eyes widening as he looks up. "Ziva? What can I do for you?"

I force a smile, though it's fragile, as if it could shatter at any moment. My pulse quickens, but I push forward. "I was wondering if we could talk after our shift ends. There's something I'd like to discuss."

"What's on your mind?" he asks, his bushy brows furrowing, a flicker of suspicion mingling with curiosity in his dark eyes.

My mind stalls for an excuse. I can't reveal too much, not here where it isn't safe. "It's… sensitive. We could meet at the old recycling factory?"

He hesitates, the doubt in his features shifting like a cloud passing over his face. I want to shake him, force him to understand how vital this is. But I can't. I need him to trust me.

"I don't know, Ziva. That's not exactly a sanctioned meeting place," he replies slowly, the words spilling from his lips, each syllable laced with doubt.

Leaning in, I lower my voice. "That's kind of the point. Please, Marcus. I wouldn't ask if it weren't important."

He studies me for a moment, and I wonder what he sees. A fellow Technician? A potential threat? Or maybe, hopefully, a kindred spirit yearning for freedom.

Finally, he nods. "Alright. After shift's end. But this better not get us into any trouble."

Relief floods through me, but I force myself to appear calm. "It wont, I promise. Thank you, Marcus."

Turning to leave, I pray this doesn't all blow up in my face.

* * *

I race through the dimly lit streets towards the recycling factory. Long shadows stretch in the fading light, and a chill creeps up my spine, as if I'm being watched. I haven't told Myall about this meeting—the risk is too great. The less he knows, the better. At least if Marcus betrays me, I know Myall will be safe from the fallout.

I slip through a gap in the chain-link fence, the rusted metal snagging at my uniform. The factory's hulking walls loom ominously, casting eerie shadows that dance in the dying light. Scanning the area, my heartbeat slams in my chest with each passing second as I double check for any hidden cameras or patrol drones.

Where is he? Did I misread him? Is he going to turn me in?

The questions cycle through my mind, but then I see him—a wiry figure slipping through the gap in the chain link fence. Relief washes over me, so intense it's almost dizzying.

"Marcus," I breathe, "you came."

He approaches cautiously, eyes darting around no doubt searching for surveillance. "This better be good, Ziva. We're taking a huge risk just being here."

I nod, steeling myself.

This is it.

"I need your help," I say, keeping my voice low. "I've discovered a glitch in the NeuroMod system. And I think that if we can exploit it, we can break the emotional control network."

Marcus's dark eyes widen, a mix of shock and intrigue flashing across his face as he realizes the implications of my words. "That's...that's impossible. And illegal. Very illegal Ziva."

"Is it?" I challenge, leaning towards him. "You've seen the inconsistencies, Marcus. The moments when the readings don't always match up. I know you have."

Marcus shifts uncomfortably, rubbing the back of his neck, his fingers twitching as if searching for an escape and I can see the internal struggle playing out across his features. I press on, determined to sway him to my cause. "We have a chance to break free, to feel again. Don't you want that?"

He runs a hand through his graying hair, conflict etched in every line of his face. "Even if it were possible," he says slowly, "the consequences if we're caught—"

"I know," I interrupt. "Believe me, I know. But isn't it worth the risk? To be truly alive again?"

Watching Marcus wrestle with his decision, doubt gnaws at me—what if he turns me down? What if everything falls apart? Our future, our freedom, hangs in the balance. And all I can do is wait, and hope.

His jaw tightens, and he takes a step back. "Ziva, this is…it's madness. We can't just tamper with the NeuroMods. Do you have any idea what they'd do to us if we were caught?"

His words sting, but I've come too far to back down now. I clench my fists, feeling the familiar rush of defiance coursing through me. "And what about what they're doing to us now, Marcus? Every day, every moment, they're stealing our emotions, our humanity."

We're both silent for a moment.

"Look, you're the best technician I know," I continue. "If anyone can figure this out, it's you. Don't you dream of what it would be like to feel…everything?"

Marcus's dark eyes meet mine, and for a fleeting moment, I glimpse him beginning to waver before he looks away. "Of course I do," he mutters. "But wondering and acting are two very different things."

I brace myself, preparing to lay it all on the line. "I've seen you, Marcus. The way you look at the NeuroMods sometimes, like you're trying to solve a puzzle. You're not satisfied with just accepting things as they are, are you?"

He doesn't respond, but his silence speaks volumes. I press on. "We have a real chance here. To make a difference. To feel again. Don't you want to know what that's like?"

As I watch Marcus wrestle with his decision, I can almost see the gears turning in his analytical mind. His eyes dart around the dimly lit factory as if searching for a way out of this conversation. I hold my breath, willing him to take the leap.

"Okay," he finally says. "I'm…intrigued. But I need to know more. What exactly have you found?"

My shoulders, tight with tension, drop, but I temper my excitement. This is just the first step. I lean in closer, my words coming out in a rushed, hushed tone. "There's a vulnerability in the NeuroMod system, like I said. I've only managed it once, and haven't been able to replicate it yet—that's why I need your help. If we can, this could be our key to dismantling the entire emotional control network."

Marcus's eyebrows shoot up. "That's… a bold claim. How did you discover this so called glitch?"

Swallowing hard, I choose my next words carefully. "I was repairing a NeuroMod last week. It malfunctioned in a way I'd never seen before. The emotional suppression protocols just…stopped responding. But the data is still reporting as normal to the Sentinel system."

His eyes narrow. "And you're sure it wasn't just a one-off defect? A fluke?"

"No," I shake my head emphatically. "I've been studying it since then. There's a pattern, Marcus. A weakness we can exploit."

I watch as he processes this information, his analytical

mind no doubt running through countless scenarios and potential consequences.

"If what you're saying is true," Marcus says slowly, "the implications are…staggering."

I nod, relieved that I'm beginning to get through to him. "Exactly. That's why I need your help. Your expertise. Together, we might be able to replicate the glitch and find a way to disable the emotional control on a larger scale."

Marcus rubs his temples, a storm brewing behind his dark eyes. "This is a huge risk, Ziva. If we're caught—"

"I know," I cut him off, unable to hide the urgency in my voice. "But knowing this now, can you live with doing nothing?"

As I wait for his response, I can't help but wonder if I've said too much, pushed too hard this time. But the thought of going back to a life of muted emotions, of controlled responses, is unbearable. I need Marcus on our side, and I'm willing to risk everything to make it happen.

Marcus's eyes meet mine, and I see something I've never noticed before—a spark of defiance, quickly masked by his usual caution. He takes a deep breath, his shoulders squaring as if bracing for impact.

"Alright," he says, keeping his voice low. "I'm in."

My shoulders slump in relief and my hand reaches out, instinctively grasping his arm.

"Thank you, Marcus," I breathe, not bothering to hide my gratitude. "You have no idea what this means."

He nods, smiling faintly. "I think I do, actually." His gaze flicks around the factory, suddenly alert. "But we can't stay here. This area is too exposed."

My stomach drops as I realize he's right. "True. You don't

happen to know somewhere safer we could meet, do you?"

Marcus leans in, his voice dropping even lower. "I do actually. There's an old tech lab I know of. Completely off the grid, away from prying eyes. We can meet there tomorrow after our shift."

A hidden tech lab.

It could be exactly what we need—somewhere we can make real progress. If it's properly equipped, I might even be able to disable Myall's NeuroMod.

Stop getting ahead of yourself.

"That sounds perfect," I say, keeping my excitement in check. "How do we get there?"

Marcus gives me the directions and a code for the door. As he speaks, a surge of hope begins to rise. We're no longer alone in this fight. With his expertise and this safe meeting location, we might finally have a chance to break free from The Harmonization Authority's control. But as we part ways, a chilling thought creeps in. We might have just signed up for something far more dangerous than we could ever imagine.

Chapter Thirteen

Ziva

The sterile corridors of the Compliance Monitoring Division feel even more suffocating today. I search the sea of identical uniforms, when I spot him near the break room's glass wall. I take a deep breath, cool air filling my lungs, and step forward, Marcus's footsteps echoing softly behind me.

"Myall," I say, keeping my voice steady despite the tension coiling in my chest "There's someone I'd like you to officially meet."

Myall's green eyes flick to Marcus, his expression a blend of curiosity and wariness. I try to avoid glancing around at our colleagues, and just have to hope that they're too preoccupied to take any notice of us. This could go terribly wrong. What if Myall misjudges him? Or worse, what if I'm betting everything on a fragile alliance?

"This is Marcus Holt. He's a Technician, like me, but with experience as a Compliance Monitor."

Marcus nods, his face unreadable. "Pleasure," he says, his tone cool but not unkind.

Myall eyes flick over Marcus, brow furrowing. He's likely trying to piece together why I'm introducing them.

"Marcus has some…unique insights that could be valuable to our project," I say, glancing at him for confirmation. His expression remains inscrutable, but I catch a flicker of uncertainty in his eyes, and my heart sinks momentarily as I turn back to Myall.

Myall's posture relaxes, his gaze sharpening with under-standing. "Is that so?" he asks, tone deceptively neutral. "I'd be interested to hear more about your experiences, Marcus."

I finally risk glancing around to make sure no one's watching. Most people are either absorbed in the vid-screen or eating. "Perhaps we could continue this in a more private setting," I suggest, my eyes conveying the urgency I can't put into words.

Marcus clears his throat. "I know a place," he whispers. "An old tech lab, abandoned but still functional. We could meet there after our shift ends."

I watch Myall closely, silently willing him to understand. His eyes meet mine, and I see the moment it clicks. "That sounds…productive," he says slowly. "I'd be happy to join you both."

Relief washes over me, though I keep my expression guarded. "Excellent," I say, allowing a small smile. "We'll met at shift's end and walk there together."

As we part ways, I can't shake the uneasy feeling in the pit of my stomach. We're taking a huge risk, but the potential rewards are too great to ignore.

* * *

The building where Marcus's abandoned tech lab is located looms ahead, a hulking shadow in the twilight. Marcus said the lab was on the ground floor, which means an easy escape if things go wrong. I approach the rusted door, Myall and Marcus close behind. I can't shake the feeling we're being watched, but I push it aside, trying to let go of my worry.

"Here we are," I whisper, my fingers tracing the outline of the hidden keypad Marcus told me about last night. "Let's hope that override code still works."

"It will," Marcus reassures. "I've been here several times in the past."

I punch in the sequence, holding my breath until the lock clicks open. We slip inside. The musty air hits us like a wall, heavy with the scent of forgotten machinery and dust that clogs my lungs with every breath.

"This way," Marcus murmurs, leading us through a maze of abandoned equipment. "I have a workspace set up in the back. I like to come here from time to time."

As we enter the small workroom, I can't help but gasp. Gutted NeuroMods litter every surface, their innards exposed like mechanical corpses. I wonder how long this place has been here and how Marcus discovered it.

"Impressive," Myall breathes, his eyes wide as he takes in the room.

Nodding, I move toward the workbench. "We can't risk being here too long so we'd better get started. Marcus, can you walk us through what you know of the NeuroMod system?"

As Marcus explains, I disassemble my malfunctioning NeuroMod, the cool metal against my fingertips and the faint scent of burnt circuitry making my stomach churn.

"Okay. So, see this circuit here?" I interrupt, pointing to a tiny component. "This is where I think the vulnerability lies."

Myall leans in close, his breath warm on my neck. "How so?"

I swallow hard, the flutter in my chest impossible to ignore. "The emotional suppression relies on this loop. If we disrupt it—"

"We could potentially disable the entire system," Marcus finishes, his eyes gleaming with newfound excitement.

As we work through our theories, I guide them through the intricacies of the NeuroMods glitch I've discovered, welcoming their questions and insights. Finally sharing this knowledge is exhilarating, working toward a common goal. For the past week, I've been stuck trying to replicate the glitch, but bringing Marcus in with his expertise could be the key.

"So, I'm guessing the device we were tasked to repair gave you the idea?" Myall asks, pointing to a tiny component hidden beneath a tiny cluster of wires.

I smile ruefully at him. "Yeah. I was fiddling with it," I say, pointing to the tiny component, "when the malfunction happened."

Myall nods in understanding and takes a closer look at the device. My fingers brush against his as we reach for it at the same time. A jolt of electricity shoots up my arm, but I don't pull back right away. For a moment, I let it linger, my breath catching. I force myself to focus, ignore it. It's just a touch.

Still, I can't help the way my pulse quickens when I glance up at him. He's already looking at me, his eyes lingering for a second longer than they should. I turn back to the workbench quickly, trying to focus on what we're doing. My hands move on their own now, disconnected from my brain.

"Careful doing that part," he says, his voice quieter this time, as his hand grazes mine again when he adjusts something near the wires. I try to ignore the heat that rises in my cheeks. It's stupid, how every little touch seems to matter now.

I should be thinking about the device in my hand, but all I can think about is the way he's standing so close. My skin's too aware of him, and I hate it. It's hard to concentrate with him right there, the air between us tight with something I don't want to name. My fingers fumble a little with the NeuroMod in my hand.

Focus, Ziva.

"You know," Myall says, his voice low, "I never thought I'd find anyone else who felt the same way about…all of this." He gestures vaguely at the lab around us, but I know he means so much more.

I nod, throat tight. "Me neither. It's…it's everything I've dreamed of, but never dared hope for."

We share a smile, neither of us acknowledging this growing thing between us, before turning back to the NeuroMod.

Marcus clears his throat, startling us both. "I think I might have another idea," he says, his usual caution giving way to excitement. "What if we could create a feedback loop within the emotional suppression circuit? It could potentially overload the system—"

I lean in, intrigued. "Go on. What are you thinking?"

Marcus explains his theory and his insights are brilliant, building on what Myall and I have already discussed.

"That's…that's genius, Marcus," I breathe, mind racing to catch up with the implications. "If we can pull this off, it be enough to bring down the whole system."

Myall nods enthusiastically. "We actually make a good team, the three of us."

Myall and Marcus hunch over the disassembled Neuro-Mod, their heads nearly touching as they begin debating the finer points of its circuitry.

"What if we rerouted this connection here to create the feedback loop?" Myall suggests, his finger tracing a path along the circuit board.

Marcus shakes his head. "Too risky. It might trigger a failsafe. But—" He pauses, a mischievous glint in his eye. "What if we disguised our modifications by adding in an additional connection?"

"Marcus, that's brilliant!" I exclaim, excitement bubbling up. "That could actually work."

I catch Myall's eye again, and my breath catches at how close he is to me. The warmth in his gaze sends my heart racing. Desire and fear swirl inside me. I quickly look away, but I feel the heat rising in my cheeks.

"I think I've found something else," Marcus says, his usually stoic face animated with excitement. "Look at this anomaly in the emotion suppression module."

Leaning in, Myall's proximity is all but forgotten. "That could be our way in," I whisper, conscious of the need for secrecy even here.

Myall's shoulder brushes mine as he leans in to take a better look. The contact sends a shiver down my spine that has nothing to do with the chill of the lab.

"If we can exploit that weakness," he says, "we could disable the entire network at once, turn off all the NeuroMods in one go."

I nod, trying to focus on the task at hand and not on the warmth radiating from Myall's proximity. "That sounds almost too good to be true. We'll need to test it carefully," I say as the others nod in agreement.

"We're really doing this, aren't we?" I say, half to myself. "We're going to break the system."

Myall's hand finds mine under the table, giving it a gentle squeeze. "Yeah, we are," he affirms, his eyes meeting mine with an intensity that makes my breath catch.

Why is it that when he looks at me like that, I feel my resolve wavering?

Chapter Fourteen

Myall

The NeuroMod on my wrist seems to grow heavier with every hour. I swear it pulses in time with my heartbeat.

The memory of almost kissing Ziva in my grandmother's house still haunts me. Her fingers brushing mine, the way we always seem to gravitate toward each other—it's like we're magnets, helpless to resist each other. The ghost of her touch lingers, stirring something dangerous within me, something my NeuroMod is having difficulty suppressing. Something the Harmonization Authority would deem a malfunction.

"Another day of keeping the masses in line?" Marcus asks, his tone dry as he approaches my workstation.

I nod, slipping into the role of the dutiful Compliance Monitor. "Just doing my part for societal harmony."

The words taste bitter as they leave my mouth. How can

there be true harmony when we're all smothering the very essence of our humanity?

Marcus's gaze lingers on me for a moment before he shakes his head and moves across the row to Ziva's workstation. I can tell he senses something is off with me today, but he doesn't press any further.

Turning back to today's NeuroMod logs, the glow of the screen illuminates my face as I input data from the citizens' mandatory emotional checks—each line a reminder of the laughter they bury and the joy they suppress. It's a monotonous task, but it needs to be done in order to identify any outliers who may pose a threat to the system. Or, to identify any individuals who might be easily swayed to our cause.

As I input the data, my mind wanders to the faces of those I monitor. What dreams do they bury? What laughter do they silence? My heart aches at the thought of being complicit in their suffering.

The shift bell rings, and a familiar anticipation stirs in my chest. Soon, I'll be back in the lab, watching Ziva's brow furrow as she works her magic on the NeuroMods. Her focus is magnetic, and I can't help but look forward to those moments with her more than I want to admit.

"Ready for another late night?" Ziva asks, her voice tinged with fatigue. Shadows begin to pool under her eyes—proof of our long hours in the lab this week. It's clear the toll is starting to show.

"Always," I reply, perhaps too eagerly. Marcus raises an eyebrow as he stands beside her, but says nothing.

We agreed to put any personal feelings aside, to focus on the rebellion. But every glance she gives me pulls me closer to the edge of wanting something more.

Making our way through the corridors of the Compliance Monitoring Division, our footsteps echo in the eerie silence, the sterile air carrying a faint metallic tang. Once outside, cool fresh air hits my face along with the soft sent of something that is undeniably Ziva.

We stroll through the streets, keeping our mouths shut out of caution as we know we're violating rules being seen in a group of more than two. The noise from the city around us only amplifies our silent commute.

Once inside the lab, Ziva wastes no time , "I think I'm close to replicating the glitch," she announces, her eyes alight with excitement. "Myall, I'll need to use your NeuroMod to test it."

My heart races as I move towards her makeshift workstation and angle my wrist with the NeuroMod for her to access it's circuitry. This is it—the moment we've been working towards all week. If Ziva can replicate the malfunction, we might have a real chance at dismantling the entire system.

And I might have a real chance at knowing if what I'm beginning to feel for Ziva is real.

"Are you sure we're ready to test it?" Marcus asks, his usual caution evident in his tone as he huddles beside Ziva.

Ziva's response is firm. "We have to try. It's the only way to give people back their right to feel. We need to test it on ourselves first to ensure I can replicate it properly."

Maneuvering my wrist into position, Ziva's touch lingers a moment too long on my wrist, sending a shiver down my spine as her warmth seeps into my skin. This time, I don't try to suppress the jolt of electricity that courses through me, making my stomach tighten. I meet her gaze, and for a moment, I swear I see a flicker of the same intensity reflected back at me.

"Let's do this," I say, sounding more confident than I feel.

When Ziva's shoulder brushes mine, her breath quickens, and I feel the warmth radiating from her. Every fleeting glance between us speaks volumes.

Her fingers move deftly over the NeuroMods, her lips pursed in concentration. I can't tear my eyes away as she connects wires and fine-tunes settings. The hum of the room is heavy, mirroring the tight knot of anticipation building in my chest.

"Almost there," Ziva mutters, her eyes fixed on the devices. "Just need to…ah!"

A sudden spark leaps between the NeuroMods, making us all jump. My heart leaps into my throat as I watch a thin arc of blue electricity connect the two devices for a split second. Then, with a soft whine, both devices flicker, and go dark.

The room falls silent.

"Did it work?" I ask, my voice hoarse with anticipation.

Before Ziva can answer, a surge crashes over me, a chaotic whirlpool that overwhelms my senses and steals my breath. My mind floods with feelings I've never known—joy, fear, anger, love—all crashing together in a dizzying tide. Colors explode around me, vibrant and overwhelming. Laughter that vibrates in my chest, yet it mingles with a sobering sorrow.

Gasping, I stagger back against the wall, my heart rate spiking. "I…I can feel everything," I choke out, my eyes wide as a wave of nausea washes through me. The intensity of it all is almost painful, yet exhilarating at the same time.

Ziva rushes to my side, her face a mix of concern and

excitement. "Myall? Are you okay?"

Meeting her gaze, it's as if I'm seeing her for the first time. The depth of my feelings crashes over me, leaving me breathless.

"I've never been better," I whisper, a smile spreading across my face despite the maelstrom of emotions inside me.

My hands shake as I try to steady myself against the cold metal workbench. The lab is suddenly too small, too confining. I need air. I need space to process this flood of sensations.

"I need...I need to step outside for a minute," I manage to say, my voice trembling with the effort of maintaining composure in front of the others.

Ziva nods, understanding in her eyes. "Of course. Take your time."

Stumbling out of the lab into the dim corridor, I gasp for breath, every sound amplified in the sudden silence.

"How could they do this to us?" I mutter, my voice thick with disbelief. "How could they take everything we've fought for?"

The weight of years of muted emotions crashes down on me. Anger bubbles up, hot and fierce as it surges its way out of me. "It's not right," I growl, slamming my fist against the wall. The pain is sharp, real, and I welcome it.

But beneath the anger, something else stirs—a warmth, a tenderness when I think of Ziva. It's always been there, but now it's magnified. Leaning against the cool wall, I close my eyes.

Is this what it means to truly be human? To feel so much that it hurts?

The sound of footsteps approaching forces me to open my

eyes. Ziva steps cautiously, likes she's approaching a wild animal, her face a mixture of concern and hope.

"Myall?" she says softly. "How are you feeling?"

My pulse quickens as I look at her. "Like I'm finally awake," I reply, my voice thick. "Ziva, we have to stop them. We can't let them keep doing this."

She nods, determination glinting in her eyes. "I know," she says softly. "We will."

A deep breath steadies me as Ziva moves to stand beside me, leaning against the wall, our shoulders brushing. Her presence surrounds me, a heady mix of comfort and longing that tightens my chest. I've never felt so bare, so vulnerable.

"It's overwhelming, isn't it?" Ziva says, inching closer, and I can see the vulnerability in her eyes as she meets my gaze. "I remember when it first happened to me. It was like…like being born again."

I nod, struggling to find the right words to convey what I'm feeling. "It's like I'm seeing everything for the first time. Colors are brighter, sounds are sharper. And you—" I trail off, my heart pounding.

You are so beautiful.

Ziva's lips curl into a small smile. "I know," she says softly. "I feel it too."

We stand there for a moment, and I resist the urge to touch her, afraid of the intensity it might stir.

"How do you handle it every day?" I ask, my voice trembling slightly. "All these feelings?"

Ziva takes a deep breath. "It's not easy," she admits. "But it's worth it. This is what makes us human, Myall. This is what they've been taking away from us."

Clenching my fists at my side, I feel a surge of determination along with the burning ache of my sore palm. "We can't let them do this anymore," I growl. "We have to fight back."

Ziva's eyes light up with fierce resolve, but there's also a flicker of fear—a fear of the consequences of our rebellion, of losing the fleeting moments we share.

"That's exactly what we're going to do," she says. "Now that you've experienced it yourself, you understand what's at stake."

I nod, the connection with Ziva beyond words. We're in this together now, now more than ever.

"So," I say, a hint of a smile playing on my lips, "what's our next move?"

Ziva guides me back inside the lab and together, the three of us start forming plans.

Marcus verifies my emotions, as detected by the Sentinel system, indicate that my NeuroMod is working correctly. This means that even though my device is currently offline, only the three of us are aware of it.

Our top priority is now figuring out how to safely replicate the glitch on a larger scale. Ziva believes she can recreate it for each person, but Marcus seems wary of having his own NeuroMod deactivated. Surprisingly, Ziva doesn't push the matter further.

After another hour of debating the next steps for our growing rebellion, Marcus stretches, his joints popping as he rises from his chair. "I think that's enough for tonight," he says, his eyes darting between Ziva and me. "You two seem to have things under control here."

A glint in Marcus's eyes makes my cheeks flush, and I quickly look away, hoping he doesn't see.

"Yeah, we'll wrap up soon," Ziva says, her fingers absently

fiddling with a NeuroMod. Her voice is steady, but I catch the slight tremor in her hand.

Marcus nods, a slight smirk tugging at his lips. "Don't stay up too late, kids," he says, heading for the door. "And remember, discretion is key."

Marcus is usually the last of us to leave, as he doesn't like us being in the lab without him, but I guess he wanted to give us a moment alone together. I silently thank him for it.

As the door clicks shut behind him, the air in the lab seems to thicken. Ziva and I are alone, truly alone, for the first time since the glitch. My heart hammers against my ribs, each beat a thunderous reminder of my newfound emotional freedom.

"So," I begin, my throat suddenly dry. "What now?"

Ziva turns to me, her hazel eyes wide. "Now we start finding others to bring into our cause," she says. "No more hiding."

I take a tentative step towards her. "I'm scared, Ziva," I admit. "These feelings...they're overwhelming. More overwhelming than I expected."

Her hand gently moves towards me, her fingers delicately pushing my hair away from my face before she lets her hand drop. "I know," she whispers. "But like you said...we're in this together."

I intertwine my fingers with hers, marveling at the softness of her skin. "How do you do it?" I ask. "How do you stay so strong all the time?"

Her laugh is tinged with sadness. "I'm not strong, Myall. I'm terrified. But the alternative of going back to that numb existence, it's unthinkable now."

Pulling her closer, I feel the warmth of her body against

mine as we stand inches apart, our breaths twining together. "We'll figure this out," I say, surprised by the conviction in my voice.

I breathe in deeply, savoring the scent of Ziva—a mix of burnt circuitry and something floral—something uniquely her. Every beat of my heart is a testament to the chaos inside me.

"Ziva," I say, pulling back slightly to search her eyes. "What we're doing…it's going to be dangerous. The Harmonization Authority—"

She cuts me off, her voice fierce. "Is wrong. They're robbing us of our humanity, Myall."

I nod, feeling the slight shift in my mood. "I know. But how do we fight them? How do we stop them?"

"We start small. We replicate the glitch, spread it. Give people a taste of what they're missing. Eventually they'll join us."

I stop to consider the possibilities of what she's suggesting. "You want to spark a revolution."

"Exactly," she grins, and my breath catches at the sight.

Her smile is radiant, full of hope, and something about it catches in my throat. I run a hand through my hair, conflicting emotions warring within me. Doubt gnaws at me, a persistent whisper that echoes in my mind.

What if our rebellion fails? What if something happens to us? What if something happens to Ziva?

The thought claws at my insides, twisting my stomach into knots. "That's exhilarating and terrifying all at once," I admit.

She leans in, her forehead resting against mine, our breaths intermingling. "That's what living feels like, Myall."

"Whatever comes next," I whisper, leaning in closer, "It will all be worth it."

Our faces hover inches apart, the silence between us filled with the weight of everything we haven't said. Her breath is soft against my skin, but it feels like the room is vibrating with the tension.

Every part of me wants to close the gap. To finally let go of all the emotions I've been holding back. But something stops me. I move slightly, pulling in a sharp breath. The space between us feels like an insurmountable distance now, and the pull to close it is almost unbearable. But I can't. Not yet. Not like this. There's too much riding on what happens next. The rebellion. The people who need us. The world we're trying to change.

Taking a half step back, my heart protests at the distance. My hand trembles at my side, wanting to reach out, wanting to pull her close, but I force myself to keep it still. She doesn't move, doesn't push. She's waiting, watching, and I can feel the patience in her eyes. It's like she knows I'm struggling with something bigger than just this moment.

We stand there, just close enough to feel the other's presence, but not enough to act on it. The tension isn't gone. It's still there, thick in the air, but I'm not ready to cross that line—not yet.

Chapter Fifteen

Ziva

The flickering glow of the lab's monitors casts eerie light, stretching long shadows across the cluttered workbench. Marcus hunches over a workbench, his fingers restless. Myall gives me a subtle nod, indicating he's waiting for me to make the first move.

During our shift today, I didn't have much opportunity to check in with Myall and see how he was coping with his emotions resurfacing. But when we returned to the tech lab this evening, Myall and I quietly exchanged words while Marcus was occupied reviewing my notes from the night before.

Our plan is to persuade Marcus into letting me disable his NeuroMod.

Last night, I tried to bring up the idea to Marcus, but he seemed hesitant, and I felt it wasn't best to push him just yet.

But I need to know if how we recreated that glitch isn't a total fluke, and the only way to know for certain is to test it again, on Marcus.

"We need to talk about your NeuroMod, Marcus," I say, my heart fluttering with nervous energy.

"What about it?" His shoulders tense as if weighed down by invisible chains, his breath hitching slightly.

I take a deep breath, choosing my words carefully. "I can disable it. Just like I did for Myall and myself."

What if I've pushed too far?

Marcus's dark eyes widen, darting between Myall and me. "I...I'm not sure that's wise just yet."

"Why not?" Myall's voice is low, urgent, but I catch the slight tremor in his hand as he gestures, a telltale sign of the anxiety bubbling beneath his calm facade. "It's overwhelming at first, but—"

"Overwhelming?" Marcus interrupts, panic edging into his voice before it's swiftly dulled. He tugs at his short-cropped hair, and I can see the faint remnants of the boy he once was, buried beneath layers of fear and conditioning. What does he truly want? Can he even remember?

Out of the three of us, Marcus is the only one who was old enough to truly comprehend the events that unfolded when The Authority seized power. I assume he's about the same age as our parents, and I wonder what emotional wounds the NeuroMod has been masking for Marcus all these years.

"It's not just about feeling everything again," I say, leaning in. "It's about being human. About connecting in ways The Authority can never control."

Marcus's gaze shifts to Myall, who gives a small, encouraging nod. I hold my breath, watching the internal struggle play out on Marcus's features.

He exhales shakily. "Fine. I'll do it."

Relief floods through me, yet there's a gnawing regret in the pit of my stomach, a shadow of doubt about whether this is the right choice for Marcus. I gather the supplies, my fingers trembling as I sift through the tools. The sharp click of metal breaks the silence. Myall and Marcus watch me intently as I prepare to recreate the glitch.

"This might feel strange at first," I warn as I maneuver Marcus's wrist into position. "Try to stay calm."

Marcus nods, his jaw tight. His pulse throbs visibly in his neck, his breath shallow and uneven. Myall moves closer, placing a reassuring hand on Marcus's shoulder.

"You've got this," Myall murmurs. "Remember, it's just the real you coming back."

I tune his words out, focusing on recreating the glitch and the familiar sequence of commands. "Almost there," I mutter, more to myself than the others.

As I input the final command, Marcus gasps, his breath hitching in his throat. His eyes widen, pupils dilating as a whirlwind of feelings cascades over him. His brows lift in disbelief, struggling to reconcile the flood of emotions with the numbness he's known for the past eighteen years.

"How do you feel?" I ask, unable to keep the excitement from my voice.

Marcus opens his mouth to respond, but no words come out. Instead, a single tear slides down his cheek. It trembles on his skin before dropping to the floor, and I realize that this might be the first time he's cried real tears in years.

Marcus's hands tremble as he touches his face, feeling the wetness of his tears. His breath comes in short, ragged gasps, and I can see the muscles in his jaw working as he struggles to process the flood of emotions vying for dominance within him.

"I…I feel everything," he chokes out, his voice raw and unfamiliar. "It's so intense. I didn't know…I'd forgotten…" His words stumble over each other in a jumbled mess.

He sways slightly, caught in the emotional storm, and I worry he might collapse under the weight. I reach out instinctively, but hesitate. Touch feels heavier now, more meaningful than it ever was before. Myall seems to sense my uncertainty and steps in, gripping Marcus's shoulder more firmly.

"Take deep breaths," Myall instructs, his tone gentle. "It's overwhelming at first, but you'll adjust."

Marcus nods, his eyes darting around the room as if seeing it for the first time. "The colors…they're so vibrant. And I can notice the air on my skin. It's. It's all too much."

He runs his hands through his hair, tugging at it slightly as if to ground himself. The sight stirs something in me. I push the feeling aside, focusing on keeping Marcus calm.

I can successfully replicate the glitch, which means I can now help others. We just need to figure out a way to persuade them to let me deactivate their NeuroMods.

"Perhaps we should call it a night," Marcus says suddenly, his voice strained, cutting through my thoughts. "I need…I need to process this. Alone."

Myall and I exchange a glance, a silent conversation passing between us. We both understand Marcus' need for solitude, but there's also an unspoken desire to stay, neither of us ready to part ways for the night. I'm not sure Marcus will want us staying here alone for a second night—it's his hideout, after all.

"Of course," I say aloud, forcing a reassuring smile. "We'll pack up here and get you home to rest."

As Marcus gathers his things, his movements jerky and unsure, I catch Myall's eye again. A slight nod, a raised eyebrow—it's enough. We'll meet back here later, after Marcus is safely home.

"Myall, you'd better leave first," Marcus says as he reaches the door, his voice almost gruff. "I'll go next, then Ziva."

Myall simply nods and slips out the door. Alone with Marcus, I ask "Are you sure you're going to be alright? I know it's a lot to process at first."

Marcus turns to face me and it's clear that he's struggling with the sudden onslaught of his emotions. I feel guilty for forcing him to have his NeuroMod disabled but I needed to be sure that recreating the glitch for Myall's NeuroMod wasn't a fluke.

"I think I just need some space to work through all these emotions in private," is all he says before he slips out the door, nodding for me to follow.

I reluctantly follow behind him. Once outside, I force myself to walk at a normal pace, as I say goodnight to Marcus and head toward my unit, the familiar streets feeling unfamiliar in my heightened state.

Inside, I go through the motions of my evening routine, counting the minutes in my head. As I brush my teeth, I catch my reflection in the mirror. My eyes are too bright, my cheeks flushed. I steady my breathing, willing my features into something neutral.

Calm down, Ziva.

After what feels like forever, though it's only been about

five minutes, I decide it's safe to leave. I slip out of the unit, blending into the shadows as I make my way back to the lab. Every sound makes me jump—a distant siren, a drone's whir. My skin prickles as if unseen eyes are watching from the dark.

Guilt tightens in my chest as I scan the dimly lit street, but I force it back. There's no time for second-guessing now. I inhale slowly, trying to ground myself. With trembling fingers, I key in the access code and slip inside.

The lab is dark and quiet, but I can sense Myall's presence before I see him. He steps out of the shadows, and the look on his face makes my breath catch.

"You came back," he says softly, relief evident in his voice.

I nod, unable to speak for a moment as I catch my breath and will my heart rate to slow. "Any trouble getting back here?" I finally manage to ask.

He answers with a faint smile, his eyes betraying the weight of his exhaustion."Took a roundabout way, just to be safe. You?"

"Same," I reply, moving closer. "I kept expecting to run into Marcus around every corner," I say, trying to laugh.

Myall raises an eyebrow. "So you're saying you didn't want to bump into him?" he teases, his grin making my heart skip.

"Very funny." I say, "I know he needed some space to process his emotions, but I can't shake this paranoid feeling that he's going to walk back in and catch us here when we said we were going home."

I want to lean in, to close that gap, but fear makes my legs feel heavy, as if the world outside could come crashing in at any moment.

"So," I say, forcing myself to focus on why we're really here.

I study Myall's face, searching for signs of the emotional storm I know must be raging beneath the surface. "I didn't get the chance to ask you how you're handling it?" I say, my voice softening. "The full extent of your emotions, I mean. Now that your NeuroMod is offline."

Myall's shoulders tense as he runs a hand through his hair. "It's…a lot," he admits, his measured tone cracking slightly. "At work today, I felt like I was going to burst. Every little frustration, every moment of anger—it all felt amplified."

I give a tight lipped smile, understanding all too well. "You look like you managed to keep it hidden pretty well?"

"Barely," he says with a wry smile. "I kept ducking into the supply closet to collect myself. Tara probably thinks I have some kind of stomach bug."

We share a quiet laugh, but there's an undercurrent of fear. If anyone had noticed, if Myall had slipped up even once, this would all be over for us.

"It's terrifying," I confess, voicing the thought we're both avoiding, as I lean against a workbench. "But also exhilarating, isn't it? To feel so much, after years of dampened emotions?"

Myall's eyes meet mine, and I see a vulnerability there that makes my heart ache. "Yeah," he whispers. "It is."

The air between us thickens, and it feels as if the world outside has vanished, leaving only this moment suspended in time.

The urge to comfort him is overwhelming, but I hold back. Instead, I ask, "What's the hardest part for you?"

Myall is quiet for a long moment. "The memories," he finally says, as he shifts from one foot to the other. "They come flooding back, all the losses, the pain my NeuroMod had buried. My parents…"

As he speaks, I see the vulnerability in his gaze, a mirror reflecting my own pain. There's an intensity there that makes a lump rises in my throat.

"I know," I say softly. "For me, it's remembering the orphanage. The loneliness. I never realized how lonely I was. How much I craved connection. Until you."

Without thinking, I reach out and take his hand, our fingers intertwining. His palm against mine sends a flutter through my stomach, an unfamiliar warmth that stirs something deep within. I find myself wanting to linger in this moment, to memorize the feel of his fingers intertwined with mine.

I open my mouth to say something, anything, but the words catch in my throat. Instead, I watch his eyes, hoping they'll reveal what he's thinking, what he wants.

"At least we've got each other now," he murmurs, his thumb brushing my hand.

I'm suddenly aware of Myall's gaze, intense and focused on me. Our breaths mingle, creating a heady atmosphere that makes my heart race. His gaze flickers to my lips, and I freeze, my breath catching. Our eyes lock, and for a heartbeat, the world narrows to just us.

Clearing my throat, I take a step back, letting go of his hand, mine trembling slightly. "So, um, what do you think our next move should be?"

Myall blinks, as if coming out of a daze. He runs a hand through his hair, collecting himself. "Right. The rebellion."

"We need more people," I say, latching onto the safer topic. "But how do we bring others in without exposing ourselves?"

Myall's brow furrows in concentration. "We could start small. Test the waters with subtle comments, gauge reactions."

"What about Kellen? He's always voicing his objections about Colvin."

"Good eye," Myall says, a hint of admiration in his voice. "We'll need to be careful though. Kellan's also got a loud mouth."

Myall's warning hits me full force. Are we insane to even consider this? I swallow hard, throat suddenly tight. "Myall, I'm I'm scared. If we're caught, it's not just us who'll suffer. Grandma Elara, Marcus—anyone we care about could be punished."

Myall's green eyes darken with understanding. "I know," he says softly. "I lie awake at night thinking about it. The consequences—they're unimaginable. I don't know how either of our parents did this."

I wrap my arms around myself, suddenly cold despite the stuffy warmth of the lab. "Sometimes I wonder if we're doing the right thing. Is emotional freedom worth the risk? Are we being selfish for wanting this? Do the people even want to be free?"

"Hey," Myall says, his voice gentle. He reaches out, hesitating for a moment before taking my hand in his once more. His touch sends a jolt through me, and I find myself holding my breath. "We're fighting for something real, Ziva. For the right to feel, to love. That's always worth it."

I look down at our joined hands, marveling at how such a simple gesture can feel so profound. Without thinking, I intertwine our fingers, savoring the warmth of his skin against mine.

"You're right," I whisper, meeting his gaze. My heart races, and for once, I don't try to suppress it. "I just...I can't bear the thought of losing you or losing any of this."

Myall's thumb traces small circles on the back of my hand, and I feel myself melting into the touch. "We'll protect each other," he promises. "Whatever happens next."

I nod, my chest unbearably heavy. "Right," I say, playing with the whispy ends of my hair to avoid his gaze. "We need to stay focused. The NeuroMods are our only shot."

Myall nods, his expression shifting from tender to determined. "You mentioned earlier needing two types?"

I pace the lab. "Yeah, we need an unattached NeuroMod and one that's still connected to someone so that I can recreate that glitch. It's crucial for figuring out how to mass-produce the dismantling process."

"Getting an unattached one shouldn't be too hard," Myall muses as he glances about the room, taking in the scattered, broken NeuroMods around the place. "But a working, attached one? That means we definitely need to bring someone else into this."

Although we are both aware of Grandma Elara's Neuro-Mod, neither of us suggest using it. The thought of getting her to leave the safety of her home and come to the lab is too much, and taking the equipment to her house is not an option.

I bite my lip, considering our options. "What if we 'borrowed' one during a routine check? I could claim it's malfunctioning, take it for 'repairs'..."

The idea has been playing on my mind for days now.

Myall's eyes widen. "Ziva, that's...that's incredibly dangerous. If they catch you—"

"I know," I cut him off, my voice tight. "But what choice do we have? Every day more people lose themselves to these things. We have to act."

He runs a hand down his face, clearly frustrated. "You're right. I just…I can't stand the thought of you getting caught."

His concern comforts me, though fear still claws at my chest. "We knew the risks when we started this," I remind him, and myself.

Myall nods slowly. "Okay. But we plan this meticulously. Leave no room for error."

My wrist tingles with the absence of my NeuroMod, the blank screen a reminder of what we're risking. "It's getting late," I say reluctantly. "We should go, It's well past curfew."

Myall's eyes meet mine, a storm of emotions swirling in their green depths. "Yeah," he agrees, his voice rough. "We can't risk staying too long."

We stand, and I find myself drawn to him, wanting to prolong this moment. My fingers twitch, aching to reach out and touch him. Instead, I clench my fists at my sides.

"Ziva," Myall says softly, taking a step closer. "Be careful out there. Please."

I nod, my throat tight. "You too. Remember, act normal. Don't let anyone see—"

"I know," he interrupts gently. "I've gotten pretty good at sticking to the shadows."

A sad smile tugs at my lips. "I wish we didn't have to hide."

Myall's hand brushes mine, and I want so desperately to lean in to his touch. "Someday, we won't have to," he promises.

I turn away, forcing myself to move towards the exit. Every step feels like I'm leaving a part of myself behind. At the door, I pause, looking back at Myall.

"See you tomorrow?" I ask, hating how hopeful I sound.

He nods. "Tomorrow."

Just before I step out, I catch a glimpse of Myall's lips parting as if he's about to say something, but then it's gone, leaving me with a rush of unspoken words hanging in the air.

Chapter Sixteen

Myall

Lingering by the window of the hidden tech lab, my gaze is drawn to the distant glow of the city lights. It's been three weeks since Ziva disabled my NeuroMod. Three weeks of experiencing life in vivid color instead of muted grays.

"We're making progress," I mutter, mostly to myself.

Ziva's fingers twitch, her brows knitting as she concentrates on the delicate components before her. She looks up from the workbench where she's tinkering with spare NeuroMod parts. "What was that?"

I turn to face her, drinking in the sight of her long brown hair falling over her shoulder as she works. My chest tightens. "I said we're making progress. You, me, Marcus—we're building something here. A real resistance."

She nods, her entire face lighting up. "Damn right we are.

And we're just getting started."

I clear my throat. "Also, I overheard something at work today. Something big."

Ziva's eyebrows shoot up as her hands still. "What is it?"

"There are rumors circulating that The Authority is developing a new type of NeuroMod. Something more invasive, with deeper neural integration. I think it has something to do with that repair request from Regent Colvin we were assigned to work on. If they succeed, it'll be nearly impossible to disable them like we've been planning."

"Shit," Ziva breathes. Her fingers clench around the screwdriver she's holding. "That changes things."

I nod grimly. "We can't afford to waste any time," I say, my voice tight. "We need to stop this—before it's too late."

"Do you think this has anything to do with whoever stole the blueprints to the NeuroMod framework?" she asks, chewing on her bottom lip.

"Yeah, I think so," is all I say.

Marcus paces the cramped space, his brow furrowed in concentration. "Then we need to intercept the plans for this new NeuroMod," he says, his voice growing urgent. "If we can get our hands on the schematics, maybe we can find a weakness and an easier way to disable them."

I nod, leaning against a workbench. "I know. But how do we get access? Security's tightened after the breach. There's no way we would be able to access anything now."

Ziva's eyes light up. "What if we create a diversion? Trigger a malfunction elsewhere to draw attention away from what we're doing?"

"That could work," I muse, the idea catching hold of me.

Marcus interjects, "We could also try hacking into their

system remotely. It'll take time, since none of us are exactly hackers, but it's much safer."

"We could try to ask around, see what information we could find out about it first?" Ziva suggests.

As we debate strategies, an idea strikes. "We could..," I begin. "Kellan was the one who told me about the rumor. He might know more about it. We could ask him. He's always voicing his opinion about The Authority when he thinks no ones paying attention. He might even be willing to join us."

Ziva's eyes meet mine, brows furrowing. "I'm not sure that's such a great idea. You mentioned he's quite open about his opinion, which would make him noticeable to The Authority if they get wind about what we're doing."

We start brainstorm ways to intercept the plans for the new NeuroMods—none of them any good when I notice Ziva fidgeting, her gaze darting to her bag. There's something she's not saying.

When Marcus steps out for a moment to use the bathroom, Ziva turns to me, her voice almost a whisper. "Myall, I need to tell you something."

Why is it when she says that, my stomach drops. "What is it?"

She takes a deep breath. "I...I stole a NeuroMod. One that's still linked to a citizen."

A cold weight settles in my gut. "Ziva, we talked about this. The risks—"

"I know," she cuts me off, her eyes pleading. "But I had to. It's the only way I can perfect the deactivation process. We *need* this, Myall."

Her gaze drops, and she bites her lip, a flush creeping up her neck. I open my mouth to protest, but the fire in her eyes tells me it's pointless. And deep down, I know she's right. We're running out of time.

I sigh, running a hand through my hair. "Just...be more careful, okay? If anything happened to you..."

Ziva's eyes soften, a flicker of something I can't quite name passing through them. "I will be," she says, keeping her voice low. "But we can't afford to play it safe anymore."

I know she's right, that we can't play it safe forever. But the idea of her recklessness getting her caught fills me with dread. I want to protect her, keep her from harm, but I know that's not what she needs. Not what any of us need right now.

"Show me," I say, my voice rougher than I intended.

She nods, reaching into her bag to pull out the stolen NeuroMod. It looks innocuous enough, but it feels like a ticking time bomb in our midst.

"Ziva," I start, unable to keep the worry from my voice, "if they trace this back to you—"

"They won't," she interrupts, her tone sharp. "I've taken precautions. Trust me, Myall."

I do trust her. That's not the problem. It's the system I don't trust, the unseen eyes always watching. "And if something goes wrong?"

She meets my gaze, unflinching. "Then we'll deal with it. Together, like you said."

A jolt runs through me at her words, the weight of 'we' sinking in. I watch as she begins to fiddle with the NeuroMod, her nimble fingers tracing over its surface. Despite my fear, I can't help but admire her focus, her determination.

"What exactly are you trying to do?" I ask, leaning in closer.

"Recreate the glitch," she murmurs, eyes never leaving the device. "If I can figure out how to trigger it consistently, we can free more people."

I nod, watching her work. As I observe her, I'm struck by her quiet beauty—the way her dark lashes frame her eyes, the slight flush that tints her cheeks. Her bottom lip is slightly fuller than her top one and my eyes are drawn to that detail every time she bites her lip.

"There," she says suddenly pulling me from my dangerous thoughts. "I think I've got it."

I hold my breath as Ziva activates the NeuroMod, expecting to see the familiar flickering spark that signals deactivation. Instead, the device emits a high-pitched whine, its screen flashing an angry red. The whine pierces through the stillness, a shrieking alarm that vibrates through my bones, each pulse matching the frantic beat of my heart.

"No, no, no," Ziva mutters, her fingers frantically dancing across the circuitry. "This isn't right."

The alarm intensifies, and I feel my heart rate spike. "Ziva, what's happening?"

"I don't know," she says, frustration evident in her voice. "It's like they've added some kind of new failsafe. If I can't shut it down—"

"It could alert the authorities," I finish, the realization hitting me like a punch to the gut.

We lock eyes, the gravity of the situation settling over us. In that moment, I see a flicker of fear in Ziva's usually confident gaze, and it spurs me into action.

I race through all the possible outcomes if we can't deactivate this NeuroMod. We could be discovered, arrested, or worse. The thought of Enforcers storming in, dragging us away into the night, tightens my chest, each scenario worse than the last.

"Okay, think," I say, brushing my hair from my eyes. "What if we…what if we overloaded it?"

Ziva's eyes widen. "Overload it? That could work, but we'd need—"

"A power surge," we say in unison.

Without hesitation, I dash to the corner of the lab, rummaging through a box of discarded tech. "Here," I call out, holding up a small battery pack. "Will this do?"

Ziva nods, her focus razor-sharp once more. "Perfect. Quick, bring it here."

I dart back, slamming the battery pack into her hands.

"Hold this," she orders, thrusting the shrieking NeuroMod into my grip. "And whatever you do, don't drop it."

The whine continues to grow louder and more persistent, almost drowning out our frantic movements. I watch, heart in my throat, as Ziva connects the battery pack to the NeuroMod. For a terrifying moment, nothing happens. Then, with a sudden burst of light and a sharp crack, the device goes dark.

A wave of tension ebbs from my chest as I catch Ziva's gaze. Her face mirrors my relief. We stare at each other, breathless. A shared sigh of relief escapes us, and our shoulders slump. Rubbing the back of my neck, I try to calm my racing heart.

"That was fucking scary," Ziva whispers, a slow smile spreading across her face.

"Yeah, I'll say," I mutter, still feeling shaken by how easily things could have gone wrong if we hadn't been able to deactivate the NeuroMod.

As the adrenaline fades, I'm struck by how close we're

standing, how easy it would be to lean in and—

The lab door swings open with a creak, and we jump apart. Marcus steps in, his eyes darting between us and the smoking NeuroMod.

"What did I miss?" he asks, raising an eyebrow.

Ziva and I exchange a quick glance, unsure how much we should tell him.

"What happened?" he asks, gesturing to the smoking device.

"We had a bit of a mishap," Ziva says, stepping forward to take the blame. "I accidentally overloaded it while trying to deactivate it."

Marcus nods thoughtfully, examining the device. "Well, at least you were able to shut it down. We'll have to be more careful in the future."

* * *

As I enter the brightly-lit workroom, the hum of machinery fills the air. I slide into my chair, fingers trembling as I access the Sentinel system, my heart pounding with the fear of what I might find. The screen's glow reflects my unease as I scan the reports, paranoid that Ziva's little mishap last night is documented in the system. Fortunately, it isn't.

I can't stop thinking about last night's close call as I monitor the compliance feeds, my eyes keep drifting to Ziva across the aisle. She catches my gaze and gives me a subtle smile, soft yet defiant—like a flicker of hope in the shadows.

"Hey," Marcus's voice startles me. He leans in, pretending to check my screen. "I think I've found someone," he whispers.

My breath catches. "Who?"

"New transfer, Yenna Reeves. I've noticed her hesitating before her weekly mood adjustments. Could be nothing, but…"

I nod, understanding. It's a start. "Good pick up. If we approach her, we'll have to do it carefully."

As Marcus walks off, I catch Ziva's eye. She tilts her head, questioning. I offer a small smile, hoping it reassures her.

Trying to refocus on the compliance feeds, my mind keeps circling back to the risk of approaching Yenna. What if she betrays us? Maybe it's better if only one of us speaks with her—like Ziva did with Marcus. That way, if we get caught, only one of us would face arrest. The sound of my supervisors voice barking at me to get back to work and focus on my productivity, distracts me from any more thoughts about Yenna Reeves.

The lights flicker as I make my way to the exit at the end of my shift. I catch sight of Ziva, her silhouette framed by the fading light of dusk, and my heart lifts at the sight of her.

She falls into step beside me, and we head towards my grandmother's house for our weekly visit. We decided to start visiting Grandma Elara mid-week instead, so we could use our day off working with Marcus in the lab. I can tell that Ziva is eager to hear about my interaction with Marcus earlier, but she'll have to wait until we are out of earshot from any prying eyes or ears.

"I have someone in mind who could potentially join our trio and make us a…whatever the proper term for four people is," Ziva mutters quietly as we walk.

"Quartet," I reply automatically as we stop to let a passing vehicle by before crossing the street.

I wonder if it's the same person Marcus suggested.

As we resume walking, I can't shake the feeling of eyes on us. A prickling sensation races down my spine, and I glance around, every sound amplified—the rustle of leaves, the distant sound of patrol drones. The hairs on the back of my neck stand up, instincts telling me that something is off.

"Ziva," I mutter, "don't react, but I think we're being followed."

Her stride doesn't falter, but I see her shoulders tense. "How many?" she asks, keeping her voice low.

"Can't tell. One, maybe two." I resist the urge to look back, instead scanning our surroundings and noticing that the streets are emptying. "We need to lose them before we reach Grandma's."

Ziva's hand finds mine, squeezing tight. "Next turn, we run. Ready?"

I nod, fear and adrenaline rushing through me. We round the corner and break into a sprint. Ziva pulls me into a narrow alley, the rough brick scraping my back as we huddle behind a stack of crates. Our breaths are loud in the suffocating silence, the distant sounds of the street fading away.

"Stay quiet," she hisses, peeking out of the alley towards the street. I follow her gaze and spot two figures walking past, their heads down as they scan the area.

My stomach twists into knots as I spot the black uniforms of Authority Enforcers, their presence a reminder of the ever-looming threat that hangs over us. Panic surges through me—they're searching for someone—and that someone could easily be us.

Once they pass by, Ziva gives me a small nod and we cautiously make our way out of the alleyway heading back the way we came. We're halfway down the alley when a figure steps out from the shadows, blocking our path. I skid to a stop, Ziva crashing into my back. My stomach drops as I recognize the shock of red hair.

"Well, well." Her figure steps out of the shadows. Her smile flashes perfectly white teeth, but it's devoid of warmth. It's a predator's grin that sends a shiver down my spine. "Looks like I'm not the only one with a rebellious streak."

"Arden," I breathe, memories of that day in the alley much like this one flooding back. Ziva's grip on my hand tightens in warning.

"The one and only," Arden grins, but there's an edge to it. She takes a step forward, and I instinctively move in front of Ziva. "Relax, lovebirds. If I wanted to turn you in, I'd have done it already."

"Then what do you want?" Ziva demands, her voice steady despite our precarious situation.

Arden's expression shifts, losing its playful edge. "The same thing you do. Freedom. A chance to feel again." She taps her NeuroMod, the faint glow reflecting in her eyes. "I know you've been disabling them. I want in."

My heart stops. This could be a trap, or it could be the break we've been waiting for. I exchange a quick glance with Ziva, seeing my own uncertainty mirrored in her eyes.

"How do we know we can trust you?" I ask, trying to keep my voice level.

Arden's lips quirk up in a sardonic smile. "You don't. But I'm guessing you need all the help you can get."

She holds out her hand, palm up. Her hand opens slowly, revealing a small device that glints in the dim light, intricate and small. My breath catches—it could be the key to our freedom—or a trap that leads us deeper into The Authority's grip.

"I've got something that might interest you."

Chapter Seventeen

Ziva

The alleyway feels like a trap. Damp, cold bricks press against me, the stench of mildew hanging heavy in the air. I hear the distant hum of the city, muffled but relentless, as Arden's silhouette emerges from the shadows.

I instinctively step closer to Myall, our shoulders brushing. His presence steadies me, but the tight coil of wariness in my gut reminds me how fragile trust can be.

Arden smirks as she extends her hand, revealing a small, intricate device nestled in her palm. "I've got something that might interest you."

My breath catches. It's a data chip. Sleek, inconspicuous, and a treasure trove of information packed into one tiny, highly illegal device.

"Recognize this, Ziva?" Arden's lips curl into a knowing

smirk as I give a brief nod, unable to tear my gaze from the chip. "I thought you might."

"Where did you get that?" I ask, barely containing my surprise.

Arden's hair catches the dim light as she tosses her head. "Let's just say I have my ways. But here's the deal—it's yours, if you let me join your little rebellion."

Myall tenses beside me. I risk a glance at him, seeing my own uncertainty mirrored in his eyes.

Can we trust her? Should we trust her?

"How do you even know about our…activities?" Myall's voice is low, controlled, but I hear the edge beneath.

Arden's laugh is sharp. "Please. You two aren't exactly subtle. But don't worry, I'm on your side."

I bite my lip, thoughts racing between what information could be on the chip, and the fear of trusting someone we barely know.

"What's on it?" I ask, stalling for time even though I already suspect the answer. I feel Myall's tension, a taut wire ready to snap.

Arden's eyes dance with excitement. "Oh, just a little thing called NeuroMod blueprints. Thought that might interest you."

So, it was her.

My heart skips a beat. With this, we could disable the entire emotion-suppression network. It's almost too good to be true. Turning to Myall, I search his face. His jaw is set, though a flicker of hope lingers in his eyes. We've dreamed of this, of finding an easier way to disable the NeuroMods. Now, the key to it all is within reach.

"What do you think?" I murmur, leaning close in an effort

to create some measure of privacy.

Myall's breath is warm on my cheek as he whispers back, "I don't know, but we might not get another chance like this."

I nod, knowing he's right. Turning back to Arden, I square my shoulders. "Alright," I say, though I'm still not entirely trusting. "But if this is a trap…"

Arden's grin is triumphant as she steps forward. "Trust me," she says, "This is just the beginning."

Why does it feel like we've just crossed a point of no return?

Myall's deep green eyes meet mine, a silent understanding passing between us. His jaw tightens, the gears turning in his head. Suddenly, he turns to Arden, keeping his voice low.

"My grandmother's house. It's not far from here. We can talk more freely there, without risking exposure."

I inhale sharply, surprised by Myall's boldness. His grandmother's house—our sanctuary—now a place for a stranger. I trust Myall, but I'm not quite ready to trust Arden.

Her eyebrows shoot up, a mischievous glint in her eyes. "Well, well. Meeting the family already? I'm flattered."

A heat spreads through my chest at her bold implication.

Myall ignores her quip, his tone serious. "It's two blocks east, then one north. The house with the faded blue paint. Wait five minutes after we leave, then follow. We obviously can't be seen together."

I watch Arden carefully, trying to gauge her reaction. She only nods.

"Smart. I'll be there. Don't worry, I'm good at staying under the radar."

As we prepare to part ways, I can't help but wonder if we're making a terrible mistake.

"Ready?" Myall asks softly, his hand brushing mine.

I nod and after a quick glance around, we step out of the alley, leaving Arden behind.

We step onto the cracked pavement, the chill of the evening air biting at my skin, and I whisper to Myall, "Are you sure about this?" My voice trembles with uncertainty, barely rising above the rustle of dead leaves swirling around us.

He squeezes my hand, his touch grounding me.

"No," he admits. "But sometimes you have to take a leap of faith."

Or a leap right off a cliff.

We're silent as we approach Grandma Elara's house—its faded blue paint standing out against the gray twilight. The familiar sight that usually brings comfort. Today, it feels like a harbinger of change. This house has always been a refuge, but tonight, it feels like a fragile bubble, ready to burst. Myall's hand is warm in mine, our fingers intertwined.

As we reach the porch, the door swings open to reveal Grandma Elara, her weathered face lighting up into a warm smile, eyes twinkling at the corners.

"There you are, my dears. I got nervous when you didn't show up on time," she exclaims, pulling us both into a tight embrace. I breathe in her scent—lavender and cinnamon— and for a moment, the world feels right again.

"Come in, come in," she ushers us inside. "I've been dying to hear about your week. Any progress with…that project you're both working on?"

Elara's excitement has already been replaced by the numbness of her NeuroMod as she takes a seat in her favorite armchair. I exchange a quick glance with Myall as we settle onto the sofa. His eyes are clouded with worry, and I know he's thinking the same thing I am—how do we explain

Arden?

"Actually, Grandma," Myall begins, cutting right to the chase, "something happened today. We were cornered in an alley by a woman named Arden. She—"

I interrupt, unable to contain my mounting anxiety. "She knows about the rebellion. Somehow, she found out, and now she wants to join us."

Grandma Elara's eyebrows shoot up in surprise. "Well, that's certainly unexpected. Do you trust her?"

"We don't know," I admit, fidgeting with a loose thread on the soft. "That's why we brought her here. We thought maybe you could help us figure out if—"

My stomach drops like a stone as the sharp knock echoes through the house, cutting me off mid-sentence. Arden has arrived earlier than expected. Myall and I lock eyes, a silent conversation passing between us. Should we trust her? Can we afford not to?

Before we can decide, another knock sounds, more insistent this time. The choice has been made for us.

I watch as Myall rises from the sofa, his shoulders tense. He moves cautiously to the back door, his hand hesitating on the knob. I hold my breath as he cracks it open, peering out.

"It's her," he confirms softly, then opens the door wider. Elara and I both rise from our seats and wait in the doorway to the kitchen.

Arden slips inside, her vibrant red hair clashing with the muted, cozy hues of Grandma Elara's kitchen. Her eyes dart around, drinking in every detail as she scans the room. Her alertness is hard to ignore, even as suspicion gnaws at my gut.

"Arden," Myall says, his voice hesitant, "this is my grand-mother, Elara. Grandma, this is Arden."

Grandma Elara steps forward, her unease hidden behind a polite smile. "Welcome to my home, dear."

Arden's mischievous smile flashes. "Thank you for having me. I've heard so much about you—well, overheard, really."

The casual admission of her eavesdropping sends a chill down my spine. How much does she really know?

We make our way back to the living room, an awkward silence settling over us. I can't take it anymore. The question that's been burning inside me since the alley bursts out.

"How did you find out about our rebellion?" I demand once we've all taken our seats, my voice sharper than intended. "Who told you?"

Arden's eyes lock onto mine, her gaze unflinching. "No one told me, Ziva. I figured it out on my own. You two aren't as subtle as you think."

My heart stutters. If she could figure it out, who else might have? Are we already compromised?

I start to press further, but Myall's hand on my arm holds me back. His touch is gentle, grounding. "Let's hear her out," he murmurs, his breath warm against my ear.

I respond with a silent nod, trying to quell the storm of emotions inside me. Fear, curiosity, and a flicker of hope war within my chest as I wait for Arden to explain herself.

Arden leans forward. "It all started the day Myall spotted me attempting to disable my NeuroMod in that alley," she begins, her words rapid and tinged with excitement. "I'll be honest, that wasn't a smart move on my part. I'd had a shitty day at work, and reached an all time low. Anyway…I noticed him watching, and well, curiosity got the better of me. So, I followed him, which led me to you, Ziva."

My stomach churns. How did we miss this? How did we miss someone following us, watching us, all this time?

"Once I put two and two together," Arden continues, pulling out the small device she'd shown us earlier, "I knew I needed something to prove my worth. So, I hacked into the Compliance Monitoring Division."

Myall's sharp intake of breath mirrors my own shock. "You what?" he asks, his usually calm voice strained.

A sly grin tugs at her lips. "It wasn't easy, but I got my hands on the NeuroMod blueprints. Took a while to crack them cause they were double encrypted," she waves the tiny chip between her fingers. "My peace offering. My ticket to join your little rebellion."

"I can't believe you managed to hack into the Compliance Monitoring Division," I murmur in disbelief, "How did you learn to code so well?"

Arden squirms in her seat, clearly uncomfortable. It's almost satisfying.

"Well," she starts, "I taught myself how to code when I was young. I always knew it was something I wanted to do professionally once I realized I had a knack for it—plus there wasn't much else to do in the orphanage."

I freeze, the weight of her words sinking in.

She grew up in an orphanage just like me.

"Now, I work in the Systems Integrity Office as a Security Code Specialist. My job is to program all the security systems in the city." She ends with a nonchalant shrug of her thin shoulders.

The room falls silent. Myall is rigid beside me, his indecision palpable. Elara's gaze flickers between us, assessing.

"Perhaps," Elara says softly, breaking the heavy silence, "it would be best if Arden shared her story with us. Help us understand why she wants to join our cause."

I nod, grateful for Elara's levelheadedness. Arden grimaces, then nods reluctantly. I find myself torn between suspicion and a growing curiosity about this fiery, determined woman who's thrust herself into our lives.

Arden starts, her voice soft. "I grew up in Sector 7, where The Authority's grip was looser. My parents…" Her voice falters. "They were part of a secret network, always working to chip away at The Authority's control."

I lean forward, intrigued despite myself.

"I learned early on how to slip through restricted zones, how to evade enforcers and how to hack into secure systems," she continues, a hint of pride coloring her tone. "But it wasn't just about the thrill. It was about freedom. Real, raw emotion."

Myall shifts beside me, his eyes fixed on Arden. I can sense his empathy, his desire to believe her.

"When I saw you in that alley, Myall," Arden says, her voice softening, "watching me try to disable my NeuroMod…I knew I'd found kindred spirit. Someone who might be willing to fight back."

Myall's expression softens, and he nods in understanding. "I can relate to that," he admits quietly. "But why join us? Why not continue the fight with your parents?"

Arden's face darkens and she gazes out the window. "My parents were discovered by The Harmonization Authority when I was ten," she says. "They were taken…and never seen again. I was lucky to escape the detention centers, and I've been on my own ever since. I've been too afraid to let myself get close to anyone over the years, for fear of losing them, like I lost my parents. As Arden finishes her story, silence falls over the room. Suspicion, hope, and sadness swirl inside me.

On one hand, I can empathize with Arden. I too lost my parents at a young age. I know the loneliness she's referring to, about growing up an orphan, the fear of letting anyone close to me. Maybe it's that fear that's stopping me from being able to trust her now.

"So you want revenge," Myall says, dragging me from my thoughts.

Arden shakes her head. "No, not just revenge. I want to make a difference. To take down The Authority and free our city from their grasp."

I can see the sincerity in her gaze, and my suspicion wavers slightly.

Grandma Elara speaks up again, breaking the tension tha's been building between us all. "We must be cautious," she warns, her eyes moving between Arden and Myall. "But if Arden truly wants to help us in our cause, then we should give her a chance."

I sense Myall's hesitation, but also his respect for Elara's wisdom. He turns to me, silently seeking my opinion. I give him a non-committal shrug, because I haven't made my mind up yet.

Grandma Elara's gentle voice breaks the silence once more. "Thank you for sharing, Arden. Ziva, perhaps you'd like to share your story next? Maybe if you all got to know and understand each other a little better, it might help."

When I hesitate to share my own story, Myall gently squeezes my hand, his thumb tracing soothing circles over my knuckles. The warmth of his touch calms my racing heart, reassuring me. I've never told my full story to anyone but Myall. I look around at the faces watching me—Myall's encouraging nod, Arden's curious gaze, Elara's warm smile— I take a deep breath and begin.

"My parents were taken by The Authority when I was six," I start, swallowing past the lump in my throat that the memory brings. "I also grew up in The Harmonization Authority's orphanage. It was…cold. Sterile. They tried to strip away every shred of individuality, but my curiosity burned like a flame that no one could extinguish. I guess that's why I've always had trouble letting people in. I've always been too afraid to make any real friends, because I've always been so terrified of someone discovering my rebellious thoughts."

As I recount my past, I glance at Myall, who listens intently, his expression softening with each word. There's a flicker of something deeper in his eyes—a silent promise that he understands my pain.

"I became a NeuroMod Technician to learn more, to find a way to break their control." My voice grows stronger, as I realize I no longer want to keep this bottled up inside of me. "I want more than just *existence*. I want to feel, to love, to be truly free. I've spent years trying to figure out how to disable my own NeuroMod in the hopes that one day…I might be able to do that for others."

As I finish, Myall's hand finds mine once more, squeezing gently. He clears his throat, his eyes fixed on mine. "I guess it's my turn," he murmurs. "My story really begins with Grandma Elara."

I lean forward, and Myall's rugged exterior softens as he speaks about his grandmother

"Grandma's stories…they opened my eyes to what we've lost," Myall continues. "She'd tell me about concerts where people danced freely, about spontaneous laughter in the streets. It made me realize how much The Authority has taken from us."

Once more, his knee brushes against mine and he lets it linger there. "I couldn't just sit by and watch our humanity slip away. I took a job at the Compliance Monitoring Division in an effort to keep an eye on The Authority and have spent years waiting for the right moment to do something, anything. It wasn't until I realized that Ziva felt the same way about The Authority that I did, that I finally decided to take that first step."

I find myself nodding, knowing full well that if Myall hadn't reached out his hand to me, hadn't made that first leap of faith, we would both have continued in our lonely existence until the day we died.

Grandma Elara's gentle voice breaks the spell. "Perhaps I could share a story from the old days?" she offers. As she begins to speak, painting vivid pictures of a world bursting with color and feeling, I notice Arden leaning forward, hanging on every word.

As Elara describes a first kiss from her youth, I can't help but imagine Myall's lips on mine. The desire is almost overwhelming. I force myself to look away, but not before catching the flush creeping up Myall's neck.

In this moment, surrounded by stories of a freer world and the warmth of human connection, I've never felt more alive—or more terrified of what these feelings might mean.

His warmth radiates next to me, his presence comforting as Grandma Elara finishes her story. My stomach drops as I realize we need to make a choice about Arden.

I study Arden's determined expression, noting the resolve in her pale face. "Arden," I murmur, "your skills…they could be invaluable to our cause."

Myall gives a slight nod, his gaze steady. "We've been operating blind this entire time, making it up as we go along," he says, running a hand through his hair. "We could really use someone with your skillset."

My chest flutters at his words, at the way he says 'we' like it's the most natural thing in the world.

"Are you sure?" I ask, searching his face for any hint of doubt.

He leans in closer, his breath warm on my cheek. "I trust your instincts, Ziva," he says. "If you think we can trust her, I'm with you."

The intensity of his gaze makes me dizzy. I swallow hard, trying to focus.

"Arden," I say, turning back to her, "welcome to the rebellion."

Her face lights up, that mischievous spark dancing in her green eyes.

"You won't regret this," she says, her voice brimming with excitement that is quickly dulled by her device.

As we begin to discuss our next steps, I steal a glance toward Myall. Whatever comes next, I know that together, we're growing stronger than The Authority could ever imagine.

Chapter Eighteen

Myall

Blue light dances on polished metal surfaces, streaking the walls with neon as the blueprints of the NeuroMod swirl in mid-air, mocking me with their complexity.

I force my gaze back to the circuit diagram, but it's no use. Arden's face rises in my thoughts—her eager expression, eyes bright with desperate hope drift through my memories. I didn't give her the lab's location yet. Couldn't risk it without talking to Marcus first.

While staying at Grandma Elara's, we made an effort to understand Arden better. I had been serious when I told her that her coding abilities would be extremely valuable to the rebellion. Our first task for her was to create a security system for the lab, so we could be alerted if anyone tried to approach.

We couldn't risk being caught off guard by The Authority or Enforcers. Arden promised to get to work on a security system for us right away.

"Myall, you with us?" Ziva's voice cuts through the haze of my thoughts, sharp and urgent.

Her eyes scan my face, narrowing in on the tension I can't hide, her brows furrowing slightly in concern. She leans forward, her lips tight with impatience, but her fingers drum lightly on the table.

"Yeah, sorry. Just…thinking." I run a hand through my hair, pushing it out of my eyes.

"About Arden?" she asks, her tone weary.

I nod, letting out a slow breath. "I keep replaying what she said about her parents. About how they used to be part of some kind of resistance. Her timeline made it sound like it was after the rebellion our parents were involved in."

Arden's words echo in my mind like a drumbeat. Her parents, part of a resistance long since buried by The Authority. If the resistance kept going, years after The Authority claims it was wiped out, can we somehow find them and join them? I can't stop wondering—*where are they now?* The thought churns in my gut.

Ziva's expression softens as she listens, her hazel eyes fulling with understanding.

"It's a lot to process, Myall. But we can't dwell on the past. We have our own rebellion to plan." Her hand rests on my arm, anchoring me.

"You're right," I admit, turning back to the holographic display. "We can't afford to lose sight of what we're trying to achieve."

Ziva's lips quirk into a half-smile. "That's why you're our

fearless leader."

"Ha-ha very funny," I mutter, thinking back to Marcus's reaction when we told him about Arden, or rather, when I'd told him about Arden and Ziva just stood there. Marcus's face had gone hard, eyes narrowing with suspicion.

"We can't trust her," Marcus had growled, his voice low, but it carried a weight that felt like the press of a hand on my chest. His eyes narrowed, and his fingers flexed at his sides, as though restraining the urge to throw something.

"It could be a trap." The words hung in the air like smoke, thick and suffocating, leaving a bitter taste in my mouth.

I'd felt my stomach clench, torn between caution and the urge to help someone clearly yearning for change. But then Ziva had finally stepped in, determined to convince Marcus that Arden could be trusted.

"She has a data chip," Ziva had explained, "with blueprints for the NeuroMod and Sentinel systems. Think of what we could do with that information, Marcus."

I watch the hologram rotate, remembering how Marcus's expression had slowly shifted. The furrow in his brow had deepened, but there was also a keen interest as he pieced together that Arden was responsible for the stolen blueprints.

"Exactly how detailed are these blueprints?" he'd asked, leaning forward.

"Enough to potentially reverse-engineer the systems," Ziva had replied, a hint of excitement creeping into her voice. "Who needs my dodgy glitch when these blueprints *tell us* how to deactivate the NeuroMods."

I'd held my breath, watching the internal struggle play out on Marcus's face. His caution warring with the potential of such valuable information.

"Okay. It's a huge risk you're taking by bringing her in," he'd finally said, "but…if what you're saying is true…it could be worth it."

Now, as I watch the hologram rotate endlessly, a knot of hope and trepidation coils tight in my chest.

"Do you think we made the right call?" My voice is barely a whisper, a thread of doubt woven through the question. I can't look at her, afraid she'll see the fear I'm struggling to hide.

She places a hand on my arm, her touch warm against the chill of the lab, as though her proximity could absorb the worry radiating off me. The pressure of her palm is gentle, but it anchors me to the present, reminding me that she's here, that we're not alone in this.

"We need allies, Myall. Sometimes, calculated risks are the only way forward." Her words are steady, but they don't quite reach the depths of doubt swirling in my stomach.

I nod. "I just hope we're not walking into a trap."

"We'll be careful," Ziva assures me. "But think of what we could accomplish with those blueprints. It could be exactly what we need to bring down the whole system."

I exhale slowly, trying to push the tightness from my chest.

"Yeah, I guess you're right." I give her a tight nod, though it's hard to shake the unease that's settled deep in my bones. "Let's take a look at those blueprints one more time."

Chapter Nineteen

Myall

The cool air of the building's lobby does little to clear the fog in my brain. My steps feel leaden, like I'm moving through a thick fog, and a dull ache presses behind my eyes.

The contents of the data chip—the vulnerabilities in the systems—are etched into my thoughts. Arden's discovery held more than we could have imagined—detailed schematics of the NeuroMods inner workings and, even more crucially, vulnerabilities in the Sentinel system and how to exploit them.

Marcus had pored over the information, his dark eyes glinting with excitement and apprehension. "This could change everything," he'd said, hands waving in the air the way they do when he's passionate about something. "If we can exploit these weaknesses—"

The shrill blare of the buildings alarm shatters my thoughts like glass. My heart stutters. The alarm's sound claws at my nerves, setting my pulse hammering in my ears, and I can't suppress the tightness in my chest as my body braces for whatever comes next. The AI system's voice crackles through the intercom, monotone and dispassionate. "Attention all employees. Mandatory meeting in the main auditorium. Attendance is required." The words fall like a weight on the room, chilling the air as they reverberate through the sterile corridors.

This can't be good.

A knot of anxiety twists in my stomach as I move to join the stream of workers filing toward the auditorium. The buzz of whispered conversations mingles with the sound of footsteps, a low murmur of apprehension filling the hall. The air is heavy, thick with anticipation, as if every person is holding their breath. I scan the crowd for Ziva, my chest tightening when I can't find her. The sea of faces presses in on me, each expression a mask, each pair of eyes calculating and guarded.

"What's going on?" I overhear someone whisper.

"No idea," comes the hushed reply. "But it can't be good."

As we file into the cavernous room, my mind races. Could they know about our meeting last night? About Arden? The rebellion? I take slow, measured breaths, fighting to keep my face blank. The last thing I need is to draw attention to myself.

I finally catch a glimpse of Ziva a few people away. Our eyes lock for a moment, and I can see my own worry mirrored in her gaze. Moving towards her, I carefully navigate through the throng of people in the room.

A hush falls over the crowd like a wave crashing against a shore. The doors to the stage swing open, and a tall, imposing figure strides in, his boots clicking sharply against the floor, echoing through the room. My breath catches in my throat as I recognize him.

Regent Colvin.

Dressed in a sharply tailored dark suit that accentuates his lean frame, he commands attention with an air of authority. His eyes sweep over the assembled workers, and I swear I feel the temperature in the room drop. Strands of silver thread his dark hair, hinting at his age, but it's his expression—hard and unyielding—that truly sends a shiver down my spine. A coldness seeps into my bones, and I can't shake the prickling sensation along my skin.

The public figurehead of the Harmonization Authority, here in New Eden...this can't end well.

When he speaks, his voice is calm, measured, but there's an undercurrent of steel.

"Citizens of New Eden," Colvin's voice booms through the auditorium, clear and resonant. His words slice through the room like a cold wind, and I feel the hairs on my arms rise. "I come to you today with grave news. The security of our society has been compromised."

The tension in the air thickens, wrapping around my chest like a vice. Cold sweat prickles along my spine as his gaze sweeps over us, sharp as a blade. The unease in the room swells, barely contained. My heart pounds, but I force myself to breathe evenly, fighting to conceal my fear.

"The blueprints for the NeuroMod and Sentinel systems have recently been stolen, and though it's taken us some time, we've managed to isolate the breach to *this* facility." Colvin announces, allowing a pause for the room to digest his news. "This rebellion threatens the very foundation of our society."

Panic ripples through the crowd, quickly dampened by their NeuroMods. Out of the corner of my eye, I glance at Ziva. Her face is a mask of calm, but I know her well enough to see the fear in her eyes.

Colvin's gaze seems to bore into each of us as he speaks. "Rest assured, we will find those responsible. The peace and stability of our society depends on it."

I inch closer to Ziva, desperate to offer some sort of comfort. As my hand brushes against hers, her fingers intertwine with mine, squeezing tight. It's a bold move, but in this moment, I don't care. I need to touch her and know that she is alright.

"Remember," Colvin's voice cuts through my thoughts, "emotional stability is the cornerstone of our society. Any deviation, any hint of unrest, will be swiftly dealt with."

Swallowing hard, I fight to keep my expression neutral. Colvin's cold blue eyes sweep across the room, his gaze like a searchlight seeking out any flicker of dissent.

"To ensure the safety and loyalty of our workforce, we're implementing new security protocols," he announces, his voice as sharp as a blade.

My stomach sinks as he outlines the measures.

"Cameras with advanced facial recognition software will be installed throughout the facility. Random NeuroMod checks will increase in frequency." Each word is like a nail in a coffin. My stomach lurches, and my palms begin to sweat. And then, the worst part.

"In the coming weeks, each citizen will have their Neuro-Mod upgraded to a newer model, which will monitor vital signs." The thought of a newer, more invasive NeuroMods sends a jolt of dread through me, a constant reminder that we are never truly alone, never truly free.

Shit, this isn't good.

Ziva's hand tenses in mine. We lock eyes for a split second, and in her gaze, I see the storm she's fighting to control. Beneath the calm facade, fear churns—fear of being exposed, of losing everything. The thought of our deactivated NeuroMods—our rebellion—hanging by a thread in the face of Colvin's new regime…

His voice cuts through my spiraling thoughts. "Furthermore, I'll be conducting individual interviews with each of you over the coming days. Consider this your opportunity to demonstrate your unwavering loyalty to The Harmonization Authority."

The air in the room feels thick, suffocating. I struggle to keep my breathing even, knowing that any sign of distress could be detected and analyzed. Beside me, Ziva's jaw is clenched tight, her eyes fixed straight ahead.

"You're dismissed," Colvin finally says, his tone leaving no room for questions or discussion.

As we file out of the auditorium, an oppressive weight settles on my shoulders. Each step toward my workstation feels like crossing a minefield, the frantic whispers buzzing around me matching the rapid thumping of my heart. I can feel the prying gazes of colleagues, each one a potential informant, ready to report any flicker of dissent.

Ziva and I separate, moving to our respective workstations with practiced nonchalance. My mind churns for any way out, any solution that might get us the fuck out of this situation.

I power up my terminal, the familiar hum vibrating through the desk—a sound that usually grounds me but now feels eerily out of place amidst the chaos swirling in my head. The rhythmic tapping of keypads and muted conversations blur into a dull roar, mocking the normalcy that feels like a cruel joke.

How can we outsmart these new measures? Maybe we could find a way to loop the feeds, or create a program to generate false data for the new NeuroMods. But with Colvin breathing down our necks, even thinking about such things feels dangerous. And what will we do when we're faced with having our NeuroMod upgraded?

I catch Ziva's eye across the aisle and give a subtle nod toward the maintenance closet. She blinks twice in acknowledgment—our silent code. I casually make my way there, palms sweating against the cold metal of the doorknob.

In the dim space, I wait, counting each second. When the door creaks open, Ziva slips in, and her presence instantly comforts me .

"This is insane," she whispers, her voice trembling. "Colvin's going to tear this place apart. What the hell are we going to do when they try to upgrade our devices and learn they're deactivated?"

I pull her close, savoring her warmth. "We'll figure it out," I murmur. "It'll be okay."

Ziva pulls back, her voice wavering. "But at what cost, Myall?" Her voice trembles, laced with an urgency that cuts through the dim light. "What if they catch us? What if—" Her words hang heavy in the air.

I can see the fear flickering in her hazel eyes, and it mirrors my own—a reflection of the stakes we've put in play, the risks we can't ignore.

"Shh," I interrupt, cupping her face. "We knew the risks. I won't let anything happen to you."

She lets out a shaky breath. "You know it's not just me I'm worried about."

We stand in silence, the weight of this harsh reality pressing down on both of us.

"We have to be more careful," I say finally. "No more stealing NeuroMods, no recruiting, no unnecessary risks. We play it safe until Colvin leaves."

Ziva nods, determination replacing fear in her eyes. "Yeah. But we can't stop completely. The people need us to free them from this hell."

A sharp knock on the door makes us both jump. "Hansen, Emerson. My office. Now."

My blood turns to ice at the sound of Colvin's voice cutting through our conversation, each syllable a cold knife. The door creaks open, and he stands there like a specter, his presence sucking the warmth from the closet. It's as if time has stopped, the world narrowing down to this moment, where every heartbeat feels like a countdown to disaster.

As we step out, Colvin's piercing gaze pins us in place. "Fraternizing during work hours?" His tone is deceptively light. "How quaint."

I force my face into a neutral expression. "Routine maintenance check on the supplies, sir. Standard procedure."

Colvin's lip curls. "Indeed. Well, let's continue this discussion somewhere more appropriate."

I can feel the trap closing in around us as we follow him down the hallway. Steeling myself, we enter Colvin's makeshift office—a stark space devoid of any personal touches. The Regent settles behind his desk, cold blue eyes scanning us like a predator sizing up its prey. I stand rigid, hands clasped behind my back, shoulders tight.

"Hansen," he begins, his voice cutting through the tense silence. "Something's been off with your work lately. Care to elaborate?"

My mind races, carefully weighing each word before I speak. "I apologize if my work has been subpar, sir. I've been pushing myself to improve our systems, sometimes at the expense of routine tasks."

Colvin's eyebrow arches. "Improve? How so?"

"I've been analyzing patterns in emotional fluctuations," I lie smoothly, drawing on my knowledge of the system. "I believe we could refine the NeuroMods sensitivity to catch potential deviations earlier."

A flicker of interest crosses Colvin's face. "Fascinating. And what prompted this... initiative?"

Ziva tenses beside me, but I keep my voice steady. "Efficiency, sir. The more precise our control, the more stable our society."

Colvin leans forward, his gaze boring into me. "And you believe our current methods are... lacking?"

It's a trap, carefully laid. I take a measured breath. "Not lacking, sir. But there's always room for improvement, isn't there? Isn't that the core of The Harmonization Authority's mission?"

For a moment, the room is oppressively silent. Then Colvin's lips curl into what might be a smile. "Indeed, Hansen. Your dedication is...commendable."

The knot in my stomach unwinds, relief flooding through

me, but I don't let it show. Colvin turns his attention to Ziva, and I pray she can navigate this minefield as well as I did.

"Emerson," Colvin's voice is like ice as he addresses his attention to Ziva, "your technical skills are impressive, but lately, there have been reports of unauthorized access to sensitive data. Care to explain?"

Ziva meets his gaze head-on, her hazel eyes unflinching. "I've been troubleshooting some anomalies with the Neuro-Mods, sir. It's part of my effort to ensure our technology operates at peak efficiency."

Colvin leans back in his chair, steepling his fingers in front of him, his expression one of calculated amusement. I can feel Ziva's tension beside me, her fingers trembling slightly, and I wonder how long we can maintain this facade under such piercing observation.

"Efficiency seems to be a common theme today. And what do you hope to achieve by your…unauthorized troubleshooting?"

Ziva's jaw sets with determination. "I aim to prevent any potential malfunctions that could jeopardize the stability of the NeuroMod readings, sir. It's crucial for maintaining emotional harmony among the citizens."

A tense silence follows her response, and I can practically hear the gears turning in Colvin's mind.

Finally, he nods slowly. "Your commitment to our cause is…admirable, Emerson. Keep me updated on your progress."

Ziva and I exchange a glance, relief flooding through us, though we try to hide it. Colvin's intense scrutiny feels like a physical weight, but for now, we've managed to navigate his suspicions.

"Dismissed," he finally says, waving a hand in a dismissive gesture.

As we step out of his office and into the corridor, Ziva exhales a shaky breath, her body still rigid with the aftershocks of the encounter.

"Holy fuck, that was close," she whispers, her voice a little breathless. I nod, my chest still tight, as if the air around me has only just started to breathe again.

I grasp her hand tightly, the rush of surviving that encounter still thrumming through my veins. "We need to be even more careful from now on," I say, pulling her further down the corridor.

Ziva nods. "Yeah. We can't afford any slip-ups."

But as we head down the corridor from Colvin's office and back to our workstations, I know that the real battle is only just beginning.

Chapter Twenty

Ziva

The familiar gray building of the Compliance Monitoring Division looms before me, yet something seems different today. It's like every step echoes, amplifying the silence. Even the guards blend into the surroundings, their rigid forms like sentinels of the city's control.

"Shit," I mutter under my breath, forcing my face into a mask of indifference.

The guards' gaze pierces me as I pass, the visor reflecting nothing but my own anxious face. I feel their eyes before I see them. The cold lenses scan my every movement, dissecting me, making my skin crawl. It's like being naked under glass, exposed for all to see, yet invisible to anyone who might care. I force myself to keep walking, to *appear* normal, but every part of me screams to flee.

Regent Colvin wasn't exaggerating when he warned us of the increased security measures yesterday. I can only hope that he hasn't begun implementing the new NeuroMods yet. The idea of what will happen when we get called in to have our devices upgraded, only to discover ours are deactivated, kept me awake most of the night.

Joining the line of employees shuffling toward the entrance, I try to quell the tremor in my hands at the security checkpoint. Hushed whispers pass between my co-workers.

"Did you hear about the interviews starting this morning?" a woman in front of me murmurs to her companion. "Regent Colvin himself…"

I swallow the lump forming in the back of my throat and clench my fists at my sides.

Stay calm, Ziva. You've prepared for this all night. You can do it.

The line inches forward, each step bringing me closer to the entrance. Closer to him. I flex my fingers, feeling the weight of the encrypted communicator hidden in my sleeve. My lifeline to Myall, now that we can no longer take the risk of sneaking into the supply closet every time we want to talk.

A guard's voice cuts through my thoughts. "Next!"

I step forward, forcing a polite smile as I present my ID. The guard's eyes narrow, scanning my face, then the card, then back again. My heart rate increases to the point where I can feel it throbbing throughout my entire body.

"You are to report for interviewing prior to commencing your shift. Proceed," he grunts, waving me through.

Swallowing my dread, I enter the facility, the familiar hum of machinery a stark contrast to the unnatural quiet of my colleagues. As I make my way to the interview waiting area,

I catch snippets of conversation.

"...looking for traitors..."

"...increased monitoring..."

"...no one's safe..."

I take my place in line, sandwiched between anxious faces and trembling hands. Ahead, a door opens and closes with metronomic precision, each soft click marking another fate decided.

My turn is coming. I can feel it, taste it in the recycled air. Regent Colvin waits beyond that door, ready to peel back layers of loyalty and obedience, searching for any hint of defiance.

Straightening my shoulders, I lift my chin slightly. Let him search. Let him try to break through the walls I've built. I was convincing enough yesterday. I can be convincing enough today.

The door opens again, and a voice calls out, "Ziva Emerson."

I step forward, my heart a war drum in my chest.

Time to face the inquisitor.

I enter the small room, my eyes drawn immediately to the imposing figure behind the desk. Colvin sits motionless, his presence suffocating, as though he's swallowed the very air in the room. The chair beneath him is angled just enough that I can't look away from his unblinking blue eyes—eyes that seem to peel back every layer of my thoughts and expose my most vulnerable fears.

His fingers are steepled, the slow tap of one knuckle against his thumb a steady reminder that *he* is in control.

"Ms. Emerson," he says, his voice a glacier. "Please, have a seat."

Taking my seat, my hands betray me with a barely perceptible tremor as I place them flat on my thighs. My mind screams for escape, but I force it all down. His eyes are still on me, cold and calculating, and I wonder if he hears my heart racing. The silence stretches, suffocating. I fight the urge to swallow, the lump in my throat threatening to choke me.

"Thank you for your patience," Colvin continues, his words a formality devoid of warmth. "We're conducting these interviews to ensure the continued efficiency of our operation."

I nod, my throat dry. "Of course, Regent. I'm happy to assist in any way I can."

His eyes narrow slightly, searching for cracks in my facade. I meet his gaze, willing my face to remain neutral and devoid of any emotion.

"Tell me, Ms. Emerson," he leans forward, hands clasped on the desk, "how do you view your role within our society?"

That's a loaded question.

I choose my words carefully, aware of the weight they carry. "I see my work as essential to maintaining societal balance," I say, relieved my voice is steady. "The emotional control system protects us all from the chaos of unchecked feelings."

Every word that leaves my mouth feels like a betrayal. The lie sits heavy in my throat, thick and bitter, but I swallow it down, forced to play my part. I can feel the tension in my jaw, the way my teeth grind together to stop the truth from spilling out.

He'll know. He'll see right through me.

Colvin leans forward, and for the briefest moment, I see

something in his eyes—an almost imperceptible flicker of satisfaction at my discomfort. I hold my breath, forcing my face into a perfect mask, though my pulse quickens, and my fingers tighten, the skin raw from how hard I'm gripping the edges of my seat.

Colvin's lips twitch into something like a smile. "Indeed. And yet, some might argue that true humanity lies in those very emotions we seek to control."

It's a trap. He's fishing for dissent. I force a small laugh, praying it sounds as hollow as it feels. "A romantic notion, perhaps. But we've seen the destruction unchecked feelings can cause throughout history."

Colvin's gaze sharpens, his cold blue eyes boring into mine. "Have you ever encountered anyone expressing… dissatisfaction with our system, Ms. Emerson?"

My heart stalls, but I keep my voice steady. "Occasionally, there are those who struggle to adapt. But it's often just a matter of proper calibration and guidance." I pause, allowing a hint of carefully crafted doubt to seep into my tone. "Though I sometimes wonder if our methods could be…refined. To better serve those who find it challenging."

Colvin leans back, his expression unreadable. "I see. And what refinements would you suggest?"

It's a dangerous line I'm walking. I tilt my head, feigning thoughtfulness. "Perhaps a more individualized approach? Everyone's emotional landscape is unique, after all."

"A bold proposition," Colvin says, his voice carrying a note of warning. "One might think you're questioning the efficacy of our current protocols."

Sweat beads on my lower back. "Not at all, Regent. I'm merely considering ways to improve upon our already successful system. For the greater good, of course."

I silently curse myself the moment the words leave my mouth. Have I pushed too far? Colvin's piercing stare gives nothing away, and I find myself holding my breath, waiting for his response.

His eyes narrow once more, as if he's dissecting every micro-expression on my face. My skin prickles under his scrutiny, but I force myself to maintain eye contact, fighting the urge to look away.

"For the greater good," he echoes, his voice carrying a glacial edge. "An admirable sentiment, Ms. Emerson. But I wonder, what do you truly believe is for the greater good?"

"Harmony, of course. Stability. The well-being of all citizens." Even as I speak, I can hear the hollowness in my words. Does he sense it too? I swallow hard, my throat suddenly dry. My mind spins. Does he believe me, or is he waiting for a slip in my composure? I can't afford to show him anything but unwavering loyalty, even if my heart feels like it's about to shatter under the weight of all the lies I have to tell.

Colvin leans forward, his fingers steepled on the desk once more. "And you believe our current system doesn't achieve that?"

"I believe it does," I say quickly, then add, "But there's always room for improvement, isn't there? In any system?"

The silence that follows is deafening. I can almost feel the weight of his judgment as he assesses me.

Finally, he speaks. "Your interview is concluded, Ms. Emerson. You're dismissed."

Standing on shaky legs, relief and fear war within me. "Thank you, Regent Colvin."

As I turn to leave, his cold voice stops me. "Remember, we're always watching. For the greater good."

I nod, unable to trust my voice, and hurry out of the room. Once outside, I lean against the wall, my breath coming in short gasps.

How the hell are we going to keep this up?

There's no way my answers cleared me of suspicion, so why did he dismiss me?

I slip down the corridor and into a secluded alcove, hidden from the ever-present cameras. With trembling fingers, I pull out the modified communicator I spent all night perfecting, ensuring that no one would be able to trace our communication. I activate the encrypted channel and type out a message, disguising it as a routine work update, praying it works.

There's a soft beep from my comm device and I quickly read the coded message from Myall. "Ziva? Are you alright?"

Relief floods through and I start tying out a coded reply. "I'm okay, but the interview Colvin was strange. I think he suspects something."

"Did you maintain your cover?" Myall asks, concern evident even in encrypted form.

Closing my eyes, I replay the conversation in my mind. "I tried, but... I'm not sure. He has a way of seeing right through you."

"We knew this was a risk," Myall messages, his words steadying me. "But we can't back down now. We need to regroup, strategize our next move."

Nodding, I forget he can't see me from my hiding spot. "Agreed. But where? The usual spots might be compromised."

There's a brief pause before Myall's next response, "The tech lab. It's our only safe option right now."

I'm concerned that the tech lab may not be secure enough, but we have no other location that is off-the-grid to meet. Hopefully Arden has managed to put together some sort of security system which might help us.

"Okay," I type, glancing around to ensure I'm still alone and that no cameras have moved to spot me. "When?"

"After shifts end. We'll take separate routes for now on, throw off any potential tails."

A flutter stirs in my chest. "I'll be there," I promise.

Chapter Twenty One

Ziva

The remainder of the day drags on in frustrating slowness. I go through the tasks of recalibrating NeuroMods and listening for any information my colleagues might offer. Myall and I do not risk attempting to communicate during work hours, and I make a concerted effort to avoid even glancing in his direction.

As soon as I hear the end bell for my shift, I swiftly gather my belongings and head straight for the exit. Before I can leave, I have to go through a new security process that involves a body scan. Presumably they are checking for stolen items from the facility.

I slip through the shadows of the city, the scent of rain on the breeze. Every footstep feels like a thunderclap in the eerie silence of the fading light. I've taken a circuitous route, doubling back and weaving through rarely used streets. I feel eyes on my back, and I hope I'm just being paranoid.

Finally, I reach the hidden building that leads to our sanctuary. With practiced ease, I key in the complex sequence and slip inside as the door slides shut behind me. The tech lab materializes before me, a cave of blinking lights and humming machinery. And there, hunched over a workstation, is Myall.

He looks up as I enter, his green eyes catching the dim light. "Thank god," he breathes, relief evident in the slump of his shoulders.

I stride quickly across the room, drinking in the sight of him. His dark hair is more disheveled than usual, and the set of his jaw speaks volumes about the stress he's under. Yet seeing him here, safe, causes something warm in my chest.

"Any trouble getting here?" I ask, keeping my voice low out of habit, but I've been dying to speak with him all day.

Myall shakes his head. "Nothing I couldn't handle. But Ziva, the way they're tightening security—it's worse than we thought."

"I know. Colvin's interview was just the beginning. What are we going to do when he implements the new Neuro-Mods? I'm scared, Myall."

He reaches out, his hand hovering near mine before he thinks better of it. I wish he hadn't stopped himself.

"We'll figure it out," he says, his tone a mix of determination and something softer. "We'll keep each other safe."

Looking around the room, I take in the meager fruits of our labor. "But for how long?" I whisper, voicing the fear that's been gnawing at me since Colvin's arrival from Elysium. "This isn't just about disabling NeuroMods anymore, is it?"

"No." His words crack slightly, betraying the tension

beneath the calm facade. "We can't turn back now. Not after everything."

He runs a hand through his hair. I can see the exhaustion in his eyes—the same weariness I feel every day. But then he looks at me, and something softer passes through him. Leaning against the workbench, my fingers trace the edge of a disassembled device.

"Colvin's questions…they were probing, searching for cracks." I shudder, remembering his piercing gaze. "He asked about my loyalty, my connections. It's like he could smell the rebellion on me."

Myall's brow furrows. "Did he give anything away? Any weakness we could exploit?"

Closing my eyes, I replay the interview in my mind. "He's… meticulous. Controlled. But there was a moment…" I pause, uncertain. "When I mentioned the slight flaw in the system, something flickered in his eyes. Fear, maybe?"

"That's something," Myall nods, his eyes lighting up. "If he's worried about a flaw in their system, it means there really is a vulnerability. One we might be able to exploit."

Leaning in, I lower my voice further. "But how do we keep meeting like this? They're watching everything now."

Myall rubs the back of his neck, thinking. "We need to blend in better when we meet, especially now that it's the four of us. We'll need to be careful with the tech as well. It might mean no more direct comms."

I nod, having already suspected he'd say that. "What about old tech? Pre-Harmonization stuff? They might not be monitoring for that."

As we dive deeper into planning, I can't shake the feeling that we're crossing a point of no return. But looking at

Myall, seeing the fire in his eyes that matches my own, I know there's no going back.

"Ziva," Myall says, angling his face towards me. "Are you sure about this? Disabling NeuroMods for people is one thing, taking down The Authority is another. And with Colvin sniffing around, things are only going to get worse."

I take a deep, steadying breath. "I've never been more sure of anything in my life," I reply, surprised by the fierceness in my own voice. "This system…it's killing us slowly. I can't stand by and watch anymore."

Myall nods, his green eyes blazing with a mix of determination and something else I can't quite name. "Then we taken it all down," he says, squeezing my hand.

The touch lingers, and I find myself fighting the urge to close the distance between us. But I know that any chance of a romantic connection with Myall is doomed as long as we remain trapped in this oppressive system.

"We should go," I say reluctantly. "Any longer and we'll raise suspicion. I'll figure out a way to communicate a meeting time with Marcus and Arden."

We quickly gather our makeshift plans and destroy any evidence of our meeting.

As we prepare to leave, Myall catches my arm. "Be careful out there," he says softly, brushing a stray lock of hair behind my ear. "You know I couldn't bear it if anything happened to you."

"You too," I manage to reply. His touch lingers for a moment longer, everything left unspoken passing between us.

He leans in closer, his warm breath tickling my cheek. His lips brush mine, tentative at first, then more certain. My mouth opens for his on instinct, my fingers twining into his hair as he deepens the kiss. Myall kisses me deeply, and the world falls away, leaving only this moment. The heat of him spreads through me, and suddenly, nothing else matters— no Colvin, no system, no surveillance. Time stops. For a heartbeat, it's just us, alive and human in a world that wants to strip us of both.

I pull back, my breath shallow, and I forget everything— *everything*—except him. His warmth, his touch. I should have pulled away sooner. I *should* have. But the taste of freedom lingers on my lips, and the thought that this—*us*—could be the last bit of humanity left to hold onto, makes the weight of the world seem insignificant for a moment.

"We should go," I finally whisper, my voice barely more than a breath as I reluctantly break the spell between us. Myall nods silently, his hand lingering on mine for a heartbeat longer before we turn to leave the lab behind.

I watch Myall disappear into the night, his figure blends seamlessly with the darkness. The walk home feels longer and lonelier without him beside me. As I walk, I realize that I am willing to go do whatever it takes for a chance at a relationship with Myall. I've been so alone, for so long. I can't bear the thought of returning to that suffocating, isolating existence.

I slip into my unit, the door hissing shut behind me. My heart still races from the meeting with Myall, the taste of his kiss lingering in my mind.

"Lights, dim," I command, and the harsh illumination softens to a gentle glow. As I move toward my narrow bed, a realization hits me with the force of a malfunctioning NeuroMod. I sink onto the edge of the mattress, gripping the synthetic fabric.

"He's right. It's not just about the NeuroMods," I whisper. "We'll have to take down the entire Harmonization Authority if we want to be free."

The enormity of the task makes my head spin. I close my eyes, steadying my breath. Images flash through my mind—the stern face of Regent Colvin, the expressionless guards, the citizens lost in a haze of regulated emotion.

"Can we even do this? Are we just two idealistic fools?" I whisper to the empty room.

But I can't stop thinking about Myall's lips on mine, that stolen moment. I stand abruptly, pacing the small confines of my unit. My uniform constricts, and I tug at the collar. We have to try—for everyone lost to this system, for more than stolen moments.

A soft beep from my comm device startles me. It's a message from Myall, encrypted and disguised as a work update. I decode it quickly, my heart picking up speed.

"Z, I can't stop thinking about that kiss, and about what we discussed. The risks are huge, but so is the potential reward. We're not alone in this. Remember that."

I clutch the device to my chest, the pulse of fear and exhilaration sharp in my veins. "We're not alone," I whisper, drawing strength from it.

But is it enough?

Chapter Twenty Two

Myall

My footsteps are muffled on the polished floor, the stillness of the tech lab almost oppressive. The encrypted channel Ziva set up is supposed to be untraceable, but with the recent security increases, I'm more paranoid than ever.

We agreed to meet after shifts' end, to come separately. This is too important to risk, especially with Arden joining us for the first time. The dangers, the potential fallout if we're caught, play on my mind in an endless loop.

I rub the back of my neck, my fingers digging into the tight knots of muscle. Regent Colvin's arrival in the city feels like a weight pressing down, the strain crawling under my skin. My shoulders are so stiff now, they feel like they belong to someone else, someone who's been carrying too much for too long. I haven't had a proper rest in days, but there's no time for it—not with the city on the brink of rebellion.

The door creaks open, and Ziva steps inside. She scans the room, and when her gaze finally settles on me, it lights up. She smiles, brief and tentative, but it's enough to send a jolt of something through me. Then she looks away, and the warmth inside me turns into something heavier—something like longing—like I've been burned by the very thing I crave. Her cheeks flush, and I ache with the knowledge that I'll never be brave enough to say what we both already know.

I can still taste her on my lips—salt and something sweeter, something I can't name. The kiss was brief, a clash of need and fear. It felt like surrender and defiance all at once. Her lips trembled against mine as she broke the kiss, pulling away. Her eyes were wide, wide with fear, and something darker—something that made my chest tighten in a way that has nothing to do with the rebellion. I don't know what it is, but it hurts, sharp and raw. Was it regret? Or was it just fear of what we could become?

It was a moment of weakness on my part. But I wonder if we were too hasty in putting any potential relationship on hold for the rebellion. Being around her every day only adds to my doubts. Would it be such a terrible idea to pursue something between us? After all, we could be caught any day. Wouldn't it be better to spend what time we have left, no matter how fleeting, together?

"Any word from Arden?" Ziva asks, her voice low, avoiding my gaze as she fiddles with the console.

"Not yet," I say, trying to keep the disappointment from my voice. I'm not even sure if it's about Arden or Ziva. Probably both. "She knows the about the increased security measures Colvin's introduced, and the risks we're now taking."

Ziva nods, still not meeting my eyes. "She's smart. She'll be fine." I glance at Ziva, her face unreadable, but I know she's just as on edge as I am.

I want to tell her that I'm more worried about us, that I don't know how to balance this thing growing between us with the cause. But I stay silent, watching her slender fingers dance over the controls. She's so sure of herself, so determined. I envy that.

The door creaks open once more, and we both stiffen. Marcus slips into the room, looking even more drawn than usual. His eyes dart around, skimming the corners like he's expecting someone to leap out of the shadows. His tawny skin is unusually pale, his jaw tense, as though he's been running on nothing but fear for days. Every movement feels sharp, jerky, like a cornered animal that's nervous, desperate.

"We need to talk," he says, his tone brokering no room for argument.

Ziva steps back from the workbench, folding her arms across her chest. She remains silent, watching Marcus with a wary eye, waiting for him to elaborate.

"I had my interview with Colvin today," Marcus continues. "He's asking a *lot* of questions. He knows something's up. I think others have mentioned our newly formed friendships to him."

Ziva's eyes narrow. "What did you tell him?"

"Nothing. I played dumb, but he's not an idiot. He's definitely sniffing around, looking for any hints of a rebellion." Marcus tugs at his hair, his fingers trembling. "You should know so you can get your story straight, Myall. You're the only one who hasn't been interviewed yet."

The three of us fall into a heavy silence. If Colvin is this close, our entire rebellion could unravel before it even starts.

The door creaks open, and Arden strides in, her presence like a gust of wind through a stifling room. "Sorry I'm late. Had to lose a tail."

The tension breaks, but only just. "Looks like I'm not the only one who's nervous," Arden adds, reading the tension in the room.

"We're always nervous," Ziva says, but there's a hint of warmth in her tone. She respects Arden, I know. Maybe even likes her. I'm not so sure.

We need her—there's no doubt about that. Her skills are unmatched, and without her, we're dead in the water. But Arden's a wildcard, and wildcards are unpredictable. You can't control them, can't trust them to play by the rules.

Arden shrugs and sets down a small duffle bag. "Got the gear Ziva, just like you asked."

Ziva finally looks at me, then back to Arden, guilt washing across her features. "It's better if you don't know," she mutters quietly to me.

I hold back a groan. If Ziva's been stealing more equipment, we're all going to get caught.

Arden raises an eyebrow, glancing between us, but doesn't press. "So, who's your friend?"

Realizing she's referring to Marcus, I clear my throat and step into the uneasy silence. "Marcus, this is Arden." I gesture to her. "She'll handle the software and security side of things."

Arden extends a slender hand, and Marcus takes it with hesitation. "Nice to meet you." Her eyes, however, are already elsewhere, her mind clearly elsewhere. "I've also got news." She doesn't wait for us to speak before adding,

"The Harmonization Authority's network is more vulnerable than we thought."

Ziva perks up, her skepticism momentarily set aside. "You're sure?"

Arden nods, her eyes bright. "Yep. I've spent the last few days looking into it like you asked. There are ways to get around the new security protocols. It won't be easy, but I think it's doable."

Marcus opens his mouth, but quickly shuts it, his lips pressed into a thin line. I wonder if he's beginning to have second thoughts. Doubt isn't something we can afford now.

"So, what's the plan?" Ziva asks, turning to face me.

All eyes are on me. I feel the weight of their expectations, their fears, their hopes. Regent Colvin. The looming interview. The NeuroMods. The Reconditioning and Detention Centers. The people silenced by The Authority.

"First, we have to figure out a solution to make our NeuroMods appear active and show that we are still under The Authority's control. It will be difficult, but if we can give off the impression of being harmonized while still experiencing all of our emotions—"

"That way, we won't have to worry about Regent Colvin's 'random' NeuroMod checks," Ziva adds, finishing my thought.

I can see the wheels turning in her mind, already strategizing the next steps.

Arden lets out a low whistle, impressed. "That's some next-level coding we're talking about."

Marcus watches us all, his expression unreadable. He finally speaks up. "It would have to be flawless work. This kind of deception is almost impossible. But that will also only protect us from his random checks, it won't help us if he decides to upgrade our devices." His words hang heavy in the air, a reminder of the consequences we're facing.

Arden outlines it quickly, her voice brimming with confidence. Hacking the system, reprogramming the NeuroMods—it sounds both insane and brilliantly simple in her hands. I nod in agreement, absorbing every detail. The others chime in with questions, concerns, and Arden swats them down with the ease.

"We'll need a diversion in the system when we hack into it," Marcus says, his brow furrowed. "Something big enough to cover our tracks, but not so big it brings down the entire Authority on us."

Arden smirks. "Leave that to me. I've got tricks up my sleeve."

I steal a glance at Ziva. She's been uncharacteristically quiet tonight, her usual sharp-edged commentary replaced with a soft, almost resigned silence. I wonder if she, like me, is thinking about the people we've lost—about the people we stand to lose.

"So, what about recruiting more members?" Arden asks, breaking the silence. "We seem stretched thin as it is. Can we even pull this off without more bodies?"

The room goes still. This is the crux of it. We can plan and scheme all we want, but without enough hands, any plan we have has room for error.

"You're right. We need to expand," Ziva agrees. "We can't keep operating at this pace. The more people we have, the stronger we are."

"Or the more vulnerable," Marcus counters. "One weak link, one person who cracks, and we're all in the Detention

Center."

They turn to me. Their trust. Their doubt. It weighs on me. Expanding the rebellion was once our priority, but now with Regent Colvin tightening his grip on the city, recruiting more is a dangerous gamble. We're playing with loaded dice.

"We have to be smart about it," I say. "Careful. We vet everyone, make sure they're committed. But Marcus is right—we can't afford to rush this."

Arden leans back, crossing her arms over her chest. "We don't have time for a long vetting process. The Authority's closing in. We need to take a shot at them before we miss the chance. It's now or never."

I want to believe her. I want to believe that we can just charge forward, that sheer force of will can see us through. But I know better. I've seen what happens to the reckless, to the impatient—to my parents.

"We proceed as planned." My voice cuts through the tension. "We recruit, but cautiously. No mistakes—no rushing. We can't afford to alienate potential allies, but we can't afford to be naive either."

The room quiets again, heavy with unspoken tension. They know I'm right, but it's clear they're not ready to face it. We're a tightrope walker's breath from disaster, and every new person we bring in is another step out onto the wire.

"We should deactivate Arden's NeuroMod before anything else," I point out, realizing that deactivating Arden's Neuro-Mod should have been our first step. I berate myself for not considering it earlier.

"You don't have to tell me twice," Arden grumbles in agreement, but her expression still shines with excitement, despite the dampening effects of her device.

Ziva doesn't hesitate, but there's a tension in the air as she heads toward the workstation. The others follow her, quietly. This is it. The first real step in the plan, and it could go wrong in so many ways.

Marcus and Ziva exchange a few hushed words, going over the blueprint again, double—checking everything. Their eyes flick between the screens, scanning lines of code with the kind of concentration that feels almost too deliberate. Time seems to stretch with every passing second. I wish I could say something, offer reassurance—but I'm not even sure I believe the words myself.

As they finish, they turn to Arden. "Ready?" Ziva asks, her voice steady, but I can hear the hint of uncertainty beneath it.

Arden doesn't respond immediately. She just stares at the screen, eyes wide, her breath catching slightly. I can see the hesitation in her posture, the way she bites her lip as she considers the gravity of what she's about to do. She's not the type to back down, but she can't deny the weight of this moment.

Finally, she nods, voice trembling with the strain. "Let's do it."

"It won't take long," Ziva says, her voice steady with concentration as she deftly maneuvers Arden's wrist into position and connects it to her datapad through a wire. "Just need to enter in the worlds most complicated command sequence—"

I catch Arden's glance, wide with a mix of fear and excitement. I want to reach out, to offer some comfort, knowing firsthand what she is about to experience—but I hold back.

"Got it," Ziva murmurs, her voice a quiet victory. She leans back in her chair, eyes glued to the screen as a series of incomprehensible codes flash across the monitor, the machine beeping its approval.

I glance at Arden, who stands there, eyes wide, one hand twitching at her side. For a moment, everything stops. I see the muscles in Arden's throat constrict, her face pale, eyes squeezed shut for just a second—like she's preparing herself for the wave that's about to crash over her.

Then, her eyes snap open, and her hand flies to her chest, like she's suddenly suffocating. Her breath hitches in her throat, and she gasps, the air rattling out of her in sharp, frantic bursts.

"Holy shit," she whispers, her voice barely above a breath. Her chest rises and falls erratically. "I...I feel...all of it." The words seem to come from some distant part of her, distant and jagged, like she's not entirely *herself* right now. She's struggling to breathe, her chest heaving in sharp, uneven gasps as her eyes dart around the room.

I watch her face—emotions flickering like a storm, raw and unfiltered. Joy. Fear. Anger. Sadness. They flash one after another, too fast for anyone to follow. Her thoughts seem to collide, each one fighting for dominance. This is too much, too fast for any of us.

"You okay?" I say, my voice softer now, like I'm afraid she might break if I speak too loudly. She looks up at me, and I can see it in her eyes before she even speaks—the storm that's brewing there. She's not just overwhelmed by what she's feeling now—she's drowning in it. She's reacting more acutely to the sudden onslaught of emotions than the rest of us did.

"I...I don't know," she says, her voice unsteady, a thin tremor running through it. It's as if she's trying to hold herself together, but her emotions are too big, too intense. Her hands shake slightly as she reaches up to wipe at her eyes, though the gesture doesn't really help. The tears are already there, hovering just beneath the surface.

"Wow," she breathes, her chest heaving in a mixture of wonder and fear. "This is so overwhelming." Her words don't capture the chaos inside her. What she's experiencing goes beyond simple emotion. It's like she's seeing the world for the first time, and she can't decide if it's beautiful or terrifying.

I step closer, unsure how to reassure her. The word 'okay' feels meaningless now. I place a hand on her shoulder, tentative, hoping it might offer some comfort.

A sudden tightness in my chest pulls me back to the moment when my own device was deactivated. It felt like I was being pulled apart from the inside, like I was waking up from a dream I didn't want to leave. The emotions were too much, too real—like a flood breaking through a dam. I see it in Arden's face now, the rawness of it. Her eyes widen, her breath catching as the weight of every repressed feeling breaks loose all at once. I glance over at Marcus and see him watching Arden with a pitying expression. I worry that this might be too much for her resolve to handle.

"Take deep breaths," I advise, not knowing what else to say to offer her comfort. "It'll pass. You'll adjust."

Arden nods, closing her eyes and inhaling deeply. When she opens them again, there's a new fire burning in their depths.

"I feel alive," she says, her voice filled with wonder. "For the first time in…god I can't even remember how long, I feel truly alive."

A smile tugs at my lips, and I catch Ziva's eye. She gives me a small nod, her own expression a mix of pride and relief.

"Welcome to the resistance," I say softly, finally allowing myself to reach out and squeeze Arden's hand. "The real fight starts now."

Chapter Twenty Three

Myall

We get stuck into the next phase of planning and I glance at each of them—Ziva, Arden, Marcus. They're more than comrades now— they're becoming a makeshift family. And like any family, we're riven with conflicts, with different visions of the future. But for now, we're united in our purpose.

I just hope it's enough.

Arden leans in, her eyes flicking between the others. "I can hack The Authority's records. Pull up a list of potential recruits who've shown signs of discontent. If anyone's been flagged after their interviews with Colvin, I can track them down."

There's a beat of silence as the team digests her words. I look at Ziva and Marcus, both of them silently weighing the risks. Ziva's face remains unreadable, but Marcus—there's something in his eyes—a flicker of doubt, though he doesn't speak up. They both know that trusting Arden—trusting anyone—is a gamble. But we need her—now.

"Okay," Ziva finally says. "But lets plan it properly. We need to make sure any of the people flagged by Colvin aren't being monitored. If they are and then we approach them, we're basically just giving ourselves away."

Arden nods, though the fire behind her eyes isn't dimmed. She stands, an edge of impatience creeping into her movements. "Fine," she says, her voice clipped. "But don't blame me if we're all 'Harmonized' before we even get started with this rebellion."

She storms out, the door slamming closed behind her with a sharp finality. I wince, knowing she can't help the highs and lows of her mood right now.

Her words hang in the air, thick with truth and tension. I can't shake the gnawing feeling in my chest. She's not wrong. We're on borrowed time. The ground beneath us feels like it's shifting, fast, and if we're not careful, it'll swallow us whole.

"She'll come around, we just need to give her some time to adjust to her full emotions," Ziva says, but her eyes are on the door, her voice less certain than usual.

I nod. Arden's always been unpredictable, like the first crack of thunder before a storm. But a small part of me wonders why Arden's emotional outbursts are stronger than ours ever were.

"We need her," Marcus says, breaking the uneasy quiet. "But we also need to be smart. Cautious. I fear she may be too hotheaded...too abrasive."

I turn to him, surprised. He's right, of course, but his

caution often borders on reluctance.

"I'm more worried about the rest of us," I admit. "We're stretching too thin."

He shrugs, but the weight of it pulls him down. "It was always going to be a long shot. But we have to try."

I look at him, really look, and see the tired lines around his eyes, the set of his jaw. We've been at this for weeks now, and the toll is starting to show. On all of us.

"Do you ever think," I start, then stop. I don't want to ask this, don't want to know the answer. But I have to. "Do you ever think it's not worth it? That we should just…give in?"

His eyes meet mine, and for a moment I see the depth of his past hurt, his conflict. "Every day," he says quietly, his voice rough. He rubs the back of his neck, eyes flicking to the door, as though something on the other side might offer him an answer. "But you know…isn't trying, even failing, better than doing nothing at all?"

His words hit me like a slap. I want to argue. I want to say something that will make this all seem possible, but I don't. He's right. *If* we even survive long enough to try.

I hope we're not fooling ourselves. I hope we're not just a group of desperate people chasing an illusion, pretending that we can actually change anything. But deep down, I know the truth. The odds are stacked against us, and no matter how many plans we make, how many risks we take, there's a part of me that's already bracing for failure. The real question isn't if we'll win—it's if we'll survive long enough to see it through.

* * *

An hour later, Ziva has taken charge of analyzing the system blueprints, trying to make a start on the plan to make our NeuroMods appear active and functioning when they are, in reality, under our control.

Meanwhile, Marcus and I have been discussing the potential risks and benefits of recruiting new members. I lean back in my chair, the old leather squeaking beneath me as I stretch my sore neck. The muscles in my back protest, stiff from too many hours spent hunched over data. A low ache spreads from my spine to my shoulders, but it's nothing compared to the pounding in my head.

"Don't start celebrating yet. We still have to—"

Arden bursts back into the room, her usual swagger amplified by an obvious excitement. "Guys, you're not going to believe this."

"We're kind of in the middle of something," I mutter, but Arden is already beside Marcus, tugging him from his seat.

"While you've been busy playing whack-a-mole with the systems blueprints, I've been accessing these old relics," she says, gesturing to the computers and datapads scattered around the room. "Some of them still have a trace of access to The Authority's mainframe."

My eyes widen in alarm. "Arden, you didn't—"

"I figured out a way to hack into their network," she says, a triumphant grin spreading across her face. "We can get everything—plans, security protocols, even the list of known potential rebels."

The room goes silent. I can almost hear the gears in everyone's heads grinding. This is huge.

Marcus is the first to speak. "It's suicide. The moment you breach their firewall, they'll trace it back here. We're not ready for that kind of heat."

"We're not ready for a lot of things. Doesn't mean we can just sit on our hands." Arden's voice is laced with scorn.

I look at Ziva, waiting for her to weigh in. Her fingers tap against the datapad, the sound sharp in the silence. Her eyes flicker to the screen and away, a tell I know all too well. She's thinking, but her face is still a mask, unreadable. I attempt to catch her eye, but she looks away, her fingers brushing through her hair in a nervous gesture. My stomach tightens—she's pulling back, and that's never a good sign.

"It's risky," she says, her voice quiet but firm. "But that data could change everything. We'd need to move fast—and relocate immediately."

"Assuming we even have time to run," Marcus interjects. "This is insane. We have a plan. We should stick to it."

All eyes turn to me. I hate this part, being the one to make the final call. It's not like we're a democracy, but we do try to reach consensus. When we can't, it falls to me, and I'm never sure I'm right.

"We need to weigh the pros and cons," I say, stalling. "If we had that information, it could make our job easier. But if it gets us compromised—"

Arden crosses her arms, her grin fading but not entirely gone. "We're compromised just by existing. This could give us everything we need to take down The Authority."

I bite my lip, the salt of sweat clinging to my skin. My hands tremble, gripping the table for stability as my mind races through the potential fallout of Arden's plan. She's not wrong, but neither is Marcus. It's a gamble, and we're already stretched too thin to take more risks.

"Let's make a list," I say. "Pros and cons. Then we decide."

Ziva grabs a datapad and starts jotting down notes as we all throw out ideas. The room feels heavy with unspoken anxiety, each argument sharp and laden with consequences—data that could turn the tide, but also the threat of discovery, a risk that could cost us everything.

"Con: We don't even know if she can pull it off," Marcus says, and I see Arden bristle.

"I've hacked more secure systems than this," she snaps. "Have a little faith."

God, I'd love to hear that story someday.

"Enough," I say, rubbing my temples. "We get it. This is dangerous, but so is what we're already doing."

Ziva sets the datapad down. "It comes down to this—are we willing to bet everything on a maybe?"

I look at the list, at the faces of my friends. We're tired, scared, and hoping for a miracle. But beneath the fear lies something deeper—a quiet certainty that every choice could be our last. I catch Ziva's eye, and I see the same worn-out resolve mirrored there. We're no longer just fighting to survive. We're fighting to win—and that's a whole different kind of fear.

"I say we sleep on it," I finally declare. "No rash decisions. We'll vote tomorrow."

Arden looks like she wants to argue, but she holds her tongue. That, more than anything, scares me. She's always so sure, so fearless.

The group disperses, each of us lost in our own thoughts. I stare at the schematic, praying we're not cutting the wrong thread. The whole plan hinges on it.

Chapter Twenty Four

Myall

I can't tear my eyes away from Arden's face. Her eyes are wide, sparkling with an intensity I've never seen before. It's like looking at a completely different person today.

"You were right. It was…overwhelming," Arden says, her voice trembling slightly. "I felt everything all at once—joy, fear, anger, excitement. It was beautiful and terrifying."

I feel myself smiling as I watch her speak.

Ziva nods eagerly. "I remember that feeling. It's like waking up from a deep, endless sleep. It was so disorienting."

"You seemed like you were handling it just fine," Marcus says, his usual stoic expression softened with concern. "The sudden flood of emotions, I mean."

Arden exhales sharply, her chest rising and falling as she forces herself to speak. "Oh no," she says, voice trembling. "When I got home, I cried. A lot. My body shook like I was finally waking from a deep sleep. Then I laughed—just because I could. And after that, anger. So much anger at everything The Authority has stolen from us. It was…a long night." She looks away, her fists clenched at her sides as if trying to physically suppress the flood of emotion that threatens to overtake her again.

We sit in silence for a moment. The hum of the lab, the soft rhythm of our breathing—it's almost peaceful.

"I felt that too," I say softly. "When my device first shut down, I realized how much I'd been missing. All the little moments of joy and connection I'd never fully experienced." My voice catches, the memory of those first days rushing back with the force of a tidal wave. The raw, unfiltered sensations of feeling too much at once—the warmth of sunlight on my skin, the sharp bitterness of coffee, the overwhelming joy of laughter—are so vivid now, they almost hurt. The weight of their gazes settles over me, a quiet understanding in their eyes. For a moment, the space between us narrows, as if we're all suspended in the same fragile thread of humanity, desperately trying to hold on.

"What about you, Marcus?" Ziva asks, turning to our most reserved member. "How did you handle the emotional overload? I don't think we ever really checked in on you after."

Marcus is quiet for a moment, his dark eyes distant. "It was…difficult," he says finally. "I've spent years suppressing what happened when The Authority took over, learning to function without emotion. When it all came rushing back, I felt…exposed. Vulnerable."

I nod, understanding exactly what he means. The Authority has trained us all to view emotions as weakness, as something to be controlled and eliminated. Learning to embrace them again is a constant struggle. I understand why Marcus wanted to hurry back to his own home, to process his emotions in the privacy and comfort of familiar surroundings. The weight of all that unprocessed feeling must be suffocating. It makes me worry about the long term effect of emotional suppression.

"But it's worth it, isn't it?" Arden says fiercely. "To feel alive again, to be truly human?"

"Absolutely," I agree, meeting her gaze as the room falls silent once more.

"Speaking of human," Ziva says with a lightness that seems almost out of place, "I've got some news that might help us keep our newfound freedom."

We all turn to her, curiosity piqued. Ziva's always been the most technically savvy among us, her quick mind constantly seeking ways to subvert the system.

"I've figured out how to make our NeuroMods *look* like they're still functioning," she announces, a hint of pride in her voice. "No more blank screens. Even if Regent Colvin drags one of us in for a 'random' check, we won't get caught."

"How?" I ask, leaning closer.

Ziva grins, her hazel eyes sparkling with mischief. "I've been studying the blueprints non-stop. There's a way to create a false feedback loop in the NeuroMods circuitry. It'll report normal emotional suppression from our old data to the Sentinel system, even when we're feeling everything. I can switch our devices back on and they'll appear active, but they won't have any effect on us."

Arden lets out a low whistle. "That's brilliant, Ziva. You're a genius."

I watch as Ziva's cheeks flush slightly at the compliment. It's strange how captivating these small displays of emotion have become, now that we're free to express them.

Marcus, ever the pragmatist, leans forward. "How do you know for certain it'll work the way you intend?"

As Ziva launches into a detailed explanation, I catch Arden's eye. She gives me a small, knowing smile, the corners of her lips curving up just slightly. There's something in her gaze—soft, yet intense—that settles in my chest, a warmth spreading from the pit of my stomach to my fingertips. Is this what real connection, real friendship feels like?

"Earth to Myall," Marcus says, nudging me. "You with us?"

I blink, realizing I've missed part of the conversation. "Sorry, just…processing everything."

Ziva looks at me with understanding. "It's a lot, isn't it? Sometimes I still can't believe we're doing this."

"Speaking of which," Arden chimes in, "I think we need a name for our little rebel group. Something catchy."

We spend the several minutes tossing around increasingly ridiculous suggestions, laughing more freely than I can ever remember. Even Marcus cracks a smile, the hard lines of his face softening. The corners of his mouth twitch, as though the act itself feels foreign—but freeing. There's a lightness in the room that wasn't there before, a warmth that spreads slowly through the space.

As the night wears on, our conversation drifts from rebellion planning to more personal topics. We share stories from our childhoods, stories about times where we each rebelled against the system. Arden regales us with tales of her misspent youth, sneaking into restricted areas and causing mischief, even with her emotions dampened. Her stories of sneaking through the city are almost unbelievable, given The Authority's grip on everything.

I find myself opening up about my own past, sharing hopes and dreams I'd long forgotten. The others listen with genuine interest, their faces open, unguarded. For once, I don't feel like a ghost, drifting through life unnoticed. The small, almost imperceptible shift in the air when someone acknowledges you—so subtle, but so powerful—fills me with a warmth I've forgotten existed. I don't just feel *seen*—I feel heard, understood, like I finally matter.

I lean forward, resting my elbows on my knees. "So, what's our next move? We've been avoiding the topic all night. Have we made a decision?"

Arden's eyes light up with pure Arden energy. "I've been thinking more about that hack I mentioned yesterday. I know it's a risk, but if we can pull it off, we could access The Authority's entire network, it will make everything we're doing so much easier."

Marcus frowns, his brow furrowing. "That's a big 'if,' Arden. The consequences if we're caught…"

"Are no worse than if we do nothing," Ziva interjects, her voice sharp. "We can't keep playing it safe forever."

Their eyes are heavy with expectation, silently asking for my opinion. I try to calm my racing heart, but it's hard to ignore the gnawing feeling in my stomach, like a hundred small doubts are clawing at me from the inside. What are we really doing? Are we ready for the consequences? I've never been more certain about something in my life—and yet, uncertainty weighs heavy in my chest. The line between passive resistance and full-blown rebellion is razor-thin.

Once we cross it, there's no going back.

"Arden," I say slowly, "walk us through this hack. What exactly would it involve?"

As Arden outlines her plan, I watch the others' reactions. Marcus listens intently, his analytical mind no doubt cataloging every potential flaw.

"It's not without risks," Arden concludes, "but think of what we could uncover. The truth about the NeuroMods and why we 'need' them, the extent of The Authority's control, who the people in The Authority even are—it could change everything."

A tense silence falls over the room. I break it, voicing the thought we're all having.

"If we do this, we can't come back here afterward," I say, the words tasting bitter on my tongue. The thought of leaving this refuge sinks into me like a stone, my chest tightening. "This lab will be compromised."

Ziva nods grimly. "We'll need a fallback location. Somewhere they won't think to look."

"I might have an idea," Marcus says, surprising us all. "There's an abandoned warehouse in the industrial district. It's been empty for years, forgotten by everyone."

I inhale sharply, pushing down the fear threatening to rise in my throat. This is it. The decision has been made, but something in me—something deep in my gut—claws at me, begging for one last moment of hesitation.

Their gazes settle on me, all of them waiting. The thought of failure churns in my stomach, but something else rises to meet it.

Hope.

I meet each of their eyes—Ziva's fierce determination,

Arden's barely-contained excitement, Marcus's quiet resolve. They're ready. But am I? For a moment, the world feels impossibly still. The decision should be simple, but it's not.

When I finally speak, my voice is steadier than I feel. "Alright. Let's do this. Let's hack The Authority."

Chapter Twenty Five

Ziva

In the end, we agreed that Arden should attempt the hack today. The decision sits like a stone in my stomach, cold and unforgiving. We're betting everything on her skill, on a maybe.

Myall still hasn't been interviewed by Regent Colvin, and I can't decide whether that's a sign of relief, or the calm before disaster strikes.

At the end of our shifts, we gather back at the lab as usual. The hum of machinery vibrates through the concrete walls, a low, constant pulse that seems to sync with the quickening beat of my heart.

Myall takes the lead, his green eyes scanning each of us with a calm intensity. He raises a hand, cutting off Arden before she can make one of her trademark quips.

"You all remember the plan," Myall says, his voice low and

measured. "But let's run through it one more time. We can't afford any mistakes."

Marcus crosses his arms, his serious expression even more pronounced in the flickering light. "We went over it a dozen times last night. We're ready."

"Humor me," Myall replies, not missing a beat. He turns to Arden, who is already fidgeting with a portable terminal. "Arden, you're the key here. You need to follow each step exactly as we laid out. One wrong move, and they'll trace us in a heartbeat."

Arden rolls her eyes but nods. "I got this."

Myall and Arden exchange a glance that speaks volumes. The tension between them is a thread I can feel, stretching tight in the air, pulling at something inside me. It gnaws at me like hunger—intense and unrelenting.

What is it between them? And why does it make my stomach twist? Is it just the tension of this task, or is something else stirring inside me, something I'm not ready to face yet?

"First," Myall continues, ignoring Arden's last jab, "we spoof the access codes. That buys us a ten-minute window where their system thinks we're one of them. Ziva, you'll monitor the feeds and alert us if anything looks off."

I nod, though my thoughts are miles away. What if this is the moment everything changes? What if we actually pull this off? The rebellion, our future—my feelings for Myall— all hang in the balance.

"Marcus," Myall says, "you'll be on standby with the jammer. If they start to trace us, you knock out their signal. But *only* as a last resort—it'll raise a red flag."

"Understood," Marcus replies, his tone as precise as the

machinery he loves.

"And I'll be—" Myall starts, but Arden cuts him off.

"You'll be hovering like a worried mother hen. We know."

Despite the tension, a small, crooked smile tugs at Myall's lips. "I'll be overseeing. Just remember, this isn't a sprint. It's a marathon."

Arden shrugs. "I run fast marathons."

Marcus helps Arden set up the equipment she'll need for the hack. His expression is unreadable, every line of his face carved in concentration.

"That should do it," he says, stepping back from the terminal. He wipes his hands on his pants, leaving smudges of grease on the fabric. "Arden, you're up."

Arden slides into the chair in one fluid motion, her fingers already tapping the keys in a rhythm I can barely follow. The sharp clicks echo in the silence, a rapid-fire percussion against the backdrop of the lab's low hum. The glow of the screens flickers in her eyes, the sharp light cutting through the surrounding darkness.

She presses her lips together for a moment, something flickering in her eyes that almost betrays her usual bravado. But in an instant, her familiar smirk is back, and the vulnerability vanishes.

"How long will this take?" I ask, not because I need to know the answer but because the tension is crushing me.

"Depends on how good their new security is," Marcus says. He crosses his arms, leaning against the table, his eyes never leaving the screens. "Could be a few minutes. Could be longer."

"Ready?" Myall asks as we take our positions. I can feel my heart pounding in my chest, each beat a countdown to something I can't fully predict.

Arden's fingers hover over the terminal. "You bet."

"Go."

The first few seconds stretch into an eternity. Arden's hands move with the grace of a conductor, each keystroke a note in a dangerous symphony. I watch the screens, my eyes darting from feed to feed, looking for any sign that we've been detected. So far, everything is as it should be.

"Already past the first firewall," Arden announces, a triumphant note in her voice. "I'm in the outer shell. Just need to crack the core."

I can't help but admire her. Everything she does is with such confidence, such reckless assurance. I wonder what it's like to be so sure of yourself, to dive headfirst into danger without hesitating.

"Access codes spoofed," Arden announces. "We're in."

A collective breath is held. Myall's voice sounds from across the room, softer now, almost tender. "Good. Now, Arden, start the data pull. *Slowly.*"

My gaze flickers across to Myall, caught by something in the softness of his voice. I force myself to look away, focusing back on the screens, the moment lost before I can understand it.

One screen shows a schematic of The Authority's network; another displays lines of code streaming past like digital rain. The rest are security feeds from various locations around the city that Arden set up. All seem quiet, too quiet.

"Something's wrong," I say, my fingers tapping nervously against the console. "It's too easy."

"Paranoid much?" Arden mutters, but even she sounds uneasy.

"Ziva has a point," Marcus says. "They should have tighter protocols."

"Just keep going," Myall instructs. "We're committed now."

The next few minutes blur by, broken only by Arden's occasional status updates. My mind races through a thousand scenarios—getting caught, escaping, the future we're trying to build. And always, the question of what Myall and I are to each other—friends, comrades, something more—hangs over me.

"Data's almost done," Arden says. "Another thirty seconds."

Right as she makes her announcement, the screens flash red, the sharp sound of an alarm screeching through the lab like a knife through the silence. My pulse spikes, thundering in my ears, and my breath feels too shallow, too fast. Arden swears under her breath, her fingers dancing over the keys with renewed urgency, but her hands shake, betraying her composure. Every second stretches into an eternity as the countdown begins in my mind.

"Shit," Marcus says. "Did they trace us?"

"Not yet," Arden says. "It's a trapdoor. I can disarm it, but I need time."

Time is the one thing we don't have. I see it before I hear it—a red flash on one of the security feeds I'm monitoring, then another. My heart skips a beat. "Guys, we've got company. Patrol drones, two blocks away and closing fast."

"Shit." Marcus reaches for the jammer.

"Not yet!" Myall barks. "Arden, hurry."

"I'm not baking a fucking cake here," she snaps, not taking her eyes off the screens. "It takes as long as it takes."

I switch my focus between the feeds and the group. Marcus is tense, ready to act with his hand hovering over the button on the jamming device. Arden is laser-focused on the screens before her, her usual flippancy replaced with grim determination. Myall look conflicted as he monitors the window. This was his call, his gamble, and he knows what's at stake for all of us.

"Ten more seconds," Arden .mutters

The drones are almost here. Their whine cuts through the walls, a mechanical whir that chills me to the bone. My fists clench, breath shallow—just a few more seconds, please.

"Five…four…three… two…one. Got it!"

"Kill the link!" Myall shouts as he ducks below the window and out of sight of the patrol drones as they pass the building.

Marcus slams a hand down on the jammer, and the screens go dark. We're plunged into an eerie silence, broken only by the fading whine of the drones outside as they move past our building.

We freeze. An eternity passes before Myall exhales slowly. "I think we're safe."

Relief floods me, but it's tinged with dread. We have the data, but at what cost? We came too close. What if the patrol drones are able to re-triangulate our location?

Arden stands and stretches, a victorious grin spreading across her face. "Told you I run fast."

Marcus places the jamming device on the table, his usual stern demeanor momentarily softened. "Nice work. Though I don't think my heart could take any more close calls like that."

I look to Myall across the lab, who meets my gaze with an intensity that makes me want to look away—and not.

"This is just the beginning," he says, but I wonder if he's talking about the rebellion or something more personal.

I move closer to Arden, the screens casting a blue glow over both our faces. Myall and Marcus move to hover nearby.

"Ready for the next part?" I ask.

Arden cracks her knuckles. "Born ready."

I plug in the data chip, and Arden's fingers dance over the keyboard once more. Lines of code scroll past, a blur of green on black. I can almost hear her mind working with every keystroke, a symphony of hacking brilliance.

"First layer down," she says, not even pausing to take a breath. "Your turn."

I take the keyboard and run the program I wrote last night. It's a brute-force decryptor, something I swore I'd never create. Just having it on my data chip is enough to get me killed. The progress bar inches forward, and I feel my pulse sync with its slow, agonizing crawl.

"How long?" Arden asks. Her impatience makes me smile—she's always in such a rush.

"Another minute," I say, hoping it's true. "Maybe two."

She leans back and stretches, her shirt riding up to reveal a sliver of toned stomach.

The progress bar hits 100 percent, and a new screen pops up. Encrypted files, dozens of them. I click one at random, and a wall of gibberish text fills the screen.

"Shit," I say. "They're double-encrypted."

Arden straightens, biting her lower lip in concentration. "We expected this. It's not a problem."

'Not a problem' means it's a huge fucking problem. Every second we spend here increases the risk. My decryptor needs additional time to bypass the next level of encryption, time that we don't have.

"We can pull the plug and try again later," I say. "It's not worth getting caught, we need to abandon this place and get to the fallback location."

Arden stops typing and looks at me, her green eyes piercing. "Ziva, if we don't do this now, there might not be a later."

I know she's right. The crackdowns are escalating, and rumors of a new NeuroMod threaten our rebellion.

"Fine," I say. "But let me—" Before I can finish, an alarm blares from outside. Myall bursts into action, eyes wide. "Enforcers!"

"Fuck," Arden says, yanking the datapad from the terminal. "We weren't supposed to—"

"No time," Myall interrupts. "Get outside, now!"

We scramble for the exit. "Ziva," Myall says, grabbing my arm as we run. "We can still—"

He doesn't get to finish. We reach the corridor and start running, my mind racing with the implications of what we've just done.

At the door leading to the outside of the building, Marcus holds up a hand and we stop. He cracks the door open a sliver and peers out into the alleyway. "Clear," he says, and we spill into the street, trying to look casual.

The city hums with its usual, disjointed rhythm, the distant noises amplifying as we weave through the streets. Every sound feels amplified, every step echoing in the back of my mind like a countdown to discovery.

"This way," Arden whispers, pulling me toward a narrow passage between two buildings. We duck and weave through the maze of alleys, the sounds of the city growing louder and more chaotic.

We slip onto a main street, merging with the small crowd

that's slowly gathering, curious about the commotion. I glance back to see Myall and Marcus trailing a few paces behind, their heads close together, voices sharp but carrying.

"Split up," Myall calls. "We'll meet at the fallback like we agreed."

Arden looks at me, waiting for a signal. For a moment, I hesitate—caught between the comfort of staying together and risk of separating.

"Go," I say. "I'll catch up."

She squeezes my hand, then melts into the crowd. I watch her go, then turn to Myall. His stare is so intense, it's almost as if he's saying goodbye. But before I can process his expression, he quickly turns and dashes across the street, leaving me behind and alone.

I inhale sharply, forcing my feet to move, my pulse thundering so fiercely it drowns out the world around me.

* * *

I reach the fallback—an old warehouse in the industrial district—exactly where we planned. The trip through the city had my heart hammering in my throat the entire time. Myall and Marcus are already here, speaking in low tones. They stop when they see me.

"Where's Arden?" Myall asks as he grabs me and pulls me into him, tightening his arms around me.

"She's coming," I say, but even I can't convince myself it's certain. I exhale, breathing in the scent of him as my heart rate begins to slow. His grasp loosens and I step back, catching Marcus' curious gaze.

We wait in tense silence. I check my watch, then glance

toward the door. After what feels like a lifetime, the door creaks open, and Arden slips inside. She looks tired, but her eyes are bright.

"All in one piece," she says, holding up the datapad.

Relief washes over me, but it's tempered by the knowledge of what comes next.

"Let's see it," Marcus says, and Arden hands him the datapad she carried as we fled. Hopefully the decryptor has finished by now.

Marcus works the datapad, and we crowd close, the dim glow of the screen casting anxious shadows on the cramped warehouse office. Myall's hand brushes mine, and I flinch, the jolt of contact sharp, electric. He pulls away, his face flushed.

"Here," Marcus says, his voice a low, almost reverent as he angles the datapad so we can all see.

A series of documents flicker to life on the screen, their titles a jumble of acronyms and technical jargon. One catches my eye: "NeuroMod Emotional Regulation: Initial Theories and Applications."

Arden leans in, her breath quickening. "This is it. This is the fucking motherlode."

We take turns reading, our eyes skimming over dense text, struggling to make sense of the jargon. The weight of it hits me in waves—this isn't just theory; it's a blueprint for control. The NeuroMods didn't begin as tools of control. They were meant to help—designed to balance emotions, make people more resilient, better equipped to handle life's challenges.

They began as a mental health resource.

"Look at this," Myall says, pointing to a section near the bottom of one document. "Authored by Dr. Elena Vance.

These are her notes."

A silence falls over us, heavy and pregnant with implications. Dr. Vance isn't just a faceless bureaucrat—she's a true believer—someone who thought she was making the world better. The realization twists something inside me, a knot of understanding and anger.

"She wasn't always a villain," Marcus mutters. "She really thought she was helping."

"Doesn't change what The Authority's done," Arden adds, a cold edge to her voice.

Myall's face is lit by the screen's glow, eyes narrowed with focus. For a moment, I wonder if he's thinking the same thing I am—or if he's as unreadable as I feel right now.

If Elena Vance could change, could we? Could we become the very thing we're fighting against? The very force we despise?

"There's more," Marcus says, not taking his gaze off the data port and pulling up another file. It's an old video, grainy and washed out, like something from a forgotten past.

A younger Dr. Vance appears on screen, her blonde hair and blue eyes unmistakable even through the pixelated haze. She speaks with passion, explaining the potential of the NeuroMod technology, how it could revolutionize mental health.

We watch in silence, the dimly lit room growing colder with each word she speaks. This isn't just propaganda—it's a heartfelt plea. She truly believes in what she's saying.

The video ends, and no one moves. I can almost hear the thoughts ricocheting off the walls, the calculus of our rebellion being reworked in real time.

"This is a game-changer," Marcus says, breaking the spell. "If people knew the truth, if they saw that the NeuroMods were meant to help… It could turn public opinion. It could make them question The Authority."

"Or it could make them more afraid," I say. "Sometimes the truth is more dangerous than a lie."

Arden scoffs. "We didn't come this far to protect people from the truth, Ziva. We're trying to set them free."

I know she's right, but that doesn't make it any easier. The truth is a blade, and we're about to hand it to a populace that's already bleeding.

"So what do we do?" Myall asks, looking to me. I see the conflict in his eyes, the same war that's raging in my chest. He wants this to be simple, but he knows it never is.

I hesitate, trying to steady myself on the tightrope of our ideals. "We release it. Carefully. Anonymously. We let the people decide what to do with it."

"We can't just sit on this," Arden says, her green eyes blazing with urgency. "People need to know the truth. This could change everything."

Marcus rubs his chin, deep in thought. "If we release it too soon, without a plan, it could backfire. The regime will crack down even harder. We need to be strategic."

"Strategic?" Arden scoffs. "We don't have time for a ten-year plan, Marcus. This is a fucking ticking bomb."

I glance at Myall, hoping for some middle ground. He's always the one who can see both sides, who can calm the storm. He shrugs, his hair falling into his eyes. "Arden's right that we need to act quickly. But Marcus also has a point. We can't just throw this out there and hope for the best."

"So what then?" Arden demands. "We sit and wait for the perfect moment that never comes?"

I feel the weight of their expectations. "We prepare. We

build a network. We make sure that when we do release it, people are ready to act. We can't afford to be reckless."

Arden opens her mouth to argue, then closes it, her shoulders slumping. "Fine. But we move as fast as we can."

"Agreed," Marcus says, and I see a flicker of respect in his eyes. "I'll make copies. We can distribute them through the old resistance channels."

"We'll need to be careful," Myall adds, passing me back the datapad. "The regime's surveillance is tighter than ever."

I take the datapad from Myall, my gaze instantly drawn to the dozens of files on the screen. One catches my eye: "Project Equilibrium."

"That's the new NeuroMod," I say, pointing. "The one they're planning to roll out."

Everyone quickly stops their debate, and I click on the file and a schematic opens, along with a block of text. When the final document opens, I can barely process the words on the screen.

"It's not just a NeuroMod," Arden whispers, her voice trembling with a mix of disbelief and horror. She leans over my shoulder, her breath warm on my neck as she points to the screen. "It's a control device. They're going to implant them."

The words hit me like a physical blow, and my stomach churns, the blood draining from my face. This isn't just about surveillance anymore. This is something worse, something irreversible. The Authority isn't just watching us—they're planning to *own* us.

"We have to stop them," I say, and this time there's no doubt in my voice. No conflict. Just the stark, terrifying clarity of knowing what must be done.

"How?" Marcus asks. "We can't just waltz into The Harmonization Center in Elysium and shut it down."

All eyes turn to Myall. He's the strategist, the leader. He'll have a plan.

"We leak all the documents we found," he says. "Let the public see what's coming. Create an outcry."

"You think they'll care about some data leak?" Arden scoffs. "People are too dosed up to utter a complaint, let alone riot in the streets. We need more than that."

She's right, of course. The Authority has crushed dissent for so long that most people can't even remember what defiance feels like.

"We could use the data as leverage," I suggest. "Threaten to release the files unless they back down."

"And if they call our bluff?" Marcus says. "If they come after us?"

I look to Arden, then to Myall. "Then we burn the bridges. We release everything and stand firm."

The room falls silent. This is the line. Once crossed, there's no going back.

"Are we agreed?" Myall asks, his gaze sweeping over each of us.

Arden nods first, then Marcus. I take a breath and close my eyes, seeing the future we're trying to build, the lives we're trying to save.

The decision feels like a weight I can't shake. The idea of releasing this data, of showing the world the truth—it's liberating, yes. But it's also terrifying. If the people rise up, we may be their leaders. If they don't, we'll be the ones who ignited the fire. Either way, we're out of control.

I think of the lives that could be lost, the faces I know we may never see again. But I can't turn back now. We've made our choice.

"Yes," I say. "We're agreed."

"We're agreed," Myall echoes. His voice is firm, but I can hear the exhaustion in it. "Let's make sure it counts."

Chapter Twenty Six

Myall

The aftershocks of last night's close call still rattle my bones. My head aches from lack of sleep, the taste of stale air and adrenaline lingering on my tongue. The Authority's true nature churns in my mind, the stolen data pulsing with sickening urgency. The implications of their plans—the new NeuroMods—gnaws at me, a suffocating presence with every breath.

If we don't act, we might lose everything.

I take a deep breath, trying to calm my nerves as I arrive at work, passing through the new security measures.

Stepping onto the main floor, my skin prickles with the silent gaze of the ever-present cameras, their mechanical whir impossible to ignore. I can almost feel Colvin's eyes boring into me, a constant pressure that I can't shake.

Sitting down, my fingers are already dancing over the keys,

but my mind races ahead, a thousand thoughts colliding. The stolen data. Neck implants that can track and control emotions even more precisely than before. It's a chilling prospect.

Around me, my colleagues work in eerie silence, the only sound the clicking of keys and the hum of machines. I can't help but wonder how many of them harbor secret doubts, hidden rebellious thoughts that they dare not voice.

"Hansen."

I flinch at the sound of my name, turning to see my supervisor standing behind me. Her face is impassive, but there's tension in her jaw.

"Regent Colvin wants to see you for your interview. Now."

My heart pounds as I nod, rising from my chair on unsteady legs. It feels like my body is going through the motions, but my mind is a million miles away. I can feel Ziva's eyes on me as I walk past her, but I don't dare look in her direction.

I pause outside Colvin's office, the sterile metal door cold against my fingertips as I brace myself. My stomach churns, and my throat tightens with the taste of iron—fear, I realize. I try to steady my breath, but it feels shallow, panicked.

No matter what happens in this room, I know one thing for certain—I won't let him break me. With a final steadying breath, I knock on the door, ready to face my fate.

It swings open, revealing the austere interior of Colvin's temporary office. He sits behind a sleek metal desk, his piercing eyes fixed on me as I step inside. The room is eerily quiet, the only sound the soft swiveling of the surveillance cameras mounted in each corner.

"Myall Hansen," Colvin says, his voice cool and measured.

"Please, have a seat."

I sink into the chair opposite him, my palms damp with sweat. Up close, Regent Colvin is even more imposing, his angular features carved from stone. He regards me silently for a moment, his gaze seeming to strip away every layer of my carefully constructed facade.

"I trust you know why you're here," he says at last, leaning back in his chair. "I've been conducting interviews with all personnel, to ensure their loyalty to The Harmonization Authority."

I force myself to nod, swallowing past the lump in my throat. "Of course, Regent Colvin. I'm happy to answer any questions you may have."

He smiles, but there's no warmth in it. "Good. Let's begin, shall we?"

Colvin leans forward, his chair creaking under his weight as his cold blue eyes pierce through mine, like a blade trying to find its mark. His stare is like a vise, tightening with every passing second, trying to wring the truth from me.

"Tell me, Compliance Monitor Hansen, have you ever witnessed any suspicious behavior among your colleagues? Any signs of dissent or disloyalty?"

My mouth goes dry as my mind races, tumbling through a thousand possible answers, but none of them feel right. The thud of my pulse fills my ears.

"No, sir. Everyone here is fully committed to The Authority's mission. We understand the importance of maintaining emotional stability for the greater good."

Even as the words leave my lips, I feel a twinge of guilt, a sharp twist in my gut. My heart hammers, as if it knows what I'm doing, as if it wants to scream the truth. But I push it down, forcing myself to keep my voice steady, to maintain the mask of compliance. I can't afford to slip now.

Colvin nods, but I can see the skepticism in his gaze. "And what about you, Hansen? Any doubts about the system? Any sympathy for the rebels who seek to undermine our way of life?"

My heart continues to pound, but I force myself to meet his eyes with unwavering conviction. "Absolutely not, sir. I believe in The Authority's vision. Emotion is a weakness that must be controlled for the sake of order and progress."

He leans back in his chair, his eyes never leaving mine. "Tell me, Hansen, what do you think about the recent rumors of a new NeuroMod device? One that would be implanted directly into the necks of citizens for even more precise emotional monitoring?"

A chill runs down my spine, but I keep my face impassive. I can't let him sense that I already know—or that the thought of such invasive technology makes my stomach turn.

"I haven't heard much about it, sir," I lie smoothly, keeping my tone even despite the pounding of my pulse. "But if The Authority deems it necessary, I'm sure it will be for the greater good."

Colvin nods, a hint of a smirk playing at the corners of his mouth. "Indeed, Hansen. The Authority always acts in the best interests of society. But tell me, what are your thoughts on the growing rebellion? Surely you must have *some* opinions on those who would seek to undermine our perfect order."

A bead of sweat trickles down my spine, but I refuse to let my nerves show. "I think the rebels are misguided, sir. They don't understand the importance of emotional control, the chaos and violence that would ensue if we allowed ourselves to be ruled by our base instincts."

His gaze is piercing and intense as he studies me. "And what would you do, Hansen, if you discovered someone close to you was involved with the rebellion? A coworker, perhaps, or even a friend?"

The thought that he could be referring to Grandma Elara, Ziva, Marcus, and Arden— the only ones who truly understand me—makes my heart clench.

"I would report them immediately," I say, my voice cold and detached. "The Authority's laws exist for a reason, and anyone who violates them must face the consequences."

"Even if it was someone you cared about...deeply?" he asks with a pointed look, the question hangs heavy in the air. My stomach twists in knots at the mere thought of it. Is he referring to Ziva?

Fuck.

I force a calm facade, my voice devoid of emotion. "I would report them without hesitation, sir," I state firmly, though my heart is pounding so loudly I fear he can hear it.

Colvin's gaze locks onto mine, narrowing as he leans forward. "I'll ask you one more time, Mr. Hansen. Have you had any contact with rebels or dissidents?"

I meet his stare, keeping my voice steady. "No, sir. I have no knowledge of any rebel activities."

He studies me, looking for any sign of deception. I keep my expression neutral, my hands clasped tightly in my lap to hide their trembling.

Finally, He sits back in his chair, a thin smile playing across his lips. "Very well, Mr. Hansen. It seems your loyalty to The Authority is intact."

Relief floods through me, but I dare not let it show. I nod respectfully. "Thank you, sir. I am committed to serving The Authority and maintaining the harmony of our society."

Colvin's smile doesn't reach his eyes. "See that you continue to do so. The Authority has no tolerance for those who seek to disrupt our carefully crafted order."

I incline my head, a silent acknowledgment of his warning. Inside, my mind races with the knowledge of the data chip hidden in my pocket, the information that could bring The Authority crumbling down.

Colvin rises, signaling the end of the interview. "You may return to your duties, Mr. Hansen. But remember, The Authority is always watching."

I stand, my legs shaky, and head for the door. Just as I'm about to exit, Colvin's voice stops me.

"One more thing."

I pause, my heart in my throat as I turn back to face him.

His eyes glint with suspicion. "If you do happen to come across any information about rebel activities, you will report it immediately. Failure to do so will have… dire consequences."

I swallow hard, nodding once more. "Of course, sir. I understand."

With that, I step out of his office, the door closing behind me with a soft click. I take a moment to steady myself, drawing in a deep breath.

I've made it through the interview, but I know Colvin's suspicions haven't been completely dispelled. I'll have to be more cautious than ever, even as I work to undermine the very system he represents.

I square my shoulders, feeling the weight of the world

on them, and make my way back to my workstation. My thoughts are already racing, spinning in chaotic loops—plans for the resistance, for how we can turn the stolen data into something that will make The Authority tremble. My heart beats faster, fueled by the knowledge that every second counts.

I settle into the seat of my wokstation, fingers moving mechanically to the keyboard. The day's tasks fill the screen, but my mind keeps replaying the interview on a loop.

Did I give anything away? Did Colvin see through my carefully crafted responses? The questions swirl in my head, and I have to force myself to focus on the screen before me.

Around me, my colleagues work in silence, their faces drawn and tense. Since Colvin arrived, the atmosphere has shifted, a palpable sense of fear settling over us all—even those with muted emotions.

I catch Ziva's eye from across the isle, the rest of the world falling away. In that brief glance, I can see the same fear and determination that I feel reflected back at me.

She gives me a questioning look, and I respond with a slight nod. We both know that we can't risk talking openly, not with The Authority's surveillance constantly monitoring our every move, and not after Colvin caught us in the supply closet.

I tear my gaze away from Ziva's, focusing on my work once more. But even as I work, my mind is already racing ahead, plotting our next move, trying to figure out the best method to get the information we stole into the hands of the public.

The day drags on, the tension in my body building, a coiled spring ready to snap. I move through the motions of my tasks, but my mind is preoccupied.

I think back to the interview with Colvin, the way he probed for any hint of disloyalty. It took everything I had to maintain my composure, to keep my mask of compliance in place. But even as I lied through my teeth, I could feel the weight of the truth pressing down on me—the new NeuroMods, The Authority's plans.

It's too much to bear alone. We need to act, and soon. Every delay gives The Authority more time to tighten its grip. We can't let them win.

But how? How do we make people see the truth?

We need help. We need to recruit, to build a network of resistance from the inside out.

It's a risk, I know. Every new recruit is a potential weak link, a chance for The Authority to discover us. But we can't do this alone anymore and Arden's right, we need to move faster.

The world blurs around me as I meet Ziva's gaze, a silent understanding passing between us. Tomorrow on our day off, it starts. We will fight back, together. I know it's dangerous, but it feels like the only choice now. We won't stop until we've brought The Authority to its knees.

Chapter Twenty Seven

Myall

I stand outside Grandma Elara's house, the familiar sight doing little to calm the storm raging inside me. The door swings open before I can knock. I step inside, the dim light and the scent of cinnamon wrapping around me like an old, familiar blanket. Ziva's sharp gaze pulls me back to the present, her voice sharp but tinged with something softer I can't quite place.

"Thought you'd bailed," she says, the sarcasm in her voice failing to hide her real concern.

"Traffic," I lie, my voice steady enough despite the tension. I follow her inside the house.

Marcus and Arden are already seated at the old oak table in the kitchen, a relic from a time when families supposedly gathered for meals and conversations. Marcus nods, his usually stern face softening for a moment. Arden just grins, her enthusiasm always a bit out of place. Grandma Elara sits in her favorite chair by the window, a soft smile on her wrinkled face as she watches us.

"Glad you made it," Marcus says, nodding. "We were about to start without you."

I sit beside Grandma Elara, the hard wood pressing through my thin jacket. She gently pats my hand in greeting. "You know I wouldn't miss this," I tell her.

Ziva leans against the counter, arms crossed. "So, how'd it go with Colvin yesterday?"

All eyes turn to me. I can see the tension in their faces. They're scared. Colvin's been interviewing everyone, sniffing out dissent like a bloodhound. I was the last of us to sit in his hot seat, well, aside from Arden that is.

I swallow hard, the memory of Colvin's piercing gaze still fresh. My hands, despite my best efforts, tremble again, and I clench them into fists at my sides.

"He's suspicious, but I think he bought my story. For now."

Arden's grin falters. "For now?"

I shrug. "We're all on his radar. He's not stupid. But he has no proof."

Yet.

Marcus sighs, running a hand through his short-cropped hair. "We need to be more careful. If one of us goes down—"

"None of us are going down," Ziva interrupts, her voice like steel. "We've come too far to back out now."

The room falls silent. Ziva's right, but it's never felt more dangerous. I glance around at the faces I've come to trust—Marcus, his brow furrowed in cautious resolve, Arden, her eyes burning with fierce energy, Elara, her wrinkled hands resting on the table with a tenderness that feels like a balm. In this room, amid the tension and fear, they're not just rebels. They're my family, and nothing The Authority does will ever change that.

Grandma Elara leans toward me, placing a hand on my shoulder and I feel a rush of warmth and worry. Her skin is paper-thin, yet her grip is firm. The worry in her eyes, the slight tremble of her hand, tells me all I need to know—she knows the danger, perhaps more than any of us.

"Myall, you need to be careful dear," she says, her voice soft but unyielding.

"I know, Grandma," I reply, meeting her gaze. They're the same deep green as mine, and they shine with the kind of emotion the rest of the world has forgotten. "We all do."

She squeezes my shoulder, then turns to the rest of the group. "You're always welcome here, but remember, the most important thing is to stay safe."

Ziva uncrosses her arms, her usual defiance giving way, just for a moment, to Elara's concern. "Thanks, Elara. We know the risks."

Do we?

Every day it feels like we're playing a game where the rules keep changing, and the stakes get higher and higher.

"Grandma, I need to tell you something," I say, breaking the silence that has settled among the group. Elara pauses, her back half-turned as she gazes out the window. She turns her attention back towards me.

With a quick glance, I signal to the others that I need a moment alone with my grandmother and they quietly exit the kitchen. Ziva catches my eye and gives me one of her faint, encouraging smiles.

"The information we stole from The Authority the other

night…" I hesitate, the weight of it making my chest tighten. "It's worse than we could have imagined."

Elara's face pales, and I can almost feel her heart race beneath her frail chest. Her eyes search mine, the concern in them growing. "What did you find?"

"They're planning to introduce new NeuroMods," I say, keeping my voice low. "Ones that will be implanted in our necks. They won't just monitor emotions—they'll control them directly."

Elara's hand goes to her throat, her fingers trembling. "This…this is monstrous."

"They've also got files on the origins of the NeuroMod system," I continue. "It shows how they gradually took control, how they manipulated people into believing it was for their own good. It's all there, Grandma. The lies, the coercion. We have the proof now, proof that The Authority's way of life is wrong."

She leans back, her eyes closing for a moment as if the weight of this new knowledge is too much to bear.

"The stakes are higher than I thought." She sighs softly.

Elara's soft voice is the only thing holding me together, but even her calm cannot erase the panic brewing in my chest. I stand and start to pace, the energy in me too restless to sit still. The pressure in my chest tightens, as if someone's squeezing my heart every time I pause to think.

Should we grow our ranks? Should we hold back?

Every time I think I've made a decision on our next steps, I hesitate. The cost of a single wrong step could be irreversible.

"I don't know what to do but I do know we need to be smart about this. If we just release the information without a plan, it could backfire. The Authority will crack down even harder. We need to grow our numbers, gather more allies. People who are willing to take a stand."

Elara opens her eyes and looks at me, and I see the years of struggle and hope etched into her face. "Myall, this is a dangerous path. You know that."

"I do," I say, stopping to face her. "But it's the only path that leads to real change. We can't just sit back anymore and hope things will get better on their own."

She sighs, a long, deep exhalation that seems to come from the very core of her being. "You're right," she says, though her agreement offers no comfort. "But remember, revolutions are not won overnight. They are long, and they are costly."

"I know," I say, my voice hardening with the resolve I need to convince not just her, but myself. "That's why we need to be strategic. We need to build a network, create a plan that has a chance of success. We can't rush this."

Elara rises slowly, the effort showing in her weary bones. She comes over and places a hand on my cheek, her touch as tender as a mother's kiss. "I believe in you, Myall. Though the thought of losing you like I've lost your parents…just promise me you'll be careful."

"I promise," I say, and this time I want the words to be true. I need them to be true.

We regather around the worn kitchen table, anxiety hangs in the air as we stare at the list Arden has compiled, each name a potential recruit—or a death sentence. Arden is the first to break the silence, her voice crackling with the same energy that seems to animate her entire being.

"I've gone through The Authority's files," she states, tapping the names. "They've all made their stance clear—skipped Harmonization sessions, attended underground meetups, some even involved in sabotage. We can use that."

I have to give her credit, she's worked diligently to get through that massive amount of data in just one day.

"It's too risky," Marcus says, his frustration palpable. "Recruiting more people means more chances for infiltration, more eyes on us. Especially with Colvin here. I say we look to release the information we gathered first and gauge people's reaction."

I lean back in my chair, arms crossed. "We need the numbers, Marcus. We're too small to keep this going alone."

He glares at me, his dark eyes intense. "You're not listening. Colvin has been sniffing around for rebels, that's why he's here. One wrong move and we're all in a detention center—or worse."

I know he's right. Colvin's presence in New Eden has put everyone on edge.

"We don't have a choice," I say. "If we don't grow, we stagnate. And if we stagnate, we die."

Marcus shakes his head, but I can see the conflict in him. He wants this as badly as I do, but he's always been the cautious one.

"What if we take a different approach?" I offer. "Instead of mass recruiting, we identify individuals with specific skills or connections. People who can bring something unique to the table. That way, we minimize the risk and maximize the benefit."

He considers this, his serious expression unchanging. "Like who?"

"Technicians who can sabotage NeuroMods without getting caught. Historians who have access to the archives. Maybe even someone within The Harmonization Authority who's disillusioned with the regime. We start small, but we make every addition count."

Marcus groans, rubbing his temples. "It's still dangerous. Every person we bring in is a risk."

"I know," I say, leaning closer, trying to keep my temper in check. "But it's a gamble we have to take. We'll be strategic. Precise."

He looks up at me, and for a moment I see the flicker of hope in his eyes. "Alright," he says slowly. "But we vet them thoroughly. No rushing."

"Let's hear the list," I say, though a part of me dreads the discussion that's about to unfold.

Arden flips her hair back and leans in, her eyes alight with purpose. "First up, Jarek Reyes. He's a dockworker with a big mouth. He's been stirring up trouble in the labor union for years."

"Too hot-headed," I automatically answer. "He'll get us all killed before we even start."

Arden shrugs. "Yeah maybe. But he's got the kind of anger we can channel. Next, there's Liora Chen. She runs a free clinic in the lower districts. Half her patients are old resistance fighters from the last rebellion, and she's patched them up without asking questions."

"She's got a family," I say, glancing at the datapad. "People with something to lose are less likely to take the plunge."

Arden shoots me a look that's almost hurt. "We all have something to lose, Myall. That doesn't make us any less committed."

I don't respond. I can't. She's right, of course, but it's

easier to believe we're different, that our sacrifice will mean something.

"Go on," says Elara, her voice cutting through the tension. She has been silent so far, but when she speaks, it always puts me at ease.

"Right," Arden says, glancing down at the datapad to check her list. "Jorel Simmons is one of our best bets. He's a maintenance worker from Sector 7 with access to the maintenance tunnels. If we get him, we'll have movement through the city, unseen."

Ziva perks up at the mention of Jorel. "Access to the maintenance tunnels would come in handy."

I nod in agreement. The maintenance tunnels are a labyrinthine network beneath the city, used for utilities and maintenance. If we had someone with access to those tunnels—it would be invaluable.

"Last one," Arden says, though her enthusiasm has dimmed. "Tariq Al-Masri. He's a journalist—well, *was* a journalist about twenty years ago before The Authority shut down the press. He's likely got connections and would know how to spread a message."

"Can we even trust him?" Marcus asks, crossing his arms. "He could be an informant."

"Everyone could be an informant," Arden snaps. "These are the people who have already stuck their necks out. They're the most likely to join us."

"Or the most likely to be under surveillance," I say, trying to inject some pragmatism into the increasingly heated debate. "If one of them gets picked up, they could lead The Authority straight to us."

Elara finally speaks, her voice the calm center of our

growing maelstrom. "Every revolution is a gamble. The question is whether we play it safe and accomplish nothing, or take the risks and go all in."

All eyes turn to me. As the de-facto leader, it's my call, but the lines of fracture are forming. We're not even in the thick of it yet, and already we're divided.

"I think we start by feeling them out," I say slowly. "See where their loyalties lie, how much they're willing to risk. We don't rush this."

"We need people who are already discontent," Ziva adds, her eyes sharp and calculating. "Recruiting non believers will be easier and less risky."

"But non believers are more likely to act rashly," Marcus counters, tapping his fingers on the table. "We can't afford hotheads who might blow our cover like that Jarek fellow."

Arden, leaning back in her chair with her arms crossed, shrugs. "Every person's a risk. But sometimes, those risks are what get us the edge we need. If we sit back, we won't make any progress."

The room falls silent for a moment as we all absorb her words. I break the silence, my voice steady with the idea that's forming. "What if we start by setting up a secure communication network? We could recruit people anonymously, assess their loyalties before bringing them in. Encrypted channels, hidden locations—things that will keep us safer."

Ziva's eyes flicker with interest. "I can set that up. I already have an encrypted channel—it just needs some tweaking."

Marcus leans forward, resting his elbows on the table. "How long would it take?"

"A few days, could be less if I can get the right materials,"

Ziva replies, her mind already calculating the steps she'll need to take.

"Encryption is tricky," I say, cutting in. "The Harmonization Authority has tech light-years ahead of ours. We need to perfect it before we even consider using it."

Marcus leans back in his chair. "What about using old tech? Analog methods? They're less likely to monitor those."

"Like what? Carrier pigeons?" Arden scoffs, but I see a hint of interest in her eyes. She's not entirely dismissive.

"Handwritten notes, perhaps," Marcus continues, unfazed. "Or landlines, if we can find any still operational. Even runners—people we trust to carry messages directly."

The room falls silent as we weigh the options. Each method carries its own risks and potential for disaster.

Elara, who has been quietly observing our exchange, leans forward. "You know," she begins, her voice soft but commanding, "this isn't the first time people have had to communicate in secret. During the early days of The Authority, we faced similar challenges."

All eyes turn to her. Even Marcus, who tends to bristle at her nostalgic interjections, listens with a grudging respect.

"We used a mix of methods," she continues. "Some as simple as code words in public conversations, others as complex as hidden compartments in everyday objects. The key was always trust—in the people delivering the messages and in the methods we used."

I think about the trust she's placed in us by letting us meet in her home now that we've lost the tech lab. It's a fragile thing, easily shattered, and yet it's the foundation of everything we're trying to build.

"Your parents were masters of this," Elara says, her gaze

flicking between Ziva and me. "They knew how to balance caution with boldness. It's a dangerous dance, but it can be done."

The mention of our parents hits like a punch to the gut. They were taken when we were young, leaving us to navigate this world alone. I wonder what they would think of our little rebellion.

"So we do it the old-fashioned way," Ziva says, breaking the silence. "We build the network slowly, person by person. We use every trick in the book and then some."

"It's not going to be easy," Marcus says, though his tone has shifted. There's a note of resolve, of acceptance.

"No," I agree. "But nothing worth doing ever is."

The tension in the room shifts, taking on a new form—less about fear and more about the daunting tasks ahead.

"So, we build the network first," I say, looking around the room. "No rushing into recruitment until we're ready."

"Agreed," they answer, each with their own tone—Ziva and Arden determined, Marcus reluctantly on board.

"Alright," I say, taking the datapad from Arden. "Let's assign tasks. Ziva, you handle the tech. We need those encrypted channels up and running as soon as possible."

Ziva nods, already lost in thoughts of the algorithms she'll write and the hardware she'll need to scavenge.

"Arden," I continue, "start mapping out potential safe houses. We need places where we can meet these new recruits and where people can lay low if things go south."

"Got it," she says.

"Marcus and I will work on identifying potential recruits. Quietly," I add, glancing at Arden. "We'll make a list and approach them only when we're sure it's safe to do so.

A murmur of agreement rises before the room falls silent again.

Ziva's voice slices through the silence, her hazel eyes sharp with determination. "Screening potential allies is one thing, but how do we convince them to take the risk?"

Nodding, I consider her words.

"What if," Ziva continues, leaning forward, her long hair falling across the table, "we left them information? Something concrete they could review in private before we approach them?"

My pulse quickens. It's a bold idea, exactly the kind of creative thinking we need.

"You mean like a data chip?" Arden asks, a spark of excitement in her eyes.

Ziva nods. "Yeah. We could include details about the NeuroMod implants. Show them what The Authority really has planned. It will help sway them to our cause."

"That's a big risk," I say, choosing my words carefully. "If the wrong person found that chip—"

Marcus cuts in, his voice low and measured. "The risk might be worth it. People need to know what's coming."

"Alright," I concede. "Let's talk about how we make this happen."

Arden leans forward, her green eyes sparkling with intensity. "The data chips can't be too obvious, or they'll raise suspicion."

"Yeah. They need to blend in with everyday items." I add.

Ziva's quick mind is already at work. "What about disguising them as credit chips? Everyone carries those."

Marcus frowns, his dark eyes narrowing. "No. If someone accidentally tries to use it that would be a disaster."

Disappointment ripples through the room, my own pulse quickening with it.

"What about hiding them in common household items?" I suggest. "Things people wouldn't think twice about, like Grandma suggested."

Ziva snaps her fingers. "Yes. We could use anything from keychains to styluses."

I can't help but smile at Ziva's enthusiasm.

Marcus clears his throat. "I can work on creating the chips. I have access to the necessary equipment from parts I've already taken from the tech lab."

Elara, who's been quietly observing, speaks up. "Once you've vetted a recruit, you should find a suitable drop point. Somewhere they frequent but isn't too conspicuous."

I nod, impressed by her strategic thinking before I remember that she's done this before. "And we'll need to monitor their reaction. See if they take the bait."

Ziva's eyes gleam with intensity. "Once we're sure they're ready to join us, we'll reach out with the encrypted channel I'll make." Her fingers drum a restless rhythm on the table.

Nodding, I feel a spark of excitement despite the danger. "Yeah, but we'd need to be careful about the meetup locations."

Arden speaks up. "Leave that to me. I can scout some safe spots around the city while I'm looking for new hideouts for us."

Looking around the table, I take in the determined faces of my friends—my family. We're in this together, for better or worse. "Same time next week?" I ask, already knowing the answer.

A chorus of affirmatives follows, and as we start to disperse,

I catch Ziva's eye. For a brief second, something shifts in her—an emotion I can't quite place. Her gaze softens, but before I can make sense of it, her usual mask slides back into place, leaving me questioning whether I imagined it. We step out into the night, feeling a sense of accomplishment, tinged with fear. But beneath the fear, there's a glimmer of hope. We might just pull this off.

Chapter Twenty Eight

Ziva

The shadows of our rebellion stretch farther with each passing day. I run my fingers along the cool, slick metal of the encrypted communicator, its weight a constant, unshakable presence in my palm.

For a week now, we've been plotting in the shadows, our eyes constantly darting for watchful Authority drones or the ever-present gaze of Regent Colvin.

He's been tightening his grip on the city, conducting unexpected searches of public spaces. It won't be long until he begins invading people's personal living spaces.

Myall's voice echoes in my mind, soft but resolute. "Please be careful, Ziva. I can't do this without you."

I nod, though he's not here to see it. I think of the data chip Marcus and Myall planted for Liora Chen to find.

Will she take the bait, or turn us in?

I can't help but imagine Liora's face when she finds the truth—the permanent NeuroMods embedded into our necks, a leash tethered to our very biology.

Will she recoil in horror, turning away from the truth? Or will she, like the rest of us, feel the same spark of defiance, that raw, reckless urge to fight back against something bigger than ourselves?

Pausing, I press my forehead against the cool glass of the window. The lower district—a subsection of Sector 7—sprawls before me in the distance, a maze of despair and hidden hope. Somewhere out there, Liora is making her decision. And we're all holding our breath.

Arden's bright determination flashes through my mind. "We're changing the world, Ziva," she'd said, her eyes ablaze. "One recruit at a time."

I close my eyes, willing myself to believe it. We're walking a razor's edge, and one misstep could mean the end of everything.

Slipping out of my unit before dawn, I make my way to the lower district. The medical clinic looms ahead, its stark walls standing out against the grimy streets. I find my planned hiding spot behind a stack of discarded wooden crates that I'd mapped out the day before, the acrid smell of disinfectant hanging in the air.

"Come on, Liora," I whisper, scanning the alley. My fingers twitch, longing for the familiar weight of a screwdriver. Anything to distract myself.

Minutes crawl by like hours, each one stretching longer than the last. My body is on edge, every nerve singing with the anticipation of what's to come. I scan the alley, watching every shadow and flicker of movement, replaying our encrypted conversation in my head.

Was there something I missed? A slip of the tongue? An unintended signal to the wrong people? My stomach churns, a ball of acid and dread. What if she's already reported us? Or worse, what if The Authority is already lying in wait?

The alley feels narrower now, the walls closing in, pressing against me as if the city itself is holding its breath.

A flicker of movement catches my eye. I tense, ready to bolt, but it's just a stray cat slinking past. I exhale slowly, trying to calm my frayed nerves.

Get it together, Ziva. Calm the fuck down.

The stakes have never been higher. If Liora joins us, we gain a valuable ally in the medical field.

If she betrays us...

I push the thought away, focusing on the mouth of the alley.

That's when I see her. Liora Chen, her salt-and-pepper hair pulled back in a tight bun. Her almond eyes flick from side to side, darting nervously as she approaches, each step tentative as if terrified she's about to walk into a trap.

That makes two of us.

I hold my breath, watching as she passes my hiding spot. My muscles coil, ready to spring into action. But first, I need to be certain. I need to know she hasn't led The Authority straight to us.

"Trust, but verify," Myall's voice echoes in my head. His concern for my safety warms me, even as I prepare to put myself in danger.

I count to ten, giving Liora time to reach our meeting point.

Liora's eyes widen as I step out of the shadows. Her breath

catches, and her hand flies to her neck, trembling fingers pressing against her pulse as if to steady her heart. It's a raw, unguarded moment—fear written all over her face—and I can almost feel the thud of her heart from where I stand. For a brief moment, I wonder if I made the wrong call, if we're both in over our heads.

"You're…you're just a girl," she whispers, her voice trembling.

Approaching slowly, I raise my hands to show I'm unarmed. "Age is irrelevant when you're fighting for freedom," I say, my tone carefully neutral. "Did you come alone, Liora?"

She nods, still staring at me with a mixture of fear and fascination. "Yes, I…I followed your instructions to the letter. No one knows I'm here."

I scan her face, searching for any hint of deception. Heart pounding, I keep my expression calm. "Good. Now, tell me about the data chip. What did you learn?"

Liora glances around nervously before leaning in closer. "It's absolutely horrible" she murmurs. "The Authority… they're planning something big. Something permanent."

"You're right, Liora. The Authority is planning to introduce permanent NeuroMods, implanted directly into our necks." My hand unconsciously rises to my own throat, fingertips grazing the spot where such a device would sit. "But there's more you need to know."

Liora's eyes widen, her gaze flickering between fear and something deeper, a vulnerability that mirrors my own. Her hand trembles slightly where it rests at her side.

I press on, "there's a rebellion forming. People who want to fight back, to reclaim our right to feel." I pause, giving her space to absorb the weight of what I'm saying.

She doesn't speak for a long moment, her gaze dropping to the ground, as if weighing her own thoughts against everything she's ever known. The silence stretches between us.

Wiping my sweaty palms on my trousers, my fingers brush against the communicator device in my pocket.

"Only use it for an emergency, Ziva." Myall had warned.

My heart pounds in my chest as I wait for her response. This moment could change everything—for better or worse. Finally, she looks up, her eyes clearer now, steely with determination.

"I've seen too much," she says, voice steadier than before. "Too many lives broken by these infernal devices. You're right. I've never been brave enough to do anything about it, but now I...I have no choice. Count me in."

Relief washes over me, and I can't help but return her smile. "You have no idea how glad I am to hear that," I say, allowing some of my usual sarcasm to creep back into my tone. "There are others who'll be thrilled to meet you. People who've been risking everything to build this rebellion."

Glancing around the alley, I confirm we're still alone.

"Listen carefully," I say, leaning in close. "There's a small, blueish painted house in the old residential district. Third street past the broken neon sign. Be there in half an hour. And Liora?" I lock eyes with her. "Be careful. Trust no one until then."

As I watch her nod and slip away towards the medical clinic, a mix of excitement and anxiety churns in my stomach. We're one step closer to our goal, I can only hope we're ready for whatever comes next.

* * *

I hurry back through the winding streets of the lower district, my pulse loud in my ears. The city feels alive with quiet threats, its shadows stretching long as the sun begins to rise. I can't shake the feeling of being watched, of every passing face being a potential betrayer. I know I'm just being paranoid, but my thoughts race faster than my feet.

As Elara's house comes into view, something inside me shifts. The danger, the weight of the plan, it all takes a backseat for a moment. I inhale sharply, the air filling my lungs. I've made it this far. I've done what needed to be done.

I knock, and the door swings open almost immediately, revealing a chorus of anxious faces. Relief floods through me—though it's quickly replaced by the sharp awareness that this was just the first step. But for now, in this moment, I let myself exhale.

"Ziva!" Myall's voice breaks the tension, relief flooding his features. His green eyes search mine through the doorway, and I feel a flutter in my chest that has nothing to do with fear. "You're okay."

I step inside, and the others immediately gather around me.

"Of course I'm okay," I say, injecting a lightness into my tone I don't entirely feel. "You think I can't handle a simple recruitment?"

Elara's warm hand finds my shoulder. "We've all been on edge, dear. Times like these don't leave room for complacency."

I nod, my bravado faltering under her knowing gaze. "It went well. Liora's in. She'll meet us soon."

The room collectively exhales and Arden pumps her fist. It's Myall's reaction that catches me off guard. He doesn't rush toward me like the others. Instead, he moves slowly, deliberately, his gaze lingering on mine.

"I'm glad you're safe." His voice is a whisper, rough with relief, cutting through the chatter in the room.

Glancing up, I meet his eyes, and I see a vulnerability there, a flicker of something deep and unguarded. It makes my breath catch, and my stomach tightens—this feeling, this connection between us, is like a secret we both keep, even if we can't say it aloud. His concern, his care for me, it's a weight I hadn't expected to feel so acutely.

I swallow the urge to reach for him and instead say, my voice steady, "We're all in this together. One more ally means one step closer to bringing down The Authority."

A sharp rap followed by two softer ones at the door silences the room. My heart leaps into my throat as we exchange tense glances. Elara moves towards the entrance, her weathered hand hovering over the handle. She looks back at us, her eyes seeking confirmation. I give a slight nod, and she opens the door.

The door creaks open, and there she is. Liora. Her expression is a mix of determination and uncertainty, as if stepping into the room means stepping into something she can't turn back from.

Elara's warm smile breaks the tension. "Come in, dear," she says, ushering Liora inside with a gentle hand on her back. "We've been expecting you."

As Liora steps into the room, I can feel the others' eyes on her, assessing, wondering.

I clear my throat, suddenly aware of how awkward this is.

"Everyone," I say, sounding steadier than I feel, "this is Liora Chen."

I gesture to each person in turn. "Liora, meet Grandma Elara, our wise counsel and heart." Elara's eyes crinkle with kindness as she nods to Liora. "This is Myall," I continue, my voice catching slightly as his green eyes meet mine. "Our strategist and…" I hesitate, struggling to define what he is to me, to us. "…and unwavering support."

Arden shoots me a look and snickers. "And Marcus and Arden," I finish quickly, indicating the last two. Arden seems to be bouncing with nervous energy as she grins at Liora, while Marcus offers a solemn nod.

Liora's gaze scans the room, assessing each face. "I…" she begins, her voice trembling slightly. "I never thought I'd find others who felt the same way. Who were willing to fight."

I step closer to her. "We're more than willing," I say, and I almost believe it. "We're ready to burn the whole system to the ground." As the words leave my mouth, I feel a strange rush of power.

Arden nearly vibrates with enthusiasm, her grin widening as she looks to Liora. "So, Liora, what's it like working in the clinic? Any juicy Authority secrets you can share?"

I catch Myall's eye, noting his slight frown at Arden's over eagerness. He steps in, his calm voice a counterpoint to Arden's exuberance. "Perhaps we should give Liora a moment to settle in. This is probably a lot for her to take in."

Liora shakes her head, a determined set to her jaw. "No, it's alright. I've been holding this in for so long, I'm ready to talk." She takes a deep breath, and I can see the weight of secrets in her eyes. "The things I've seen in the clinic…the 'treatments' they force on people who show even a hint of nonconformity…"

My fists clench involuntarily as Liora speaks. The familiar rage bubbles up inside me, and I have to force myself to take slow, measured breaths. Myall notices, his hand ghosting over my arm in a gesture of comfort that sends a flutter through my stomach.

"You okay?" he mouths, concern etched in his eyes.

I nod, feeling his hand brush my lower back, and the warmth of his hand through my thin sweater.

"We need to move fast," Arden interjects, her usually animated face creased with concern. "The Authority are planning to implement those new NeuroMods, we don't know when, but we need to be one step ahead of them before they do."

I nod, my mind already switching focus from Myall to the rebellion.

"You're right." I turn to the group. "Our next step is clear. We need to reach out to Jarek, Jorel, and Tariq."

Marcus's eyebrows shoot up. "All three? At once? Are we sure that's wise?"

"We don't have much choice," I reply, meeting each of their gazes in turn. "We're running out of time, and we need all the help we can get."

Marcus gives in with a sigh and agrees, "Fine."

I turn to Liora, our newest addition to the team, and ask, "Are you ready to have your NeuroMod deactivated?"

Chapter Twenty Nine

Ziva

My boots scrape against the cracked floor, a sound that feels louder with each step, echoing in my skull. I can't keep still. My mind is spinning, and no matter how hard I try to ground myself, it's like my thoughts are a thousand miles ahead, too far gone to reach. What if Arden doesn't come back? What if we're too late? I try to shove it down, but that suffocating thought won't leave.

What if it's over before we even start?

The smell of rust and dust clings to the air, making it harder to breathe. Every flicker of movement from the clock on the wall makes my stomach tighten further.

Myall sits on a crate, his posture straight, green eyes tracking my restless movements with unsettling calm. He looks calm, like he's mastered the art of patience—but I can see the way his fingers flex, the slight tightness around his eyes. He's as anxious as I am, just hiding it better.

"She'll be fine," he says, his voice steady, measured. It's the kind of tone that could convince anyone of anything, but it doesn't work on me.

"She's late," I snap, then soften. "It's not like her. Something's *wrong*."

It's been three weeks since Liora joined our group. Within this time, we also successfully recruited Jarek, Jorel, and Tariq—increasing our numbers to nine with Elara included.

I have effectively deactivated the NeuroMods of all the new recruits, while making them seem like they are still operational in case Regent Colvin decides to interrogate us—which could be any day now.

Regent Colvin's shadow hangs over everything we do. His Enforcers have been dragging people off the streets, raiding houses in the dead of night, and making examples of anyone who dares to resist. Recalibration numbers are the highest they've been since the last rebellion. The city's fear has taken on a new weight under his reign. We don't just fear capture— we fear what he'll do to us once we're in his hands. Every move we make could be our last.

Our latest hideout is a forgotten storage room in the basement of an abandoned factory, deep in the belly of the city's outskirts. The walls are caked in grime, and the ceiling sags under the weight of years of neglect. Every time I inhale, I get a waft of mildew and decay. It feels like the room is closing in on me.

We found this place by accident, a lucky stumble in our desperate search for somewhere safe after the tech lab became compromised. The dim light flickers above, casting long shadows over the rusted machinery that has long since ceased to work.

In the past few weeks, we've set up an encrypted communication system here. It's allowed us to screen and approach potential recruits without getting caught. The work has been exhausting, but necessary. Marcus was right to be overly cautious. Regent Colvin's crackdown on dissent has made every move a gamble. People are scared, and with good reason. The Harmonization Authority isn't playing around anymore.

I stop pacing and lean against the wall, crossing my arms over my chest. "Do you think it's worth it? Going after new recruits when we can barely keep ourselves safe anymore?"

Myall takes a moment before answering, his eyes thoughtful. "We need numbers, Ziva. Numbers equal strength. It's what we all agreed on."

I know he's right, that Arden's right to push us to recruit more members, but it doesn't erase the suffocating fear that plagues me. Before we started all this, I was looking at the world with rose colored glasses, thinking that starting a rebellion would be easy. It's the furthest thing from easy. We have to be so careful of every move we make, of every choice we make. The more people we bring in, the harder it becomes for us to collectively agree on anything. At the rate we're going, it feels like we're accomplishing nothing.

"Remember when it was just the two of us?" I say, almost wistfully. "It was simpler back then."

"Lonelier," he counters, but there's a flicker of something in his eyes—perhaps a memory, perhaps a longing. I can't tell, and I don't dare ask.

Uncrossing my arms, I resume my pacing. Myall and I have

always had a complicated dynamic. We rely on each other, we care for each other, but there's an unspoken tension that neither of us is willing to address.

"She has to be okay," I say, more to myself than to him. Arden is fearless, almost recklessly so, but she's also the heart of our little rebellion. Her bravado is infectious and without her, I don't know if I could keep going. I've never had friends. I've always been too afraid to allow anyone to get too close. But with Arden, she has this way of getting under your skin without you realizing.

Myall stands, his boots scraping the floor softly as he crosses the distance between us. I can feel his warmth before he touches me, and wonder if he feels the same pull. He places a hand on my shoulder. His touch is light, but it carries more weight than it should. It's like a promise I'm not ready to face.

"Ziva, she'll be fine. You know how resourceful Arden is."

It should be comforting, but instead, it feels like a reminder of everything we're trying to ignore. My heart stutters in my chest, the rush of it drowning out everything else for a moment.

I want to believe him. I need to believe him. But more than that, I want to lose myself in this moment, to let the tension between us break and wash over me like a wave. His hand slides down my arm, and I shiver. Every nerve in my body is on high alert, screaming for something I know I can't have.

"We can't lose her," I say, my voice barely a whisper.

It's not just about Arden. It's about what she represents. She's the heart of this rebellion, the one who makes us *believe* we have a chance. If we lose her, we lose everything we've worked for. I can't let that happen.

He lets out a deep sigh. "She'll be fine, Ziva. I promise."

The door to the storage room slams open, its rusted hinges shrieking in protest. My body jerks, instinctively pulling away from Myall, as if the very air between us has caught fire.

A young man, no older than seventeen, bursts through the threshold, his face pale, eyes wide with fear. His breath comes in ragged gasps, like he's been running for his life, and for a split second, I wonder if he's just brought more danger with him. His name is Khynan, and he's the potential recruit that Arden was meeting with.

The silence that follows is suffocating.

"They've got Arden." His words hit like a blow. "Regent Colvin himself. She's been taken to the Detention Center."

A cold hand grips my heart and squeezes. The Detention Center is part of Regent Colvin's latest crackdown—a place where the regime extracts more than just information. New Eden has never had it's own detention center before, but I suppose he wanted to bring something across from Elysium with him.

"Are you sure?" Myall asks, though we both know the boy wouldn't risk coming here with news like this unless he was certain.

Khynan nods, breath ragged. "I saw it all. She didn't resist. She told me where to find you…said not to worry. That she'd be alright."

I glance at Myall, whose jaw is set in a hard line. His promises dissolve in the harsh light of reality, and I feel the fragile hope he gave me shatter.

"Go," I tell Khynan. "Get somewhere safe and lie low for a while."

The boy hesitates, his wide eyes flicking between us and the door, as if searching for a way to make his words matter. But there's nothing more to say. He bolts out the door, disappearing into the night like a shadow swallowed by the darkness.

"Fuck," I say, turning back to Myall. He's staring at the ground, lost in thought. When he looks up, the conflict in his eyes mirrors my own.

"Ziva," he starts, but I cut him off.

"Don't. We don't have time. We have to figure out a way to get her out."

I know what he's going to say, and I can't bear to hear it. We have to focus on Arden now, on the rebellion.

He takes a step back, and the space between us feels like a chasm. "You're right. Let's call the others."

Nodding, I reach for the communicator, but my hands are shaking too much to hold it steady. Myall takes it from me gently, his fingers brushing mine, and for a moment I think I might break. But I don't. I can't afford to.

Myall speaks into the communicator, his tone calm and authoritative, summoning our small network. I sink into a chair, my mind spinning with visions of failure—Arden in the hands of the Enforcers, the rebellion scattered, everything we've fought for slipping away.

The sounds of our rebellion members fill the room from the communicator. Myall doesn't waste a second.

"Arden's been captured," he announces. A murmur of shocked voices flow from the device. "We need to find out how it happened and, more importantly, how we're going to get her out."

One of the members, Jorell, speaks up. "Are we sure this

isn't just a temporary setback? Maybe she's just lying low somewhere."

"A kid from her sector came to warn us," Myall says. "He saw the Enforcers take her. This is very real."

Myall takes charge, laying out the facts and delegating tasks. He's always been the reluctant leader, but in moments like this, his natural ability shines through. It should comfort me, seeing him so composed, but instead, it deepens the pit in my stomach.

"Ziva," Myall says, breaking into my thoughts. "Can you check the Sentinel logs for any spikes in emotional output? Maybe someone tipped the Enforcers off."

I nod, though the last thing I want to do is leave the room and be alone with my thoughts. The old terminal in the corner hums softly as I access its interface. Myall continues to strategize with the others, his voice steady, unyielding.

The logs are a mess of data. I scan through them quickly, looking for anything that stands out. Emotional spikes can mean anything—an argument, a moment of illicit joy, fear. I'm looking for something unusual, something that would draw the Enforcers' attention.

I glance back at Myall. He catches my eye, and for a brief second, I see the worry he's hiding, the fear for Arden, for us. For me. I refocus on the terminal, my chest tight.

"Got something," I say, walking back to Myall and the others on the line. "There was a huge spike in her sector two hours ago. It looks like it could be one of Colvin's surprise searches."

"So, it wasn't just her they were after," says Liora. "They could've been cracking down on the whole sector and she got caught up in it."

"Which means we don't have much time," Myall says. "We need to act before they try interrogating her."

"How do we even get close?" asks Jorell. "The detention center would be a fortress of security measures, and Arden's the one who looked after that."

"We'll find a way," I say, my voice stronger than I feel. "Arden would do the same for any of us."

A flicker of something passes in Myall's gaze at my resolve.

"Alright," he says. "Let's map out the possible routes we could take and identify the weakest points in their security. We'll need a diversion, something big enough to draw their resources away."

The group starts to brainstorm, throwing out ideas and shooting them down just as quickly. To my surprise, it's Marcus who is determined to do whatever it takes to rescue Arden. She must have really grown on him.

"Ziva," Myall says softly. I look up, and the rest of the group falls silent on the line. "We need your expertise on this. Is it possible to create a device that could overload a NeuroMod? Something that would emotionally overload a large group?"

I hesitate. Overloading a NeuroMod is a gamble. It could kill the wearer. Could kill them all. But the risk isn't just about getting Arden back—it's about what we're willing to sacrifice.

"It's possible," I say. "But It would definitely be a risk to those wearing the devices."

"We'll figure that out later," Myall says, but we all know he's already considering how to get around the problem of overloading a device without killing the wearer. "For now, we need to prepare and gather the resources. Ziva, can you start working on the device?"

"Yeah," I say. "I'll need some old NeuroMods, and a lot of wiring."

Marcus offers to help find the supplies I'll need. They sound more determined now, as if having a plan—no matter how tenuous—has given them something to hold onto.

"Lie low and stay safe everyone," Myall says, ending the call.

The communicator goes dark, and the room feels colder, like a weight has settled in the air. I stand to leave, but Myall blocks the doorway.

"Ziva," he says, and this time I let him continue. "I'm sorry. I never wanted to put you in this position."

I know he means more than just the rebellion, more than just Arden. He means us, the thing growing between us that neither of us can afford to acknowledge.

He steps aside, and I walk out into the cold night air. The stars are hidden behind a blanket of clouds, and the city hums with its usual, dispassionate rhythm. I pull my jacket tighter around me and start to make my way home, but then I stop.

I can't go back to my empty unit, not after tonight. I turn and head towards the old workshop we found last week, near our new base of operations. If I'm going to save Arden, if we're going to have any chance at all, I need to start now.

Chapter Thirty

Ziva

The door to the workshop creaks as I push it open. The sharp, familiar scent of metal and oil hits me, grounding me in a way the cold night air never could. I breathe it in deeply, flicking on a small lamp, its warm glow casting long shadows on the walls. The workbench is cluttered with parts and schematics, a chaotic mess that only I can navigate.

Sitting, my eyes fix on the pile of old NeuroMods, the cold metal seeming to mock me. I remember how simple it was, back when I first tinkered with them—just a twist of a dial, a quick adjustment. Now, it feels much messier.

My hands move on their own, disassembling the device with practiced ease. I need to create something that works like an emotional bomb, something that will overload the

Enforcers long enough to create a distraction. The irony isn't lost on me; I'm building a device to simulate the very thing we're fighting for.

Hours pass, and I lose myself in the work. The tightness in my chest eases slightly as I focus on each wire, each resistor. Working on NeuroMods is the only time I ever feel in control.

A soft knock on the door pulls me from my trance. I turn to see Myall standing in the doorway, his silhouette backlit by the corridor's harsh lighting.

"I thought you'd gone home," he says, stepping inside.

"I needed to get started," I wipe my hands on a rag, avoiding his gaze as I speak. "What are you doing here?"

He holds up a small nutrient bar. "Food. You never remember to eat when your working."

I hadn't realized how hungry I was until he mentioned it. Myall sets the nutrient bar on the workbench, the gesture alone makes my stomach growl.

"Thanks," I say, though I'm not sure if I should take it, I have too much to do tonight.

"Eat," he pulls up a stool beside me, his tone brokering no argument.

I take the nutrient bar off the counter and take small bites. We sit in silence for a while, the tension between us thick, but not unbearable.

"How's it coming?" he asks, nodding towards the device in my hands.

"Slow without all the equipment from the tech lab," I say. "But I think it's doable."

He watches me work for a moment, and I can feel his thoughts weighing heavy. He wants to say something, and I brace myself for whatever it is.

"I meant what I said earlier," he starts. "About being sorry. I didn't expect things to go south this quickly."

I set the NeuroMod down with a sharp exhale. "What did you expect, Myall?" I can barely hold back the frustration in my voice. "A nice, easy rebellion? We knew the risks and we took them anyway, and now Arden is in danger."

He runs a hand through his hair, sighing. "I know. And I understand now why you pushed to put the idea of 'us' on hold. What's happening to Arden makes my stomach turn. The thought of losing you…it's unbearable, Ziva."

"I know," I say, fiddling with a lose wire to avoid his gaze. "I sometimes question whether we made the right call, in choosing this fight. But then I remember that we could never truly be together, not with The Authority in charge."

There are moments when I question everything we've done—the lives we've risked, the choices we've made. But then I remember—it's not about our comfort, it's about freedom. I think of our parents, of the sacrifices they made for a chance to save us from The Authority. If they were willing to sacrifice the possibility of never seeing their children again, then I can sacrifice my feelings for Myall. So why is it that I'm still so afraid to act?

Myall nods, and the tension in his shoulders seems to ease a fraction. "You're right. I just…I don't know how to let you walk into danger."

"We'll figure it out," I say, though I'm not sure how.

An hour later, Myall and I meet the others in the storage room of the old factory. The tension in the air is palpable, and I'm not sure whether to feel relieved or more anxious.

"It must have been Khynan," Jorel says the moment we enter the storage room, and my stomach twists. "He was the one Arden was going to meet. He must have turned her in."

I look at Myall. His eyes are stormy, the kind of unsettled that can break either way—toward action or despair. I think he knew, or at least, suspected, that it was Khynan.

"Why?" Tariq's voice cuts through the murmur. "Why would he do that? He said he believed in our cause, that he wanted to join us."

I clench my fists, the anger in the room is contagious. We're all thinking the same thing—If Khynan could betray us so easily, who else might fold under pressure? Who else isn't as committed as we thought?

"Enough," Myall says, and the room falls into a sullen silence. "We don't know the whole story."

I can't hold it in. "The story is simple. He sold her out to save his own skin. Cowardice is a pretty straightforward plotline."

Myall's eyes flick to me, and I see the hurt there. Not just for Arden, but for Khynan, for a young boy who was scared. "Ziva," he says, but I'm not done.

"We thought he believed in what we're doing. We thought he could be one of us. How many more like him are going to turn us over to The Authority rather than risk their necks for a chance at freedom?"

Restlessness consumes me. I can't stay still, not with this rage simmering under my skin. "We can't just sit here and hope the Enforcers don't come knocking. We need to get her out, Myall."

"Ziva," Myall says again, more firmly this time. "We will. But rushing in without a plan will just get us all captured—or worse."

I stop and look at him, he's right, of course. He's always the rational one, the strategist. But rational doesn't cut it for me right now. Rational feels like giving up.

"She knew the risks," someone mutters, and I can't even tell who.

I turn to the door. I can't take the defeat in their voices, the resignation seeping into every word they say. Their faces, drawn with exhaustion and fear, blur in front of me. These are the people who are supposed to fight beside me, but right now, they look like they're ready to surrender.

It's a weight in my chest, something cold and heavy, pressing me down. I can feel my own pulse in my temples, the heat of anger surging through me, raw and unfiltered. Every breath tastes bitter, like dust and desperation.

I can't just sit here. I can't let this be the end.

"Where are you going?" Myall asks.

"To finish the device," I say. "It's the only thing that might give us a chance."

I leave before he can say anything else, before he can temper my anger with his reason. I walk quickly back towards the workshop, my shoulders braced against the cool night air.

We thought we were so clever, so prepared. We thought our cause was enough to inspire unshakable loyalty. But one boy's fear has undone us, and now the cracks in our rebellion are starting to show, and we've barely even begun.

Arden's the last person who deserves to be sitting in a Harmonization cell, waiting for the NeuroMods to drain her of everything that makes her *Arden*. Waiting for us to rescue her—or not.

The heat of my anger cools, replaced by a sharper, more determined focus. This isn't just about us anymore—it's about proving we can win.

We have to save her, not just because she's one of us, but because if we can't save Arden, then we can't save anyone. And if we can't save anyone, what's the point of all this?

I close the workshop door behind me with a soft click and exhale. The familiar clink of metal against metal echoes in the room as I set to work, each motion fluid, automatic. My hands move, steady despite the turmoil inside me.

This is the only place where I don't feel like I'm drowning.

The device feels cold against my skin as I turn it over in my hands. It's a brilliant piece of work, if I do say so myself. The kind of brilliance that could change everything—if it works.

Gently, I set it down—like it's made of glass and start to tinker. Every twist of a screwdriver, every spark of a soldering iron, is a small act of rebellion. A way to channel my anger into something useful. I promised him I'd keep fighting, but fighting isn't enough. We need to start *winning*.

I'm nearly done, when I hear the door creak open. Myall stands in the doorway, his face a flood of conflicting emotions. He steps in and closes the door behind him.

"Ziva," he says, and I brace for whatever comes next. "We have a plan."

I let out a deep breath. "Good," I say, though a part of me is still prepared to go in alone if I have to.

He walks over and looks at the device in my hands. "Is it ready?"

I nod. "It'll work. At least, it has to."

He reaches out and touches my hand, the contact startling

in its tenderness.

"We will get her back," he says, and I believe him—or at least, I believe he believes it. Right now, that's enough.

"Tell me the plan," I say, and he does.

As he speaks, the anger inside me begins to cool, settling into something stronger—more durable. A quiet resolve. A flicker of hope. We're not as broken as I thought. The cracks are there, but they're not fissures. For now, that's enough.

Chapter Thirty One

Ziva

A few days later, we meet in the storage room of the decrepit factory. The only light comes from a flickering bulb overhead, casting sharp shadows across the piles of forgotten equipment.

The floor is covered in dust, settled over years of neglect, while the table in the center looks untouched—except for the hand-drawn map spread across it. The edges are frayed, dotted with red-pen annotations.

Myall points to a large building at the map's center. "This is The Authority's detention center in New Eden."

He taps the map again, but this time his hand lingers, his finger trembling just slightly, as if even he's unsure of what's next. The rest of us lean in to get a closer look.

There are seven of us—Myall, Marcus, me, and the four others. Each of them looks worn but resolute, their faces a gallery of suppressed emotions. We've been meeting like this for days, ever since Arden was taken during the raid. Every session has ended in frustration, until now.

"The main entrance is too heavily guarded," Liora says, her scowl deepening as she crosses her arms. "We'd never make it past the checkpoints—"

"We're not going through the main entrance," Myall says, cutting her off. "We're going in through the maintenance tunnels."

Jarek, a stocky man with nervous eyes, asks, "Are you sure they're not monitored?"

Myall nods. "The Authority doesn't have the manpower to watch them all. We have a map of the tunnels and a key to the maintenance hatches thanks to Jorel. Once we're inside, it's a straight shot to the building's sub-basement."

My stomach tightens as I trace the route on the map again, fingers grazing the frayed edges. We agreed to only use non-digitized maps and schematics, in an effort to minimize the chance of our plans being discovered. The problem with non-digitized maps, is that they're outdated. The uneasy thought lingers.

"What about once we're inside?" I ask. "The building will be crawling with Enforcers."

"We create a diversion," Myall says. "Something big enough to impact anyone else in the building."

"Like what?" Liora asks, skepticism heavy in her voice.

"Like an emotional overload," says Myall. The room goes silent. "From the device Ziva's been working on," he adds. "We set it off in the lobby, and if it goes right, the emotional overload should knock out everyone in the building."

I glance at Myall. Given that there is no way to test this

plan, we have no guarantee the device I've designed will function the way we'd hope. It's a clever idea, but the kind of thing that can easily go wrong. The others exchange looks, weighing the new information.

"While they're all knocked out, or dealing with our diversion, that's when we'll go up and get Arden," Myall continues. "We'll have fake access card's and uniforms to blend in."

He looks at me, and I know what he's going to say next. "Ziva and I will lead the extraction team."

"Why you?" Jarek asks, not bothering to hide his suspicion.

"Because we're the leaders of this rebellion," Myall says. "And because we're the ones who got the uniforms."

I don't bring up the fact that Grandma Elara was the one who obtained the uniforms. She had kept all of the resources from our parents' involvement in the resistance, neatly stored away in her attic.

The room is quiet for a moment, then Marcus speaks. "It's a good plan," he says, and I'm almost surprised to hear him concede. "But if it goes wrong—"

"It won't," Myall interrupts. "This is our best shot. We have to believe it will work."

One by one, the others nod. It's a reluctant agreement, but it's enough. We disband with instructions to gather supplies and prepare for the infiltration. As the others file out, I stay behind.

"Myall," I say. He stops and turns to me. "I don't even know if the device can work the way you just described. At least, not to that extent."

"I know," he says softly.

I walk over to the map and run my fingers along the route again. "It's a solid plan," I say, "but it relies on too many variables. If even one thing goes wrong—"

"We'll adapt," he says, stepping closer. "The plan will work."

"Will it?" I ask, looking up at him.

He doesn't answer right away, and I can see the conflict in his eyes. "Ziva," he says finally, "if you don't want to do this—"

"I want to," I interrupt. "She'd do the same for us."

When Myall takes my hand, his fingers are warm, but his grip trembles—just enough to mirror the uncertainty in his eyes. I squeeze back, trying to reassure him, but inside, the same nervous knot twists deeper.

"We will get her back," he says softly.

I squeeze his hand again. "I know."

We stand like that for a moment, holding on to the fragile thing we've built. Then he pulls me into an embrace, and I let him. His arms are strong and sure, and for a brief moment, I feel safe.

When he pulls back, he looks into my eyes, searching for something. "Ziva," he says, and his voice is softer now, almost pleading. "I need you to be careful tomorrow."

I nod, but we both know that caution won't be enough to save us if things go wrong.

Myall leans in, his breath warm against my lips. His kiss is soft at first, testing, before it deepens—a slow, deliberate promise. It's more than a kiss. It's an unspoken vow, a plea wrapped in a moment we know might be our last.

When our lips part, I can still feel the heat of his touch. We're silent, knowing that anything we say now would only dilute the moment. He gives my hand one last squeeze, then turns and walks out the door.

I watch him walk away, the echoes of his footsteps too

loud in the silence that follows. My lips still tingle from his kiss, but it's the quiet, gnawing doubt that lingers longer. I know what we're up against, and part of me wonders if this fragile plan, this hope, is enough to save Arden. Or if it will crumble before we even get close.

I glance at the map one last time before rolling it up and tucking it under my arm. We have twenty-four hours. It's not enough, but it's all we've got.

Chapter Thirty Two

Ziva

My heart pounds as I slip through the rusted factory door, its jagged edges scraping my skin. The creak of the hinges echoes too loudly, making my nerves jump like they're about to snap.

I rub my bleary eyes, exhaustion dragging at me after a restless night. Each time I tried to sleep, my mind replayed visions of the plan falling apart. What if we're caught? What if Arden's already been recalibrated? The doubts gnaw at me, but I can't afford to let them take hold.

"You made it," Myall's low voice cuts through the gloom. His usual warmth replaced by sharp focus as he scans me from head to toe, noting the dark clothing and steel-toed boots before nodding in approval.

"Wouldn't miss it," I quip, masking my anxiety with sarcasm, the way Arden would. "Nothing like spending my day off planning a jailbreak."

Myall's lips twitch, but the smile doesn't reach his eyes. "Let's hope it's worth the overtime."

We head to the storage room, the faint hum of machinery and the rustle of movement inside the only sounds in the abandoned factory. A small window, coated in grime and located high up on the wall, provides the only source of natural light in the room.

Marcus hunches over a makeshift workbench, fiddling with communication devices. His forehead is creased in concentration, reminding me how crucial his role is, even if he can't join us in the field.

"Everything set?" I ask, scanning the room. Liora's figure looms by a stack of freshly folded uniforms, the smell of fabric softener cutting through the air.

She gestures to the pile, each one meticulously pressed, its fabric stiff and dark blue. "Elara came through. These should get us past the first checkpoint without a second glance."

Tariq hefts a small, dark duffel bag. "Got the maintenance tunnel key in here. Jorel's sure it'll work?"

"It has to," I mutter, more to myself than anyone else. I glance at Jorel, who is preoccupied with Marcus as he connects our earpieces.

As the others continue preparations, I catch Myall's eye. He moves closer, his voice low, meant only for my ears. "You okay? You look like you haven't slept."

My heart is racing, but not just from the mission. It's the thought that I might never have the courage to tell him how I feel. How, what began as a confusing mess of feelings, has slowly evolved, to the point that I cannot bear the idea of anything happening to him. Ever since Arden was captured, the idea of losing Myall has been plaguing my mind. The thought of everything that might go wrong today, kept me up all night.

"I...I'm worried," I admit. "There's so much that could go wrong."

Myall's hand finds mine, his thumb rubbing over my knuckles like it always does. "We've planned for every contingency. We'll get Arden out."

Or die trying.

I squeeze his hand, drawing strength from his touch, letting the simple connection steady me. But as I look around at our ragtag group—friends turned rebels—it feels like after today, nothing will ever be the same.

Jorel steps forward, his face set with determination as he hands us each an earpiece. "Alright, people. Let's get this over with."

Marcus assures us that he will keep an eye on all the surveillance feeds we still have access to from Arden, and wishes us luck. I'm too afraid to say a proper goodbye, I don't want it to be our last one. Besides, I know I need to remain strong for the others.

We weave through the factory, dodging piles of broken machinery until we reach the door to the alleyway. Jorel leads us to the closest maintenance hatch in the far corner of the alley, gesturing for us to follow. He pulls a set of keys from the duffle bag Jarek hands him, and unlocks the hatch, revealing a narrow passageway illuminated by dim overhead lights.

We file into the maintenance tunnels, the stale air hitting my nostrils as Jorel seals the entrance behind us. The dim emergency lighting casts long shadows, turning familiar faces into ghostly apparitions.

"Watch your step," Jorel warns, as we squeeze through the narrow tunnel. "And keep your eyes peeled for cameras. I've mapped most of them, but The Authority's been adding new ones since Colvin's crackdowns began."

The walls close in, damp and cold, and each step echoes through the tunnel. I trail close behind him, my nerves alive with every sound.

"How often do other maintenance workers come down here?" I ask, scanning the murky corners.

Jorel shakes his head, his dark curls bouncing. "Not often, but we can't risk getting comfortable." His voice is low, laced with caution. "There's a junction up ahead where we'll need to be extra careful of the cameras."

As we approach the junction, Jorel holds up a hand, signaling us to stop. He peers around the corner, then motions us forward. "Clear for now, but move quickly."

My heart races, breath catching as we hurry across the exposed area. I can't shake the image forming in my mind of alarms blaring and guards swarming toward us. But we make it through undetected.

After what feels like hours of tense silence, Jorel finally pauses. A rusted hatch looms before us, identical to the one we entered.

"This is it," he whispers. "The sub-basement access."

He pulls out the key, his hands steady. It slides into the old fashioned lock, and for a heart-stopping moment, nothing happens. Then, with a soft click, the hatch unlocks. Jorel eases it open, revealing the dark expanse of the detention center's sub-basement beyond.

As we prepare to enter, I take a deep breath to steady

my racing nerves. There's no turning back now. Whatever happens next, we're committed to seeing this through.

Emerging from the hatch last, my eyes adjusting to the dim light of the sub-basement. The air is thick with the scent of mildew and rust. Pipes snake along the low ceiling, their steady drip punctuating the stillness.

"Everyone okay?" Myall whispers, his eyes scanning our faces, lingering a moment too long on mine.

His hand brushes my arm, a silent reassurance lost in the damp air of the sub-basement. Somewhere deep in the walls, the faint hum of machinery makes the silence unbearable.

I nod, swallowing hard. We're deep in enemy territory now, and if we're caught, we're done for.

Liora's voice trembles slightly. "It's so…empty." Her words float in the stagnant air, and for a moment, the emptiness seems to swallow us whole.

"That's good," Jarek mutters. "Empty means no guards."

We gather in a tight circle, our breaths mingling in the stale air. I can feel the tension radiating from each of us, a palpable force in this confined space.

"Ziva," Myall says, his tone steady despite the tension in the room. "You ready?"

I pat the pocket where my homemade device rests. "Don't really have much of a choice."

He nods, then addresses the group. "Alright, Ziva and I are heading to the lobby. The rest of you, stay put and keep comm silence unless absolutely necessary."

As we prepare to leave, Tariq grabs my arm, pulling at the stiff fabric of my maintenance uniform. "Be careful up there," he whispers, his coffee-colored eyes wide with concern.

Managing a smirk, I try to project more confidence than I

feel. "We will."

Myall and I move towards the stairwell, our footsteps echoing softly in the dampness of the sub-basement's cement walls. As we climb, it feels like I'm leaving part of myself behind with the others. While Myall and I work on planting the device in the lobby, I know my mind will be split between the task at hand and worrying about the safety of the others.

"You okay?" Myall asks, his voice low yet still carrying in the cramped stairwell.

I nod, not trusting myself to speak. My mind lingers with all the ways this could go wrong, all the lives at stake if we fail.

After climbing up three flights of stairs, we finally reach a door with a small sign that reads 'ground floor'. We come to a stop, knowing that once we open this door, there's no going back.

Reaching for the metal door, I pause, my hand on the handle. "Myall," I whisper, "if this all goes horribly wrong…"

I've never told him how much he means to me—how much I rely on him. That I need him. Want him. Now, when I need the words most, they won't come.

He places his hand over mine, his touch warm and reassuring. "It won't. You've got this, Ziva."

"Right," I murmur, steeling myself. "Let's make this count."

Chapter Thirty Three

Ziva

We slip into the lobby, the door clicking shut behind us. The space is stark, the white walls and polished floors reflecting the harsh lighting. My pulse quickens as I grab for my earpiece, a knot forming in my chest. "Marcus, status?"

His voice crackles through, tense but steady. "All clear, Ziva. No unexpected movement detected on any of the security feeds outside."

Scanning the lobby, I count the bystanders who might become collateral. I nod to Myall, my fingers trembling as I pull out the device. It's small, innocuous-looking, but loaded with potential. The culmination of countless hours of work and if done incorrectly, could result in the death of anyone wearing a NeuroMod within this building, potentially even on the street outside.

"Here goes everything," I mutter, strolling in a casual pace towards the center of the lobby, my boots echoing off the polished floors.

I focus on the floor, aware of the cameras that might trigger an alarm. With a deep breath, I strategically position myself near the main entrance, hidden in plain sight beside a cluster of artificial potted plants.

Myall takes position by the glass doors, ready for any surprises. His eyes meet mine, a silent encouragement passing between us from across the lobby.

I activate the device, and for a moment, nothing happens. Then, a soft whir emits, followed by a wave of energy that pulses outward, invisible to the untrained eye but I can feel it passing through my body. The device vibrates in my hand, and I grit my teeth against the rising panic.

Suddenly, the atmosphere shifts. People passing by slow their steps, their expressions changing subtly. A woman glances up from her datapad, her brow furrowed in confusion. A man talking on his communicator frowns and raises a hand to his chest.

"It's working," Myall murmurs, his voice lost in the lobby's hum.

Around us, we hear thuds and crashes as people collapse.

Light-headedness envelopes me, and I'm not sure if it's from the fear that I may have caused harm to all these individuals, or a reaction from holding onto the device so tightly in my hand.

"Ziva! Are you alright?" Myall's strong arms steady me.

Breathless, I nod. "I'm fine. Just a little lightheaded."

He helps me pry the device from my grip, my fingers relaxing instantly, then touches his earpiece. "Marcus, confirm status."

"Confirmed," comes Marcus' reply. "All NeuroMods in the building have overloaded. You did it, Ziva."

Relief washes over me, so potent it nearly brings me to my knees again. Myall squeezes my hand.

"I'll tell the others," he says softly as he activates his comm. "It's safe. Join us in the lobby. Jorel, stay put and keep our exit clear."

"You got it," Jorel replies.

As we wait for the others, Marcus confirms the feedback loop he created, through a backdoor in the Sentinel system, is reporting no inaccuracies to the NeuroMods we just overloaded. As long as we don't trigger any other alarms in the building, our break-in will go unnoticed.

"We actually did it," I whisper, a smile breaking across my face as I meet Myall's gaze.

He smiles back, a rare, genuine expression that makes my heart skip. "No, Ziva. *You* did it."

The sound of approaching footsteps breaks the moment, and we turn to face our approaching teammates, ready for the next phase of our plan.

Once we're all assembled, I lead our group through the eerily silent corridors. The sprawled bodies of unconscious guards litter our path, a testament to the power of my device. I try not to look at their faces as we step over them, but I can't help feeling a twinge of guilt. Were the employees here by choice, or were they merely pawns controlled by The Authority?

At least they're still breathing.

"Keep an eye out," I whisper to the others, my voice barely audible above the rapid beating of my heart. "We don't know how long they'll be out."

Myall nods, his eyes scanning our surroundings. "Which way, Ziva?"

I consult the mental map I've constructed of the detention center. "Left here, then two rights."

We move swiftly, our footsteps echoing in the empty hallways. The sterile white walls seem to close in on us and every corner we turn makes the place feel like one giant maze.

As we round the final corner, my heart sinks. A massive security door blocks our path, standing at least 10 feet tall. Its surface made of sturdy metal and dotted with buttons and a numeric keypad. The control panel glows a pulsating red, warning anyone who dares to try and tamper with it.

"Shit," Jarek hisses. "Now what?"

I step forward, my mind running through the options as I assess the locking mechanism.

Fortunately, it appears to be a numerical access code, which is convenient, because they are easier to hack than biometric scanners. It also means less wires to pick from.

"I've got this." I mutter.

As the others form a protective circle around me, I approach the panel and pry open the circuitry. My fingers trail over the wires, searching for one in particular.

"Come on," I mutter, frustration building as the seconds tick by.

I find the right wire, and a grin spreads across my face. Pulling a pair of pliers from my pocket, I isolate the wire, and cut. The access panel emits a faint click that's barely audible.

"We're in," I announce, triumphant as the heavy door

swings open with a soft hiss.

Myall's hand rests on my shoulder, grounding me. "You never cease to amaze me, Ziva."

I turn to face him, our eyes locking and my chest becoming tight. For a moment, the world falls away, and it's just us. Then reality crashes back in.

"Let's go," I say, tearing my gaze from his. "Arden's waiting."

As we step through the doorway, the holding cells stretch ahead, their steel doors echoing with a grim finality. My eyes dart from door to door, searching desperately for any sign of Arden.

The flickering lights cast long shadows across the cells, turning the place into a maze of metal and despair. Each cell contains a metal door with a small window. A quick glance through one of the window's shows only a narrow bunk bed and a small toilet— the absolute bare minimum.

Suddenly, a flash of red at a door catches my attention. "There!" I whisper urgently, pointing to a cell at the far end.

We rush forward, and I freeze when I see Arden's face pressed against the small window. She looks up, her eyes wide with recognition.

"Ziva! Myall!" she calls out, her voice muffled, but unmistakable.

As I gaze beyond Arden further into the cell, I notice another figure behind her—an older woman with wavy blonde hair and glasses. She stands against the far wall, her shoulders hunched slightly. Something about her seems oddly familiar, but I push the thought aside, focusing on the sight of Arden.

"Stand back," I warn, already working on bypassing the lock. My fingers wrench open the access panel, fueled by adrenaline and determination. I find the wire that I need. "Almost there…"

With a satisfying click, the door swings open. Arden bursts out, throwing her arms around me in a tight embrace. I hug her back, relief washing over me in waves.

"I knew you'd come for me," she whispers as she holds onto me tightly, her voice thick. She trembles in my arms, but it's hard to tell whether it's from the thrill of seeing us or as a resut of what she's been through. I run my hand down the length of her curls, offering what comfort I can.

As we pull apart, Myall embraces Arden in a bear hug. "Glad to have you back, troublemaker," he says, his usual calm tone carrying an unexpected warmth as he wraps an arm around her waist.

The older woman emerges from the cell, her posture rigid and uncertain. Arden turns to her, then back to us, her expression suddenly serious.

"Umm…this is Dr. Elena Vance," she announces, and my blood runs cold as I gaze at the woman. "She has crucial information about The Authority. We need to bring her with us."

I exchange a shocked glance with Myall, my mind spinning. Dr. Vance—the architect of the very system we oppose— here, in front of us.

"Are you insane?" I hiss, struggling to keep my voice low as I cast a quick glance at the older woman. My muscles instantly tighten at the sight of her. "She's the enemy, Arden!"

Dr. Vance steps forward, her blue eyes pleading. "I understand your hesitation, but please, hear me out. What I've learned…it changes everything."

Myall adjusts his earpiece. "Marcus, please tell me you're

getting this." He listens for a moment. "Yeah, I know. It's a huge fucking risk."

I watch Dr. Vance as she takes in the sight of Myall and me. My thoughts are a chaotic whirlwind. Can we trust her? Why is she a prisoner in our city? Is this a trap? But the desperation in her eyes—it seems genuine.

"We don't have time for this," Jarek interrupts, his voice tense. "We need to move. Now. Let's just bring her with us."

I take a deep breath, the gravity of the situation sinking in. "Fine," I say finally, locking eyes with Dr. Vance. "But one wrong move, and you'll wish we'd left you here. Understood?"

She nods solemnly. "Perfectly."

As we turn to leave, Arden's hand finds mine, squeezing it tight. Despite the unexpected complication, I can't help but feel a surge of triumph. We did it. We got her back.

Now we just have to make it out alive.

Taking point, I lead our ragtag group back through the maze of white corridors. My eyes dart from corner to corner, hyperaware of every sound, every movement.

"Left here," I whisper, gesturing to a narrow hallway. "We're almost back to the lobby."

As we round the last corner, a groan echoes from behind us, making my blood run cold.

"They're waking up," Myall hisses, his voice tight with tension.

Fuck.

Spinning around, I see the first stirrings of movement from the unconscious guards we'd passed earlier, his fingers twitching against the white marble floor.

"Run!" I command, abandoning all pretense of stealth.

We sprint down the corridor, our feet slapping the polished floor. I hear Arden's labored breathing behind me, and the uneven shuffle of Dr. Vance's footsteps.

"Ziva," Marcus's voice crackles in my ear. "You've got company headed your way. North corridor."

"Understood," I pant, desperately glancing about the hallway for a solution. "Everyone, in here!" I yank open a maintenance closet, ushering the group inside.

We huddle in the darkness, our bodies pressed tight together. Arden trembles against me, and I wrap an arm around her, trying to soothe her. I lean against a shelf and feel something hard pressing into my lower back, but I don't dare move.

"What now?" Liora whispers, her voice barely audible as someone—likely Arden—whimpers.

Closing my eyes, I force myself to think. We're so close. I can't let us fail now.

"The ventilation system," I murmur, an idea forming as I recall the near invisible grate along the wall of the hallway. "It connects to the sub-basement. It'll be tight, but—"

"It's our only shot of getting out of here," Myall finishes grimly. It's too dark to see him in the storage closet, but I know he must be frowning. His eyebrows, usually so dark and smooth, will be furrowed with concern.

Myall cautiously peeks out of the closet, making sure no one is nearby. Once he's confident the coast is clear, he opens the door wider for us to quietly exit into the hallway.

We emerge from the closet, and I begin working on prying open the closest vent cover.

One by one, we squeeze into the cramped ventilation shaft and follow Marcus's instructions through our earpieces to make our way back down to the sub-basement. Every muscle in my body is tense with fear as I crawl through the narrow ventilation shaft.

Jorel's anxiety is palpable as I crawl out of the ventilation shaft. He grips a broken pipe, ready for anything. His shoulders slump when he sees that it's us coming out of the shaft, and throws his pipe to the ground with a loud clang that makes me wince.

We quickly and quietly return to the maintenance hatch and Jorel leads us back through the tunnels towards the factory, taking care not to make any noise or draw attention to ourselves. Arden and Dr. Vance don't question our directions and simply follow us through the winding tunnels, placing their trust in us to guide them to safety.

* * *

The storage room erupts in a cacophony of cheers and laughter as we burst through the door. Upon seeing all of us, Marcus visibly lets out a sigh of relief. He quickly removes his earpiece and tosses it onto the workbench in front of him. The adrenaline still buzzes in my veins, making my hands shake as I pull Arden into a tight embrace.

"We did it," I breathe into her hair, hardly believing the words myself. "We actually fucking did it."

I can feel the adrenaline fading, but there's no easing of the pressure in my chest. Arden's safe, we've pulled this off, but Myall….he's not just a partner in this rebellion. He's something more, and I've never told him. What if something happens and I never get the chance to tell him how I really feel?

Myall's deep voice slices through the celebration, and he steps forward, his eyes locking onto Dr. Vance. "We're not out of the woods yet," Myall says, his tone cutting through the tension.

The doctor stands apart from our group, her pristine lab coat now wrinkled and smudged with dust. Her blue eyes dart nervously, her posture stiff, like a trapped animal.

"You're right," I say, reluctantly releasing Arden. My fingers twitch with the urge to hold on, but I let go, turning to face Dr. Vance.

Myall steps forward, his eyes weary as he faces Dr. Vance. "It's time for you to prove you can be trusted, doctor. Why should we believe you're not here to betray us to The Authority?"

Dr. Vance straightens, pushing her glasses up her nose and squaring her shoulders.

"I understand your suspicion," she says, her voice calm but with an undercurrent of tension. "But I assure you, my presence here is not what you think."

I can't help but scoff. "Really? Because from where I'm standing, it looks like we just invited the wolf into our den."

"Ziva," Arden interjects as she places a hand on my forearm in warning. "She helped me. She's not what we thought."

I want to trust Arden, but the gnawing fear of what Dr. Vance represents—of everything she's been a part of—twists in my gut.

Dr. Vance takes a deep breath. Her blue eyes flicker—not with the confidence I expected, but with something that resembles regret. She straightens, pushing her glasses up once more.

"I've been blind for too long," she says, her clinical tone

faltering. "The work I've done…I thought I was helping people. But I've seen the truth now, and I want to make it right."

Myall's eyes narrow. "Pretty words, doctor. But we need more than that. What can you offer us that's worth the risk of harboring you?"

I watch Dr. Vance closely, my heart pounding, my fists clenched so tightly my nails dig into my palms. Our entire rebellion hangs in the balance of her next words.

Chapter Thirty Four

Myall

The air in the abandoned factory is thick, cloying with the scent of rust and decay as we confront Dr. Vance. Ziva's eyes narrow, her fingers drumming against the side of her leg. Her jaw tightens, like she's holding herself back from charging forward, fingers twitching near the pliers in her pocket, every muscle on alert.

Jarek's breath brushes against my neck, hot and unsettling. His proximity sends a ripple of unease down my spine. I have to take control before his temper explodes.

"Pretty words, doctor. But we need more than that. What can you offer us that's worth the risk of harboring you?" I demand. "Give us one good reason not to turn you back over to The Authority right now."

Dr. Vance's blue eyes lock onto mine. There's no hesitation in them, no softness—just cold, clinical assessment. Her gaze doesn't waver, but I notice the tightness in her throat, as if she's swallowing something she doesn't want to say.

"Because I created the very thing that's oppressing us all," she says, her voice steady but tinged with regret. "And I want to make it right."

Is this be the break we've been waiting for, or just another trap? What if she's working for Colvin?

"Explain," Ziva snaps, taking a step towards Dr. Vance, her anger barely masking her curiosity.

Dr. Vance takes a deep breath, her slender shoulders rising and falling with the motion. "The NeuroMods weren't meant to control emotions. They were designed to help people understand and manage their feelings." Her hands tremble slightly as she adjusts her glasses. "I wanted to cure depression, anxiety, PTSD. But The Authority saw potential for something far more sinister."

I clench my fists at my sides, fighting the urge to lash out. How many lives have been destroyed because of her creation? But I force myself to take a deep breath, and listen.

The rest of the group stands behind us in tense silence for Dr. Vance to continue.

"They threatened my family, my colleagues. Said they'd 'disappear' if I didn't cooperate." Dr. Vance's voice cracks as she gazes at the concrete floor. "I thought I could work from the inside, find a way to sabotage the project. But they were always one step ahead."

Arden steps forward, her lip trembling slightly. "It's true," she says softly. "When they captured me, I saw firsthand how they treated her. She was as much a prisoner as I was."

Jarek's voice drops to a low growl, his shoulders tense, his fists balling at his sides, but he doesn't move. "Why was she even in that detention center then? She's not from our city." The question cuts through the air, sharp and unforgiving.

Dr. Vance visibly shrinks, hunching her shoulders inward.

"Colvin brought her here for a reason," Arden snaps back.

What possible reason would Colvin have for needing Dr. Vance in our city?

Dr. Vance acknowledges with a slight nod, whispering, "Regent Colvin had me moved from the detention center in Elysium to here because he said he needed my assistance in implementing a new version of NeuroMods throughout your city."

Ziva's face pales slightly as she asks, "What are you saying?"

Dr. Vance runs her hands up and down her arms, as if trying to comfort herself. "The Authority wanted to use this city as a test case for their new version of NeuroMods. They've been developing it for years and they thought it would help quell the unrest in your city. You were all just supposed to be part of the experiment, and I was brought here to oversee it."

Nausea churns in my stomach, and I can feel bile rising in my throat. A swift glance at Ziva confirms that she shares my disgust. I can hear Jarek muttering behind me, struggling to keep his temper under control. The rest of our group stands behind us in silence, but I can sense their discomfort as they shift and fidget.

I study Dr. Vance's angular face, searching for any sign of deception. "So how exactly can you help us take down The Authority?"

Her eyes flicker with a desperate light, as though I've offered her a thread of hope she's been starving for. Her hands ball into fists, like she's ready to fight for it.

"I know the weaknesses in the NeuroMod system. The backdoors, the fail-safes. With my knowledge and your resources, we could create a device to disrupt the entire network in this city."

Could this really be our chance, or am I about to make the same mistake I've always feared? If she betrays us, I'm not just putting myself in danger—I'm putting all of us at risk. Glancing at Ziva, I see my own conflicted emotions reflected in her eyes. She nods slightly, signaling for me to continue questioning Dr. Vance

Dr. Vance continues, her voice barely audible. "I can't undo the harm I've caused. But I can help you free everyone from the emotional prison I helped create. Please, let me try to make this right."

The weight of her words fills the space between us, thick and suffocating. It presses against my chest. The silence that follows is almost a physical thing, settling into the corners of the room like dust. I can feel it, heavy and choking, like we're all holding our breath, waiting for something to give.

The eyes of my fellow rebels are on me, waiting for my decision. Their eyes flicker between me and Dr. Vance, each of them trying to gauge where the conversation will go, what side they need to take.

I lean back against the rusted shelf, the rough metal digging into my back. My fingers trace it's grooves, thinking over Dr. Vance's proposition. Her story stirs a mixture of curiosity and a caution I can't shake.

"Dr. Vance," I say hesitantly, "you mentioned being manipulated by The Authority. Can you elaborate on that? What exactly drove you to collaborate with them in the first place?"

She meets my gaze, her blue eyes magnified behind her glasses. A flicker of pain crosses her face before she composes herself, crossing her arms across her chest.

"It wasn't a simple decision," she says, taking a deep breath. "When I first developed the NeuroMod technology, I truly believed it could help people manage their emotions in a healthy way. You see, mental health had been rapidly declining across the globe, and there wasn't enough access to healthcare providers. There were too many vulnerable people out there, with no understanding of their condition, or how to manage it. That's what the NeuroMods were supposed to be for. Took me years to develop a prototype, and when I applied to various government agencies for funding, The Authority approached me with promises of unlimited funding and resources to further my research."

My jaw sets into a hard line of anger. "And you didn't see through their facade?"

Dr. Vance sighs, her pristine facade crumbling as she rubs her face in exhaustion. "I was young and naive, perhaps willfully so. They persuaded me that if everyone wore a NeuroMod, it would solve the worlds mental health crisis. They painted a picture of a world free from emotional turmoil, where people could live in harmony. It was...very seductive."

Ziva scoffs from the corner, leaning against a pile of crates. "Seductive enough to ignore the loss of free will?"

"No," Dr. Vance says firmly as she glances between Ziva and me, seemingly realizing that we're the ones in charge. "That came later, gradually. By the time I realized the full extent of The Authority's plans, I was in too deep. They had my research, my prototypes—and they made it clear that my cooperation was no longer optional."

I push off from the shelf, pacing the small floor space in the room that isn't piled with crates or our supplies from the heist. My mind races, trying to reconcile her words with the suffering I've witnessed for so long.

"So you just went along with it? For how long?"

"Years," she admits, looking down at the floor once more, her voice barely above a whisper. "I told myself I was minimizing the damage, working on safeguards. But in reality, I was trapped in a prison of my own making."

The tension in the room is thick enough to cut with a knife. Marcus stands with his arms crossed, skepticism etched on his face. Arden looks torn, her recent experiences clearly influencing her perspective.

Liora, Jorell, and Tariq try to conceal their revulsion, but their quick glances at each other show they're just as disgusted as the rest of us. They may be better at hiding it, but they're not fooling anyone.

My pacing ceases as I turn to face Dr. Vance directly, doing my best to ignore the others in the room. "And now? Why should we believe your change of heart is genuine?"

She meets my gaze unflinchingly. "Because I've seen the true cost of my work. The broken families, the hollow shells of people. I can't undo what I've done, but I can try to make it right. And frankly, young man, I have nowhere else to go. The Authority wants me silenced, and you…you're my only hope for redemption."

Her words hang in the air. I want to trust her, but a nagging doubt tells me we might be walking into a trap.

I glance at Ziva, still dressed in her dark blue uniform, her gaze meeting mine. She gives me a look, as if to ask, 'Do you really believe this crap?'.

Dr. Vance's shoulders slump, her pristine facade crumbling. "You can't imagine the pressure," she says, her voice cracking. "Every day, I'd wake up knowing my work could save lives, or destroy them. Waking up not knowing if my family were safe or even alive. The Authority…they weren't just my employers. They were my jailers."

My chest twinges at the thought of not knowing if your family are safe. We all know that fear. Dr. Vance's piercing blue eyes, once so clinical, now shine with unshed tears.

"They threatened my family," she continues, wringing her hands. "My sister, her children…they made it clear that one misstep, one hint of disobedience, and they'd disappear. I was trapped. Every breakthrough felt like a new chain. I haven't heard from my family in years…I can only imagine what's happened to them."

My fists clench, knuckles whitening under the strain. Every part of me aches to reach out, to soothe her, but I can't—can't show any weakness now.

"But you still did it," I say, struggling to keep my voice from rising. "You kept developing the NeuroMods, knowing what they'd be used for."

Dr. Vance nods, her jaw tight. "I did. And that guilt…it eats at me every day. But I thought I could change things from the inside, make the technology less invasive, more humane. I created a new version of the device, one that doesn't dose the wearer in chemical suppressants. "

The room falls silent, wondering if there's any truth to this so called alternative device. Part of me wants to believe her, to see the woman behind the lab coat. But can I trust those instincts?

"It wasn't enough," she utters. "I realized too late that there's no 'humane' way to strip someone of their emotional autonomy. When I finally tried to sabotage the project, to leak information…that's when they turned on me."

My stomach tightens. This is it—the moment of truth.

"They came for me in the middle of the night," Dr. Vance continues, her words tumbling out in a rush. "Dragged me from my bed, threw me in a cell. They…they used my own creations against me. Do you know what it's like to have your emotions twisted, amplified, shut off at someone else's whim?"

I swallow hard, imagining the horror. Despite my reservations, I find myself taking a step closer to her.

"I'm sorry," I say softly, surprising myself. "No one should have to endure that."

Jarek scoffs from behind me as Dr. Vance looks up, her gaze meeting my own, hope flickering in her eyes. "I know I don't deserve your trust," she says. "But please, I'm asking for it nonetheless. Let me help. Let me try to undo some of the damage I've caused."

I hesitate, acutely aware of the weight of this decision. The fate of our rebellion, of countless lives, hangs in the balance. Can we afford to trust her? Can we afford not to?

When we extracted her from that cell, I don't think any of us truly considered the consequences of taking her with us. Or the extreme measures Colvin might take to retrieve her.

Arden steps forward, her green eyes, usually sparkling with mischief, are shadowed now. I swallow the lump forming in my throat as I take in the way she holds herself, slightly hunched, as if bracing for a blow.

"I can vouch for her," Arden says, her voice rough. "We

were in the same cell. She helped me stay sane when they tried to break me."

I lean in, torn between my desperate desire for more information and my fear of what it might reveal. "What happened?"

Arden's gaze flicks to Dr. Vance, then back to me. "At first, I thought she was just another Authority lackey. But…it didn't take me long to realize that she was a prisoner too. She helped me. Kept me sane when they were messing with my head, using those damn psychological torture techniques."

The memory clearly pains her. I fight the urge to reach out and comfort her, knowing she'd hate to appear weak in front of the others. Later, once we get through this, she'll need our help to overcome what she's been through. I don't know the first thing about helping someone through a traumatic event.

"Dr. Vance taught me how to resist," Arden continues softly, interupting my thoughts. "How to build mental defenses against their psychological manipulation. Without her, I might have broken. Might have given up everything about our rebellion."

Dr. Vance's gaze lingers on Arden before dropping to the floor. It's hard to reconcile the woman before me with the cold scientist I'd imagined.

Arden takes a deep, measured breath. "Look, I know it's a risk. But she wants to help us. And frankly, we need her expertise if we're going to have any chance of taking down The Authority."

The strain in Arden's face is unmistakable as she makes her case. Her hands tremble slightly, and there's a haunted look in her eyes that wasn't there before her capture. It's clear that trusting anyone associated with The Authority is difficult for her.

"She saved my life," Arden adds softly. "I think...I think she deserves a chance to save others, too."

My jaw tightens as Dr. Vance's confession and Arden's impassioned plea settle over me, a storm of emotions brewing inside. Anger bubbles up first—hot and fierce—at the thought of all the suffering Dr. Vance's work has caused. The NeuroMods, the very tools of our oppression, born from her mind.

"You created the instruments of our enslavement," I spit out, unable to keep the bitterness from my voice. Dr. Vance flinches and takes a step backwards, her eyes downcast.

But as quickly as the anger flares, a wave of disappointment crashes over me, making my shoulders slump. I'd hoped, foolishly perhaps, that she was different. That someone within The Authority had seen the truth and fought against it from the start.

"I...I understand your anger, young man," Dr. Vance says softly. "I've made terrible mistakes. But I want to make them right."

Her words stir something deep inside me—memories of my grandmother's stories, a time when people believed in second chances and redemption. Elara would've scolded me for my lack of empathy, urged me to show compassion to the woman standing before me.

Scanning the room, I gauge the others' reactions. Arden's eyes are imploring, but the others all appear unconvinced.

"We can't ignore the risk," Ziva finally speaks up as someone scuffs their boot across the concrete. "This could all be some elaborate trap—"

"It's not!" Arden cuts in, her voice sharp, rounding on Ziva. "I swear it."

"But how can we be sure?" Marcus counters. "The Authority's deception knows no bounds."

"My suggestion is to kick her out and leave this place behind and—." Jarek starts before Arden interrupts him.

"We can't just abandon her," Arden pushes back, her voice rising with the tension.

I watch Dr. Vance closely as the debate swirls around us. A part of me really wants to believe that she is on our side and wants to make things right. She can't change what she did in the past, but she does deserve the chance to redeem herself from her own actions.

"If we turn her away," I find myself saying, surprising even myself, "we lose a valuable asset. And we prove we're no better than The Authority—unwilling to see the humanity in those who've made mistakes."

The room goes still, the weight of my decision settling all around us. I know the others will respect my choice, even if they don't fully agree with it.

I draw in a shaky breath, feeling the weight of all eyes on me. Every muscle in my body locks up, the pressure of their eyes like an invisible hand on my chest, squeezing tighter with each passing second. I know I can't back down now. Not after everything that's been said, everything that's been lost.

"Dr. Vance's knowledge of the NeuroMods could be invaluable," I say, my voice growing steadier. "She knows their weaknesses, their inner workings. That kind of insight could turn the tide of our fight."

Ziva nods slowly, her hazel eyes thoughtful. "You're not

wrong, Myall. But can we trust her?"

I turn to Dr. Vance, studying her face. The lines around her eyes speak of years of worry, of guilt. "Dr. Vance," I say, as I turn to address her directly. "If we accept you, what exactly can you offer us?"

She straightens, a hint of her earlier confidence returning. "I can help you disable the NeuroMods by guiding you through the process of building a device that can shut down the mainframe," she says. "And I know the layout of The Authority's Compliance Monitoring Division here and in Elysium. I can guide you through their defenses and how to shut down the NeuroMod and Sentinel systems for good."

With that kind of information, we could strike at the very heart of The Authority.

"It's too dangerous," Marcus cuts in, uncrossing his arms. "She could be feeding us false information, leading us into a trap."

The tug-of-war inside me pulls hard—hope fighting suspicion, trust battling caution. "We'd need to verify everything she tells us," I admit slowly. "But if it checks out—"

Arden steps forward, her eyes blazing. "I've seen her suffer at the hands of The Authority," she says fiercely. "Trust me when I say she's not loyal to them anymore."

"This can't just be my decision. We need to vote," I say, gazing at each person in the room. "But before we do, I want to hear from everyone. What are your thoughts?"

As the others begin to voice their opinions, arguing the pros and cons of trusting the woman who helped create our emotional prison, I watch Dr. Vance. She stands quietly, her hands clasped tightly in front of her. I lock eyes with Dr. Vance, searching for any hint of deception. Her piercing blue eyes hold mine, unwavering as she waits for us to decide.

"Alright," I say, my voice cutting through the noise of the room. "We've heard everyone out. It's time to decide. This isn't just a decision for me—it's for all of us. Dr. Vance knows more about the NeuroMods than anyone. If we're going to defeat The Authority, we need her. But don't think for a second that I'm blind to the risk."

Ziva's sharp intake of breath is audible. "Myall, are you sure about this?" she asks, concern etched across her face as she meets my gaze.

I nod, though my stomach churns with uncertainty. "We'll take precautions. Dr. Vance won't have unrestricted access to our plans or locations. But we need her expertise."

Dr. Vance's shoulders visibly relax, and I catch a glimpse of relief in her eyes. "Thank you," she says softly. "I won't let you down."

"See that you don't," I reply, my tone firm. "Because if you do, the consequences will be severe."

As the others begin to discuss the logistics of integrating Dr. Vance into our operations and where would be the smartest location to hide her from Regent Colvin, I find myself lost in thought. Have I just made a decision that will save us all, or have I invited a viper into our midst?

Chapter Thirty Five

Ziva

With the adrenaline fading and a joint decision made about Dr. Vance, I finally have a moment to reflect on what has been gnawing at me since Arden was taken. As the others begin integrating Dr. Vance into our operations, their voices a low murmur in the cramped storage room, I find myself drawn to Myall, leaning against the shelf, his figure silhouetted against the dim light.

When he meets my gaze, a rush of heat floods my cheeks. My breath catches, sharp and shallow—my body recognizing something my mind still refuses to admit. A flutter of nerves knot in my stomach, and the warmth from his steady stare feels like an unspoken invitation. I gesture for him to join me in the shadows, craving the privacy that feels almost sacred in this moment.

"We need to talk," I whisper, my voice trembling slightly

against the backdrop of their chatter. His green eyes lock onto mine, understanding flickering in their depths like a distant flame.

"I might know a place," he murmurs, a teasing glint in his eye that makes my pulse quicken.

I raise an eyebrow. "How do we ditch the others?"

His hand closes around mine, warmth radiating from his touch, a stark contrast to the cold of the storage room. My eyes flick to Arden, who catches my gaze with a knowing glance, and a rush of heat floods my cheeks.

Myall begins leading me from the room, and we slip out of the storage room unnoticed by all except Arden. The heavy, metallic scent of the factory lingers, but as soon as we step into the cool twilight air, it's like a veil lifts.

The silence wraps around us, amplifying every sound— the rustle of leaves, the distant hum of machinery. My heartbeat is loud in my ears as we navigate the shadowy streets, paranoia prickling at my skin.

We walk in silence, Myall leading us toward the outskirts of the sector, the buildings looming like skeletons, their decaying facades crumbling under the weight of time.

Every creaking sign, every broken window, makes my skin prickle, and the hairs on the back of my neck stand up. Yet with Myall's hand in mine, I push the fear aside, the adrenaline making my pulse race even faster.

"Are you sure this is the best place to talk?" I ask, my voice taut with tension as we enter the forbidden zone, its edges draped in shadows.

Myall squeezes my hand reassuringly. "Trust me, Ziva. We've been here before and didn't get caught." His smile warms something within me, a flicker of courage that pushes me forward.

"Yeah, but that was before Colvin arrived. Before the rebellion." I say, checking our surroundings once more.

As we approach the abandoned theater, a familiar ache stabs through me. The cracked stone, the tattered remnants of curtains fluttering in broken windows—each detail brings me back to the first time Myall and I explored this forgotten place.

I remember how we'd joked about the ghosts that might haunt this place, how his laughter had been the only thing that kept the fear at bay. Now, it feels different. The air is thicker with tension, with the weight of everything unsaid between us.

"It's perfect," I breathe, drinking in the sight of the crumbling structure.

We slip inside through the cracked doorway and approach the stage. I run my fingers along the dusty velvet curtain, marveling at its texture, surprised it hasn't disintegrated under my touch.

Myall's voice pulls me from my reverie. "What did you want to talk about?" I can see the flicker of concern in his eyes, urging me to find the words I've been holding back.

I turn to face him fully, my heart fluttering in my chest. There's so much I want to say, so many feelings I've kept bottled up that are threatening to spill out of me. The weight of everything I want to say is almost unbearable, as if speaking could shatter this fragile moment.

How can I put into words the storm of emotions raging inside me? How can I tell him how much I need him, how terrified I am of losing him?

The silence between us stretches out, unbearable and

heavy, as if the very air knows what I'm afraid to voice.

Myall's patient gaze is fixed on me, waiting for my response. I take his hand, his fingers warm in mine, and lead him towards the stage. We wind past rows of dust-covered chairs. As we step up onto the worn wooden boards, I feel exposed, vulnerable. The empty seats stretch out before us, silent witnesses to what I'm about to confess.

My eyes catch sight of a worn and dusty chaise at the back of the stage, and I briefly consider suggesting to Myall that we should sit. But then I think better of it.

"Myall," I begin, my voice barely audible in the silence of the theater. He's watching me intently, his eyes never leaving mine. "I've been an idiot."

His eyes search mine in the dim light, brows furrowing. "What do you mean?"

I take a shaky breath, trying to steady myself. My chest tightens as if the emotion will burst out of me.

"When we started this rebellion, I thought…I thought I was doing the right thing by putting the possibility of 'us' on hold. I told myself I just didn't understand what it was that I was feeling. But now…" My voice cracks, and I clench my fists to steady myself.

"Now what?" Myall prompts gently, his hand still in mine, warm and reassuring as he gently rubs his thumb across my knuckles.

"Now, I understand now just how easily I could lose you," I confess, the words tumbling out in a rush. "When we were rescuing Arden, all I could think about was how I'd feel if something happened to you. How I'd never forgive myself for wasting the time we could have had together."

Myall's eyes soften, and he steps closer. "Ziva, you don't

have to explain—"

"But I do," I interrupt, pressing on before I lose my nerve. "I've been so focused on fighting The Authority, on breaking the chains, that I forgot why we're doing this—to love freely, without fear."

I hesitate, breath catching in my chest. The words weigh heavy, but they're all that matter now.

"I love you, Myall." It's a quiet admission, but it feels louder than any battle cry. It's the truth I've been afraid to face, but the only one that can free me.

I exhale shakily, my pulse racing in my ears. The dusty stage beneath our feet feels unsteady as I continue. "I dream of a world where we can walk hand in hand without fear, where our emotions aren't crimes to be punished. Where we can build a life together, free from The Authority's control. And I want that so badly, that life with you."

My gaze fixes on the row of seats below, avoiding his gaze. "I thought that we could just wait, wait until we were free from The Authority's grip to be together. That I was being selfless, putting the rebellion before my own wants and desires. But now, now I realize that there might not be a tomorrow, and I don't want to spend what could be my last moments denying how I feel."

The words hang in the air between us, heavy with meaning. I hold my breath, waiting for his response, terrified that I've ruined everything.

Myall's grip on my hand tightens, his calloused fingers intertwining with mine as he pulls me closer to him, until we're centimeters apart. The warmth of his touch gives me goosebumps, reminding me of the connection we've been denying ourselves for so long.

"I want that too, Ziva," he breathes, his voice low. "More than anything. But I'm terrified."

His admission surprises me. Myall has always been so steady and sure, he rarely shows vulnerability.

"Of what?" I ask, searching his face. We're standing so close together, our breaths mingling in the small space between us.

He swallows hard, his eyes meeting mine. His voice cracks slightly, a tremor of rawness that surprises me.

"Of losing you. Of failing you. Every day we risk everything, and sometimes I wonder if we're just delaying the inevitable. That we're walking toward something that might never come." His confession is a weight, but it's also a relief—because it means he feels the same.

I feel a surge of protectiveness, wanting to chase away his doubts. But before I can speak, he continues.

"But then I remember why we're doing this. For a future where we can feel without shame, love without fear. And I know that no matter what happens, I'll never regret fighting for that. For us."

I can't look away from Myall, his deep green eyes conveying a silent question, a flicker of understanding.

"Myall," I whisper, my voice barely audible in the stillness of the theater. "I don't want to wait anymore."

Chapter Thirty Six

Ziva

His gaze flickers to my lips, then back to my eyes. "Neither," he breathes, wetting his lips.

We lean in simultaneously, drawn by an irresistible force. Our lips meet, and it's like a dam breaking. Everything I've been holding back, everything we've been hiding—our fear, our hope, our desperation—collides in the space between us.

The kiss is charged with warmth and need, but his lips are soft, a kind of tenderness that pulls me deeper. My hands slowly trace the contours of his jaw, fingers curling into his hair, reveling in the softness of his locks.

His strong arms wrap around my waist, pulling me tightly against him. All my doubts dissolve as I press closer to him, unable to ignore how perfectly this feels. For the first time, I understand why we're fighting. Not just for survival, but for a future where moments like this are possible.

Myall deepens the kiss, our bodies pressed together as if trying to meld into one. I am consumed by the overwhelming sensations, savoring the taste of him, in the way his touch lights every nerve ending in my body, making me burn with desire.

Is this real? Are we really about to do this?

But I can't pull away, can't break the contact that feels like a promise finally being fulfilled. His touch, warm and sure against my skin, grounds me in the reality of the moment, and yet, my mind refuses to accept it.

Every part of me wants to retreat, to protect myself from what comes after, but his lips, his hands—everything about him is pulling me deeper. We've denied ourselves this for so long, and now, it feels like a truth I've been too afraid to face.

Myall's hands roam the contours of my back as he kisses me, leaving trails of fire in their wake. I melt into him, a quiet moan escaping as his touch ignites something deep within me. He responds with a low growl, making my toes curl in my boots.

With a gentle whisper, he speaks my name, his lips brushing against mine. I feel the intensity of his desire in every breath, sending goosebumps over my skin.

Breaking away from his lips, my cheeks are flushed, my breaths coming out in ragged pants. I look into his eyes, searching for any hesitation or doubt, but all I see is an unbridled longing mirroring my own.

I've studied the anatomy of desire, but this—this raw need—is something I've only read about in forbidden books. The heroines in those stories always seemed to experience overwhelming pleasure. I want that—want it with him.

"Show me," I whisper, my voice trembling, raw with desire I've only dreamed of. I sound bolder than I feel, but I can't hold back now, not when he's made me feel everything I've been hiding from.

His fingers move with purpose, undressing me slowly, almost reverently. With each movement, the coolness of the room against my exposed skin heightens the warmth spreading from his touch. Our eyes lock and I am entranced by the intensity of his gaze, unable to break away.

He undoes each button carefully, fingers grazing my collarbone, sending a rush of heat through my veins. With each inch of fabric that falls away, my breath quickens, a mixture of anticipation and nerves flooding me. Slowly, he slides the garment off my shoulders, his eyes never leaving mine.

"I've dreamed of this…with you," I whisper, my voice thick with longing.

"Me too," he rasps, throat bobbing. His fingers work with practiced ease, pulling my uniform until it falls in a heap around my ankles, stirring up dust motes. The cool air brushes my skin, but a searing heat pulses within me, consuming every inch.

Myall drops to his knees on the dusty stage, his hands trailing down my bare legs, sending shivers up my spine. He undoes my boot laces with deliberate slowness, pulling each one off as if savoring the moment. The sight of him kneeling at my feet, so focused and close, nearly shatters my control. Standing before him in nothing but my underwear, I've never felt so exposed—and yet so powerful. His calloused fingers trace over me as he stands, sending another shiver of pleasure through me, my inner muscles clenching involuntarily.

Our gazes lock and hold for a beat before my fingers move toward the buttons on his uniform, hesitant but determined. Every nerve in my body trembles as I fumble with them, my hands shaky with urgency, terrified I'll make a fool of myself. Myall's heartbeat thrums through the fabric, wild and uneven, syncing with the frantic pulse in my chest.

As his uniform drops to the floor, my gaze sweeps over his bare form, the only fabric his underwear. His body is sculpted from muscle, a faint trail of dark hair across his chest, leading down to his waistband. He mirrors my tension, his body vibrating with anticipation, and I feel my throat tighten, dry and aching, as the air between us thickens with heat. My hands shake as I reach for his boots, eager to strip them away, but his quiet voice halts me.

"Let me." Before I can react, he drops to his knees in front of me. His hands grip the worn leather of his boots, peeling them off with a soft scrape. There's a raw, primal energy in his motions, and I can't look away, mesmerized by every pull of his hands, every controlled breath.

When he rises, the heat in his gaze makes my breath falter. He takes my hand, guiding me toward the chaise at the back of the stage, my legs trembling as if they might collapse beneath me.

His voice, soft and deep, hums against my skin. "You're so beautiful Ziva." His lips graze my shoulder, a rush of warmth flooding through me. His fingers glide gently down my arm, raising goosebumps, each stroke a spark that races to my chest. I can't find my voice, consumed by the sensations he stirs within me. His touch ignites something deep inside me, a flame that spreads through every nerve, and I crave more.

"I want you, Ziva," he says, his voice raw with need. I shiver under his touch, heat radiates from his fingertips as he gently explores my body.

"I've wanted you since the moment I met you, I just didn't understand it at the time,"

he confesses.

"I know," I breathe, unable to resist as he guides me towards the chaise.

Myall pulls us down, our bodies entwined as we disturb the quiet air, sending a flurry of dust motes swirling around us. The chaise groans beneath us, creaking under the weight of our bodies.

My skin tingles as he caresses every inch of it, sending waves of pleasure through my body. I grip the worn chaise, desperately seeking support.

He presses soft, heated kisses along the curve of my neck, his lips leaving a burning trail on my skin. "I want to taste every inch of you," he murmurs, moving to kiss my mouth.

His hardness presses against me through our underwear, and I moan into his mouth, wanting nothing more than to remove this barrier between us.

Desperate for more, I flip us over, straddling him. My hands roam down to his waistband, feeling the outline of his arousal through the fabric. Our eyes lock as I slowly remove his underwear, his hips lifting, assisting me before flipping us again.

With a gentle touch, he reaches to unclasp my bra, sliding the straps down my arms. He trails his hand lower and removes my underwear, the fabric slightly damp, revealing my most intimate parts to him. In the dim light, Myall's eyes devour me before he leans in, lips brushing against mine.

When his lips meet mine, it's more than hunger, more than

desire. It's release—a floodgate opening. Every part of me that's been locked away for so long floods to the surface in an unstoppable force. His arms tighten around me, and I melt into him, the fear of tomorrow dissolving. In this moment, it's just him and me, and I let myself believe, for the first time, that this is real—that he feels the same.

Breaking our kiss, his lips trail down my body. Every touch fills me with a wave of pleasure, my breasts growing heavy and sensitive. His lips brush against my pebbled nipple, tingles of pleasure coursing through my body. I arch into him, a low moan escaping. Myall's tongue delicately explores and swirls around my hardened peak, making my core tighten.

"God..that feels so good," I whimper, fingers tangling in his hair, guiding him back to my throbbing nipple. The cool night air already settling over my sensitive peak.

He smiles devilishly before giving the same attention to my other nipple. My whole body shudders as he teases and caresses it with his tongue, the sensation almost too much to bear, my core trembling and aching for more

"More," I moan, voice breaking, breaths coming in short and shallow. "I need more."

His touch is delicate as he traces a line down my torso, eyes never leaving mine. He parts my legs and slowly, ever so slowly, slips a finger inside of me.

A small gasp escapes me at the overwhelming sensation.

"You're so wet," he breathes in my ear, his voice husky with desire.

He slides another finger inside me, stretching and filling me in a way I've never felt before. But with Myall, I feel safe, complete.

A low moan escapes my lips, head falling back against the chaise. My inner muscles tighten like something is building, begging for release. His hardness presses against my thigh, and I ache to trace my fingers along its length.

Myall continues his steady rhythm, each stroke of his fingers sending waves of pleasure through my body. My core tightens with every stroke, the gentle pressure building.

His thumb circles and rubs against my sensitive nub, pushing me further over the edge, our ragged breathing and Myall's steady rhythm the only sounds in the theater.

He slowly curls his fingers, and I am instantly consumed by a burst of light. My body arches off the chaise, a loud moan ripping out of me. Pins and needles course through my entire body as my orgasm washes over me like wave. Every sensation is amplified, from the warmth of his touch to the tightening of my inner muscles. His fingers continue their expert movements, prolonging my release until I finally collapse, breathless and spent.

A surge of euphoria floods through me, leaving a dizzying warmth in its wake. I've never known such bliss, and in this moment, I'm thankful I waited to share it with Myall.

He softly presses his lips to mine before pulling away, gaze locking with mine. His eyes are soft, a reflection of the longing, desire, and something deeper—love—shines through in his gaze.

"Are you ready?" he says, his voice low and husky, thick with anticipation. He presses another gentle kiss to my swollen lips, his touch tender and teasing.

"Yes," I nod, gripping the edge of the chaise for support.

Every nerve in my body is on fire. Slowly removing his fingers from inside me, he positions himself at my entrance.

He brushes a stray lock of hair from my face and I can smell myself on his fingers—musky and slightly sweet.

"We'll go at your pace, and if you ever want to stop, we will," he assures me as he meets my gaze.

I know, without a doubt, that if I told him to stop, he would do so without a second thought. But I trust him completely, with every part of me. I nod, my gaze locked on his, my heart beating in sync with his.

With excruciating slowness, he enters me, inch by agonizing inch. I bite my lip, trying to muffle the moans threatening to escape. His size is almost unbearable, stretching me in the most delicious way possible. His eyes remain locked on mine, silently gauging my reaction.

I let out a strangled cry of pleasure-pain as he bottoms out, our hips flush against each other.

"Ziva," he whispers, voice tight. "Are you alright?"

"Yes," I moan, my breath coming in short, shallow bursts.

This is more than I expected. The feeling is indescribable— a mix of pain and pleasure that makes my entire body ache with longing.

"Keep going," I beg, rocking my hips against his, craving more friction.

My heart thumps steadily, matching the rhythm of Myall's movements within me. Each thrust of his hips is a perfectly coordinated dance of slow thrusts and sudden surges. My legs instinctively wrap around him, drawing him closer as we move together, the chaise shuddering beneath us.

"Oh gods," I moan, my voice trembling with pleasure as he pulls out and slams back in. "Again."

He complies, slowly pulling out, almost fully withdrawn before slamming back in. A guttural moan escapes my parted lips as he continues to repeat the motion until his movements begin to become unsteady.

"Ziva," he pants in my ear, breath warm against my cheek, "I can't hold on much longer."

Breath catching in my throat, I gasp, "Neither can I," as my inner muscles tense with each powerful thrust.

Myall's mouth finds mine and we kiss hungrily. He moans, mouth mostly missing mine. With each erratic movement, the edge draws closer.

With one last thrust, he plunges deep inside me. A powerful wave of pleasure consumes me as his name escapes my lips in a strangled moan. My body convulses, my inner muscles tightening around his length. My entire being is overtaken by the overwhelming sensations as I climax.

We lie there for a few moments as we catch our breath. Myall gently withdraws, lying down beside me on the chaise. His skin warm against mine, his breathing equally ragged. Our bodies are clammy with sweat, and the heady, musky scent of him fills the air.

His arm rests around me, and I can feel the steady rhythm of his heart. This quiet is strange—almost tangible, as if we've crossed some unspoken threshold we can't unwrite. But for once, it doesn't feel unsettling. It feels like we've found exactly where we belong.

"I love you," he whispers, pressing gentle kisses to my lips, his eyes locked on mine, full of tenderness and unguarded emotion.

"I love you too," I whisper, my voice raw and tender as the words spill out. For a long moment, neither of us speaks, the quiet stretching between us like a delicate thread. His breath against my ear is the only sound I can hear, slow and steady, grounding me. I close my eyes, letting the silence sink into my bones.

I've never been one to trust easily, never known how to let anyone close. But now, in the warmth of his arms, I understand something I've denied for too long: my love for him isn't just an act of defiance against The Authority. It's a quiet act of rebellion against every fear I've been taught to carry.

My fingers trace slow, lazy circles on his chest, the steady rhythm of his heartbeat a grounding pulse beneath my palm as I shift my body to face him, my hand resting against his chest.

"I can't believe we waited so long for this," I whisper into the crook of his neck.

Myall's fingers weave through my hair, sending shivers of delight down my spine.

"It was worth the wait," he murmurs, eyes meeting mine.

Nodding, I rest my cheek against his chest. It was more than worth it. Every moment of anticipation, every stolen glance, every touch that left me wanting more—they all led up to this perfect moment.

"I just wish we didn't have to hide," I whisper, a pang of sadness tightening in my chest, my voice trembling slightly.

Myall's fingers trace the line of my jaw, his touch reverent. "I know," he whispers, his voice thick. "I've been afraid too. Afraid of losing you, of everything we've fought for slipping through our fingers. But right now, it feels like it's all been worth it. You're worth it, Ziva."

I prop myself up on an elbow, studying his face in the dim light. "I was so afraid too," I confess, the words tumbling out. "Of losing you, of never getting the chance to show you how

I feel."

His hand cups my cheek, his thumb brushing across my skin. "Ziva, you've always shown me. Every act of rebellion, every risk you've taken—it's all been for us, for a future where we can be together freely."

My eyes sting with unshed tears, the weight of his words heavy yet liberating. "But what if we get caught? What if The Authority—"

"Hey," Myall interrupts gently, pulling me closer, his breath warm against my skin. "We're in this together, remember? Whatever comes, we face it side by side."

Nodding, I bury my face in the crook of his neck, inhaling the scent of him—earthy and familiar. "I love you, Myall," I whisper, the words feeling both terrifying and liberating each time that I say them. "I love you, and I don't want to wait to be together anymore."

His arms tighten around me. "I love you too, Ziva. More than I ever thought possible."

I want to let go, to forget everything for just a moment and stay here forever, wrapped in his arms. But the world outside this room is still there.

"Whatever comes," he says again pulling me closer, "we'll face it together. I promise." His words settle over me like a comforting warmth, and for the first time in a long while, I let myself believe, deep down, that maybe we can survive this, together.

Chapter Thirty Seven

Myall

I stare at my reflection in the small, foggy mirror, watching the beads of steam form and disappear on the glass as my fingers fumble with the buttons of my gray uniform. The collar digs into my throat as I finish the last button. I hate the way it conforms to my body, a constant reminder of who I am—and who I must pretend to be.

The events of yesterday flash through my mind like fragments of a vivid dream—breaking into the detention center to rescue Arden, Dr. Vance joining our ranks, and then…Ziva.

For a moment, I close my eyes, savoring the image of her in the abandoned theater, the heat of her body pressed against mine, her breath warm in my ear as we whispered in the dark. My hands tremble, remembering her touch, the way her body responded to mine, the way it felt… real. But reality crashes back as soon I open my eyes, met with the harsh light of the room and my own troubled gaze in the mirror.

"Stop thinking about it," I mutter to myself, straightening my collar as a flush creeps up my neck.

Grabbing my ID badge, my palms sweat, and I swipe a shaky hand through my hair, trying to steady my breath. The door handle is slick beneath my fingers as I pause, almost paralyzed by the idea that we've crossed a line that can't be uncrossed—a line that hangs between us like a blade ready to drop. With a deep breath, I step out into the hallway and make my way towards the lift, my mind returning to Ziva once more.

"Morning, Hansen," a neighbor calls out, his voice flat and emotionless as he holds the lobby door.

Nodding, I force a neutral expression. "Morning."

I brush past my neighbor and step outside, the enormity of our situation hitting me full force. The Harmonization Authority's reach is vast, its control nearly absolute. And after yesterday's rescue, we've made ourselves their prime targets.

We're in too deep. There's no going back now, and I can't let anything happen to her.

My eyes scan the streets for any sign of increased surveillance, noting the usual flow of early morning commuters, their faces expressionless. A nearby propaganda screen flickers to life as I walk down the street, Regent Colvin's stern face filling the display, his eyes unblinking and accusatory. The sound of his voice cuts through the still morning air, harsh and authoritative, like nails scraping against metal. My stomach churns, muscles tightening as if his words are physically pressing in on me. The cold breeze does nothing to ease the sweat gathering at the base of my neck.

"Citizens, remain vigilant. Report any suspicious activity immediately. The harmony of our society depends on your compliance."

I clench my fists, a mix of fear and determination coursing through me with each step. This is what we're up against—not just an oppressive system, but the very fabric of society itself.

Joining the steady stream of workers heading towards the maglev station, my resolve strengthens. Yes, the risks are enormous. Yes, the odds are stacked against us. But the possible future that Ziva and I've been imagining for weeks now, that's worth fighting for.

The maglev approaches, its sleek form a symbol of the progress and order The Authority prizes so highly. I board, blending in with the sea of gray uniforms, scanning the car, looking for any signs of suspicion or surveillance, but the faces around me remain blank, their eyes soulless.

My mind replays the feel of her lips against mine, the softness of her skin under my fingertips. The memory is almost too real, a moment so vivid I can almost taste it again, as if the distance between us is nothing more than an illusion. After I'd returned to my apartment late last night, I lay awake in bed replaying those stolen moments with Ziva on a loop. If we get taken in by The Authority after our stunt rescuing Arden yesterday, at least I will always have that memory of Ziva.

"Approaching Central Station," the automated voice announces. "Please prepare for disembarkation."

I join the throng of blank-faced workers exiting the maglev, my feet carrying me towards the imposing steel and glass structure, the anticipation of seeing Ziva building with each step.

At the security checkpoint, I present my ID card. "Hansen, Myall. Compliance Monitor, Level 3," I state, keeping my voice steady.

The guard's eyes flick to his screen. "Proceed," he nods.

Passing through the biometric scanner, I will my heartbeat to slow, taking a few deep breaths for good measure.

It's just another day. Act normal.

Inside, I head to my workstation, scanning the workroom for a glimpse of Ziva. My palms are slick as I log into my terminal.

"Morning, Mr. Hansen," Tara mumbles as she passes, her gaze downcast like always.

I nod, unable to trust my voice, my eyes flicking to each footstep, hoping to see her. The anticipation is nearly unbearable.

I try to focus on the screen, but her smile lingers in my mind, the warmth of her touch, the softness of her lips whispering that she loves me. I close my eyes for a second, seeing the intensity of her gaze—how it pierced through the walls I've built. My skin still tingles with the echo of her presence, warmth lingering against the cold of the room.

Shit. Get it together, Myall.

But God, how I long to see her face again, to meet her gaze across the room, to see that smile that makes everything feel right. I sigh, forcing my focus back to the work in front of me, but my senses are still tuned to the door, waiting for her to walk through.

Approaching footsteps becomes audible, and my heart leaps as Ziva glides into the room, her eyes immediately finding mine across the space. For a split second, her face lights up with a radiance that takes my breath away. Her lips curve into a suppressed smile, her eyes dancing with barely contained joy.

Transfixed, I watch her glide to her workstation, a new energy in her step. She tucks a strand of hair behind her ear, a gesture so familiar yet suddenly intimate. My fingers itch to reach out and run my fingers through her hair, feeling it's softness.

"Morning, Emerson," I manage to say, relieved that my voice doesn't betray the storm of emotions brewing inside me.

"Hansen," she replies, her tone neutral, but her gaze lingering on mine a heartbeat longer than necessary.

Turning back to my screen, my mind is far from the data scrolling before me. Instead, I'm acutely aware of Ziva's presence, just a few meters away. The air between us seems charged with an invisible current, like two magnets drawn to each other.

I force myself through the motions of my work, mechanically reviewing compliance reports and flagging anomalies. But it's agony, knowing Ziva is so close yet so untouchable. I ache to look at her, to cross the room and hold her.

A stern voice cuts through my reverie. "Hansen, your productivity seems to have dipped this morning."

Snapping to attention, my heart rate spikes as I meet my supervisors cold, gray eyes. She glares down at me, clearly expecting an appropriate response.

"Apologies, ma'am," I say, keeping my voice steady and respectful. "I'll pick up the pace."

As my supervisor moves on, Ziva's concerned gaze lands

on me.

Look away, Ziva. We can't risk it, not with Colvin prowling around.

The hours crawl by, a torturous dance of stolen glances and carefully maintained distance. I never knew silence could be so deafening, or that simply existing in the same space as someone could be both heaven and hell.

The overhead speakers crackle to life, startling me. Regent Colvin's voice, cold and authoritative, fills the room. "Attention all personnel. Please proceed to the auditorium for a mandatory meeting, effective immediately."

Ziva's hazel eyes meet mine, a fleeting but meaningful exchange. In that moment, we both understand—the meeting is likely about Arden and Dr. Vance's escape.

Unease twists in my stomach, but I push it down, rising from my workstation. With a shared nod, we fall into step alongside our colleagues, moving as one towards the auditorium.

The thrum of nervous energy pulsates through the crowd as we enter the cavernous space. My eyes automatically begin searching for an exit strategy, a plan forming in my mind should things take a turn for the worse.

Regent Colvin stands on the raised platform, his icy gaze scanning over the crowd as we file into the room. He's dressed in his usual Navy blue uniform, his graying hair standing out harshly against the dark material.

Ziva joins me, her hand lightly brushing against mine in a way that could easily be overlooked as accidental. I know we probably shouldn't be seen anywhere near each other, but in this moment, I'm glad she's right beside me.

"Last night, two highly dangerous criminals escaped from

the detention center." Regent Colvin addresses the room, his voice carrying with ease. "These individuals pose a severe threat to our harmonious society, as do the rebels who aided and abetted their escape. All citizens are required to report any suspicious activity immediately."

As soon as Colvin reveals the information, whispers fill the expansive room. Every person exchanging hushed comments with their neighbor about what they just heard.

Although I anticipated this meeting would revolve around Arden and Dr. Vance, my stomach still tightens at his words. I fight to keep my expression guarded, even as my mind races.

Did we leave any traces? Could they have tracked us?

Colvin observes the room closely, keeping track of all our reactions. Ziva and I make sure to convincingly mimic the reactions of those around us.

Colvin continues, his tone hardening. "Let me be clear. Anyone found to be aiding or harboring these fugitives will face the harshest penalties. We will not rest until these disruptors are back in custody, along with any rebel sympathizers."

I risk a sidelong glance at Ziva. Her face is a mask of dutiful compliance, but the set of her shoulders betray her. We both know the stakes just got higher.

"Sir," a sycophantic voice pipes up, "what should we be on the lookout for?"

Colvin's lips curl into a cold smile. "Excellent question. We're dealing with a young woman with pale skin and red hair, known for her cunning, and an older woman, a former scientist with blonde hair and glasses. Both are skilled manipulators and highly dangerous."

Swallowing hard, I think of Arden's telltale hair color. We'll need to be more careful, perhaps even figure out a way to change the color. Elara will be able to disguise Arden's red hair. I remember the stories she used to share about the bold and vibrant hair colors she tried out during her rebellious teenage days.

"Remember," Colvin's voice drops to a menacing whisper, capturing my attention once more, "The Authority sees all. We will root out this infection, no matter the cost."

As Colvin stalks off the stage, the air seems to thicken, heavy with fear and suspicion, every person in the room tense and on edge. I can feel the hairs on the back of my neck rise, the oppressive heat of the room now amplified by the cold dread settling deep in my gut. We're all marked now, trapped in the same invisible net.

The audible sound of NeuroMods buzzing in warning before dosing their wearers makes me seethe with anger. The room falls silent as the mind-numbing effects of the emotionally suppressing drugs take effect.

I want nothing more than to reach out to Ziva, to reassure her, to feel the comfort of her touch. But I can't. We're surrounded by potential informants, our every move scrutinized.

So I turn and follow the crowd slowly exiting the room, my mind already plotting our next move.

Chapter Thirty Eight

Myall

The musty air of the factory's storage room fills my lungs as I enter, and I exhale slowly, trying to shake off the day's tension. Ever since Colvin's announcement, I've been on edge constantly, my shoulder blades aching.

Ziva stands near the window, her silhouette framed by the fading glow of the sunset. The light catches in her hair, turning the dark strands to bronze. I can't help but feel her absence in the world around me, as if everything sharpens into focus when she's near. She turns, and the sight of her steals my breath away.

"Hey," I say, keeping my voice low, even though it's just the two of us.

"Hey yourself," she replies, a smile playing at her lips. "Anything interesting at work today?"

I let out a dry chuckle. "Oh, you know, the usual soul-crushing grind." My attempt at levity falls flat, the weight of Colvin's threats still heavy on my mind.

Ziva picks up on my unease. "Myall? What is it?"

I shake my head, hair falling into my eyes as I struggle for the right words."It's just… Colvin's really ramping up the search. And after last night…we need to be more careful than ever."

She nods, her hazel eyes darkening with concern. "I heard whispers today. They're increasing patrols in the lower sectors of the city."

"Yeah, I heard that too. Good thing Arden and Dr. Vance are lying low at Grandma Elara's," I murmur.

"I also heard they're considering sending more Authority personnel from Elysium to help Colvin crack down on the dissent here," she adds, a hint of trepidation in her tone.

Shit.

"If they bring more Authority members here—"

"I know," she says as she cuts me off, her voice rising to meet mine "We need to act before that happens."

We both fall silent, and I feel myself drawn to her like a magnet. Without thinking, my hand reaches for hers, and as our fingers tangle, heat and relief flood through me. The warmth of her skin against mine is like a grounding force, an anchor to something real in this world that seems to be spinning out of control. Her hand is smaller than mine, but firm, holding onto me with a quiet strength I never knew I needed. In that simple touch, I feel both comfort and the weight of everything we stand to lose.

"Ziva," I murmur, marveling at how her name feels on my tongue. Last night replays in my mind—the softness of her lips, the curve of her body against mine. My pulse quickens at the thought.

She squeezes my hand, her eyes meeting mine before softening slightly. "I know," she whispers, and in those two words, I hear all the fear, hope, and fierce determination burning between us.

She leans in, her voice low, breath warm against my ear. "We're only torturing ourselves, thinking about what could happen if we're caught," she whispers, her breath tickling my neck. "I've been thinking about…after. As a way to distract myself." Her fingers trace patterns on my palm, a jolt of sensation running up my arm. "What if we could build a home together, somewhere clean, where we can see the stars?"

I feel her vulnerability in the tremor of her voice, the way her eyes dart to mine and then away. She's sharing a piece of herself, fragile and precious.

"Tell me more," I urge softly, squeezing her hand.

Her voice softens as she speaks, and I can hear the longing in it, that quiet hope she's always kept hidden. "I want a garden, Myall. Flowers that breathe—jasmine, I think, for their sweet scent. Not the fake, sterile blooms we're surrounded by here. Something alive, something that breathes with us." Her words leave a fragile silence in the air, a dream we can almost touch, if we reach out far enough.

"And children, Myall. Children who can laugh those deep belly laughs Elara is always going on about."

"What about a big tree in the yard, with a swing on it?" I add, imagining it as I speak. "For the children, I mean."

She smiles wistfully, "one that has enough shade so I can read under it on a warm, sunny day."

Her words stir something deep within me, and I pull her closer, resting my forehead against hers. "We'll have that, Ziva. A world where emotions aren't crimes, where we can just be ourselves."

I pause, gathering my thoughts. "I see us dismantling the NeuroMods—reprogramming them to *enhance* emotions instead of suppressing them. We'll use your genius to turn their weapons against them."

Ziva's eyes light up at the idea. "And education," she adds eagerly. "Real history, art, literature—all the things they've taken from us."

"Yeah," I nod, my enthusiasm building to meet hers. "We'll build schools, libraries. People will rediscover what it means to feel, to create, to be human."

The future we're dreaming of comes into focus—a life with Ziva, a life worth fighting for. The intensity of our shared vision is overwhelming, and I can't hold back anymore. I lean in, cupping her face gently in my hands, and kiss her.

It's a collision of everything—heat, hunger, an urgent need to hold onto something real. Her lips are soft, but there's fire behind them, a spark that ignites something deep inside me. The taste of her—sweet, intoxicating, like strawberries— lingers long after the kiss ends. I lose myself in the feel of her, in the way her breath mingles with mine, and for a moment, the world fades away. It's just us.

I breathe her in, the scent of flowers and something uniquely Ziva filling my senses. My fingers tangle in her long hair as she presses herself closer, warmth seeping through the fabric of our uniforms.

We pull apart, breathless. Neither of us speak. We don't need to. I watch the play of emotions across her face—wonder, hope, a fierce protectiveness that mirrors my own feelings. Her fingers are still entwined in my uniform, the slight tremor unmistakable. It hits me then, how monumental this is.

I can't help myself. My hand moves of its own accord, reaching out to brush a wayward strand of Ziva's hair behind her ear. The simple gesture feels intimate in a way that surpasses even our kiss. My fingers linger, tracing the curve of her cheek with a gentleness I didn't know I possessed.

"Ziva," I whisper, my voice low and full of unspoken promises.

She leans into my touch, her eyes fluttering closed for a moment. "I know," she murmurs, her voice wavering.

A tremor runs through her, and I pull her closer, her body fitting against mine as if we've always belonged together. The warmth of her chases away the coldness of the room.

"Are you scared?" I whisper, the fear gnawing at me.

She hesitates, the walls she's built around herself beginning to crack.

"I'm terrified, Myall. Not of us—not of this—but of losing it. Losing this…feeling. That when all of this is over, we'll be left with nothing but the emptiness again. A hollow space where everything I've learned to feel is erased. I don't think I could survive that." Her gaze drops, unable to hold mine, as if saying it aloud might make it real.

I swallow hard, understanding completely. "We won't let that happen," I promise fiercely. "Whatever it takes, we'll fight to keep this. To give everyone a chance at real emotion."

She nods, determination hardening her gaze. But beneath it, I see a vulnerability that she rarely allows anyone to glimpse. In this moment, Ziva isn't the brilliant technician or the defiant rebel. She's simply a woman, allowing herself to be loved, perhaps for the first time. I press a soft kiss to her forehead, marveling at how natural it feels.

The sound of footsteps echoing through the old factory jolts us back to reality. Ziva and I spring apart, exchanging a look that speaks volumes. Her hazel eyes, usually so guarded, soften with lingering affection.

As the others file in—Marcus, Arden, Tariq, Liora, Jarek, Jorel and Dr. Vance—I force my face to remain impassive, a mask I've worn for years, but the rush of warmth in my chest is impossible to hide. The tug of a smile threatens to form, a fleeting reminder of the joy I've just tasted. But I swallow it down—this isn't the place for it.

Arden zeroes in on us immediately. "Well, well," she drawls, "Where did you two sneak off to last night?"

A flush creeps up my neck, but it's nothing compared to the deep color on Ziva's cheeks. Her attention falls to a loose thread on her uniform, avoiding my gaze.

Without thinking, I take her hand, intertwining our fingers again. "We figured there's no time left to waste," I say, my voice steady despite the fluttering in my chest. "Not in this world."

Ziva's fingers tighten around mine, and when I glance at her, the radiance of her smile takes my breath away.

Yes, this is happening, and I'm not ashamed.

"About damn time," Arden chuckles.

I want to say more, to shout our love from the rooftops. But even here, surrounded by allies, old habits of secrecy die hard. Instead, I simply nod, hoping they can see the depth of what we've found in each other.

As the group settles in, preparing to discuss our next

moves, I can't help but marvel at how quickly everything has changed. When we began, Ziva and I just wanted to find a way to switch off our NeuroMods. But now, we're not just fighting for freedom. We're fighting for a future where love like ours isn't an act of defiance, but a basic human right.

Marcus catches my eye, his usual stern expression softening for a moment. He gives me a subtle nod, and for once, words aren't necessary. The others in the room shift awkwardly, mumbling congratulations that sound more like clearing their throats. I feel Ziva's hand tense in mine, and I give it a reassuring squeeze.

Arden's voice breaks through the moment. "Alright, lovebirds," she says with a grin. "As heartwarming as this is, we've got a revolution to plan."

I clear my throat. "Right. Dr. Vance, what can you tell us about your inside knowledge of The Harmonization Authority?"

Dr. Vance leans forward and readjusts her glasses. "Well… as you know, they're developing a new type of NeuroMod. One that can read and manipulate emotions on a deeper level. To do so, it must be implanted in the wearer's neck."

A chill runs through me as I recall the semantics we uncovered. "We saw the blueprints for it. But how does that work?"

"It's a combination of nanotech and advanced neuroscience," Dr. Vance says, shrugging. "If they succeed, they'll be able to rewrite emotions entirely. It will essentially give them complete control over every citizen. Though I do wonder if any consideration has been given to the long term effect of such a device."

The room falls silent as the implications sink in. Ziva's

grip tightens, her fingers interlocking with mine, and I'm struck by a terrifying thought—in that world, would what we feel for each other even be real?

"We have to stop them before they release it on the city," I say, my voice low but firm. "What's our next move?"

"Figuring out a way to warn the public, I'd say." Arden mutters from her spot in the corner.

We begin planing our next move. This isn't just about freedom anymore. It's about preserving what makes us human. I glance at Ziva, catching her eye. In that moment, I see my own determination reflected back at me. Whatever comes next, we'll face it together. And somehow, that makes me believe we might just have a chance.

Chapter Thirty Nine

Ziva

My footsteps echo in the dimly lit room, the soft light casting long shadows on the walls. I pace restlessly, the stale air mingling with the lingering scent of my bergamot soap. My mind is a tempest, swirling with doubts and fears and the unshakable sense that we've crossed a line we can never uncross.

I collapse onto the bed, its soft mattress shifting beneath me. Almost instantly, my knee starts bouncing—quick, jittery—as though trying to escape the weight of my thoughts. The information we leaked overnight about The Authority's plans for the new NeuroMods weighs heavily on me.

The data is out there now, circulating through the city like wildfire. Every datapad and propaganda screen now carries our message. I try not to imagine the chaos it could spark, the risk to our loved ones—but the gnawing dread in my chest won't let up. Arden ensured it could not be traced back to us.

But what if we've miscalculated? What if the citizens don't revolt?

Myall and I came to a mutual decision not to show up at work today. We know we have to act fast and move on to the next phase before The Authority can regroup. Since the initial resistance, we've never needed The Authority's presence in the city. The NeuroMods have kept order, enabling The Authority to govern us from a distance. But now that's all changing.

I glance at the manual clock on the wall, its soft ticking a counterpoint to my racing heartbeat. Myall should be here any moment. My stomach twists with nervous anticipation—this is the first time he'll be in my living unit. I push myself off the bed, about to pace again when a soft knock interrupts, followed by two sharp raps.

Moving to unlock the front door, it slides open with a soft hiss, and Myall's flushed face greets me.

"Morning, beautiful," he says, his voice low and tinged with warmth as he steps into the room. Before I can respond, he pulls me into his arms, the stubble on his jaw brushing against my cheek.

I relax into his embrace, the warmth of his body a welcome comfort. His familiar scent of lemon soap floods my senses, and I close my eyes for a moment, allowing the sound of my heartbeat to slow, to sync with his. For just a moment, I allow myself to feel safe, to forget the enormity of what we've set in motion.

"Did you see anyone on your way here?" I murmur against his chest, the sound of his heartbeat audible through his thin sweater.

Myall pulls back slightly, his eyes meeting mine. "Not many, the streets were eerily quiet. I think we calculated correctly that people would refuse to go about their daily lives once we leaked the information."

We had remained in the factory well into the night, gathering and organizing crucial information—with Dr. Vance guiding us on what would have the greatest impact on the public. Arden and Tariq ensured the information would spread without a trace back to us.

I nod, a mixture of relief and apprehension coursing through me. "Good. That's…good."

"Are you okay?" Myall asks, his brow furrowing with concern as he releases me.

Hesitating, my fingers grip the hem of my worn black shirt, the fabric thin under my touch. "I'm…I don't know," I whisper, my voice shaking. "Part of me is terrified we've made a huge mistake. What if we're wrong? What if we've just doomed everyone?" I feel the weight of it pressing on my chest, as if I can't breathe around this impossible decision.

His hands settle on my shoulders, warm and steady, grounding me in a way I didn't know I needed. He traces small circles near my collarbone, the motion gentle, almost tender. I feel his touch seep through my skin, reaching the anxious parts of me that have been on edge since last night.

"Ziva, look at me," he says softly, drawing my gaze.

"I know it's hard. That guilt you're feeling, that hesitation?" He pauses, making sure I'm really hearing him. "It just proves that you're more human than The Authority ever were."

I blink at him, the truth of his words hovering just out of reach.

"They didn't hesitate," he goes on. "Not when they stripped us of our emotions. Not when they turned people into empty shells in the name of control."

His jaw tightens. "They never cared about the long-term impact. About what it would do to us—our memories, our relationships, or the effect on our nervous system."

My throat tightens, but I stay silent, letting him speak.

"But you?" He lifts one hand, brushing a strand of hair behind my ear. "You're still questioning. Still worrying about the consequences. That's because you *care*. About what comes next. About the people who will have to live with what we've done."

He lets that sit for a moment before finishing, softer now. "That's how I know we're doing the right thing. The Authority can't be allowed to implant those new NeuroMods. They have to be stopped."

Nodding, I try to draw strength from his conviction. "You're right. It's just…the weight of it all, you know?"

"I do," he says softly, his thumbs continuing their lazy circular motion.

I square my shoulders, sighing faintly. "Okay. So what's our next move?"

Myall's eyes flick towards the kitchen. "We take the day to review our plans, make sure that nothing is left to chance. We only get one shot at this."

We move toward the kitchen table, Myall seeming completely at ease in my space which is comforting, yet unnerving all at once. Under different circumstances, I might have savored this moment—sharing space with someone who understands me in a way no one else does.

"It's strange, isn't it?" I say, gesturing vaguely around my living unit as we make our way towards my kitchen. "Being here, together, when we should be at work—pretending everything's normal. I've never skipped a shift."

Myall's lips quirk into a small, knowing smile. "Nothing about this is normal, Ziva. But that's kind of the point, isn't it? To break the cycle."

Returning his smile, I feel a flicker of the rebellious spirit that first drew us together. "I suppose you're right."

We settle at my small kitchen table, Myall pulls out my chair with an easy, unspoken familiarity. My fingers trace the outline of the Compliance Monitoring Division on one of the blueprints Jorel obtained, thoughts swirling as I consider our options.

"The city's in disarray," Myall says, his voice sounding tight as he takes the seat across from me. "The Maglev was nearly empty this morning. Streets are quiet. It's like everyone's holding their breath, waiting for something to happen."

I meet his gaze across the table. "Good. That means our message got through. People are resisting, even if they don't fully understand why yet."

Myall nods, leaning in closer and resting his elbows on the table. "But we can't let this momentum fade. We need to strike while The Authority is unsteady, before they can call in reinforcements."

I pull up a holographic display of the NeuroMod blueprints on my datapad. "Our access codes and I.D badges should get us past the initial security checkpoints, assuming that they haven't been flagged yet. But after that, we're in uncharted territory."

We can only hope our access is still valid, despite our absence today. That's why Marcus made sure to go in today, so at least one of us would still have entry into the facility. He also promised to report back with any new information he gathers during his shift today.

"What about these maintenance tunnels?" Myall gestures toward a faint line on the blueprint spread across the table. "If we can get a small team of us through there, we might be able to bypass most of their internal security."

Biting my lip, I consider. "If we're caught in there, we'd be trapped."

"Better than walking through the front gates and getting caught, Ziva," Myall says, his hand finding mine across the table. "But it might be our only way to reach the core of the network."

He's right. If we want to dismantle the entire NeuroMod system, we need to find a way into the building and locate the central hub of the network. Only then can we successfully disable it.

Slowly I nod, my mind already planning the next steps. "We'll need to coordinate with the others. Make sure everyone knows their role."

I hope that Arden and Dr. Vance have successfully finished the device to deactivate the NeuroMod system while they're lying low at Elara's house. Dr. Vance promised that she'd knew how to dismantle the NeuroMods as they currently are. But once they upgrade to their newer version, that's when her knowledge would become limited. They kept her in the dark about so many things, it makes me wonder who has been developing this newer version, if it wasn't her.

"Do you think Dr. Vance will go through with this?" I ask, the doubt in my voice unmistakable. My chest tightens, and a nagging feeling creeps up my spine. I want to believe in her—and in the cause—but I can't shake the image of her eyes, so haunted when she spoke of the NeuroMods. She's been part of the system for so long, how much of her is still tethered to it?

Myall's expression grows serious as he considers my words. "I believe she will. Remember her face when she told us what the new NeuroMods would do. She looked… haunted."

She did, but a small part of me still holds a kernel of doubt that she can't be entirely trusted. My hands tremble as I trace the outline of the Compliance Monitoring Division on the map. A rush of excitement and fear pulses through me, making my grip unsteady. Myall notices, reaching out to gently place his hand over mine. His touch is warm, reassuring, and instantly calms my fraying nerves.

"We can do this, Ziva," he says softly, his eyes meeting mine with unwavering conviction.

Slowly I inhale, trying to calm my racing heart and steady my shaking hands. "I know. It's just…there's so much at stake if this goes wrong."

"I know," he says as he leans in closer,. "I've been thinking more about how we can get inside. There's a service entrance here," he points to a spot on the blueprint, "that would be less guarded. If we time it right, during shift change, we could slip in unnoticed."

Listening intently, my mind is already cataloging possibilities and potential obstacles. "What about the internal security systems? They'll have cameras, motion sensors—"

"That's where Marcus comes in," Myall interrupts. "He'll remain behind and work his magic to create a blind spot for us on the software Arden created."

I pause, considering. "It could work, but do you think

Arden's ready for this after what she just went through…"

We continue to refine the plan, and I can't help but marvel at how in sync we are. Myall's strategic mind complements my technical knowledge perfectly.

"Do you really think we can pull this off?" I ask, glancing sidelong at Myall, voicing the doubt that's been gnawing at me. "Don't sugar coat it, be honest with me."

Myall's hand tightens over mine as he meets my gaze, unwaveringly. "I believe in us, Ziva. In you. If anyone can bring down The Authority and free people from these damned NeuroMods, it's you. It's always been you."

My cheeks flush, his words fill me with a warmth that has nothing to do with the plan and everything to do with the man before me.

Taking a deep breath, I try to calm the storm of emotions swirling inside me and the way my body instantly reacts to Myall. "We should run through the contingencies one more time," I say, clearing my throat and forcing myself to focus. "If we can't access the main control room—"

"Then we fall back to Plan B," Myall finishes, his voice steady. "We use the maintenance tunnels to plant the disruptors at key junctions. It'll take longer for the effect to spread, but—"

"But it's better than nothing," I nod, appreciating his foresight.

We spend the next several hours meticulously going over every detail, every possible scenario.

Finally, Myall leans back, running a hand through his disheveled hair. "I think that's as solid as we can make it. We'll present it to the others tonight at the factory."

The mention of our impending meeting with the others

suddenly makes everything feel real. I wipe my sweaty palms on my thighs as a tremor of fear runs through me. "Myall, what if—"

He doesn't let me finish as he rises from his chair and pulls me into his arms. I bury my face in his chest, inhaling his familiar scent.

"I'm scared, Myall," I admit quietly, voicing the fears I've been trying to hide.

Myall's arms tighten around me. "Me too," he confesses, his usual confident facade cracking.

Looking up at him, I see my own fears and hopes reflected in his green eyes. Without thinking, I reach up and trace the line of his jaw. "Promise me you'll be careful," I say softly.

"Only if you promise the same," he replies, his mouth twitching at the corners.

His fingers brush mine as he guides us toward the sofa. When he pulls me down beside him, there's a slight tremor in his touch.

His arms encircle me, pulling me closer, the heat of his body pressing against mine, his heart beating in time with my own. His chest feels solid beneath my cheek, his breath steady in the dim light. For a moment, all the weight of our mission, all the danger ahead, feels distant, like it doesn't matter in this small, fragile space.

I breathe in his scent—lemon soap mixed with the faint, earthy tang of sweat—and the familiar comfort of his presence soothes the raw edges of my nerves. My fingers curl into the soft fabric of his sweater, tugging him closer, needing to feel the reassurance of his touch.

His lips graze my forehead, a feather-light kiss that makes my toes curl. I tilt my face up to meet his, the warmth between us almost tangible as his gaze meets mine. For a heartbeat, we hold each other's gaze, and the world seems to narrow down to the space between us.

Without a word, he leans in, his lips brushing mine in a tentative kiss. It deepens quickly, heat flooding through me. The sensation of his lips against mine makes everything else fade—the fear, the mission, the unknowns.

I pull him closer, my hands finding the soft locks of his hair, and he responds, his hands sliding around my waist, pulling me to him with a quiet urgency.

Breaking the kiss, lips still tingling, I rest my forehead against his. "We don't have much time," I whisper, my breath ragged.

His response is a soft chuckle, his voice low and husky. "I know. But right now…I don't care."

His lips crush against mine, hot and demanding, and I moan into his mouth. My hands claw at his hair, pulling him closer, desperate for more. He moans low in his throat, his hands gripping my waist like he's afraid I'll vanish beneath him.

The kiss deepens, his tongue slipping past my lips, tangling with mine. I can feel his length hardening against my thigh, and it sends a jolt of pure, unhinged desire straight to my core.

Breathless, I pull back for a second, my breath hitching. Myall's lips trail down my neck, sucking and biting at the sensitive skin there. I gasp, arching into him, my fingers tugging at his shirt until it's off and tossed aside.

He moves his way down my body, and my breath catches in my throat. His hands slide up my thighs and he rubs his thumbs against my heat before reaching to undo my pants. I lift my hips as he removes them and tosses them to the floor. My underwear is already soaked through with my arousal as he presses his lips against the thin fabric. I nearly come undone.

"Myall," I whimper, my voice trembling with nerves and anticipation. He looks up at me, his eyes dark with hunger. He hooks his fingers into the waistband of my underwear and pulls them down slowly, gliding them down my legs, leaving a trail of goosebumps in their wake.

I'm exposed, vulnerable, and I can see the way his gaze burns as he takes me in. He reaches out, grabbing my knee and angling my hip, opening myself for him. He doesn't waste time. He leans down, his tongue lashing out, licking from my entrance to my clit. I cry out, my hands flying to his hair, desperate for something to hold on to.

"Holy fuck," I gasp as he circles my sensitive bundle of nerves with the tip of his tongue, the sensation almost overwhelming. His hands grip my thighs, spreading me wider as he dives in, his mouth hot and wet against me.

That feels so fucking good.

He suckles at my bundle of nerves, flicking it with his tongue, and my core trembles. My breathing is short and shallow. One of his fingers slides inside me, curling just right, and I moan loud enough to wake the dead.

"That feels…so good." I moan, my fingers gripping his hair tighter. He adds another finger, stretching me wider. His fingers thrust inside me while his mouth works me over. The heat builds, coiling tighter and tighter in my core until I'm shaking, my hips bucking involuntarily. This is nothing like the other night. This isn't slow and tender, this is full of hunger and burning desire.

"Please," I whine, my voice breaking. "Don't stop."

He growls against me, the vibrations sending shockwaves through my body. I'm so close to the edge, my inner muscles tightening. His tongue circles faster, harder, and his fingers thrust deeper, hitting that spot inside me that makes my vision blur. I lose it, my orgasm crashing over me like a tidal wave. I scream his name, my thighs clamping around his head as I ride out the pleasure. He doesn't stop until I'm twitching and whimpering, oversensitive and completely wrecked.

He pulls back, wiping his mouth with the back of his hand. His gaze flickers down to my lips before meeting my eyes again.

"We don't have much time," he says, echoing my earlier words, his voice rough and dripping with desire.

I barely have the strength to respond, but I manage to whisper, "Then stop wasting it," before he pulls me to my feet, dragging me toward my bedroom.

Chapter Forty

Ziva

The sun dips lower, the faint click of the blinds opening nearly drowned out by the hum of the building's ventilation. The air is thick and warm, heavy as though a storm is just waiting to break. Time seems suspended, the fading sunlight stretching the silence in the room.

Time to go.

My heart sinks as we rise from the bed and gather our plans, carefully folding the maps and blueprints to take with us. Myall stands by the door, shoulders taut, waiting for me. As I approach, he turns to me, his gaze lingering on my face.

"Ziva," he says, his throat bobbing. "Before we go…"

He doesn't finish the sentence. Instead, he pulls me close, one hand cupping my face. I feel the warmth of his palm rough against my cheek, his calloused thumb tracing my cheekbone in slow, gentle movements.

Breath catching, I gaze up at him. "Myall, I—"

His lips press gently against mine, and I inhale sharply, tasting the faint tang of salt on his skin, the warmth of his breath mingling with mine. His body presses against mine, as though he could absorb every fragment of my fear and hope. His hands slide into my hair, tugging me closer, and I feel the tension of his muscles, the heat of his skin seeping into mine. The kiss deepens, urgent now, his tongue brushing against mine, seeking the same desperate release I feel. I lose myself in it—the softness of him, the storm swirling inside of me. When we finally break apart, we're both breathless and my heart is thumping in my chest.

Myall presses his forehead to mine. "Whatever happens," he whispers, "I love you. I will always love you."

I nod, unable to speak past the lump forming in my throat. With a deep breath, I step back and open the door, it glides open with a soft hiss. It's time to face our fate.

The city greets us with an unsettling quiet, its usual rush of evening commuters replaced by an unnatural stillness. The hum of propaganda screens echoes off the empty streets, but it feels like a whisper in a void. The air is thick, too thick, like it's holding its breath, waiting for something.

A single bird flutters past, a fleeting reminder of life, but otherwise, the city feels hollow, its heartbeat silenced. The propaganda screens, once promoting emotional stability and harmony, now display warnings about the invasive NeuroMods.

Beneath the harsh glow of a screen, someone has scrawled the words 'Emotions are what make us human.' The paint is fresh, the brushstrokes wild and bold against the drab gray of the building. The same phrase is displayed on the screen above.

The Maglev train glides by, nearly empty. A few people hurry along the sidewalks, their eyes darting nervously.

"It's working," Myall murmurs as we walk. "They're questioning the system and The Authority, just like we hoped."

Nodding, a mix of excitement and fear courses through me as I see two people stopped on the sidewalk, whispering. They immediately stop their whispering as we approach, only resuming once we've passed them.

"Let's hope it's enough," I mutter.

The walk to the factory is quiet, our minds preoccupied with what we're about to do. We take a circuitous route, avoiding the main thoroughfares. As we pass through a residential area, I spot a small group of people huddled together, speaking in hushed tones. They fall silent as we approach, watching us warily, the same way the couple we passed before did.

"They're afraid," I whisper to Myall once we're out of earshot.

He squeezes my hand in response. "Fear can be the first step towards change."

As twilight deepens, the city's unease seems to grow. I've never seen the streets this quiet, especially after shifts end. We're almost at the factory now. I can see its hulking silhouette against the darkening sky. My steps falter for a moment as the enormity of what we're about to do hits me.

Myall stops, turning to face me. "You okay?" he asks softly.

I think of all we've risked, all we stand to lose—and all we might gain.

"I guess I don't really have a choice but to be okay," I reply, squaring my shoulders, trying to appear more confident than I feel. Myall can probably sense my false bravado, but he doesn't say anything.

The heavy metal door creaks shut behind us, the sound too loud in the silence of the factory. We move quickly, slipping between the machines and empty conveyor belts that line the walls. My footsteps are muffled by the thick dust on the floor, but my heart pounds loudly in my chest, matching the rhythm of the hum that surrounds us.

As we walk into the storage room, the dim light reveals familiar faces gathered in a loose circle—Arden's usual smirk as she leans against a pile of discarded wooden crates, Marcus's intense gaze as he looks up from the workbench, Dr. Vance's sharp eyes behind her glasses as she clutches a datapad. My heart swells at the sight of our little rebellion.

"About time," Arden quips as she pushes off from the crates she was leaning against, a smirk playing on her lips. "We were starting to think Colvin nabbed you."

Forcing a chuckle, I try to shake off the tension and ignore the way her joke makes my stomach churn. "Not yet. It's pretty quiet out there."

Marcus steps forward, still dressed in his work uniform, his expression grave. "It's exactly as we hoped. People are whispering in the streets and at work, questioning. I saw a group refuse to board the Maglev this morning."

"Good," Myall nods. "That's exactly what we need—doubt."

Liora chimes in, her arms crossed. "The Authority is likely scrambling. They're trying to maintain control, but cracks will be forming. We won't have much longer before their reinforcements arrive."

As the others share their observations, I'm lost in thought. The Authority is planning to send more personnel into the city in the next few days. Dr. Vance suspects that when they arrive, it will be to implement their new devices in our city. We have a limited window of time to act before that happens. Thankfully, Marcus was able to retrieve the necessary supplies today so I can complete the last steps on the disruption device.

Myall's voice cuts through my thoughts. "Ziva," he says softly, "should we share our plan?"

I nod, clearing my throat. "Right. We think we've figured out the best way into the Compliance Monitoring Division without needing to pass through the security checkpoints at the front doors."

As Myall and I take turns explaining our strategy—the weak points we've identified, the potential allies within—I watch the faces of our friends. I see determination in Arden's eyes, careful consideration in Marcus's furrowed brow, and a flicker of something I can't quite name in Tariq's expression.

"It's a gamble," I conclude, "but it's our best shot at getting into the building undetected and getting the device activated."

A moment of heavy silence follows. Then Arden speaks up, her voice uncharacteristically serious. "We're with you. All the way."

The others nod in agreement, and I feel a surge of gratitude. Some of these people I've only known for a few weeks, and yet they are ready to put their lives on the line for a plan we hastily created this morning while sitting around my kitchen table.

As we hash out the finer details of the plan, Dr. Vance

clears her throat, her piercing blue eyes sweeping across the room. She holds us in her gaze, making sure we're all focused on her.

"I feel compelled to point out a critical factor in the plan," she says, her voice carrying easily across the room. "The strategy we're discussing will only disable the NeuroMod system within this city's jurisdiction."

My heart sinks, a heavy knot tightening in my chest. I swallow, my throat thick with tension. The plan we've built— our hope—feels suddenly fragile.

I steady my voice, but it betrays me, cracking on the last word. "What do you mean, Elena?"

She adjusts her glasses, a habit I've noticed when she's about to deliver complex information. "The NeuroMod network is decentralized. It was a contingency plan The Authority came up with years ago. Each city operates on its own sub-system. Disabling yours won't affect the global structure."

Myall stiffens beside me. "So, all of this...and it only matters for one city?" he asks, frustration evident in his tone.

Dr. Vance's expression softens slightly as she turns to face him directly. "Not 'just,' Myall. It's a crucial first step. But yes, dismantling the entire system globally will require significantly more time and resources."

The room falls silent as we process this information. Even if we managed to dismantle the systems in our city, what's to stop The Authority from regaining control? I close my eyes, trying to quell the wave of disappointment threatening to overwhelm me. When I open them, I'm surprised to see a glimmer of excitement in Arden's eyes.

"Guys don't you see?" she says, leaning forward on the balls of her toes. "This is how we start a domino effect. We free our city, we grow our numbers, and then we take on the next city, and the next."

"How do we make sure The Authority doesn't just take it all back?" Tariq asks, voicing the question I know is on everyone's mind.

Arden scoffs. "You really think once people get a taste of freedom, they'll just let The Authority take control again?" She says it with a challenging tone, daring us to disagree.

A spark of hope flickers in my chest, unexpected and wild. "She's right," I say, my voice stronger now, meeting the eyes of the small, determined group around me. "If we can pull this off here, we prove it's possible. We become a beacon of hope for other cities, other rebels."

Myall squeezes my hand, his voice filled with renewed determination. "We could create a network of free cities, each one joining the fight to liberate the next."

"We could even enlist some people from those weird hippie groups in the isolated communities. Get them to to join us in liberating the other cities." Jarek suggests, his broad arms still crossed.

As murmurs of agreement fill the room, I realize we're standing on the edge of something much bigger than I'd initially imagined. This isn't just about our city anymore; it's about igniting a global revolution.

Arden is right, once people are freed from their emotional prison, there's no way they would let The Authority take it from them again. More and more people will join our cause, and eventually, with time, we can change the entire world.

Dr. Vance clears her throat, refocusing the room. "The

people living in those 'weird hippie' communities, as you so eloquently put it, Jarek, may not be as easily swayed to join our cause."

"What do you mean?" I ask, intrigued by the isolated communities that exist outside of The Authority's control.

"Well," she begins, "They have their own governing body and rules, but those rules are designed to keep their citizens compliant. I believe they have a similar version of our NeuroMods. Though unlike ours, which chemically suppresses our emotions, I believe theirs focuses on psychological conditioning. The two elements combined form some pretty nasty emotional manipulation."

I always believed that those living under The Sanctum's governance were truly free, but according to Dr. Vance's explanation, they are just as trapped by their emotions as we are.

"So we need to find a way to liberate those cities as well," take down The Authority *and* The Sanctum." Arden interjects, her tone cutting through the tension in the room.

Leave it to Arden to want to save everyone.

"Alright," I say, feeling the adrenaline coursing through me. "Let's get back on track. We have a city to free, and after that…a world to change."

We huddle closer, pouring over maps and timelines. I can feel the energy in the room shift. The air is charged with a potent mix of anticipation, fear, and hope.

Tomorrow, we make our move. Tomorrow, we take the first step towards dismantling The Authority's control.

Chapter Forty One

Myall

The first slivers of dawn creep through the cracked factory windows, casting pale golden light across the dust-laden air. It settles on Ziva's sleeping face, her skin soft and warm against the chill that still lingers in the concrete. Her hair, tangled from the night, brushes against my cheek as I hold her, the scent of her bergamot soap mixes with the remnants of sweat and earth. For just a moment, I let myself savor the warmth of her body, the gentle rise and fall of her chest against mine.

But reality crashes in like a tidal wave.

The air smells of stale metal and the lingering stench of sweat and grime, and I can feel the dampness in the floor creeping into my bones. For a heartbeat, I wish we could just stay here forever—trapped in this brief moment of peace. But we aren't safe here. Not with what's coming.

Can we really pull this off? Overthrow The Authority? Disable the NeuroMods and break the chains that bind this city to its iron grip? Or are we marching to our doom, the way my parents did?

I've often wondered what happened to them after they were dragged away. Are they still alive? Are they out there, waiting for me to fail? Their faces flash before me—so young, so full of hope. It feels like we're teetering on the edge of a cliff, about to fall into the void.

I steady my breathing, reluctant to wake her just yet. She deserves this brief moment of peace before everything changes. My fingers trace idle patterns on her back as my mind runs through our plans, searching for any flaw, any weakness that could bring it all crashing down.

Finally, knowing we can't delay any longer, I press a soft kiss to Ziva's temple. She stirs in my arms, hazel eyes fluttering open to meet mine.

"Morning, beautiful," I say, trying to keep the tension from my voice.

A sleepy smile tugs at the corners of her lips as she shifts. "Morning," she replies, nestling closer, shifting the threadbare blanket we're both wrapped in, making me itch. "Is it time?"

Reluctant to break the moment, I nod. "Yeah. The others will be up soon."

She sighs, her fingers trailing along my jawline. "Just five more minutes?"

I chuckle softly, even as anxiety gnaws at my insides. "You know we can't. But when this is all over—"

"When we're free," Ziva corrects, her eyes sparking with that familiar defiance that can only be described as simply,

Ziva.

"When we're free," I echo, pressing a kiss to her forehead, "We'll have all the time in the world to simply….be."

We lay there for a heartbeat longer, forehead to forehead, breath mingling in the cool morning air. Then, with visible effort, Ziva throws off the worn blanket and pushes herself up. I'm immediately cold without the warmth of her beside me, goosebumps spreading over my skin in her absence.

"Let's get this done then," she mutters, her voice hardening with resolve.

As we rise and start gathering our gear, dressing in our usual drab, gray work uniforms, I can't help but marvel at her strength. Where does she find such unwavering conviction? She's been through as much as I have, yet she stands tall, like the flames of resistance burn brighter in her than they do in me.

And me? I'm just waiting for the ground to crumble beneath us. The mere thought of something happening to her—makes my stomach churn. It's like a weight pressing down on my chest, and no matter how deep I breathe, it won't lift.

"Ziva," I say softly, catching her hand. "There's still time to back out, to—"

She silences me with a fierce kiss, her warm body presses against mine as she kisses me hungrily. When she pulls back, her eyes are flashing with a fire I know too well. "Don't you dare, Myall. We're in this together, remember? To the very end."

"To the very end," I echo, my throat tight with the weight of unspoken doubts. We're walking into a trap, but we have no choice now.

Please, don't let it come true.

Ziva's hand finds mine, squeezing tight, and I draw strength from her touch. Whatever happens today, at least we're facing it side by side.

Together.

The storage room buzzes with tense anticipation as we wake the others and gather our gear. Arden stretches in her pile of blankets, bones popping. Marcus's bloodshot eyes tell me he didn't sleep at all.

Ziva's fingers move quickly over a communication device, her brow furrowed in concentration. "Frequency's clear," she mutters, more to herself than anyone else as she packs it into one of the bags. "No sign of unexpected chatter."

Nodding, I heft a heavy backpack filled with the tools we'll need to break into the Compliance Monitoring Division. The goal: disable the mainframe.

"Everyone clear on the plan?" I ask, scanning the faces of our fellow rebels.

"Yes." Arden sighs, rolling her eyes. "Please, stop asking. You're making everyone nervous."

As if for emphasis, Liora fumbles with a screwdriver, and it clatters to the floor. Tariq grabs it first. "Sorry," she says, snatching it back and shoving it into the bag.

Jorel, our maintenance insider, gives a terse nod. "I've memorized every twist and turn of those tunnels. I'll get us where we need to go."

We file out of the storage room, and I catch Ziva's eye. There's a flicker of something—fear, maybe?—before it's replaced by steely determination. I want to reach out, to offer some words of comfort, but now isn't the time for sentimentality.

We slip out of the factory, the pre-dawn air crisp against our faces as we make our way down the alleyway. The maintenance tunnel entrance looms before us, a gaping maw ready to swallow us whole. I take a deep breath, steeling myself to enter into the stale, musty tunnels beneath the city.

"Alright, let's do this."

As we descend into the tunnels, the dim emergency lighting casts everything in an eerie blue glow. The faint dripping of water from a pipe punctuates the silence, its irregular rhythm a constant reminder that we're not alone down here. The air grows thick with dampness, clinging to my skin like a second layer.

With every step, the tunnel seems to close in on us, the walls pressing tighter, the air growing heavier. Every footfall echoes too loudly, every breath too sharp, too alive. I try to swallow the knot in my throat, but it only tightens, a warning I can't ignore.

"Left here," Jorel says. "Watch your step—there's a grate coming up."

Ziva's hand brushes against mine in the darkness.

"You okay?" she whispers, her voice barely audible over the constant dripping of the pipes.

I nod, not trusting my voice. The weight of our mission— the risks, the stakes—threatens to crush me. I attempt to distract myself by thinking about the world Ziva painted for me—a place where we could have a home with a flourishing garden, filled with sounds of our children playing and laughing.

That's the future I am determined to fight for.

"Yeah, I'm fine," I whisper back, as much to convince myself as her. "Just thinking about where we're going to build that house you wanted."

Ziva's lips twitch into a small smile. "Don't forget the garden," she whispers back.

I suppress a chuckle. "I won't forget to build you your garden," I murmur, feeling a comforting warmth radiate through my chest as Ziva effortlessly soothes my frayed nerves.

The tunnels stretch endlessly before us, a labyrinth of shadows and echoes. Every footstep feels like a thunderclap, every breath a siren. I can sense the nervous energy radiating from our group, a palpable tension that threatens to choke us.

"Hold up," Jorel hisses suddenly, his hand shooting out to stop us. We freeze, hearts pounding, the air suddenly thick with the scent of sweat and fear. I feel the prickling sting of moisture on my upper lip as the first bead of sweat forms, slipping down my face. In the distance, heavy boots click sharply against the metal grating, deliberate and methodical.

"Security patrol," Ziva breathes, her eyes wide in the dim light. "We need to hide."

Scanning our surroundings frantically, I spot a narrow maintenance alcove. "There," I whisper, gesturing urgently. We squeeze into the tight space, pressed against each other, barely daring to breathe.

The heavy footsteps grow louder, voices drifting toward us.

"…increased security…"

"…Regent Colvin's orders…"

Increased security?

Did they suspect something? Or was this just The Authority's response to our data leak? Ziva tenses against me, and I know she's thinking the same thing. As the patrol passes, I catch a glimpse of their uniforms through a gap in the pipes. Standard Authority Enforcers, but their weapons look upgraded. My stomach twists in a knot.

Do the upgraded weapons mean they're after us?

Once the danger has passed, we emerge from our hiding spot.

"Fuck that was close," I mutter, trying to keep the tremor out of my voice and failing, badly.

Ziva's hand seeks mine in the darkness. "We knew it wouldn't be easy," she whispers. "But we're almost there."

After what feels like hours of creeping through the tunnels, avoiding patrols, and battling our own mounting fear, we finally reach our destination. The access point to the Compliance Monitoring Division's sub-basement looms before us, a heavily reinforced hatch that represents both our greatest hope and our greatest danger.

"This is it," I say, keeping my voice hushed as we gather around the hatch. "Once we're through, we can't turn back."

I meet each of their gazes—determination and fear in their eyes. Ziva's eyes lock with mine, a silent understanding passing between us.

"Ready?" I ask, my hand hovering over the access panel as the others nod.

With trembling fingers, I insert Jorel's stolen key into the access panel. The mechanism whirs softly, then, with a satisfying click, the hatch unlocks.

"We're in," I murmur, disbelief and exhilaration blending in my voice.

We crawl through the hatch and pile out into the sub-basement. This is it. We're inside the very heart of The Authority's stronghold in our city. Adrenaline surges through me, the salty tang of sweat stinging my lip.

This lower level brings back memories of the detention center's sub-basement—the cold, hard cement floors and the assorted pipes hanging from the cracked ceiling.

"Remember," I caution, my eyes scanning the dim room, searching for the stairwell access door, "we know this place, but we can't afford to get cocky. No one do anything stupid."

Ziva nods, her expression focused. "I've memorized the patrol schedules, but we should assume they've changed some routines."

My eyes finally catch sight of the access door we need to pass through. "You're up first," I tell her.

Ziva turns her head in the direction of my gaze and gulps.

"Okay," she breathes, walking towards the door on the opposite end of the sub-basement. She runs her fingers along the access panel beside the door, its small screen casting a dim red light.

She yanks off her backpack, plugs in the datapad, and her fingers fly over the screen as code flashes to life. The access panel emits a faint beeping sound moments before the door clicks open.

Jarek quietly mutters a curse as the rest of us let out sighs in relief.

We slip through the doorway, moving like ghosts through the facility—our footsteps barely audible on the white polished floors. Every shadow seems to hide a potential threat, every distant sound a harbinger of discovery. I lead the way, drawing on my intimate knowledge of the building's layout.

As we approach a junction, I hold up a hand, signaling the

others to stop. A security camera sweeps back and forth at the end of the corridor. I close my eyes, counting the seconds of its rotation in my head.

"Two more seconds and it will be pointing the other way," Marcus's gravelly voice says through my earpiece.

"Now," I whisper, and we dart across the open space during the camera's blind spot.

My heart hammers in my chest. It feels like we're walking into a trap, that at any moment alarms will blare and we'll be surrounded. But we've come too far to turn back now.

Ziva squeezes my hand, her touch steadies me and reminds me why we're here.

Marcus's next reply comes, "You're good." He continues, "I'm currently working on setting up the feedback loop that will make you invisible to their cameras."

"Thanks Marcus," I say, nodding to the others. We press on, and with Ziva's help, we enter the stairwell, hurrying up two flights of stairs, and emerging into another sterile looking corridor.

"This is the floor," Ziva whispers from behind me as we quietly make our way down the long corridor. Someone's boot squeaks on the polished floor, making me grit my teeth at the small noise. The control room door looms ahead at an intersection, a fortress of technology guarding the heart of our oppression.

The control room is off-limits to everyone except those with the highest level of security clearance. It's a place none of us have ever been allowed to enter before, tucked away in a secluded area of the facility that is strictly reserved for authorized personnel. Even our supervisors don't have clearance for this sector of the facility.

My pulse quickens as we approach the heavy metal door, a mix of excitement and dread coursing through my veins. This is it. The culmination of all our planning, all our risks.

"There," I whisper, pointing to the sleek panel beside the reinforced door. "The biometric lock."

Arden steps forward, her eyes glinting with that defiant spark, the one that always says she's got this. "My time to shine," she murmurs, before suddenly halting.

The scuff of a boot on the polished floor reaches my ears seconds before an Enforcer comes into view. His black uniform and visor stand out harshly against the white walls of the corridor as he continues his steady pace.

Shit, what to we do now?

Chapter Forty Two

Myall

As the Enforcer patrols the corridors, his eyes remain fixed on a datapad in his hand. He seems lost in the information displayed on the screen, not paying attention to his surroundings.

My mind begins racing, trying to figure out the best way to knock him out before he gets a chance to sound the alarm, and ruin our entire mission. Ziva's eyes meet mine, her hands gesturing erratically. A quick hand signal to the others, and we double back, pulling back down the corridor.

The purposeful footsteps stop, as if the Enforcer senses something amiss. His gaze sweeps the corridor right as we dart around the corner and out of his direct line of sight. For a heart-stopping moment, I fear he might have spotted our movement. But then his footsteps resume their steady gait as he continues on his patrol, oblivious to our presence.

As soon as he is out of sight, Ziva grabs my arm, panic flashing in her eyes.

"We need to move," she murmurs, keeping her voice as low as possible. "He's going to loop back this way."

Nodding decisively, my mind already working on a plan, I give my orders. "Jorel, you take the left side," I command quietly. "Jarek and I will flank him from the right. The rest of you stay put."

We split up without hesitation, each of us moving silently towards the spot where we last saw the Enforcer disappear. The rush of adrenaline makes my muscles tense, my stomach knotting.

Peering around the corner, my pulse thrums in my ears as I catch sight of the Enforcers black uniform. He's walking with purpose, oblivious to the danger lurking behind him as he continues gazing at his datapad. With a swift nod to Jarek, we move on silent feet in perfect synchronization, closing the distance between us and our target.

As we approach from both sides, I see Jorel out of the corner of my eye, his movements slow and controlled as he silently approaches. I stealthily position myself opposite him and Jarek, eyes locked on the Enforcer who is yet to notice our presence.

Some guard.

I nod and in one seamless motion, we strike. Jarek lunges forward, his meaty hand clamping over the Enforcers mouth to stifle any cries for help. Jorel and I move swiftly to restrain him, ensuring he can't raise an alarm or access his weapon.

We overpower and disarm him, securing his unconscious body in the stairwell. I hush the guys with a finger to my lips as we loop back towards the others by the control room door, praying that they are unharmed.

Ziva visibly relaxes, her tense shoulders slumping as she spots the three of us walking towards the group, unharmed.

"It's your turn," I whisper to Arden, gesturing towards the wall where the biometric scanner is located.

I watch in awe as Ardens fingers fly over the datapad, moving with such speed that it's almost like a dance—each tap a calculated movement, each swipe of her finger bypassing layers of security with ease.

The machines hum around us, their distant buzz fading into the background as I focus on her, on the way her brows furrow in concentration, the faint sheen of sweat on her brow. In this moment, the world seems to shrink down to just her—her mind, her hands, the only things that stand between us and our goal. It's like watching an artist create a masterpiece, each movement deliberate, each code a stroke of genius.

"How much longer?" I ask, glancing down the hall.

"It shouldn't be taking this long," Ziva mutters, eyes glued to Arden.

"Just a few more seconds," Arden snaps. "This system's more complex than I expected."

"But can you get past it?" I ask, trying and failing to hide my worry.

"I can if you let me concentrate," she snaps, her attention glued to the screen.

A soft beep breaks the tension. Arden's face lights up. "We're in," she announces, yanking the datapad free and pushing the door open.

I swiftly direct the others to keep watch from the hallway, reminding them to stay on guard and to notify us if they spot anyone or notice any attempts to enter the control room while Ziva, Arden, Dr. Vance, and I are inside.

The group isn't thrilled about being left out, but the plan was clear—if we're caught, at least half of us will get a shot at escaping.

As we file into the control room, my breath catches at the faint scent of overheated electronics. The walls are lined with rows of servers, their blinking lights casting a sickly glow, like an eerie heartbeat in the quiet. There, at the center, stands our target: the NeuroMod and Sentinel system mainframe.

It towers above us—glossy black surface reflecting the dim light. Cables snake from its base, connecting to various devices and systems around the room. The sheer power of the mainframe is both intimidating and repulsive.

"It's beautiful," Ziva whispers, her eyes wide with a mix of wonder and disgust as she gazes up at the towering mainframe. "In a terrifying sort of way."

I nod, understanding completely. "Dr. Vance, we need you now."

The older woman steps forward, her immaculate appearance slightly disheveled from our journey through the grimy tunnels. "Right," she says, her voice tight with tension as she gazes up at the mainframe.

"What are you four doing in here?" A harsh voice interrupts, making us all jump.

My heart leaps into my throat as we turn to see a man in a bone-colored uniform standing behind us by a wall of monitors, their screens casting a faint blue light.

Shit. No one is supposed to be in here.

I don't have time to question why Marcus didn't warn

us about the worker—maybe he doesn't have access to the security feeds. I try to come up with a believable explanation for why we are here.

"My name is Dr. Elena Vance," Dr. Vance's voice quivers as she introduces herself. "These three," she says, gesturing towards Ziva, Arden, and myself, "are here to assist me in resolving a small issue with the system."

The man scrutinizes us suspiciously, unsure if he should trust Dr. Vance's words or not. His fingers twitch nervously at his side, drawing my attention to the communicator device attached to his waist.

Turning to look at Dr. Vance, I silently urge her to keep the man occupied while we come up with a solution. But before Dr. Vance can respond, a thunk echoes through the room, the man collapsing to the floor.

Arden towers over him, brandishing a datapad like a weapon. "You two were taking too long," she snaps at us.

I let out a sigh that's both relieved and exasperated. "Marcus," I whisper into my earpiece, but all I hear is static.

"The communication lines are jammed," Ziva says, her eyes widening with realization. "That's why Marcus didn't warn us, and why he's not responding."

I nod, feeling uneasy about our current situation. "Let's just finish what we came here to do and get out of here as quickly as possible," I mutter under my breath.

And pray Marcus can override whatever is jamming our communication.

As we approach the mainframe, I marvel at the irony. Dr. Vance, who spent years perfecting this system, is about to be instrumental in its downfall. Her hands tremble slightly as she reaches for the access panel, as if she's thinking the same thing.

"Having second thoughts?" I ask, unable to keep the edge from my voice.

Dr. Vance hesitates for a moment, her fingers hovering over the access panel. She takes a deep breath, eyes flickering to the mainframe, and I see a flash of something—guilt? Regret?

Her voice is tight when she speaks. "What we're doing...it's right. But you have no idea how strange it feels to turn my back on everything I've worked for." She glances at the mainframe, her face a mixture of awe and disgust. "I spent years designing this system, perfecting it...and now I'm about to bring it down." Her hands shake as she presses a key, but her eyes show only resolve.

Arden places a reassuring hand on Dr. Vance's shoulder. "Your knowledge is invaluable, Elena. We couldn't do this without you."

I watch as Ziva, Arden, and Dr. Vance work in sync. Ziva easily pulls open the access panel and connects her datapad without wasting any time. Arden's fingers dance over the keypad, while Dr. Vance guides her through the system's intricacies. I stand guard, every muscle locked tight in anticipation.

"How much longer?" I ask, glancing nervously at the door, frustrated by the loss of our communication link to the others.

"No idea," Arden mutters, brow furrowed in concentration, her eyes fixed on the screen. "This firewall is a beast, but I think I've got it. Once it's down we should be able to install the device."

The room is thick with anxiety, a pressure that clings to

my skin. I think of our friends outside, creating distractions and keeping watch. Their lives are in our hands too.

Arden's fingers fly over the keypad, eyes transfixed on the datatpad as she bypasses the layers of firewalls. Sweat beads at her temple, but she remains unmoving, her focus unbroken. Her eyes flicker across the screen, and she hisses under her breath, her fingers flying faster. The numbers flicker, a living pulse of green against the black.

"Got it!" she announces, her voice sharp with relief, but her gaze remains locked on the screen, the smile of triumph on her lips barely hiding the tension in her eyes.

All I see are eerie green numbers scrolling across a black screen, but the others look relieved at the sight of it.

"Elena, the device?"

Dr. Vance hands Ziva the disruptor device, and she swiftly connects it to the mainframe's wires and the datapad. This is it. The moment we've been working towards for so long. Countless nights have been spent working as a team to create this device from stolen scraps and blueprints with Dr. Vance's knowledge. If we succeed, we'll be changing the course of history. If we fail...I push the thought away. We don't have time for doubt.

"It's connected," Dr. Vance whispers, glancing at the glowing red timer. "In ten minutes, the systems will shut down. Once they do, it will take a miracle to get them back up and running again, even if The Authority send reinforcements."

We share a look of mingled relief and apprehension. Our task is almost complete, but we're not safe yet. Not by a long shot.

"Let's get the fuck out of here," I say, taking Ziva's hand

in mine, noticing that her hand is cold from the machinery. "We need to be long gone before that system goes dark."

Suddenly, Marcus's voice crackles through our comms, urgent and panicked. "Myall…Myall are you there? We've got company! Authority Enforcers. The others can't—"

Whatever Marcus was about to warn of the others is cut off. A cold dread settles in the pit of my stomach.

No, not now. We're so close.

The heavy thud of boots and raised voices echoes from the corridor outside, growing louder with each passing second.

I yank Ziva behind the console, the cold metal digging into my back as I pull her close. The tension between us, the fear, the uncertainty—it's all so raw, so real. I hold her tighter, feeling the quick rhythm of her breath against my chest. She's trembling.

Dr. Vance crouches beside us, her eyes wide and shimmering with fear. Panic rises in my chest as I realize I've lost sight of Arden, her fierce resolve now swallowed by the panic unfolding around us.

"We need more time," I whisper, the realization hitting me with full force. "We can't escape, and that device still has about nine more minutes left."

Ziva's eyes meet mine, and I see my own panic reflected in her hazel depths. Her fingers intertwine with mine, squeezing tight but I can feel the slight tremor in them. "Together," she mouths silently.

The door crashes open, shaking the room. Footsteps echo sharply, deliberate, calculated. I peek around the edge of the console, my breath catching in my throat as the figure in the doorway emerges—Regent Colvin, flanked by his squad of Enforcers.

He steps into the room with the air of a man who already knows how this ends. His tailored suit is impeccable against the dark uniforms of his guards. His eyes scan the room with an almost amused detachment, as though he's already won.

"Well, well," he says, his voice smooth like poison. "What have we here?"

As he surveys the room, his blue eyes gleaming with triumph, a horrifying thought dawns on me. The ease of our infiltration, the lack of resistance—it all makes sense now.

"He knew," I whisper to Ziva, my voice shaking with a potent mix of fear and rage. "He let us get this far on purpose."

Ziva's face pales as the implications sink in. We've walked right into Colvin's trap, and now he has us—and all the evidence he needs to crush the rebellion once and for all.

My arms tighten around Ziva, pulling her closer as the pounding of my heart seems to drown out everything else. I can feel the rapid rise and fall of her chest against mine, her breath shallow, each inhale a silent plea for escape, my own pulse thunders in my ears. I don't know if I'm shaking because of the fear, the adrenaline, or the crushing realization that this could be the end for us.

A vision flashes through my mind—the home Ziva dreamed of, our children laughing and running in the yard. But that future…it dies here.

Chapter Forty Three

Ziva

Colvin's eyes lock onto mine, devoid of mercy, like an iron vice closing in. My heart pounds, each beat echoing the crushing weight of our miscalculations, my breath shallow and jagged like broken glass. Fear coils in my chest, but beneath it, anger rises—hot and suffocating, almost overpowering the terror.

How could we be so stupid?

"You can stop trying to hide," Colvin's sneer sends a chill down my spine. He moves closer, his polished boots clicking sharply against the floor.

He moves like a shadow, each step a measured countdown to our doom. "It seems our little band of rebels thought they could outsmart The Authority."

I steal a glance at Myall, his jaw clenched so tightly that I fear he might shatter his teeth. He releases his hold on me and rises from his crouched position like a coiled spring, ready to unleash his fury.

Dr. Vance moves to stand rigidly beside him, her face pale. I follow suit, catching Arden's eyes as they dart frantically around the room, searching for an escape that doesn't exist.

"I must admit, I'm impressed you made it this far," Colvin continues as he strides before us with the confidence of a wolf among sheep, his posture rigid, a slight curve at the corners of his mouth. "Though I suppose having an insider helped." His gaze lands on Dr. Vance, lips curling into a sneer. "I expected better from you, Elena. After all we've accomplished together."

My stomach knots as Colvin's words slice through the air, dredging up memories of my parents' whispered fears. Their anxious faces flash before me, the suffocating dread that has gnawed at my insides since they were taken—a familiar pain that intertwines with my anger. I don't see how are we going to get ourselves out of this.

Dr. Vance lifts her chin defiantly. "What we've done is monstrous Jonathan. I couldn't stand by any longer."

"Monstrous?" Colvin chuckles darkly, the sound making my skin crawl. "We've brought peace and stability to a world full of hatred. Your weakness disappoints me."

Balling my fists at my sides, I fight the urge to lash out but my anger gets the better of me. "Peace built on oppression isn't peace at all," I spit, my voice trembling with barely contained rage.

Colvin's eyes snap to mine, a cold smile playing on his lips. "Ah, Ms. Emerson. Always the troublemaker. I wonder, does your newfound rebellion stem from a genuine belief in freedom, or is it merely a desperate attempt to feel something—anything—in a world that's left you behind?"

His words hit closer to home than I'd like to admit, but I'll never admit that to him.

"You're wrong," I fire back, the words like a punch to the air.

Myall's hand brushes mine, grounding me amidst the storm of uncertainty and fear that threatens to pull me under. A surge of raw energy floods through me, fueled by the memory of everything we've lost. There *has* to be a way out of this. We can do this.

Locking eyes with Colvin, my voice is steady, though my stomach churns. "We feel more deeply than you can imagine. That's why we're fighting."

Colvin's laugh is hollow, echoing through the room, as if he feeds on our despair, each note a reminder of his power over us.

"Such passion. It's almost a shame to extinguish it." He turns his attention from me to address the room. "For those wondering about your other compatriots—Liora, Jarek, Jorel, and Tariq—they're currently enjoying the hospitality of our Enforcers outside. I'm sure they'll be joining you all in confinement shortly."

Each name cuts through me like a dagger—Liora, Jarek, Jorel, Tariq—all of them captured. But as I lock eyes with my friends, I know: we're cornered, outgunned, but not defeated. Not yet.

"What now, Jonathan?" Dr. Vance asks, her voice steady despite the circumstances. "Will you make an example of us in the streets, or lock us away again?"

Colvin's eyes glint with a malevolent fire, the kind that promises pain and suffering. My muscles tighten involuntarily, and I can't stop myself from flinching.

"The Authority always finds a use for resistance. You might be the perfect candidates for testing our latest emotional suppression tech. Or better yet, our re-population program."

The threat looms over us like a dark cloud, chilling and all too real. I don't know anything about a re-population program, but if The Authority's in charge of it, I can only assume the worst.

The seconds drag by, each one heavier than the last. Seven minutes until the device shuts down the NeuroMod and Sentinel systems. I need to keep Colvin distracted, focused on us rather than the mainframe. Just seven more minutes.

"Why us, Regent?" I ask, injecting a hint of curiosity into my voice. "Out of all the potential dissenters in the city, why were we worth this elaborate trap?"

Colvin's cold blue eyes fix on me, gleaming with something predatory. "Always the inquisitive one, aren't you? It's what made you such a promising Technician. And now, such a dangerous liability."

He paces, his shoes clicking against the marble floor. The sound echoes in the tense silence of the control room, making me flinch. Behind Colvin, the Enforcers shift uneasily, their expressions covered by their opaque visors, but their postures tense with anticipation, as if waiting for a signal to pounce.

"Over the years, there have been minor uprisings," he says, his eyes boring into mine with a cold intensity. "Your parents were probably part of the first one, given your age. But there have been other rebellions since then, all of which were swiftly dealt with."

I try to suppress the nausea rising in my throat. The way

he talks about past rebellions, as if they were just minor irritations—like nothing more than an annoying fly—makes me sick.

"You see," he continues, his voice like a serpent's hiss, coiling around my thoughts, squeezing tighter with each word. "Loyalty is the foundation of society. Without it, everything crumbles. You rebels are the cancer that must be excised."

Myall tenses beside me, his fingers brushing against mine in a silent show of support. I resist the urge to look at him, keeping my gaze locked on Colvin even though I want nothing more than to cling to him for support.

"But loyalty built on lies isn't loyalty—it's just another form of control," I counter, my voice steady despite the fear and disgust churning in my gut. "None of this," I say, gesturing around the room, "has been to make the world a better place. All it is, is the government's way of controlling us."

Colvin's lip curls in disdain. "Control is necessary for harmony. You claim to fight for freedom, but your actions would plunge us back into chaos. What the crime rates were like without the NeuroMod technology? Tell me, how many would suffer if emotions ran unchecked?"

I open my mouth to argue, but Arden beats me to it. "And how many of us are suffering now, living half-lives, stripped of what makes us human?"

The Regent's attention shifts, and I breathe an internal sigh of relief. Every second he spends debating is another second closer to our victory. If we can just keep him talking long enough for the device to finish shutting down the mainframe, it will all be worth it.

"Humanity's overrated," Colvin sneers. "War, pain,

destruction—what has it given us? The Harmonization Authority offers peace, stability, progress."

"At what cost?" Dr. Vance interjects, her voice trembling slightly, yet she stands tall. "I've seen the data, Jonathan. The long-term effects of emotional suppression—"

"Are necessary sacrifices for the greater good," Colvin cuts her off sharply. His gaze sweeps over us, calculating and ruthless. "You've all made your choices. Now, you'll face the consequences."

A bead of sweat trails down my spine as I watch the seconds tick by.

We're so close now—just a little more time.

He watches me with icy detachment and a cruel smile tugs at his thin lips. "Speaking of choices, let's discuss you and Mr. Hansen, shall we?"

My spine stiffens. I force myself not to look at Myall, but I can feel the tension radiating from him beside me.

"Your attempts at concealment are pitiful," Colvin continues, his voice dripping with contempt. "Did you really think your…affection for each other…would go unnoticed? That you weren't being monitored?"

I ball my fists, fighting to keep my expression blank, to pretend that his words aren't making bile to rise up in my throat. "I don't know what you're talking about," I say, but the slight tremor in my voice betrays me.

Colvin chuckles, a sound devoid of warmth. "Oh, I think you do. Tell me, Ms. Emerson, how does it feel to know your weakness could be his undoing?"

One of Colvin's Enforcers steps forward with a quick nod. "Ms. Emerson needs reminding of the price for emotional weakness."

"No!" The word escapes me before I can stop it. Panic surges through me as I watch the Enforcer move towards Myall. As I take a step forward, someone suddenly grabs onto my forearm and pulls me back, their bony fingers tightly squeezing in warning. I quickly glance at my captor—Arden—and see her eyes are open wide with fear, her jaw clenched tightly.

I want to rip my arm free from her tight grip, to place myself between Myall and danger, but I know I can't. Not yet. We're so close. We just a few more minutes.

"Leave him alone," I growl, the sound coming from deep within me as I meet Colvin's gaze with a fierce determination. "I'm the one you want to punish. All of this was my idea, My plan."

Colvin's eyes narrow, studying me intently. "Interesting," he murmurs, the sound barely audible over the thudding of my heart. "You're usually more… calculated in your responses. What game are you playing, Ms. Emerson?"

Fuck.

He's getting suspicious. I need to keep him focused on me, away from the device.

"No game," I reply, forcing a bitter laugh. "Just tired of your twisted version of harmony."

Colvin's lips curl into a cruel smile. "And yet, you willingly served The Harmonization Authority for years. How does that make you any different from me?"

"I only wanted to become a Technician so that I could find a way to free myself from my NeuroMod," I say through gritted teeth. "This rebellion may have started from selfish reasons, but at least I'm willing to admit it, and fight for what's right."

"You naive child. You have no idea of the chaos you're inviting. The consequences of emotional suppression, even if the NeuroMod is removed from the person, will be severe in the long run." Colvin's expression darkens and he raises his hand, signaling for the Enforcer to continue with their plan to harm Myall.

"No!" Dr. Vance cries out, stepping forward to intervene, only to be violently struck by an Enforcer as he backhands her across the face, the sound almost deafening. She crumples to the ground in a heap, clutching her cheek and breathing heavily—almost choking down her breaths.

Colvin huffs a laugh and turns abruptly, striding towards the mainframe, to where the device is slowly counting down the seconds.

Not yet. Not now.

"Sir," I call out, desperate to delay him. "You're making a mistake. The system—"

"Enough!" Colvin snaps, his gaze flicking back to the device. "It's time for you to learn compliance."

He reaches for the device, his fingers mere inches away from undoing everything we've worked so hard for. Simultaneously, he nods to his Enforcers. "Show Ms. Emerson the consequences of misplaced loyalty."

The weapon glints as an Enforcer raises it toward Myall. Two more move, ripping Myall away from my side and restraining him, their hands gripping his arms tightly as he struggles in their grasp.

"Kill him," Colvin says.

My mind races, calculating angles, distances, probabilities. There has to be a way out of this, a way to save both Myall and finish shutting down the system. The Enforcers exchange glances as they tighten their grip on Myall.

Myall's dark hair falls into his eyes as he struggles against the Enforcers, his jaw hard.

I see my reflection in his eyes, my own fear made tangible through his expression. But in that moment, I can also see the unwavering determination to fight, to resist, to never give up. In that moment, I make my choice, my eyes locking with Myall. Without words, he understands.

Trust me.

Chapter Forty Four

Ziva

"Wait!" I shout, the sound echoing through the control room. Myall stops struggling, allowing the Enforcers grip to tighten around him like a vice. "I'll tell you everything. Just… pleas…don't hurt him."

Colvin pauses, his pale hand hovering over the wires connecting our device to the mainframe. "What now," he says, his voice laced with menace as he turns his attention to me once more.

Taking a deep breath, I pray I can keep his attention just a little longer. "The truth is, Regent Colvin, your perfect system has always had a flaw. And we've found it."

My eyes search the room, desperate for anything that might help. The sleek control panels, the rows of monitors, the sterile white walls—they all mock me with their unyielding neutrality. Catching Arden's gaze, I silently plead for help. She shakes her head minutely, her usually mischievous eyes now filled with grim resignation.

Dr. Vance remains frozen in place on the floor, her face a mask of pain and sorrow. The internal struggle is clear in her wide eyes—the scientist who helped build this system now forced to face its brutal reality.

"A flaw, you say?" His voice oozes with contempt as he drops his hand. "How quaint. And what, pray tell, is this supposed flaw?"

I swallow hard, my mind racing. "It's…it's in the emotional feedback loop. The way the NeuroMod interprets—"

"Spare me your technobabble," Colvin interrupts, taking a menacing step towards me. "You're stalling, Ms. Emerson. And my patience has run out."

My heart sinks as I realize the futility of our situation. A tight knot forms in my stomach, as the reality sets in. The Enforcers outnumber us, their weapons trained and ready. There will be no backup from the others outside. Colvin's eyes bore into me, seeming to strip away any illusion of control I thought I had.

My muscles lock with the strain of the decision.

"You're right," I say, forcing my voice to remain steady. "I am stalling. But not for the reasons you think."

Glancing at Myall, his eyes meet mine with a mix of concern and grim resignation as he remains held in the Enforcers vice like grip. I'm faced with an impossible choice—save the man I love, or free the city from emotional control.

How am I supposed to choose between them?

Fear and love clash within me, each vying for control.

Sweat clings to the back of my neck, my fingers twitching, desperate to take action, to make a choice. The suffocating pressure of my indecision nearly crushes me as I internally weigh the consequences.

Sabotaging the systems could liberate thousands, but at what cost? Myall's life hangs in the balance, and the thought of losing him makes my chest tighten with a pain I can barely contain. Losing my parents was only bearable because my NeuroMod dosed me into neutrality. But if I choose freedom, I won't have the emotionally suppressing drugs to numb the pain from Myall's loss.

"What's it going to be, Ms. Emerson?" Colvin's harsh voice cuts through my inner turmoil. "Your precious rebellion or your…lover?"

My nails dig into my palms. With a deep breath, I make my decision.

"I choose Myall," I declare. The words leave my mouth almost mechanically, like they're being pulled from somewhere deep inside, against every instinct that screams at me to turn away. I avoid Arden's and Dr. Vance's gaze, my stomach churning with the weight of their unspoken judgment.

Colvin's eyebrows rise in mock surprise. "How touching. And utterly predictable." His voice is cold, clipped, as if he's already decided our fate.

I step toward Myall, every muscle coiled with tension. It's like I can feel the floor beneath me, each step measured, a quiet tremor running through my legs.

"You can let him go now," I order, my voice shaking slightly as I attempt to reach for him.

"Oh, I don't think so," Colvin sneers, a cruel twist of his

lips. "You see, you've both proven to be quite the thorn in my side." His voice drips with contempt, but I'm past the point of caring. The Enforcer raises his gun once more, and takes aim at Myall's forehead.

Myall frantically resumes his struggle against the two Enforcers pinning him, his arms straining against their iron grips. Each twist of his body, each shout of frustration, sends a surge of helpless fury through me.

And then, it happens. The snapping point.

Something inside me, something primal and raw, breaks free. It's like the string of a bow that's been pulled too tight, ready to snap. A deep, guttural growl rips through my throat, primal and uncontrollable. There's a ringing in my ears and I don't even think; I just move, adrenaline flooding my veins, my vision narrowing to only Myall, and the Enforcer who has his gun aimed.

"Ziva, don't!" Myall shouts, but it's too late.

I lunge, fueled by pure adrenaline, my fingers outstretched for the Enforcers throat. My nails rake across flesh as we crash to the ground, bodies skidding over the polished floor. A loud bang echos through the room. Blood slicks my fingers, warm and metallic.

The impact is brutal. My knees slam into the unforgiving floor, sharp pain lancing up my legs, but I barely feel it. The rage is a tide, drowning out everything else, making me feel untouchable, unstoppable.

I'm on top of the Enforcer, breathing ragged, his blood coating my fingers. He grunts, disoriented, blood leaking from a wound in his torso. I take advantage of that split second, scrambling to my feet, my heart pounding against my ribs like a war drum as I kick the weapon out of his reach.

"Arden, now!" I yell, my voice hoarse, raw with the force of my desperation.

To my relief, Arden doesn't hesitate. Her long hair whips around as she tackles one of the guards restraining Myall, the sound of the guard's body hitting the floor a sickening thud. Dr. Vance, wide-eyed but determined, grabs a datapad and swings it at a third Enforcer, the metal striking with a resounding clang.

The room is chaos with the sounds of bodies crashing, the hum of tech, the wild, panicked shouting of Colvin and his Enforcers. My senses are on fire, every nerve screaming, every movement a fight for survival.

Colvin's eyes snap to me, narrowing as he realizes his control is slipping. His face hardens. "Subdue them!" he barks, his voice cutting through the noise, sharp and commanding. His gaze flickers nervously to the mainframe.

He's already moving toward it when I rush him, my boots pounding against the floor, heart a steady drumbeat in my chest. The pulse of the countdown timer flickers in my peripheral vision, each second an eternity.

"Not so fast, Regent," I spit, my words sharp, laced with fury.

Colvin whips around, his face a mask of disdain. "You foolish girl," he snarls, his fingers already closing around the datapad, the cord snaking from it like a lifeline to his doomed empire. "You have no idea what you're dealing with."

I don't care about his threats. I reach out and seize his suit jacket, tugging him closer. His suit stretches as he tries to pull away from me. My muscles burn as I pull him from the mainframe, away from the device that could undo everything we've fought for.

My elbow connects with his solar plexus with a sickening crunch, sending a shockwave of pain up my arm as he stumbles back, his breath coming out in a wheeze. A metallic tang clings to my mouth as I struggle to keep him away from the mainframe, my body trembling with the effort.

"I know exactly what I'm dealing with," I pant, my gaze snapping to the countdown timer, its blood-red digits ticking ever closer to zero. "A tyrant who's about to lose everything."

Colvin lunges, a blur of rage and violence, but I'm already moving, dodging his wild grasp. I shove him with all my strength, using his momentum against him. The datapad slips free from his grasp, the cord swinging wildly. My stomach drops as the timer's red numbers flash—each one an agonizing countdown. The deafening roar of fighting fills my ears, louder than anything else, and I know that if we fail now, there won't be another rebellion.

"Tell me, Regent," I taunt, circling him like a predator. "What does it feel like to know your perfect system is about to crumble?"

Colvin's eyes flash with fury. His breath comes in ragged gasps, but there's something else now—fear. "You underestimate the power of order. This rebellion of yours has been doomed to fail from the start." His voice cracks, just slightly, and in that moment, I can see it—his power is slipping through his fingers.

I risk a glance at Myall. His face is bruised, his expression grim as he struggles against two Enforcers. Our eyes meet for the briefest of seconds, and in that look, I see everything— the fight, the fear, the love. I won't let this be our ending.

"We're not done yet," I murmur, heart hammering, blood roaring in my ears as Colvin takes another step toward the mainframe.

A shout jerks me back to the chaos. "Ziva, catch!"

I turn just in time to see Arden toss me a datapad. My fingers wrap around it instinctively, and without a second's hesitation, I slam it into the nearest control panel that stands between Colvin, and the mainframe. Sparks explode in a brilliant burst, and the sickening screech of electrical overload fills the air.

An alarm blares overhead, its shrill wail slicing through the mayhem.

"No!" Colvin roars, his voice cracking with rage and disbelief as he lunges for me, but it's too late.

The countdown reaches zero.

A deafening silence fills the room as the machines power down. The oppressive hum of the NeuroMod and Sentinel systems—their constant, suffocating presence—vanishes, leaving only the sharp sound of our breathing. My legs threaten to give way beneath me as the full weight of what we've done crashes into me.

We did it. Against all odds, we actually did it.

"It's over, Regent," I spit. The words carry a bitter triumph, like the final blow to a weary war.

Colvin stands frozen, his face contorted with disbelief and fury. For once, I see something new in his eyes—fear. But before he can react, the Enforcers, his once-loyal soldiers, begin to move. Their bodies tense, their posture shifting as though they're emerging from a long, oppressive fog.

One by one, their hands come up to their visors, hesitant at first, unsure of what to do with the flood of emotion suddenly coursing through them.

One of them stands to my left, gripping his helmet, fingers

trembling as he slowly pulls it off. His face is flushed, eyes wide in confusion. For a long moment, he stares at the floor, as if the simple act of seeing it is a revelation—like he's encountering reality for the first time.

"God… what…?" His voice is raw, strained, like someone who hasn't spoken in years. His breath comes out in ragged gasps, as if the air itself is a shock to his system.

Another Enforcer, visor already removed, stumbles back. His hands clutch his head, the wave of regained emotion crashing over him. His face contorts, a flicker of pain crossing his features. His shoulders heave as if he's trying to shake off the weight of the years of control that have been stripped from him in an instant.

"It's…too much," he mutters, almost to himself, his voice trembling.

Colvin's head whips toward them, his fury turning to panic. "What are you doing? *Stop them!*"

But it's too late. the Enforcers are no longer under his command. One by one, they look at him—not with the blind obedience they once had, but with the raw emotion of free beings who have just tasted what it is to be human again.

The first Enforcer, the one closest to me, takes a step toward Colvin, his eyes flashing with a mix of confusion and anger. "You've…you'veused us," he says, his voice almost a snarl. "We were *nothing* but tools to you."

A flicker of fear crosses Colvin's face as he begins to understand the weight of what's happening. He stumbles back, but his Enforcers are already moving. They seize him by the arms, their grip no longer cold with obedience, but with something else. They aren't following orders. They're acting on their own will.

"Let go of me!" Colvin snarls, his voice filled with rage. "I *command* you!"

But their hands tighten. There is no command left for him to give. Colvin's strength is nothing compared to the weight of their newfound autonomy.

One of the Enforcers glances at me, and I catch the briefest flicker of something that resembles gratitude. It's fleeting, but it's there.

"It's over, Regent," the Enforcers voice is low but firm, as if reaffirming the finality of Colvin's downfall.

They begin to drag Colvin out of the control room. His struggles are weak now, futile, as if he realizes that it's over for him. His empire is crumbling, and there's nothing he can do to stop it. As they pass through the door, the silence left in their wake is almost suffocating.

My gaze meets Myall's, and his bruised face breaks into a radiant smile, his eyes glowing with pride and love. My heart swells in my chest.

"We did it," I whisper. The weight that's been pressing down on me for so long lifts, the culmination of every sacrifice, is overwhelming.

The door bursts open again, the sudden noise making my chest tighten—but it's not more Enforcers. It's our team. Liora, Jarek, Jorel, and Tariq. Their faces are flushed with exertion and triumph, their energy contagious.

Liora grins at me, her usually guarded expression cracking into something softer. "We did it," she says, nodding towards the disabled mainframe. "The plan actually worked."

Words escape me. I want to shout, to cry, to laugh, to collapse, but all that comes out is a shuddering breath. The adrenaline is wearing off, leaving only a deep, heavy fatigue.

We're not done yet. The city is free, yes—but now, we have to figure out what comes next. What kind of world will we build without Colvin's control? What will freedom really look like?

Myall steps closer, his eyes searching mine with a quiet intensity. Without a word, he pulls me into his arms. For a moment, I stiffen, startled by the intimacy, but then I relax into him, letting out a shaky breath. The warmth of his body envelops me, and for the first time, I feel safe. Truly safe.

"We actually did it," he whispers into my hair, his voice thick with emotion. "*You* did it, Ziva."

I close my eyes, pressing my face into his chest, feeling his heartbeat beneath my cheek. I inhale, and his scent fills my senses—sweat, salt, the unique essence of him. The world outside is in disarray, but in this moment, I'm with him, and that's all that matters.

"I couldn't have done it without you," I murmur, my voice wavering. "Without all of you."

His arms tighten around me, and I feel the strength in him, the certainty that we'll face whatever comes next.

"Although," he says softly, his breath warm against my ear. "At some point, we should discuss the fact that you were ready to sacrifice everything for my sake."

I pull back slightly, meeting his gaze. His eyes are tender, full of love, but there's a flicker of something else underneath it.

"It's a choice I would gladly make again," I say, my lips curling into a smile. "Because I love you, Myall."

His eyes soften, and without another word, he leans down to kiss the top of my head, his voice low, meant for only my ears. "I love you too, Ziva."

Chapter Forty Five

Myall

The workroom doors glide open, and a gust of cool air washes over me. A thick scent of sweat fills the air, mixing with the sterile antiseptic, making the whole scene feel like a grotesque dream. The once-orderly workers are in various states of emotional turmoil, their faces contorted in expressions I've never seen before.

"What's happening to me?" a woman sobs, tears streaming down her cheeks as she clutches her chest. Her body convulses, each sob shaking her as if the weight of all her suppressed emotions are breaking free, a floodgate finally giving way. Her colleague stands frozen, eyes wide with what I can only assume is fear.

Ziva's fingers quiver around my arm, her grip tight, carrying more than fear—a silent storm of unsaid things. With every step forward, triumph surges within me, but it's swiftly tainted by a shadow of guilt. Images of the workers' faces—now freed yet fractured—flash through my mind, stirring a turmoil I can hardly contain.

The grip on my arm tightens, her breath quickening. "Myall, they're experiencing it all at once. It's too much for them to handle." The fear in her eyes mirrors the panic in her voice, and I feel a surge of protectiveness wash over me.

I rub my free hand over hers to offer her comfort. "We knew this might happen. They'll adjust, but it won't be easy for them in the beginning."

As we navigate through the frenzy, I notice a man nearby laughing uncontrollably, his laughter erupting like a dam bursting. He clutches his stomach, eyes glistening with tears of joy, while another worker slams his fist against the wall, his face twisted in a mask of rage, veins bulging at his temples.

"On second thought… maybe should we stop to help them?" I ask, torn between our need to escape this hellhole, and my innate desire to comfort those in distress.

Ziva shakes her head, her long hair swaying around her. "We can't risk it. We need to get out of here before any remaining loyalists regroup."

She's right, but it doesn't make it any easier to watch. We push forward, our rebel group forming a tight formation around us. The further we move through the workroom, the more varied the reactions become. Some workers huddle together, seeking comfort in shared confusion, while others stand alone, overwhelmed by their newfound emotional freedom.

As we approach the main entrance, my heart rate increases. We're so close to freedom, yet the weight of what we've done—what we've unleashed—threatens to crush me. I glance at Ziva, seeing her already smiling up at me.

"Ready?" I ask, my voice solem. She nods, her eyes alight with the triumph of what we've accomplished today.

We push through the glass doors into the light, and the world suddenly feels alive—too alive, too loud. The sun hits my skin like a blessing, but it's almost too bright, too harsh after the artificial glow of the control room. The city's noise hits me all at once—laughter, shouting, clashing voices weaving into a chaotic symphony. It's messy—bordering on pandemonium—and yet, there's something undeniably beautiful in it.

Without hesitation, I reach for Ziva's hand, intertwining our fingers. The simple act sends a jolt through my body, and I can't help but marvel at the fact that we're doing this in public.

"We're free," I murmur, squeezing her hand. She grips mine back, wordless as her lips curve into a smile, radiant and alive. In her eyes, I see a reflection of the hope we've sparked. "It's just the beginning, Myall. Look around." she whispers tenderly.

Warmth blooms in my chest, expanding with each beat, filling the spaces once reserved for fear and doubt. In this moment, surrounded by madness, our connection feels like an unbreakable tether, anchoring us together.

Laughter erupts from a group nearby, their faces crinkled with genuine mirth, a sight I never thought I'd witness. Across the way, a woman sobs openly, her tears a testament to newfound freedom. The air is alive with an energy I can't quite name—hope, perhaps, or the intoxicating rush of possibility.

For once, I feel truly connected to the world around me.

"It's…overwhelming," I say, my eyes darting from scene to scene, trying to absorb it all.

Ziva's hand tightens in mine. "That's freedom, Myall. Messy, chaotic, beautiful freedom."

"What now?" I ask, my heart pounding in both excitement and dread. Though, as I gaze around at the joyous mayhem unfolding around me, I can't help but wonder if this new-found freedom will ultimately lead to liberation or deeper unrest.

Ziva's grip tightens on mine. "Now, we build a world where this"—she lifts our joined hands—"is the norm, not the exception."

Our fellow rebels surge past us, bumping my shoulder in the process as they whoop and embrace. Liora, her eyes shining, calls out, "I'm going to find my sister!" before disappearing into the crowd. Others follow suit, scattering to reunite with loved ones long kept at arm's length since The Authority. I nod to the others as they pass to let them know we'll catch up with them all later.

I better check on Elara later too.

Turning to Ziva, I'm suddenly unsure. "Where to now?"

She tilts her head, considering. Her hazel eyes, always so piercing, seem to look right through me. "Somewhere quiet," she decides. "Just us."

I nod, relived to know she's craving solace too. "I know just the place," I say, tugging gently on her hand.

We weave through the jubilant crowds and it's like we're standing on the precipice of something monumental. The warmth of Ziva's hand in mine is comforting as we navigate the bustling streets. The city's newfound vibrancy is intoxicating, just as it is to witness others fully express themselves for the first time.

"I never actually thought we'd make it this far," I admit, my voice barely audible above the cacophony of city noise.

Ziva's grip tightens as we walk. "There were moments I doubted too," she admits, staring ahead as we walk. "Like when you had that gun pointed at your head."

I shudder as I remember the paralyzing fear that flooded me when the gun was aimed at me, or how my heart seized when it fired. "How could I forget? I thought we were done for."

"But we weren't," Ziva replies, her voice gaining strength, yet I see the shadow of doubt lingering in her eyes. "We outsmarted Colvin, now it's time to take on the rest of The Authority."

Our footsteps echo on the pavement as silence falls between us.

"Do you think it was worth it?" I finally ask, my voice trembling under the weight of the unspoken fears hanging between us. Each word feels like it could unravel the fragile peace we've built. The silence stretches, thick with uncertainty, as I watch the flicker of doubt cross Ziva's face.

"Colvin was adamant that uncontrolled emotions would result in chaos and destruction. What if he's right?" I add. Ever since we left the control room, Colvin's last words have been lingering in my thoughts.

Ziva stops abruptly, turning to face me. Her eyes blaze with an intensity I've never seen before. "Look around, Myall. People are laughing, crying, embracing without fear. We did that. We gave them back their humanity."

I nod, a surge of emotion I can't name rising inside me.

"You're right. It's just...I don't know. Maybe he's just getting inside my head."

"I know," she says softly.

We resume walking, the familiar shape of her building coming into view. As we step inside Ziva's unit, the door clicking shut behind us feels like a barrier against the storm outside. The muffled sounds of celebration fade, leaving only the echo of our breaths. Ziva ducks into the bathroom to rinse the blood from her hands, before joining me in the living room once more.

Settling onto her worn sofa, her expression grows serious. "Once the celebrations die down, we'll need to regroup and figure out how to tackle the other cities. And Regent Colvin...he's still dangerous, even locked away. We need to be sure to have a plan for when The Authority retaliates."

Reaching out, I take Zher hand. The simple act still sends a thrill through me as I realize that I don't have to hold her hand in secret anymore.

"Yeah, I know," I say, taking a deep breath. "But what we've done here...it's more than just dismantling a system. We've sparked hope in people's hearts. That spark is going to ignite, and eventually, those flames will burn away what's left of The Authority and their system."

She looks at me, her hazel eyes searching mine. I see hesitation in her gaze, the weight of responsibility settling in.

"But how can we stand against the rest of The Authority?" she asks, her grip tightening. "They'll come for us, try to reclaim control."

I lean in, cupping her cheek. "They might try, but look at what we've accomplished already. The citizens of this city have tasted freedom. They won't give that up easily."

Her lips quirk, a tentative smile, but the doubt in her eyes mirrors the unease in my chest. "You really believe that?" she asks, her voice soft but laced with something like hope.

I nod, more certain now as I look into her eyes. "I do," I say, the surge of conviction rising up like a fire in my belly. For the first time in forever, I feel like I'm standing on solid ground. "Think about it. Every person out there experiencing joy, anger, sorrow—they're our allies now. The Authority can't fight an entire city of people who've rediscovered their humanity."

Hope blooms in Ziva's eyes, replacing the doubt. She nods slowly, her brilliant mind no doubt running through scenarios.

"You're right," she says, her voice gaining strength. "We've given them something worth fighting for."

I inhale deeply. "Ziva, this is just the beginning," I say, my voice firm despite the quiver of uncertainty that remains. "We've sparked a fire here. If we're careful, we can spread it—dismantle the system—not just here, but everywhere." The words hang in the air between us, full of promise.

Her eyes widen in understanding. "Myall, that's…that's an enormous task for just two people."

"It is," I agree, feeling a mixture of excitement and trepidation. "But think about it. If we can unite the rebellion, gather support from every freed city…we could change everything. We could prove Colvin wrong…change the world."

Ziva is quiet for a moment, as if considering my words. "Where would we even start?" she asks softly.

I comb my fingers through my hair, my fingers snagging slightly. "We can expand our reach." I rise to pace the small confines of Ziva's living unit "Recruit more members here, spread our message to other cities and once we liberate a new city—we recruit more members to liberate even more cities."

Ziva's eyes follow me, brow furrowed in concentration. "That won't be easy," she warns, her voice sharp with caution. "The Authority will be on high alert now. It will be hard enough trying to stop them regaining control of our city, let alone working to free other cities."

I nod, my body heavy with the exhaustion of the day. "You're right. We'll need to leave some of our rebellion here to maintain order and ensure The Authority can't regain control."

She leans forward, hair spilling over her shoulder. "I might have an idea," she says excitedly. "What if we create a network of rebels across different cities? Small, independent groups working towards the same goal, with one central hub for coordination and information sharing."

I pause mid-pace, turning to face her, "Ziva, that's genius." The pieces fall into place in my mind. "Each group adapts to their city's unique challenges but remains connected through this central network. It could be our way to spread our influence without overextending ourselves."

She grins, a rare flash of unrestrained joy. I feel a pang of warmth in my chest at the sight of it. "Exactly. It's decentralized enough to prevent The Authority from taking us all down at once, yet unified in purpose. It'll be a true rebellion against emotional oppression."

"You're amazing," I reach for her hand as I rejoin her on the sofa. "But we need to think bigger too. The isolated communities—we can't forget about them."

Ziva's expression turns serious. "You're right. They've been cut off for so long, who knows what kind of emotional control they're under."

"We'll need to send out scouts, gather intel. Those people deserve freedom too." I lean back on the sofa, my ribs still aching from the day's events. Ziva's warmth beside me is a comfort I never thought I'd have.

"You know," I say, "six months ago, I couldn't have imagined any of this. Us. The rebellion. Freedom."

She turns to me, her eyes searching mine. "We've both changed so much," she says, a hint of wonder in her voice. "Remember when you were just the brooding Compliance Monitor, and I was the sarcastic Technician?"

I laugh softly. "Oh, I remember. I used to love watching you work on recalibration days."

"Myall!" She laughs loudly, teasingly jabbing my shoulder, but then her expression softens. "But seriously. The strength I've found in you… it's changed me in ways I could never have imagined."

Swallowing hard, feeling a surge of gratitude towards the woman sitting before me. "And you've taught me to question, to fight. I used to think I was alone in my doubts."

Ziva's hand finds mine, her fingers intertwining with my own. "We're not alone anymore," she says softly.

I nod, Colvin's final words replaying on my mind once more. "We'll have to relearn how to live, how to feel. And there will be those who want to bring back the old system."

"We'll deal with it, if and when that happens," She says firmly, but I can see the flicker of uncertainty in her eyes. "But what about us? As a couple? We've never had the chance to just…be."

"We'll figure it out," I say softly, pressing a kiss to our joined hands.

Ziva nods, resting her head on my shoulder. "I'm scared," she whispers. "Not of the challenges out there, but of…this. Us. It's so new, so raw."

Pulling her closer, I feel how perfectly she fits against me. "Me too," I confess. "But that's okay. We'll figure it out, step by step. Just like we did with the rebellion."

I rub my thumb along the back of her hand, marveling at how that simple touch causes a warmth to travel through my body. It's as if every nerve ending awakens, and the world around us fades away, leaving just the two of us suspended in this moment.

"I promise you, whatever comes next, we face it as one. No more hiding, no more fear."

Her fingers tighten around mine, each squeeze a silent promise, a vow that we'll face whatever comes next together, side by side.

"I love you," she whispers, the words carrying a weight that makes my chest ache. "Through all of this chaos and uncertainty, you've been my anchor."

I can't help the grin that spreads across my face. "And you've been my compass, always pointing me towards what's right."

We both lean in, our lips meeting in a kiss that starts soft, but quickly increases in urgency. I cup her face, feeling the warmth of her skin, the silky strands of her hair brushing against my fingers.

Her hands roam my back, pulling me closer as she deepens the kiss, her tongue clashing against mine. I taste the salt of tears—hers or mine, I'm not sure—mingling with the sweetness of her mouth. Trailing kisses along her jaw, I revel in the soft gasp she lets out as I gently lower her further onto the sofa.

"Myall," she breathes, her voice thick with want as I continue trailing kisses down her neck. "We don't have to rush anymore. We have all the time in the world now."

Pulling back slightly, I drink in the sight of her flushed cheeks and swollen lips. "You're right," I murmur, nibbling at a spot on her slender neck. "And I intend to savor every moment with you."

Chapter Forty Six

Ziva

I wake to the steady, comforting beat of Myall's heart beneath my ear, the heat from his body a gentle weight against mine. Dawn's light is soft, hesitant, and it filters through the thin curtains in beams, casting pale stripes across Myall's face. His hair is tousled, wild from sleep, and I catch myself reaching toward him before pulling my hand back, the urge to brush it from his forehead almost overwhelming.

Myall's eyes flutter, his dark lashes grazing his cheeks. For a moment, I think he's still in the haze of sleep, but then his gaze sharpens, locking with mine, and a slow smile curves at the corners of his lips.

His voice is husky with sleep, low and warm, as he murmurs, "morning, beautiful." The sound of it stirs something deep within me, like his words are a physical caress.

"Morning," I whisper, tracing the line of his jaw with my

fingertips, feeling the roughness of his stubble against my skin.

Waking up like this feels almost unreal. After years of numbness, each touch, each word from him stirs something deep—like my heart's learning how to beat again. I catch myself savoring these moments, afraid they might slip away if I don't hold on tight enough.

Myall's warmth presses into me, but beneath it, I can still feel the echo of my NeuroMod. The silence of The Authority echoes in my mind—distant but relentless, like a nightmare I can't quite shake off, no matter how hard I try.

"We should get up," I say reluctantly, even as I make no move to leave the comfort of his embrace.

Myall nods but doesn't release me, instead he nuzzles closer. "Five more minutes," he bargains.

He presses a kiss to my forehead, his lips are tender, sending a rush of warmth through my chest. I can smell the faint hint of lemon from his soap, mixing with the earthy scent of his skin as I nestle closer to him. I close my eyes, savoring this moment before the day's responsibilities close in. The rebellion we've started, the changes we're implementing—it's been a lot of work over the last two weeks.

Reluctantly, I pull myself from Myall's arms and slip out of bed, my bare feet cool against the worn floor as I pad over to the small kitchen. My fingers are stiff from the chill, but I don't mind. The quiet of the room wraps around me as I start the small, familiar ritual of preparing our food, my mind wandering.

The air smells faintly of grease and burnt toast as I scrape together the simplest breakfast I can manage—just a few stale slices of bread and a dollop of cold, unappetizing paste that passes for butter. We've made significant progress in restructuring the city's leadership, but there's still so much to be done.

"What's on your mind?" Myall asks, coming up behind me and resting his hands on my shoulders.

I lean back into him, drawing strength from his steady presence, feeling his warmth seep into me. "Just thinking about everything we need to do. The centralized hub we're setting up, coordinating with the other rebel groups—"

"We're making a difference, Ziva," he reminds me, his voice calm and reassuring. "One day at a time."

Nodding, I bite my lower lip as I turn to face him. "I know. It's just…the responsibility of it all. We're not just changing a system, we're reshaping an entire way of life."

What if we start something that consumes us instead of freeing us?

The thought gnaws at me, twisting my stomach into knots. Can we truly wield this power without becoming the very oppressors we seek to overthrow?

Myall's eyes soften with understanding. "And that's exactly why we're the right people for this. Your passion, your determination—it's what's inspiring others to join our cause."

I breathe deeply, centering myself. "You're right. We've already established the framework for the independent groups to work together. Now we just need to fine-tune the coordination and information sharing through our central hub."

"Which we'll run together," Myall adds, a hint of pride in his voice.

The enormity of what we're undertaking hits me anew.

"It's daunting, isn't it? But also… kind of exciting. To think of all the people we could help, all the lives we could change."

Myall pulls me into his arms, his muscles tightening around me. "That's why we're doing this."

Pulling back from Myall's embrace, my heart races with a mix of exhilaration and nervousness. It's still strange, feeling so much without the dampening effects of the NeuroMods. I let out a small laugh, reveling in the sheer joy of it.

"What's so funny?" Myall asks, his eyes twinkling with curiosity.

"Everything," I reply, gesturing at nothing and everything at once. "I'm terrified and thrilled and overwhelmed all at once. It's… even after all these weeks it still feels weird."

Myall grins, running a hand through his hair. "I know exactly what you mean. Sometimes I catch myself waiting for the numbness to set in, but it never does."

We move around each other in our morning routine, but there's a new energy to our movements. I catch Myall's eye as I'm pulling on my sweater as he watches me dress, and a surge of affection washes over me.

"You know," I say, my voice sounding husky. "I think my favorite part about this new world we're creating is that we no longer have to follow the AI system's strict timekeeping."

Myall pauses, his shirt half-buttoned. "Mine too," he laughs softly, crossing the bedroom towards me.

Reaching up, I trace the line of his jaw with my fingertips. "We should probably get going," I murmur, but I make no move to step away, and neither does he.

Instead, his arms encircle my waist, pulling me closer. "Probably," he agrees, but then his lips are on mine, soft and insistent.

I melt into the kiss, my hands sliding into his hair. The world falls away, and all that exists is this moment, this feeling. We break apart, breathless, the cool air between us tinged with the lingering warmth of our shared breath, my heart racing as if I've just sprinted a mile.

"We're going to be late," I say, but there's no real concern in my voice.

Myall shrugs, a mischievous glint in his eye. "Let's be late then. We're building a revolution, I think we've earned the right to enjoy a moment of freedom."

Laughing, I pull him closer, feeling the weight of everything slip away in the rush of his kiss. "You're a bad influence, Myall Hansen."

"And you love it, Ziva Emerson," he retorts, his voice warm with affection.

As his lips meet mine, the world narrows to the intoxicating feel of his warmth against my skin, the urgency of his hands pulling me closer, as if we might dissolve into each other entirely. Suddenly I'm lost, drowning in sensation. The taste of him—lemon soap and toothpaste and something uniquely Myall. His touch sears my skin as his hands cup my face. Our kiss deepens, hungry and desperate. My hands roam over the planes of his chest, his muscles taut under my fingers.

"We shouldn't," I gasp, even as I tug his shirt free, letting it fall to the ground. "We'll be late."

"Don't care," Myall growls, nipping at my neck and making my nipples pebble. "They can wait."

A soft moan escapes me as he pushes me against the wall. His knee slides between my bare legs and I grind against him shamelessly as he kisses me. I lose myself in the pleasure, in the freedom of expressing my desire with Myall without fear or shame. Just Myall and me and the passion we share.

His fingers slip under my sweater, tracing patterns on my skin as he gently lifts the fabric over my head. His fingers trail up my stomach, leaving goosebumps in their wake.

His eyes are dark with need as he looks at me. "You're so beautiful," he whispers reverently as his calloused fingers continue their gentle trail. His fingers pinch my hardened nipple and I arch into his touch, desperate for more. "Please," I whimper.

He grabs me by the waist and lifts me into his arms, carrying me towards the bed, his urgency mirroring my own. I wrap my arms around his neck, my fingers gripping his hair.

We fall onto the bed together, a frenzy of limbs and kisses. He trails kisses down my neck, knowing exactly how to touch me, how to make me feel alive and desired.

I tug at his belt, impatient to feel him, skin against skin. He chuckles against my lips, the sound vibrating through me. "Eager this morning, aren't we?" he teases as he helps to undo his belt.

Groaning in response, I tug at his pants until they fall away. Myall moves on top of me, his weight pinning me to the bed as he trails kisses down my body. Each kiss sending shivers through me as I arch into him, wanting more.

"I need you inside of me," I whisper, a low moan escaping my lips as he kisses the sensitive spot where my legs and pelvis meet.

He doesn't hesitate, positioning himself at my entrance and entering me with deliberate, slow thrusts. His mouth meets mine in a hungry, all consuming kiss as he continues to plunge deeper and deeper until he bottoms out entirely. We both moan and he allows me a small moment to adjust before he withdraws and thrusts back in, repeating the motion slowly. My head falls back against the pillow, a moan escaping my lips as I feel the pleasure already building inside of me as I meet him thrust for thrust.

"I love you," I breathe, the words slipping out before I can stop them.

Myall's grip on me tightens, his pace increasing. "I love you too," he groans, burying his face in the crook of my neck, the raw vulnerability in his voice making my heart ache.

As the intensity builds with each thrust, I feel myself nearing the edge. "Myall," I gasp, "I'm—"

"Me too," he pants.

We lose ourselves in each other, cresting the wave of pleasure simultaneously, crying out in shared ecstasy. As my orgasm washes over me, I can't help but think this is what we're fighting for—the freedom to feel, to love, to be fully human, in all our messy, beautiful complexity. And I wouldn't have it any other way.

* * *

When we finally tear ourselves away from our unit, stepping out into the cool morning air, I feel the crispness of it on my skin, as though the air itself is breathing life into the city.

The streets, once desolate, now pulse with joy. Children race through a forgotten lot, their laughter filling the air like music—something I never thought I'd hear again, breaking through the silence we'd grown used to.

"You know," I say, turning to Myall and keeping my

voice low, "sometimes, I wonder if we're ready for all this responsibility…" I trail off, my hands clenching at my sides as the enormity of our plans settle heavily on my chest. I gesture vaguely at the world around us, the city teeming with energy, children laughing and playing, yet unease lingers. A breeze stirs the leaves of the trees around us, but it feels cool, sharp, like a warning.

Myall's fingers intertwine with mine. His voice is low, thoughtful. "I know what you mean."

I nod, squeezing his hand. "We have the power to reshape society, to give people back their emotions. But what if we mess it up?"

"That's why we have to be careful," Myall replies. "We can't just tear down the old system without considering the consequences."

A group of children, all young and carefree, rush by us, their joyful squeals and laughter filling the streets as they race each other.

"I keep thinking about how we'll help people transition," I muse, finally voicing something that's been playing on my mind these past few weeks. "It's not just about removing the NeuroMods. We need to teach people how to handle their emotions, how to deal with their trauma that's no longer being suppressed."

Myall nods thoughtfully. "You're right, but it's going to be a long process."

As we approach the former Compliance Monitoring Division building, the surrealism of it hits me again. The stark, clinical space that once felt like a cage now hums with life. Vibrant murals of bright blues and fiery oranges cover the walls, where sterile whites once reigned. The scent of fresh paint mixes with the sharp tang of coffee and the chatter of rebels filling the air. It's the same building, but it feels entirely different—alive, free, like it could never return to its old, oppressive self.

"It's still hard to believe," I whisper, taking in the sight of our fellow rebels gathered around a makeshift office space. "This place used to terrify me."

Myall squeezes my hand. "Now it's a beacon of hope."

We head toward the central meeting area, where a holographic display flickers to life. Arden catches my eye, and she flashes us a mischievous grin.

"About time you two lovebirds showed up," she teases. "Some of us have been working since dawn."

Heat rises to my cheeks. "We got caught up…discussing strategy," I lie, poorly. Arden snickers.

Myall clears his throat. "So, what did we miss?"

She begins running through the daily report as my mind wanders. We've made progress, but dismantling a worldwide system of emotional control is no small feat. The isolated communities worry me most. We've tried gathering information remotely, but Arden was only able to find surface level information before declaring that we'll need to send operatives in to access their systems directly. But the idea of sending one of our people into an unknown and potentially hostile environment absolutely terrifies me.

"I know we need eyes and ears in those communities," I interrupt, my voice tight, hesitant. "But sending in our people blind could be disastrous."

"I'll go," Arden says, her eyes flashing with challenge. "I can blend in, gather intel on The Sanctum, and report back without raising suspicion."

As Arden makes her suggestion, I catch a flicker of concern in Myall's eyes. His hand tightens around mine, his knuckles going white for a moment. I can almost feel the tension in his body—the way his shoulders are slightly stiff, as if preparing for a fight.

Arden's words are light, but her suggestion cuts through the room like a knife. Her confident smirk does little to ease the fear growing in my chest.

"No. It's too dangerous, Arden." I say. "If they realize why you're there—"

"They won't," she cuts me off, that familiar smirk playing on her lips. "I grew up dodging Enforcers, remember. I'm the best hacker you've got. This is what I'm made for."

Myall's brow furrows, doubt flickering in his eyes as I voice my concerns. I can sense the tension, like a taut wire ready to snap. "Infiltrating a community is a far cry from evading a few Enforcers," he says, but I can tell he's struggling to find a plausible excuse not to send her.

My heart races at the thought of Arden going in alone. "What if they realize why you're there, and you get caught?" I don't dare voice my concern that I'm not sure she's exactly ready for a mission like this. She doesn't like to talk about it, but she hasn't been the same since her confinement in the detention center. Whatever they did to her in there, it changed her irreparably.

"Then I'll have a partner. Someone who I can check in with every day, and will know that if I don't check in, that the worst has happened. They can sound the alert," Arden mutters, fiddling with the armrest of her chair.

I glance to Myall, hoping for support, but I see the wheels turning in his mind. He's actually considering it.

"We need a solid plan," he says slowly. "Arden's skills make her the ideal candidate, but we can't rush in without a thinking this through."

The room erupts into a flurry of tactical discussions, and I can't shake the feeling that we're playing with fire. But I can't deny Arden the right to help the rebellion. This is her fight, as much as it is mine.

As we take a break for lunch, Myall and I find ourselves alone on the small rooftop garden, the city stretching out beneath us. The garden is a patchwork of greenery, wildflowers in bursts of lavender and yellow swaying gently in the breeze, their petals rustling softly against one another. For a moment, I close my eyes and soak in the tranquility, the stillness.

"Elara is wondering if we're still planning on joining her for dinner," Myall says. Undoubtedly, he's just received a reminder comm from Elara.

"I wouldn't miss one of her dinners for anything," I reply softly, meaning it. We make it a point to have dinner at Elara's house a few times each week now. Sometimes it's just the two of us with Elara, but other times our fellow rebels join us. The dinners when we're all together at Elara's are my favorite.

Myall joins me, his shoulder brushing mine. "What's going on in that brilliant mind of yours?"

"Just...thinking." I say, letting out a sigh. "I know the isolated communities are still in the dark, and we need to know how deep The Sanctum's control runs, but I hate the idea of sending Arden of all people into such a dangerous situation."

"I know it's hard," Myall says softly. "But she's the best person for the job, and you know she won't take 'no' for an answer."

"I know," I groan, leaning my head back.

Myall's hand finds mine, steadying me. "We won't send her alone or without a solid plan."

I nod, his words solidifying my resolve, but beneath it, doubt still flickers.

We have a long road ahead, full of challenges and risks. But we're no longer alone. We have each other, and a growing army of people ready to reclaim their humanity. This fight is no longer ours to bear alone.

"Okay," I whisper. "Let's send Arden to The Sanctum."

Chapter Forty Seven

Myall

Standing before the floor-to-ceiling glass window of our resistance headquarters, I look out over the remnants of the old Compliance Monitoring Division. Below, the city sprawls, a patchwork of gleaming towers and vibrant streets. The sun hangs low, casting long shadows over the park where children play. Their carefree laughter rises up to me—a sound that would have been unthinkable just six months ago. Proof that every decision from here on carries weight.

The door slides open behind me with a soft hiss. I don't turn—I don't need to. I feel Ziva before I see her, the quiet certainty of her presence grounding me even now.

"Ready for today's meeting?" she asks gently, her hazel eyes meeting mine.

Her voice is warm, steady, like sunlight streaming through

the glass.

I let out a slow breath. "No. But I will be."

She wraps an arm around my waist, pulling me close as she rests her forehead lightly between my shoulder blades. The warmth of her steadies the tight coil in my chest, though it doesn't loosen it completely.

"I keep thinking about Arden," I admit softly. "About sending her into the isolated communities. I know why we're doing it. I know it's necessary." I swallow, taking a deep breath before continuing. "That doesn't stop it from feeling like we're crossing another line we can't uncross."

Ziva doesn't rush to answer. This is a conversation we've had many times over the past few months. Her fingers tighten just slightly in silent acknowledgment.

"The Sanctum isn't like Authority-controlled regions," I continue. "They don't just suppress emotions with NeuroMods. They've built entire cultures around emotional absence. Identity, faith, obedience—it's all woven together." I turn to face her. "If we destabilize that, even carefully… people will break. Some of them won't thank us for it."

Ziva's fingers—warm, firm—press against my forearm, and a sense of calm washes over me. It's as if her touch slices through the fog of my thoughts, a reminder that I'm not alone in this. The warmth of her hand spreads up my arm, rooting me in the present, grounding me.

"I know," she says quietly. "And that's why we're not charging in like conquerors. Recon first. Listening first. But the people of The Sanctum deserve emotional freedom as much as the rest of us."

I nod, gaze drifting back toward the city below. "The risk isn't abstract anymore," I mutter. "It's Arden. Which means we have to treat this like our highest-priority operation."

Ziva hums in agreement as I step away from the glass and run a hand through my hair, already mapping contingencies in my head. "I want safeguards. Daily check-ins. A dedicated point of contact who knows that silence isn't delay—it's failure. No improvising."

Ziva doesn't hesitate. "Already accounted for," she says, and I have no doubt that she's been meticulous in her planning. "Marcus has volunteered to be positioned on the outskirts. He knows Arden best, and he'll be in constant communication. If anything deviates from baseline, we pull her out immediately."

Good. I trust Marcus to keep a close eye on Arden. Hell, he's probably the only person, beside us, that I'd trust Arden's life with.

"And the extraction?" I ask, turning to face her fully.

"Planned and rehearsed," She replies. "Multiple exit routes. Redundancies layered on redundancies. You know I couldn't risk sending her in there without being over prepared."

Some of the tension in my chest loosens from Ziva's over preparedness. Looking into her eyes, I see my own worry mirrored there. In moments like these, when she understands not just my words but my fears, I feel closer to her than ever.

"Alright," I say, turning my attention back toward the window. "Then it's time to send her in."

Ziva steps closer, her shoulder brushing mine as she looks out at the city with me. "This is why we're co-leaders of this rebellion," she says quietly. "To make the hard decisions together."

I smile faintly at her words. "Okay, that makes me feel

better," I murmur.

"I thought it might," Ziva replies, her voice soft but filled with understanding. We're both silent, drinking in the sight of the city spread out before us.

"Remember when we first started this?" she asks after a pause, a hint of nostalgia in her voice. "We were just two people against an entire system. Now look at us."

I chuckle, remembering fondly. "Yeah, we've come a long way from secret meetings and homemade communicators."

Ziva's eyes soften, the raw emotion taking my breath away. I inch closer, closing the distance between us. A soft vibration pulses against my wrist. Arden's name flashes across the small holographic display.

Are you two lovebirds going to join us for the meeting or not?

A faint smile tugs at my mouth. "She's always so impatient." Ziva huffs a quiet laugh as we turn to leave the room. "She always is."

Filing in after Ziva, the conference room buzzes with an undercurrent of nervous energy. The walls, once sterile and impersonal, now pulse with the glow of maps, charts, and scattered data pads. The faces around the table—some familiar, some new—are lit not with fear, but with a quiet resolve. I can almost taste the change in the air, the mix of hope and fear that we're about to do the impossible.

taking my seat beside Ziva, Arden winks and grins in our direction before turning back to her hushed conversation with Liora.

"Alright, let's begin," I say, my voice calm as I address those seated at the table around me. "We need to discuss our next steps in dismantling the emotional control system *globally*."

Ziva leans forward, her long hair pulled back for once in a messy knot atop her head. "I've been analyzing the data from our operatives in Zion. It looks like The Authority is starting to crack down on any signs of emotional freedom there."

I try to piece together a strategy in my mind. "We'll need to adjust our approach there. Maybe focus on building a stronger underground network before we make any overt moves in that city."

As the discussion deepens, a familiar sense of purpose settles over me. This is what I was meant to do—strategize, fight, lead.

"What about the southern region?" one of our members asks. "We've had some success there, but progress has been slow."

I lean back in my worn leather chair, considering. "We need patience. Change doesn't happen overnight. Let's focus on education and gradual integration of emotional freedom concepts—less likely to provoke backlash."

Ziva nods, and a warm rush of affection sweeps over me. Over the past two months, we've grown closer—we make a good team, balancing each other's strengths and weaknesses. We still have our disagreements and debates, but it's clear that we have each other's backs no matter what.

What started as a spark has grown into a formidable force, with networks spanning cities. It's dangerous work, but the thought of a world free from emotional control makes every risk worth it.

"Ziva, is everything set with the NeuroMod disruptor device?" I ask.

She looks up from the datapad, meeting my gaze. "Good

to go. These devices will be wearable under clothing, masking our operatives' emotional signatures, creating the appearance that their NeuroMods are functioning normally. Their devices should report correctly to any Sentinel system that nothing is amiss."

I nod, reassured by the fact that Ziva knows exactly what she's doing and won't send anyone in without the device working flawlessly.

"Arden," I call out down the long conference table. "How's the terrain mapping coming?"

She drums her fingers on the table. "All sorted. We've got detailed layouts of every community. Hidden entrances, blind spots, the works."

A pang tightens in my chest. Her enthusiasm is infectious, but it only deepens my concern for her safety. "Good work. Just…remember, this first part is recon only. No heroics, okay?"

Arden rolls her eyes, but her smile softens. "Yes, dad. I'll eat my vegetables too."

Ziva snorts, breaking the tension in the room. "Alright, people. Final checks. We move out in an hour."

* * *

The next sixty minutes fly by in a blur of last-minute preparations. Before I know it, we're standing at the launch point, a hidden alcove on the outskirts of the city.

I pull Arden into a tight hug, the weight of her thin frame pressing into me. Her heartbeat thuds steadily against my chest, a rhythm that calms the racing in my own veins. The smell of her hair—damp with sweat from the preparations—

clings to me, and I hold her a moment longer than I should, wishing I could somehow shield her from the dangers ahead. In the press of her warmth, I feel both protective and powerless.

"Be careful out there," I say, my throat suddenly thick, each word laden with the weight of unspoken fears.

She squeezes back. "Always am. Don't worry so much, you'll get wrinkles."

"Remember, this is recon only," I say quietly. "You observe. You listen. The moment something feels wrong, you disengage. No exceptions."

Arden grins, but her eyes sharpen, focus—serious beneath the bravado. "I know. Get in, gather intel, get out."

"That's not reassuring."

"It should be," she says. Then, more seriously, "I'll check in. Same time, every day. If that changes, you'll know why."

"You're not alone out there," I add. "Check-ins are non-negotiable. Miss one, and we pull you out."

She nods once. No jokes this time. "Understood."

As she steps back, Ziva embraces her next. "Remember, if anything feels off—"

"Abort and activate the emergency beacon," Arden finishes. "I've got this, guys. Really."

We watch as Arden slips into the shadows and I can't help but feel a sense of unease settle in my stomach. Despite her confident words, I know how dangerous this assignment is. The communities we're targeting are notoriously insular and suspicious of outsiders. There's no telling what kind of reception our operatives will receive.

But Arden is a natural at blending in and winning people over with her charm. That's why she's the one going on this mission, despite our reservations. That and her amazing hacking abilities.

Ziva's hand slips into mine, grounding me in a world that suddenly feels unsteady. Her fingers lace with mine, and despite the calm in her voice, I feel the tremor in her palm, the tension in the way she holds me.

"She'll be fine," she whispers, though the words carry more uncertainty than she intends. I squeeze her hand tighter, trying to convey all the strength I don't feel.

Turning to her, I see the same storm of emotions in her eyes that I feel. "We're really doing this, aren't we?"

She nods, lips tugging into a smile. "Changing the world, one community at a time."

As the operatives fade into the shadows, I hold Ziva close, drawing strength from her presence.

Whatever comes, we'll face it together.

Epilogue

❧❧

Myall

Six years later

The sharp, earthy smell of cut grass mingles with the floral sweetness of jasmine, filling the air with an intoxicating harmony. The grass brushes against my bare feet as I chase my giggling children, their laughter ringing out in a carefree chorus that fills the air with joy.

Sunlight dapples through the jacaranda's blossoms, painting the ground in shifting patterns. The sound of my children's laughter rings out, a bright, carefree chorus that bounces off the walls of the house and rises into the sky. It's a melody of freedom, one that echoes in my heart long after the sound fades away.

"I'm gonna get you!" I call out playfully, my heart swelling with joy as my daughter shrieks with delight and my son makes a clumsy attempt to outrun me on his chubby toddler legs.

I glance up at the porch, where Ziva and Grandma Elara sit in weathered rocking chairs, their creaking rhythms in time with the gentle breeze. The wood beneath them is faded by years of sun, but their smiles are timeless—matching, content, and full of love.

Ziva's eyes gleam with a quiet joy that has only deepened over time, while Grandma Elara's face softens as she watches us, her hands resting gently in her lap, fingers curled in a reflection of the strength she's always possessed.

The house behind them—our dream home that I built with my own two hands—stands as a testament to how far we've come. It's a beautiful two-story structure with a wrap-around porch and bright blue shutters. A stone path leads from the porch to the perfectly manicured lawn.

In the front yard, there's a swing set and a playhouse for the children to enjoy. But most importantly, there's the garden I planted for Ziva, filled with her favorite flowers and herbs that she tends to with care and love.

Catching my children, I swing them into the air, their laughter fills the air—a symphony of innocence and freedom. Ziva's joyful laugh joins theirs in a chorus of happiness, and something stirs deep within me—a quiet ache that reminds me of the battles we fought, the sacrifices we made. It's a raw, almost primal feeling, a pull to protect them, to ensure that this laughter will never be taken from us again.

I think back to the world we came from, where happiness was rationed, where love was controlled. How did we survive it? But that's not us anymore. We've built something better.

Grandma Elara chuckles softly, her hands folding over each other with practiced grace. "You're truly living the dream, Myall," she says, her voice filled with pride.

Smiling, a deep sense of contentment settles over me. "We all are," I reply, glancing at Ziva with a love that still takes my breath away after all these years.

"Daddy, look!" my daughter calls out, holding up a dandelion. "I found a wish!"

Kneeling beside her, I marvel at how her hazel eyes—so like her mother's—sparkle with unbridled curiosity. "That's right, sweetheart. Why don't you make a wish?"

As she closes her eyes and blows, scattering the seeds to the wind, a wave of emotion washes over me—grief, hope, awe. This simple act—so innocent, so pure—is everything we fought for—the right to dream without fear, to hope without limitation.

I remember a time when dreams were forbidden, when to hope was to risk everything. But now, as I watch the dandelion's seeds lift into the breeze, I realize we're free. Our future is no longer written in the shadows of the past, but in the clear light of a new dawn.

"What did you wish for?" I ask, my voice thick with emotion.

She grins up at me. "Can't tell you, Daddy. It's a secret!"

Laughing, I scoop her up in my arms. "Of course it is. Come on, let's go see what Mommy and Great-Grandma are up to."

Approaching the porch, I catch Ziva's eye. In that moment, without a word spoken between us, I see in her gaze the same overwhelming gratitude and love that I feel. Grandma Elara reaches out to take my daughter from my arms, her weathered hands gentle as she settles the child on her lap.

"Now then," she says, her voice warm with the wisdom of

years, "who wants to hear a story about the old days?"

As Grandma Elara's voice weaves tales of a world before emotional control, her words feel like threads pulling us into a past that now seems like a distant nightmare. I lean back against Ziva's legs, her warmth grounding me, her steady presence a reminder of everything we've overcome. The world we live in now—where we can love freely, without fear—feels like a rare gift, one we must cherish in a way that the old world could never have understood.

Closing my eyes, I soak in the harmonious laughter around me—the sound of freedom, of dreams realized, of a legacy built on love and resilience. The weight of our past struggles lingers in the corners of my mind, but it no longer dominates.

Now, in this moment, I see only the faces of my family— each of us a thread in the tapestry of this new world we've woven together.

And for the first time, I feel truly at home, truly free. The future, like my children's laughter, is endless and bright, and it is ours to shape.

Up next in the "Chains Of Conformity" series

If you loved following Ziva and Myall's journey, get ready for the next book in the **Chains Of Conformity** series. In the upcoming sequel, the focus shifts to Arden—our daring, unpredictable rebel—as she infiltrates the isolated communities.

Ziva and Myall's chapter has closed, but Arden's is just beginning. The fight for freedom continues, but this time, the stakes are even higher, and the risks more personal. The world of the resistance expands, and with it, new dangers, alliances, and romance.

Stay tuned—this is just the beginning.

About the Author

Tristen lives in Newcastle, Australia with her husband and two kids and works full time in the insurance industry, helping people get their lives back.

Currently, Tristen is balancing the joys and challenges of motherhood with an energetic toddler and a baby. Despite her busy schedule, she's still dedicated to her writing.

Recently, she released *The Insurance of the Heart Novella Collection*, a series of interconnected romance novellas. After this, she shifted her focus to writing Dystopian Romance.

You can connect with me on:

- https://www.tristenwillis.com
- https://www.tiktok.com/@author.tristenwillis
- https://www.instagram.com/authortristenwillis
- https://www.threads.net/@authortristenwillis

Subscribe to my newsletter:

- https://subscribepage.io/jBvYk5

Also by Tristen Willis

Tristen is a multi genre author who's taste in writing varies much like her taste in reading.

Insurance Of The Heart Novella Collection
Book 1: The Happy Hour Hookup follows Ruby, who hooks up with her team leader after a tipsy night at after-work drinks.

Book 2: Love Bytes and Gossip is about Ruby's BFF, Hannah, as she rebuilds her confidence after a messy breakup, unravels juicy workplace gossip, and falls for a sexy surfer.

Book 3: Shared Secrets and Smiles, features Eliza, who accidentally fakes a boyfriend to impress her coworkers—and the office newbie offers to play the part.

Book 4: Under The Office Tree, is set to publish November 2026. It's a grumpyXsunshine Christmas romance.

Drop Your Complaints Here

The office was beige.

The solution? A fake HR complaints box.

Everyone thinks it's official. Everyone's filling it with petty drama, ridiculous demands, and unfiltered confessions.

I planned to keep it secret... until Dan caught me.

Now we're partners in crime, feeding the gossip, planting chaos, and laughing as the office slowly unravels. It's messy, it's petty, and for the first time, work is actually fun.

But secrets have consequences. And when the complaint box blows up, we'll have to face HR, our furious coworkers, and the question neither of us saw what happens when the game is over?

The Genesi Duology

Book 1: The Genesi Code follows eighteen-year-old Luka as she attempts to uncover her father's murderer, which leads her to discover a deadly government conspiracy—and secrets about her own DNA.

Book 2: The Genesi Cure, follows Luka as she is caught in a war between the humans and Genesi. With humanity's fate in her hands, will she rise as a savior or become the ultimate weapon?

www.ingramcontent.com/pod-product-compliance
Lightning Source LLC
Chambersburg PA
CBHW050956180726
48291CB00006B/1856